L.A. BYTES

P.A. BROWN

mlrpress

MLR Press Authors

Featuring a roll call of some of the best writers of gay erotica and mysteries today!

M. Jules Aedin	Drewey Wayne Gunn
Maura Anderson	Samantha Kane
Victor J. Banis	Kiernan Kelly
Jeanne Barrack	J.L. Langley
Laura Baumbach	Josh Lanyon
Alex Beecroft	Clare London
Sarah Black	William Maltese
Ally Blue	Gary Martine
J.P. Bowie	Z.A. Maxfield
Michael Breyette	Patric Michael
P..A. Brown	Jet Mykles
Brenda Bryce	Willa Okati
Jade Buchanan	L. Picaro
James Buchanan	Neil Plakcy
Charlie Cochrane	Jordan Castillo Price
Gary Cramer	Luisa Prieto
Kirby Crow	Rick R. Reed
Dick D.	A.M. Riley
Ethan Day	George Seaton
Jason Edding	Jardonn Smith
Angela Fiddler	Caro Soles
Dakota Flint	JoAnne Soper-Cook
S.J. Frost	Richard Stevenson
Kimberly Gardner	Clare Thompson
Storm Grant	Lex Valentine
Amber Green	Stevie Woods
LB Gregg	

Check out titles, both available and forthcoming, at
www.mlrpress.com

L.A. BYTES

P.A. BROWN

mlrpress

Copyright 2010 by PA Brown

Published by
MLR Press, LLC
3052 Gaines Waterport Rd.
Albion, NY 14411

Visit ManLoveRomance Press, LLC on the Internet:
www.mlrpress.com

Editing by Kris Jacen
Cover Art by Deana C. Jamroz
Printed in the United States of America.

ISBN# 978-1-60820-040-5

First Edition 2010

Monday, 10:55 am Ste. Anne's Medical Center, Rowena Avenue, Silver Lake, Los Angeles

Christopher Bellamere studied the traffic on Hyperion Avenue, eight stories below. A blanket of brown smog lay over the nearby Golden State Freeway. Behind him, Terry Corwin, the network manager at Ste. Anne's, fiddled with his Blackberry and carried on whispered conversations with himself. Terry was the anxious type.

"What are you saying?" Terry asked him. "Please don't tell me what I think you're telling me. I know I saw some anomalies, but they only started last night. You gotta be wrong."

"I'm not. You were right in your initial assessment." Chris pivoted to face him. Terry wore a custom made suit Chris recognized as a Dolce and Gabbana. Chris remembered him from CalTech, where he'd been more of a T-shirt and ripped jeans kind of guy. He never had that kind of taste—or discretionary funds. Chris was glad he'd worn his newest Versace to this meet. He hated to be upstaged.

Still, he felt bad for the news he had to deliver.

"You were hacked. By someone who knew what they were doing."

"A virus? Trojan—?"

"Nothing I've ever seen. It's got enough of a unique signature to suggest it was written just for your system."

Terry shoved his glasses up his nose. "Who?"

"Don't know that," Chris said. "Whoever it was, they're good. Covered their tracks well."

"But you were able to spot them?"

"They're not that good." Chris held up his hand to forestall Terry's next question. "There's more. The attack came from inside your network. And my guess is, it's still occurring."

Terry slumped into one of the swivel chairs crowding the oak and brass table. He stared down at the report Chris had given him earlier. "How much damage?"

"Hard to say at this point."

"Any indication our patient records were compromised?"

"That will take more time to determine."

"How much time?"

"Can't say at this point."

Terry swelled up like an angry cat. "What can you say? I need answers on this fast. We have an audit coming up, otherwise I wouldn't have called you in. I'd have taken care of it myself."

"I'll need at least two more days."

"I'll have to clear it with management." Terry was still pissed. Chris didn't blame him. "They're not likely to be as accommodating."

Chris nodded. He'd expected that. He gathered his laptop and tucked it into his carrying case. He'd make himself scarce while Terry argued with the suits about the catastrophe that had hit on Terry's watch.

Terry held up his hand.

"Don't go yet." His fingers fluttered over his tie after hanging up. "We need to talk. Let's go to my office. I've got some decent coffee. You can fill me in on how you're going to approach this so I have something more concrete to take upstairs."

Chris glanced at his watch. David would be done at the doctor's downstairs in about twenty minutes. He had time. "Sure."

He followed Terry out to the elevator. They didn't speak on the short ride down to the second floor. Terry's office mirrored his attire. His dark cherry veneer desk was clutter-free except for an IBM laptop and a picture of his wife, Cathy. They had no kids as far as Chris knew. Terry and he hadn't done much socializing over the years. He hadn't been invited to the wedding and hadn't invited Terry to his, either.

On a sideboard were a drip coffeepot, an assortment of free trade coffees, and the usual mix of large and small mugs. "What's your flavor?" Terry asked, holding up the coffee filter.

"Something dark."

"Sumatran?"

Chris nodded and looked around the small office. The walls were covered in framed certificates that spoke of Terry's long years in the industry. He'd been a real go-getter at CalTech. That drive apparently hadn't left him. There were several O'Keeffe prints showcasing New Mexico. Under the certificates and prints, something he never would have expected, an acoustic guitar with the patina of long use leaning against the wall.

Terry followed Chris's gaze. "I took it up about a year ago. Play some jazz and blues."

Chris approached the instrument. He didn't touch it, but he did notice the half dozen photos taken at small clubs on the wall above the guitar. In each one Terry was part of a trio of musicians. In them, he had eschewed his suit in favor of jeans, a T-shirt and a neon headband.

"Where do you play?"

Terry grinned. "Around town, did a couple of gigs in San Francisco." His frown returned. "Just what did you find in our system?"

Chris continued to stare at the images. You thought you knew a guy. "Besides the signs of file activity you mean? Password cracking tools. Some pretty sophisticated stuff. It can be deconstructed, which might point to who wrote it, but I'll need time to do it."

Terry opened his briefcase and drew out several pages that he handed to Chris. "This is what your final contract will look like. Check it over, let me know if you have any problems with it."

Chris skimmed the contents quickly. It looked like a standard boilerplate non-disclosure, work-for-hire four-week contract. He'd signed a similar, shorter one for the initial assessment. No unusual term that would limit his ability to do his job or bind him up afterward.

"Take it home," Terry said. "Read it over. Have your lawyer vet it."

Chris held out his hand. They shook. "I'll let you know tomorrow." He glanced at the guitar one more time. For some reason it intrigued him. "Let me know when your next gig is. I'll bring David. He loves jazz."

Terry nodded; he seemed too preoccupied to pay attention. Chris could tell his mind was already back on his computer problems.

Chris stuffed the contract into his laptop case. He strode across the dove gray carpet toward the elevator. Once inside, he pulled out his Blackberry. No messages. At least he wasn't late picking up his husband. David hated tardiness.

David's doctor had an office in a building attached to the main hospital. David, who hated needles, was due to get his allergy shot. Chris made the appointment for him, knowing David would avoid it as long as he was left to his own devices.

The receptionist showed him into a small consulting room off the main waiting room.

David scowled up at him. "They're not here yet. We have to wait."

The fierce look on David's face didn't faze him. He dropped into an uncomfortable chair beside his husband of eighteen months. "Who's not here?"

"The pharmacy." David's scowl deepened. "And my shot."

Chris rolled his eyes. "You mean I get to watch the tough as nails homicide detective take his medicine? Think of all the good that comes of it—you won't be sniffling and carrying on when the animals jump on you. And we'll save a fortune on Kleenex. You're always after us to save, right?"

"Right, a fifty dollar bottle of wine is acceptable, but a two dollar box of Kleenex isn't?"

Chris grinned. After several seconds, David followed suit. The smile lifted his dour face and reminded Chris of why he loved this man.

One of the clinic nurses bustled in. A diminutive Korean, she smiled when she saw Chris and glanced at their joined hands. "Come to comfort the patient?"

Everyone, it seemed, knew about David's aversion to needles. David quickly disengaged his hand from Chris's.

David refused to watch as she uncapped the syringe and swabbed his arm with alcohol. He winced as she deftly slid the needle into the muscle and depressed the plunger. She covered the puncture mark with a circular Band-Aid.

David rubbed the spot. The nurse deposited the used syringe in a sharps container and left the room.

"There, that wasn't so bad, was it?" He waited for David to stand. Chris reached for his arm, carefully avoiding the injection site.

David shook his head. Suddenly he blinked and swallowed convulsively.

"David?"

David wheezed, struggling to catch his breath. His face went rigid. Lips pressed together, his eyes unfocused.

"David!"

His entire body stiffened. He drew in a convulsive breath, then struggled to draw another. His face blanched as he clawed at his throat.

David arched forward and spewed out a stream of vomit across his jean clad legs and the tile floor beside the bed. Before he could take a breath, he repeated the action. The room filled with the sour stench.

Chris's stomach rolled over at the smell. He darted toward the door.

"I'll find the doctor," he said. He emerged in a waiting room full of expectant patients. Several of them turned startled eyes on him.

"Where's the doctor?" he shouted.

In the room behind him metal crashed and David's guttural cry was abruptly cut off.

CHAPTER TWO

Monday 11:55 am Rowena Medical Center, Rowena Avenue, Silver Lake, Los Angeles

The Korean nurse hurried through the door.

David's mouth moved as though he struggled to form words. His voice, when it emerged, held none of the strength Chris was familiar with. His throat was puffy and his lips were turning blue.

"Numb…" He whispered. "Can't breathe."

"What's wrong with him?" Chris hovered over David. "Get the doctor, for God's sake."

"He's on his way." The nurse grabbed an epipen and jabbed it into David's thigh. "Please, Chris. It would be best if you left—"

David's doctor, Dr. Daniel Abrahms, entered the room.

David's dark skin looked sallow and clammy. His breathing remained labored.

"What's that?" Chris asked. "What's wrong with him, Doctor?"

"David is going into anaphylactic shock. This," he said, holding up the syringe, "will stabilize him."

"Anaphylactic shock? From what? His allergy shot?"

The doctor slid the syringe into David's shoulder and depressed the plunger. "This is epinephrine," he said. "It should stabilize him."

"What's going on here?" Chris asked. "What's wrong?"

David's breathing grew more regular and his eyes cleared. He blinked and met Chris' gaze. Then he turned hard eyes on Abrahms.

"What the hell happened?"

"Anaphylactic shock—"

"He should go to the hospital, shouldn't he?" Chris wanted to touch his lover, but he knew David was reticent about physical contact in front of straights.

"I'm fine, Chris, really," David murmured.

Chris whirled on him. "Stop playing the damn martyr, David. Stop trying to prove how tough you are." He spun back toward the doctor. "I want him admitted. Now."

"I concur," Abrahms said.

Chris had never liked David's doctor. The man was too analytical, too cool. His bedside manner sucked. To have the man agree with him was unnerving. Just how bad was David?

"Go home, Chris," David's voice still sounded weak, but there was no mistaking his annoyance. "Let the professionals do their job."

That was a sore point with them. Chris had the bad habit of butting his nose into David's work. Chris didn't mean to, but sometimes he thought the LAPD was slack in their duties, especially when it came to how they treated the cops in their ranks that were "different." The LAPD had never quite reconciled itself to the number of gay officers that to them must have seemed like they were coming out of the woodwork. Several crippling and image-destroying lawsuits had made them tread lightly, so these days they tiptoed around people like David.

It didn't help that David was damned good at his job.

Chris was going to suggest again that David be admitted, but David cut him off. "I'm not going into the hospital. I'm fine, Chris, really. Dr. Abrahms?"

"I have to agree with Christopher on this, David. There are some tests—"

David shrugged his rolled up shirt sleeves back down over his muscular arms and levered himself out of the chair. "I'll come back if things don't feel right, but for now I'm going home."

Chris knew better than to argue, even if Abrahms didn't. He scooped David's jacket off the coat hook and handed it to him.

On the way out the door he looked at David's still pale face and tried again. "David—"

"Don't. I'm fine, really."

Chris made a rude noise in his throat, which his husband ignored.

Chris unlocked the kiwi green hybrid Escape he had bought to replace his first Escape wrecked in a car accident. Even with the sunshade covering the front windshield the car was still roaster hot. Chris buckled in and started the AC, knowing it would take a few minutes to cool the car's interior. In the heat stench from the vomit covering David's legs grew stronger. After a couple of minutes Chris cranked his window down and tried to breath through his mouth. David followed suit. It didn't help much.

The radio clock said it was nearly one. David flipped his cell phone out. "I better call Martinez, he'll be wondering what hole I fell into when I don't come back."

David's partner of nearly twelve years had grown comfortable with his gay partner. He had even been best man at their wedding. He still tended to eye Chris with a slightly jaundiced gaze when he thought no one was looking. The one time Chris had mentioned it, David had dismissed his complaint. "That's just Martinez," he had said. "He doesn't mean anything by it."

"Right," Chris had retorted. "And Fred Phelps is kind to his children."

Chris kept half an eye on David all the way home. A short trip, but an uneasy one. David grew paler and paler. Chris snapped, "I want to take you back."

"I won't go."

"You need to go back."

"No. No, just home. I'll be fine, Chris. Really."

David already had his key out when they drove into the cobbled drive of their Silver Lake home. A pair of nesting mourning doves flew out of the Cyprus tree beside the stone alcove. Sergeant, their rescued Doberman, greeted them enthusiastically at the door, circling David, sniffing at his jeans. Chris shut and locked the front door and turned to find David halfway up the marble steps to the second floor.

Chris took the stairs two at a time. He found David stripping his filthy pants off and tossing them in the laundry basket. After a very quick shower he slid into their king-sized bed and drew the duvet up to his chin. The dog stood beside the bed, whining. He knew there was something wrong. David patted the bed and the dog leaped onto it, settling down at his feet.

"Listen, hon, you don't need to prove how tough you are," Chris said, stroking the dog's knobby head. "A trip to the hospital isn't giving in."

"Give me a break. I just need to rest."

Chris stood in the doorway for another minute, then gave up. He took the laundry hamper downstairs and shoved the jeans in the washer. In the kitchen he rinsed out the few dishes in the sink and loaded them in the dishwasher. Preparing a pot of Indonesian coffee, he sat alone at the kitchen table. Idly, he toyed with an orange from the fruit bowl without seeing anything.

Growing restless with so many unanswered questions, he knew he needed to get back into Ste. Anne's network to see what had gone on there. David had taught him long ago that coincidences were rare. Chris knew from his preliminary work that the clinic where Abrahms worked was linked into Ste. Anne's network. He would start there. But first he had to sign Terry's contract. Only then would he get the access he needed.

He pulled his Blackberry out and punched in Terry's number. After the initial greetings Chris didn't waste time. "I want to come in and finalize the contract."

"Good. When?"

"How about now."

Chris met Terry inside his office. Signing the contract took only a minute. After Chris slid his Mont Blanc pen back into his suit pocket, he stood and shook Terry's hand. "The only other thing I'll need is physical and remote access to all your systems."

"I can do that."

"The sooner the better. I'll write you up a nightly report so you can see the direction I'm taking. Does that work for you?"

Chris waited in Terry's office while Terry collected an electronic badge that gave him access to any place in the hospital. Terry provided the necessary passwords; Chris committed them to memory.

While Terry showed Chris his system, his pager went off. Terry glanced at it. "I gotta go. You'll be okay here on your own?"

Chris nodded. After Terry left he sat down at a workstation and logged in to the main hospital system. He quickly navigated his way through files and directories, probing for signs of intrusion.

Streams of information flashed across the monitor from the intrusion detection programs he was running.

Chris glanced through some captured data logs. On the surface he saw nothing unorthodox. But he'd expected that. He'd seen how good this guy was. A quick scan of the outer firewall revealed the software gateway that protected the inner network was being hit by a lot of traffic, but that was standard—the Internet swarmed with packets designed to do nothing but probe for open ports. Nothing seemed to be getting past the perimeter. Terry had hardened his network well.

Before he went any further he stopped and took a deep breath. What he was going to do next wasn't entirely ethical; it was outside the bounds of his contract but he had to know.

What had happened to David? As much as he didn't like Dr. Abrahms, he knew the man was too good to make so simple a mistake as dosing David with the wrong medication. Chris knew David was allergic to the whole range of penicillin drugs. Had the hospital somehow delivered that instead of the anti-allergen he should have received?

He sent his probes into the heart of Ste. Anne's. It took him a while to find Dr. Abrahms' files and even longer to locate David's but eventually he was inside. He was able to look up past treatments David had received and compared them to the last one. The difference was immediately obvious. Whoever had hacked the system had made no effort to hide what he had done. Obviously no one at the pharmacy had checked the script. Why would they? They took what was delivered. He also saw the alert, warning the pharmacy of the allergy, had been removed, so there was nothing to warn anyone of the mistake they were about to make.

He didn't have to search much to find out what had replaced the drug David had received: Amoxicillin rather than the anti-allergen. No wonder David had such a violent reaction. But... it didn't make any sense. Why David? Sure he was a cop and a gay man. Both attracted the wrong kind of attention. Could the hacker have had a run in with cops? With David in particular? If he had this power he could have hit the entire hospital pharmacy records.

Chris scrambled to his feet. He had to warn Terry. If medications were compromised time was vital. He snatched up his Blackberry and punched in the network manager's cell.

He answered on the third ring. In the background Chris could hear children yelling. The sound suddenly died; Terry must have moved to another room.

"What's up?"

"You may have a bigger problem than we thought." Chris told him about David's compromised medication. There was nothing but silence at the other end.

"You think other records might have been altered?"

"I can't rule it out."

Terry swore.

"I'll be right there," Terry said.

CHAPTER THREE

Monday, 4:45 pm Ste. Anne's Medical Center, Rowena Avenue, Silver Lake, Los Angeles

"I heard about your troubles a few years ago," Terry said. He had run out to Krispy Kreme and picked up half a dozen donuts along with two coffees. "What did the paper call him? The Carpet Killer? It must have been rough."

Chris figured just about everybody had heard about that terrible time with the Carpet Killer. The press had gone on a feeding frenzy with Chris and the newly outed David at center stage for way too long. The whole mess had nearly derailed David's career. The police brass had not taken kindly to one of their homicide detectives forming a relationship with a man who had been a murder suspect at one time. Their wedding in Canada eighteen months ago had only solidified his news value.

Oddly enough, it had all provided a much-needed boost to Chris's new business. When he'd quit DataTEK, and gone solo, he'd worried about building his new client base. All the publicity had actually brought in new business. He figured it was a Hollywood thing—any publicity was good as long as they spelled your name right.

"It had its moments," Chris said. "Look, I know you've got a good system here. But this is a lot more malicious than I originally thought," Chris said. "We need to take a look at all the patient records to see if they show signs of tampering."

Terry was pale but stoic. They discussed what they were looking for and soon the two of them were seated in front of glowing monitors scanning through directories, looking for what didn't belong.

"Watch for odd timestamps," Chris said. "We'll have to look at everything that was altered within the last forty-eight hours, compare any suspicious ones against your backups." David's file had been changed roughly sixteen hours ago. "You realize we're going to have to let management know what's going on? You have to comply with the data breach laws. Those with legitimate access to those files are going to have to go through them, too."

Pain crossed Terry's face. Disclosure was mandated by law. "This is bullshit. How the hell did he get in?"

Chris hated what he had to say next. "On foot."

"You mean he just walked in and hacked my system?"

"Not quite that simple, but here, look..."

Chris had been pleased to find Terry had employed a passive protocol analyzer, which operated at the lowest levels of network operation, and was extremely difficult to evade. There was no obvious way to transmit packets on a monitored network without it being detected. It still took a trained eye to spot the bad packets from the good ones. At first glance the activity logs seemed innocuous. Terry scrubbed stiff fingers through his short hair. "I don't see anything."

Chris was looking for tunneling activity or some other TCP/IP exploit, since it was the one type of traffic that couldn't be blocked without blocking Internet access. Once inside, any savvy cracker could access the rest of the network. Chris often used something similar to run penetration tests of networks he was charged with protecting.

"It's probably some damn script kiddy," Terry muttered. "You know as well as I do that most of these guys are kids, barely out of diapers. Makes you feel old. Doesn't it?"

"I try not to think about it." Truth was, Chris did feel old sometimes, trying to keep up with teenagers with no morals, and minds like quicksilver. It was all fair game to them, and it never did any good telling them it was wrong to hack a stranger's computer. They made heroes out of the ones who got caught. Famous crackers and phreaks like Riddle and Mitnick were vilified by the mainstream media, but lived on as cyber-legends, in chat rooms and newsgroups, all over the world. Role models to a disenfranchised generation.

"How did it happen? I can't believe you're saying he just strolled in off the street."

"Not quite that simple, but yeah, he did it from inside." He tried to soften his words. "Face it, would anyone notice a stranger wearing scrubs? Carrying a stethoscope?"

"It is a big hospital," Terry admitted. "Lots of staff turnover, what with interns and teaching staff coming and going. Not to mention patients and visitors. I don't want to think about the uproar if we start refusing them entry."

"So you're not going to catch this guy in the act. All we can do is follow his trail."

"And play catch-up," Terry muttered. "Not good enough."

Chris shrugged. "We may not figure out who he is, but we can head him off. Damage control."

Terry sucked at his coffee. He dug through the box and nibbled a donut.

Chris grabbed one too and went back to scanning files. It was tedious work. He had set up a simple script that would show only those files which had been changed in forty-eight hours. It was still a load of files. Thousands at least.

He copied each file that fit the criteria and put it in a temporary folder for examination later. Time crept by and before either of them knew it was six in the morning and the hospital was coming to life.

Chris blinked and leapt up. "Jesus, David—" Under Terry's puzzled gaze, he pulled out his BlackBerry and dialed home.

A groggy sounding David answered on the fifth ring. When he realized who was calling he growled, "I told you I was fine. I've already told Martinez I won't be in today. Happy?"

Chris was, and wasn't afraid to show it. "Sleep then. I'll bring something special for dinner, okay?"

"Fine, good. I'll see you then."

Chris put his phone away, pulled his pen out, and skimmed it across a line of text on the screen. "A MAC address." A MAC address was hard-coded into every piece of network hardware and was unique to that piece of equipment. "Recognize it?" Chris asked.

"That's a 3COM card," Terry said. "Makes it a workstation."

"This is internal, then. Where is it?" They may have just found their point of entry.

At a DOS prompt Chris tapped out an nslookup command. It would give him the computer name that was linked to the MAC address. The name that came back was THD028.

"That's on the third floor." Terry scribbled in a dog-eared notebook. Like most system administrators, Terry wrote liberal notes to himself. He shared an uneasy look with Chris. "There's maybe a dozen workstations on that floor. It should be easy to find."

At one point Terry spent a heated fifteen minutes on the phone with his boss and Chris didn't need to hear the other end of the conversation to know it wasn't good. A second call confirmed that. They'd found more damning evidence of file damage. Terry looked at Chris with haunted eyes.

"Several patients on the third floor have had their medications compromised." Terry closed his eyes. "One of them just died."

Chris felt something inside him contract. He couldn't breathe for the lump in his throat. The next words out of Terry's mouth were even more chilling.

"And to make matters worse, the press is here."

Chris had far too much experience with the fifth estate. He knew too damn well how they were masters of manipulation, and how the worst of them practiced an in-your-face frontal assault. He had been badly burned by zealous reporters when David had been outed and Chris had found himself the cops' number one suspect in a series of gruesome murders.

David's career as an LAPD homicide detective had nearly been sabotaged. Chris had lost the job he'd worked years to secure and both of them survived by sheer, stubborn persistence. It had taken them months to recover from the disaster. The only good that had come of it was David. Now someone had invaded their lives, threatening David's life.

A red-hot rage threatened his thin hold on his composure. How dare they.

Chris scrubbed the grit and sleep out of his eyes. His hands rasped over his unshaven face and his mouth felt like a landfill site. Even a mug of Terry's free trade coffee hadn't helped.

Finally at eight o'clock Terry collapsed in a chair, nearly spilling onto the floor. Around him the deadening glow of the monitors cast a baleful light.

Chris sank into a chair beside him. He felt numb.

"We have to take a break," he said. "Is there anyone you can call in to take over—?"

Terry's cell rang again. Another heated conversation followed. Terry disconnected and sagged in the chair. "That was Hugh Denton, the hospital administrator. Major dickhead, but he insists on being in the middle of this. 'Keeping his hand on the pulse.'" Terry buried his head in his hands. "I am so fucked." Finally he met Chris's gaze. "I can call Yuri. He's done work for us before."

Chris glanced at his watch. "Call him then. We'll meet back here in four hours."

"My mind stopped working two hours ago."

Chris crawled out of his chair, joints creaking in protest. He arched backward, feeling his spine crackle, barely suppressing a groan.

"Now how the hell do we get out of here?" he asked. "Without running the gauntlet of reporters?"

■ □ ■ □

The elevator glided open onto the back ward. Chris poked his head out to an empty corridor. So far so good.

A few feet from the back exit, he heard his name and a voice he had never wanted to hear again. "Chris! Is it true computer hackers attacked the hospital?"

Roz Parnell was a reporter for the *L.A. Times.* Years ago, when Chris and David found infamy clinging to them like a bad smell, Roz had pursued them with a single-minded purpose.

The publicity might have helped his new business, but it left a bad taste in his mouth for the press.

How had she heard about the attack? He knew damn well neither Terry nor Denton would have told her. The hospital administrator would be having kittens if he knew Roz was here.

"How serious was it, Chris?" Roz was a red-haired brazen woman with a penchant for pink jackets and Prada heels. She also had a surprisingly dulcet voice. That voice, he was sure, had fooled more than one person into revealing things they hadn't intended. "Did you know the man who died?"

He wasn't going to play in her sandbox. He ducked away from her and muttered, "No comment."

"Do you think this was a deliberate act of sabotage?" Roz persisted. "How vulnerable are our hospitals? Will they strike again?" She shoved her perfumed cleavage into his face. "Is this the work of terrorists, Chris? Do you expect more deaths as a result of this? Or do you think it's teenage hackers?"

"Crackers," Chris said, then his curiosity got the better of him. "How did you even find out?"

Roz smiled. "Some people believe the public has a right to know this kind of thing. We were alerted—"

"You got a phone call," Chris said. "It ever occur to you the guy who broke into the hospital made the call? You like feeding the ego of a killer?"

Roz was writing furiously. "So you admit there was an attack? Is the hospital going to hire you to find out who did it?"

"No comment—"

He shoved past her. She followed him to the parking lot, trotting to keep up with his long strides.

"Is it true David was impacted by this? How serious was he affected—?"

He slammed the car door and cranked the engine. Grabbing a U2 CD he put it on and turned it up loud before rolling down the car window. "No comment," he shouted over the thunder of Bono's voice. "Now leave both of us the hell alone."

CHAPTER FOUR

Chris pulled into the driveway and shut the engine off. David's Chevy '56 two-tone sport coupe was still parked in the driveway. He had done what he said and stayed home. Unmoving, Chris sat watching a squirrel make short dashes across the lawn, finally bolting for a eucalyptus when Chris's neighbor walked by with their black lab.

Chris climbed out of the car, waved hello to the neighbor and entered the cool foyer. Sergeant rushed the door to greet him. Absently he patted the animal's blocky head. The house was quiet. David must still be in bed. A frisson of alarm skittered across his nerves. David wasn't the type to sleep in even if he was home sick.

Dumping his keys on the foyer table, he slipped his shoes off. In stocking feet he padded up the stairs. The dog followed.

The bed was empty. In fact there was no sign it had even been slept in. A quick look in the bathroom confirmed it. David was not in the house.

"Where'd he go, boy? Where's David?"

With growing alarm, Chris hurried back down the stairs into the kitchen. No sign the coffee pot had been used. An empty cup in the sink held the dregs of orange juice. His alarm faded, replaced by a growing annoyance.

Growing more pissed by the minute, Chris looked for a note he knew wasn't there. He even checked the answering machine in case David had called after leaving. Nothing. Chris knew where David was. Martinez had called or he had called Martinez. This time, David had answered his siren call. He'd gone back to work just a few hours after having a dangerous anaphylactic reaction.

Too wound up to rest now, though he knew he would pay for the neglect sooner rather than later, Chris tried David's cell. No answer. He finally broke down and called the Northeast Station. He wasn't surprised that David wasn't there, and no, he wasn't going to leave a message with the officious desk sergeant who answered the phone.

Hanging up, he set about making a pot of coffee. If he couldn't rest, he might as well make the most of his time. While he waited for the coffee, he took the clothes out of the drier and trotted back upstairs, folding and putting them away. Then he cleaned the already spotless bathroom and tidied the bedroom. Sergeant and Sweeney, the Siamese cat David had brought to their relationship, followed him around until he got the hint and fed them both. Sweeney wrapped around his ankles, purring hoarsely, throwing one jaundiced eye at the dog he had finally grown to tolerate. Barely. Chris scooped the cat up.

"You miss him too, don't you?" Chris rubbed the sleek seal-colored head. He glanced down at Sergeant. "He didn't happen to mention where he was going, did he?"

Neither animal answered.

Tuesday, 10:20 am, Carillon Street, Atwater, Los Angeles

Another body; another dead woman.

David had lost count of the number of corpses he had seen in his ten years as a homicide detective. Instead he concentrated on studying the body on the bed. Whatever struggle she might have waged, in the end it didn't show on the unmarked, vanilla plain face. In the background an air conditioner hummed loudly. David was glad for his suit jacket; the room was cold. It was also almost antiseptically clean. He rubbed his pock-marked face. His skin felt mottled with goose bumps.

"It seem cool in here to you?"

"Some people got more money than brains." Martinez, his partner of nearly twelve years narrowed his dark eyes and took in the bed and its occupant. "How long you figure she's been dead?"

The scent of decay rode the cool air. But faint, just a hint of the mordant stench to come.

"No flies."

"She kept a clean apartment."

"You really think she always kept it this cold?" David pulled on a pair of gloves and crouched beside the bed. He couldn't touch the body, but while they waited for the coroner, he could look around. "Who did you say found her?"

"Neighbor called it in," Martinez said. "Our Lady of Antarctica here didn't go to Sunday mass, something she never missed. She rarely left the place except to go to church. Neighbor thought maybe she'd gone to visit family, then she missed a very special church meeting yesterday. According to her, this proved something was wrong. So she finally convinced the super to open up this morning."

Like an under-smell that grew on his senses, the stink of decay ripened. Despite his first thought that this was a new body, David suddenly knew she'd been a corpse for a while. Instinct hewn from years of being a cop. Instinct he trusted. Atop the bedside table sat an alarm clock and a five by ten framed picture of a gangly teenage boy and Nancy Scott. Mother and son? Nephew? No way it could be grandson. Not enough age between them. He looked around. One other picture, the same boy, slightly older. No images of a man who might be the father. Never married? Didn't jibe with the woman being so religious. Divorced? Widowed? He looked back at the body.

"Somebody didn't want her found."

"ME's on her way," Martinez said, pulling on a pair of thin gloves. Powder puffed out and lingered briefly in the cool, still air. "Let's toss the place. Ten says she's been dead forty-eight."

David studied the dead woman's left hand on top of the flowered comforter. He noticed the faint purplish hue at the ends of her fingers. He crouched beside the bed, taking a closer look without touching. "Seventy-two."

"Put your money where your mouth is."

"You're on." David moved to stand up, and paused, fingers braced on the carpeted floor beside the bed. In the shadows formed by the comforter something darker lay concealed. Casually, David flipped aside the covering. He reached in and pulled out two tiny, dark brown paper wrappers.

"What have you got?"

David leaned back on his heels. He raised a wrapper to his face and gingerly sniffed. "Chocolate."

"So our victim's mowing down on chocolates in bed." Martinez glanced sourly at a book on the night table. There was an image of a half-naked man and woman entwined on the cover. "My wife reads that crap. What do they get out of it?"

"Fantasy. It's not about you."

Martinez scowled. "So, she's reading bad literature and indulging in a candy fix."

"Where's the rest of the chocolates?" David prowled the room, staring down into the wicker garbage pail. A yellow bag lined the receptacle. "Where's the empty box? Where's the rest of the *garbage?*"

They moved systematically through each room. Splitting duties, David took the bedroom, probing closets and drawers, and under the sparse furnishings that filled the pin-neat apartment. The rugs were spotless, the furniture looked like a showroom. David ran one gloved finger over the top shelf of a knick-knack showcase. It came away dust free.

Martinez took the bathroom and David could hear the rattle of the medicine cabinet as he rummaged through it, and the slam of drawers. Martinez even whisked aside the shower curtain, though what he thought he might find was anyone's guess.

Another body? No one in this place would be so bold as to die anywhere but neatly on the bed, like the woman had.

David stacked up piles of paper and scrapbooks that he found in a drawer, piling them on the kitchen table, roughly sorted by type. Receipts in one, hand-written notes in another. Doctor's appointments, grocery lists, phone numbers, addresses.

Martinez came out carrying the wicker trashcan from the bathroom. "No sign anyone but her lived here, or stayed long enough to leave anything behind. Just female stuff." He knelt and tipped the trashcan contents onto a sheet of plastic on the floor, sorting through it carefully with gloved fingers. He held up an empty vial.

"Insulin," he said. "From a Doctor Vanya Parkov, Glendale address."

She was a diabetic.

David opened the refrigerator and they peered inside. Whoever the woman was, she had been no gourmand. More vials of insulin. Homogenized milk in a plastic jug and a no-name brand of orange juice claiming to be fresh-squeezed crowded the side panel. The fridge also held a jar of pickles, ketchup, a half-empty jar of Miracle Whip, cold meat, cheese slices, raw carrots and six potatoes sprouting eyes. The cupboards were almost as empty. David pulled out a few cans of chicken noodle soup, two cream of mushroom and a boxed Kraft Dinner.

No chocolates. No candies of any kind.

"Somebody comes visiting," David mused. "Brings her chocolates, which she's not supposed to have, then takes them when they leave?"

"Maybe she tells her visitor don't leave stuff to tempt her?"

"Or maybe the chocolates are more than chocolates," David said. In his gut he knew this wasn't a natural death. "Bag it all. We take it to forensics. Let them sort it out."

■ □ ■ □

David extended his card to the tiny woman with pumpkin-colored hair.

"Mrs. Crandall? Alice Crandall?"

She took the card and held it between her finger and thumb like it might be the devil's calling card. She barely glanced at it.

Alice had been the victim's neighbor for "nigh on five years, young man," she told the two detectives. "That's why I told that young pup that there was no way Nancy committed suicide. She'd have paraded naked down Glendale Boulevard sooner than she'd have killed herself."

"We're here to listen, Mrs. Crandall." David tipped his head and kept his face neutral. He flipped open his notepad and wrote the day's date. "We'd like to ask you a few questions about your neighbor, if we could. Nancy Scott was her name, is that correct?"

"Nancy Amelia Scott," Alice said. "That was her full Christian name, rest her soul."

"You knew her five years. Did she move in five years ago, or did you?"

"I've been on this same spot of earth since before my good husband Lloyd passed, nigh on eleven years ago it was, rest his soul. He was a good man. Salt of the earth."

David scanned the room. From what he could see it looked like Alice had furnished the place during the height of the beige eighties and never recovered from it. If there was a spot of color anywhere, he couldn't find it. "So Mrs. Scott moved in five years ago. Was she by herself?"

"That man was a saint, he was. Why, even Father Barnaby used to remark as how good he was, never drank a tipple in his life and worked until they forced him to retire at sixty-five. Not that he wanted to leave, mind you, the man loved to work, almost as much as he loved to talk—"

"Yes, Mrs. Crandall," David said. "I'm sorry for your loss, but if you could just answer some questions about your neighbor."

"Lloyd would have loved Nancy. She was a pious woman, never heard a curse word come out of her mouth. Even Lloyd wasn't that good."

"When was the last time you actually saw Mrs. Scott, ma'am?" David persisted. Patience was a virtue, his own, less than saintly, mother might have said, but there were times when patience could take a flying leap. "You mentioned her missing Mass on Sunday. So if she wasn't there, when did you see her last?"

"Sunday Nancy always came with me," Alice said. "She wasn't born a Catholic; she told me that right after I first asked her to join me at Incarnation. Was born a Presbyterian but never found satisfaction in that faith." Alice dug her short, unpolished nails through the tight mass of bright hair. "She strayed, she said, and when she found her way back, she decided the good Lord meant her to be part of the true faith, so she come and joined our church. She asked for my help then," Alice said proudly. "She asked me to help her find her way back to God."

"Yes, ma'am," David said. Beside him Martinez harrumphed softly. "But I still need to know when you last saw Nancy alive."

Alice eyed Martinez coldly, then smiled at David, revealing impossibly even, white teeth. "Are you Catholic, young man?"

"No, ma'am, I'm sorry. I'm afraid I'm not."

"Pity."

"Yes, ma'am. Now ma'am—"

"I know," Alice said. "When did I last see her?"

"Yes, ma'am—"

"I'll tell you if you stop jabbering. Can't stand a man who always interrupts. Her son was like that, you know. Always cutting in, interrupting his mother like everything he had to say was pure gospel and the rest of us should just shut up and listen."

"Her son, ma'am?" David leaned closer, pen poised over his dog-eared notepad. "Mrs. Scott had a son? What about a Mr. Scott?"

"No Mr. Scott. He was her past, she used to say, she was her own future. She never spoke of him. If he was anything like her son, I can understand why."

"Would you know where we might find this son?"

"He comes around, regular as church bells," Alice said. "Every other Wednesday."

"And the last Wednesday he was here?"

The woman shrugged her thin shoulders. "Week or so ago." The corners of her mouth lifted in a smile. "Why, I guess that would be two weeks ago tomorrow."

David and Martinez traded looks. "Yes, ma'am," they both said.

"I guess you can ask him these questions." Alice smiled slyly. "Oh, and the last time I saw Nancy was Saturday morning. We walked down to the market to buy groceries."

"What did Mrs. Scott buy?" David asked, remembering the nearly empty refrigerator. And the chocolate wrapper.

Alice sniffed. "Orange juice, couple of cans of soup, bananas and a newspaper. I never saw such a one for not eating proper. I don't know how she stayed healthy." Her face suddenly screwed up. "I guess she didn't though, did she?"

"No, ma'am."

"You still think she killed herself?"

"That's up to the medical examiner to determine," David said.

"Will you be by to talk to that boy of hers tomorrow?"

"We just might do that, ma'am."

Alice smiled again. "Well, I won't tell him you're coming."

David almost smiled in return. "You have a good day now."

"You find out what happened to Nancy, and I'll have a good day."

She shut the door of her apartment behind them, leaving them standing in the musty hallway looking at each other in bemusement.

"Guess we come by to talk to junior, then," Martinez said. "Where do you think he was all this time?"

David pulled out the car keys and jangled them against his leg. "We'll have to make sure to ask, now won't we?"

CHAPTER FIVE

Tuesday 1:50 pm, North Mission Road, Los Angeles

The Los Angeles County Coroner's office was a low-slung colorless building within shotgun distance of the I5; the eternal roar of traffic drowned out any attempts at conversation. Golden afternoon light glinted off the smog rolling in off the distant freeway. The air smelled of diesel, and gas, and acrid dust.

David eased the unmarked into park and waited for Martinez to clamber out before he slipped off his seat belt. He sat in the heat and early fall sun that poured through the open car window and blinked to clear his head. The muzziness of encroaching exhaustion clouded his mind; he began to regret his haste in returning to work, but he was damned if he was going to beg off.

He pushed aside the rush of vertigo that hit him when he stood, and followed Martinez into the air-conditioned building.

They donned a plastic apron, mask, gloves, and covered their shoes with booties before entering the autopsy room. Harsh florescent lights illuminated over a dozen bodies in various stages of postmortem exam. There was a weird purple glow from the bug zappers scattered throughout the building. Every table was occupied; the Los Angeles morgue was one of the busiest in the country.

They found the deputy coroner, Teresa Lopez, prepping Nancy Scott's body. She nodded at David and Martinez and indicated the illuminated viewing box, which held the X-rays she had taken earlier.

"No visible external trauma." With gloved hands she propped one of the victim's eyelids open. "Conjunctiva's pinkish, and the pupils are dilated."

"She sick?" Martinez asked.

"Can't tell you," Teresa said. "Yet."

"We think she was diabetic," David said. "We found insulin in her fridge and an empty vial in her garbage."

Teresa nodded. Wielding a scalpel she made the Y-incision then moved aside while the morgue assistant used what looked like a pair of gardening shears to crack open the ribs and remove the sternum. Teresa flipped up the rib cage, revealing the body's internal organs.

"Interesting," she murmured. "I see signs of hemorrhaging. Not consistent with insulin shock."

David glanced away while Teresa deftly removed the heart, lungs, liver and kidneys, weighed them and prepped samples for tox screening. She also extracted blood and urine samples as well as the contents of the victim's stomach, which she would have analyzed.

"Tell me if she ate chocolates." In reality he knew she would tell him everything the woman had eaten for several hours prior to her death.

"Can you tell us when she last took an insulin shot?" Martinez asked.

"Sorry, there's no accurate way to measure that."

"Cause of death?" David finally asked, after the victim's brain and been removed, and weighed.

"Inconclusive," Teresa said, and Martinez rolled his eyes. "Sorry guys. We'll see what the tox screens show."

David stripped off his gloves as he headed for the door, a muttering Martinez trailing in his wake. They finished removing their gear and tossed them into the nearest hamper.

Outside, the late afternoon sun bounced off the car straight into David's brain. The distant rustle of heat drove air through some nearby palms. The dull headache he had been harboring during the autopsy flared into a head-pounding drill. He winced as he slid behind the wheel.

"*Dios*," Martinez said softly. "You okay? You look like shit."

"Thanks." David cranked the key and the engine rumbled to life. "It's nothing."

"Bull."

David looked at him sharply, a mistake since the sudden movement made the entire parking lot spin. He closed his eyes.

The passenger door opened and the whole car rocked when Martinez got out. Seconds later the driver's side door jerked open.

"Get out, I'm driving."

David hesitated only long enough to draw in one shuddering breath, then released the wheel and slid out. When he slipped into the seat Martinez had recently vacated, he made the mistake of meeting his partner's angry glare.

"What the hell are you thinking?" Martinez snapped. "You *loco*, man?"

"I'm fine—"

"*Mierda! Que eres un idiota loco?* You want to put *me* in the hospital this time?"

Martinez jerked the wheel around as he backed out, nearly sideswiping a coroner's wagon. The driver laid on the horn and gave them the finger.

Martinez ignored her. "I'm taking you home, and if you know what's good for you, you won't say one fucking word to me."

"It's not—"

"One more word and I tell Chris what's going on. You want me to do that, *partner*?"

David winced. Chris was already worse than a mother hen. Let Martinez breathe one word of this and Chris would lock him in his room for the next six weeks. Probably use his own handcuffs on him.

David nodded wearily. "Fine," he said. "I'll go home and rest. But I am not letting this go."

"Yes, you are. I'll interview the son."

Like hell. Martinez was a lousy interviewer. They both knew it. "Not alone you don't."

"*Estupido—*"

"I promise to go home and rest. By tomorrow I'll be fine. We do the interview, I go back home."

Martinez glared. David glared back, trying to keep his eyes from crossing. His head throbbed.

"You'll go home and rest until Friday?"

"Thursday—"

"Friday, Davey."

"Fine, Friday."

Tuesday 2:40 pm, Cove Avenue, Silver Lake, Los Angeles

Chris spent the day at the hospital. No calls from David, and another call to David's cell late in the afternoon yielded nothing. He didn't bother leaving a message.

The two-toned Chevy was still in the driveway. Where the hell was his husband?

Chris took a shower in the master bath he and David had only finished renovating back in the summer. He came out toweling his short hair into spikes.

Sweeney twined around his ankles, angling for food, so Chris followed him downstairs and fed him and the dog.

The phone rang.

It was Des, Chris's best friend since college days. "Hey, stranger, you fall off the planet?"

"Hi, Des. It hasn't been that long, has it?"

"You don't even know, do you?"

Chris sniffed. Des was always such a drama queen. "I don't

keep a calendar."

"You should. If you did, you'd know it's been positively ages. Two weeks at least, maybe even three."

"I've just been a teensy bit busy."

Des laughed. "Oh, and the rest of us aren't?"

Chris popped the fridge door open and surveyed the interior. What could he do for supper? Should he bother preparing anything—how likely was David to be home? He'd picked up a pork loin to stuff, but why make the effort just for himself?

"So aside from that, just how is everything?" Chris asked, eying a bowl of fettuccine and pesto and trying to remember when he had made it. As usual he had forgotten to label it.

"I'd like you and David to come for supper Wednesday night. I've got a little party set up for my birthday. You did tell him, I hope." Des's voice rose a notch. "I've got a surprise for both of you. Ohhh, you'll be so thrilled."

"I'll have to check with David," Chris said warily. Des's surprise could mean anything from finding a new designer to showcase in his upscale men's boutique in Beverly Hills, to his latest tuck. "But yes, I told him about it being your birthday."

"Tell him he absolutely must come. No squirming out of it for anything; not work, nothing. I've found the most fabulous sushi chef. He does amazing things with ahi and ono. You'll just die."

Chris perked up. He loved ahi. "I'll let you know. Let me talk to David." His second line beeped. "Gotta go. Talk later."

Wandering into the living room he dropped onto the white leather sofa facing the bay window overlooking the reservoir at the bottom of the hill. A trace of mist clung to the hillside as it trailed down onto the glassy surface of the lake, giving the area its name. The lake looked like it was steaming.

"Christopher Bellamere? This is Troy Garcia of the *Los Angeles Special*—"

Chris slammed the phone down with a strangled curse.

Garcia was the kind of sleaze-ball journalist who made Roz look respectable. Neither Chris nor David had forgiven him for running the sleazy images of David's former homicide partner, Jairo Hernandez, when Jairo, who had tried very hard to seduce David and take him away from Chris, had been shot and killed in a botched hostage taking crisis. That whole fiasco had nearly derailed their relationship, but ultimately led to David proposing to him and their subsequent marriage. When the phone started ringing again he let it go to voicemail. Climbing to his feet he entered his home office tucked in the back of the house. There he turned off the phone and sat down in front of his workstation.

Logging in, he opened his email program and watched the usual flurry of messages come in. He discarded the spam and moved several business-related emails into their respective folders, then skimmed the others. Just as he was about to close his mail program, a new email popped into his inbox. The subject line read "Warning for Chris" and the handle in the From column was Sandman422—no one he knew.

There were no potentially dangerous attachments. He opened it.

It contained one line.

`MIND YOUR OWN BUSINESS OR ELSE`

A second look at the email handle showed it was a Freemail account. Sandman422. Anyone with access to the Internet and five minutes could set up an anonymous account there and never worry about being traced. Okay, it was a joke. One of his online contacts playing a tasteless joke.

Then a little mail icon appeared in his system tray. New mail. Escaping out of Sandman's email, he found a second one from the same person.

He hesitated only briefly before opening it.

`IF YOU MESS WITH ME DAVID MIGHT NOT BE SO LUCKY NEXT TIME`

Shards of ice raced through Chris's gut. The skin of his face felt tight. "You bastard," he whispered to the silent screen.

This time he opened the properties of the email and looked at the message source. It told him a whole lot of things that weren't going to help him catch the prick. Sandman422 had sent his email from a Calnexxia server—Calnexxia was a local telecom company, spawned by the breakup of the telecommunications monopoly. The ISP that hosted Freemail used their servers and fiber lines as conduits for their product.

Chris ran a host lookup utility and found no surprises. The ISP matched the Calnexxia domain. Then he ran an Arin WHOIS search and got an organizational ID and a local Los Angeles address. Sandman422 had indeed used a free emailer to threaten David. He could have made the threat from anywhere. Not that Chris believed that. Sandman had to be local—how else would he know about David? He must have either been at the hospital, or—a horrible fear blossomed in his gut. Chris thought of the phone call from Troy Garcia. Had he received the same phone call Roz got? Was it Sandman who was spreading the story about his attack?

His phone rang. Chris answered, hoping it was David. "Intelligent Security, Chris speaking—"

"Hey, Chris," Terry sounded scared. "You need to get down here right now."

"Something new happen?"

"There's some serious shit going on. Denton pretty well tore me a new one," Terry said. "But he's given me support in tracking this asshole down. I've isolated that computer on the third floor. Talked to a guy I know who's done some work for the FBI and he told me how to secure it."

"Good." Chris cradled the phone between his shoulder and his chin while he sorted through some papers he had pulled together earlier for another client.

He was beginning to rethink his decision to work with Terry on this. It was promising to turn into another media circus—sure as shit this thing was going to become a public nightmare. But he'd already signed the contract, so his reluctance was moot.

"Can you come down now? Denton wants a proposal on how we're going to tackle this. I told him I'd have something on his desk for Wednesday."

Chris thought of David. No telling when he'd be home. He sure hadn't gone out of his way to let Chris know his plans. He could be gone all night.

Chris tucked the papers into a file folder. He thought of his aborted search for something to eat. "You hungry?" he asked.

"Haven't eaten yet, so I guess so," Terry said.

"Cafeteria still suck?"

"What do you think?"

"Tell me what you want and I'll be there in thirty."

It ended up taking nearly fifty minutes before Chris rolled into the hospital and had Terry paged. The system administrator loped off the elevator and grabbed Chris's arm, nearly knocking the bags of takeout out of his hand and jostling the laptop case against his hip.

"Hope there's coffee in there," Terry said.

Chris handed him an extra large.

"Come on," Terry said. "Let's sit in the cafeteria, the dinner rush is over."

Except for a pair of doctors in green scrubs and a woman nursing a bowl of soup, the small cafeteria was empty. Terry grabbed a table in the far corner.

Chris dug into his pastrami, savoring the sharp bite of stone ground mustard. He drew a yellow legal pad out of his laptop case and while he ate, made notes.

"Tell me where you are so far," Chris said.

Terry ticked off on the fingers of one hand. "I've copied all the activity logs to my workstation and I made hard copies. We can go over them later. I checked for outside connections but couldn't find anything suspicious, so I think your call that it's all coming from inside is right." Terry guzzled coffee.

"Where is the workstation now?"

"In my office."

"Can you round up another computer similar to it that we can use for the next few days?"

Terry wiped his hands on a napkin, shredding it before he stuffed it into the take-out bag with the rest of the garbage. "It's an older model, up for replacement this quarter. If memory serves me we've already replaced some on the other floors..."

Chris rounded up the rest of the leftovers and grabbed his laptop case. "Let's go check it out."

In Terry's office they found a technician hunched over a keyboard, tapping away with a classic hunt and peck method. He straightened when the door opened, his bearded face twisting into a scowl. Light from the monitor bounced off his hairless head.

"Yuri," Terry said. "This is Chris, he's helping us out for a bit, too." He nodded at the ranks of glowing monitors. "Anything up?"

"Nada."

Chris glanced at the monitor Yuri was scowling at. A helicopter zoomed into view and a rain of fire traced its flight. The helicopter vanished in a fireball. Yuri cursed. So much for due diligence. Terry seemed too distracted to notice his assistant was gaming instead of working.

"Where are those PCs we swapped off the fifth floor?"

"They're in the work room. What do you want them for?"

Terry glanced at Chris. "What do you want it for?"

"We clone the workstation," Chris said. "That way we don't damage the original files. If we catch the guy you'll need them intact to prosecute." Being married to a cop had its advantages.

Yuri nodded absently. Fishing a red stick of licorice out of a package he chewed on it while he tried to move his online character to safe ground.

Chris and Terry left Yuri to his game. They grabbed a cart and loaded the third floor machine onto it.

"Where we going?" Chris asked.

"Second floor storage room just down the hall. We stage new equipment out of it, and decommission old stuff while we wait to ship it."

They rolled the cart into the storage room, which Chris was happy to see had a properly set up staging area for several computers to sit side by side while techs worked on them. It took the two of them only a few minutes to wrestle the machine into place and find a matching computer among several sitting on a skid in the far corner. Chris hooked monitors onto the two systems and cabled them together.

Chris opened his laptop and sorted through his software. He powered on both computers and slid the disc into the third floor machine. Within minutes he had the cloning process running.

"That'll take about an hour," Chris said. "You want to keep looking over those logs?"

CHAPTER SIX

Tuesday 6:25 pm, Cove Avenue, Silver Lake, Los Angeles

Martinez dropped David off at home. "I don't want to see your face until Friday"

David didn't argue. Exhaustion rode him like a too tight shirt; even breathing was an effort.

Chris's car was gone. A single light burned over the small courtyard. The house was dark. The interior air cooled his heated face. Sergeant greeted him with glee, leaving David exhausted by his enthusiasm. He slipped his shoes off in the tile foyer and padded into the kitchen. The dog followed. He knew he needed to eat, but the thought of food roused only dull nausea.

A shower might help.

After taking the dog out for a ten-minute run, he crawled into the shower. A half hour later he managed to down a couple of pieces of toast and a glass of fresh-squeezed orange juice.

The phone rang. Chris? He gingerly picked up, expecting a blasting.

It was Des.

"I invited you and Chris for dinner Wednesday," Des said. "I don't want him to welch out without telling you."

David smiled. "Chris wouldn't do anything like that." They both knew he would, especially if he thought it was in David's best interests. "I'll let Chris know we'd be happy to come. Thanks, Des."

After he got off the phone he headed for the media room. Nothing on TV held his interest. Even a late season game between Boston and Atlanta left him yawning. His head buzzed with too many thoughts, none of which could focus. He thought of the interview tomorrow. Would the son have heard of his mother's death? He knew the propensity for "if it bleeds, it leads" meant most of the media would ignore the apparent suicide of an old woman as non-news. So if he knew what did that say? Was he involved in her death? If David's instincts were correct and it was homicide, then the son became their prime suspect. The interview was going to be a tricky one. David preferred to interview next-of-kin before releasing the bad news. He knew it often came across as harsh and unfeeling, but trying to catch a killer in a lie was more important than playing nice. Distraught families were rarely able to focus on the needs of the investigation. But the son would know something was wrong the minute he arrived at an empty apartment. What time had the nosy neighbor said the son usually arrived?

He checked his notes. She'd been fuzzy on the time and David hadn't pushed her. He called her now, hoping there wasn't a Tuesday night Mass too.

She answered on the fourth ring.

"Oh, Detective," Alice said. "I was just thinking of you. Imagine you called!"

"I just have one question, Mrs. Crandall. What time does Nancy's son usually come to visit? Do you remember if there was any pattern?"

"He always showed up around ten-thirty or so. He knew his mother and I had tea every morning and she asked him not to come then. We had Bible study and she didn't want him interrupting us."

A thought occurred to David. "Did he resent his mother's new interest in religion?" Maybe he felt she'd betrayed her old faith. It was a stretch as a motive, but he'd seen worse done for less.

"He never said anything to me and Nancy never spoke of it. He always seemed like an attentive boy. Always there for her. Always had a smile for me or anyone else he met, except..."

"Except what, Mrs. Crandall?"

"That smile never went anywhere. His eyes always looked like they was laughing at you, even when he was playing nice. I never told Nancy, it being her only blood, but I never liked that boy much."

"Thank you, Mrs. Crandall. I appreciate your time. I'll let you get back to your evening."

"Will you be along on Wednesday then, Detective?"

"I'll be there," David said, even though he knew showing up was going to piss Martinez off big time, he needed to do this. "With my partner."

"Mum's the word, right, Detective?"

"Right. Thank you, Mrs. Crandall."

David scribbled his notes. He called Martinez, giving him a heads up on the interview time, letting Martinez's anger roll off him. Stifling a jaw-stretching yawn, he returned to the media room where he turned off the game without even checking the score and climbed the Mexican tile steps to the second floor.

In the bathroom he ran a hand over his face and felt the rasp of day-old beard. Normally he shaved at night, but tonight he didn't bother. Chris wasn't around to complain and he wasn't sure he had a steady enough hand for the task.

He stared hard at the mirror. Brushing his fingers through his thick mustache, he frowned. Was that white hair? His 'stache looked frosted and the stubble on his face had a silvery sheen. Combined with the new lines under his eyes and the deepening furrows around his mouth, he was starting to look like one of those old winos who hung out around the pool hall down from the station. Old. He was getting old. Slowing down.

Seven years older than Chris, sometimes the gap seemed larger. Chris, just past thirty, looked twenty-five. Beautiful Chris. Heads still turned when he walked into a room. People watched him, young guys cruised him when they went out. Chris laughed at it, telling him they could look all they wanted. He was flattered, but he wasn't interested. David still didn't understand what

Chris saw in him. And after everything they'd been through he'd stopped asking.

He stripped down to his boxers, tossing his dirty clothes into the hamper. He refused to look at himself again. He didn't need to verify that the liberal sprinkling of gray extended to his chest hair. He needed no more reminders that age was catching up fast. Only nine years till he had his twenty in and he could retire. Chris wouldn't even be forty then.

Unwanted thoughts tumbled through his head. He climbed between the sheets and tried to read. The words on the page made no sense.

The ones in his head were altogether too clear.

Tuesday, 8:35 pm, Ste. Anne's Medical Center, Rowena Avenue, Silver Lake, Los Angeles

Chris saw the IP address after nearly an hour of dissecting the logs Terry had collected from all the hospital's servers.

Logs generated on each server recorded, among other things, the source and destination IP, the user id and the server that all incoming and outgoing messages came from.

IT people lived in a world of numbers and strings of code, much as the computers they administered did. Like a magician's sleight of hand, he was able to pull useful information out of data logs that to most people looked like gibberish.

IP addresses were like that. Nine digit numbers separated with periods, to most people random. Without meaning. Chris probably recognized at least three dozen IP addresses at a glance and matched them to a particular server, the rest he could classify instantly.

But this IP he recognized. He'd seen it only recently. It was the IP from Sandman422's email header, the one that claimed to be coming from Calnexxia. Only here, in the sniffer log, it was listed as sourcing from a server *inside* Ste. Anne's.

Chris stabbed a manicured nail at the line in the log file. "Recognize this?"

From over his shoulder Terry studied the output on the screen. "That's our web server."

Chris told him about the two threatening emails he had received from Sandman422.

"I just figured he signed up for a Freemail account," Chris said. "Instead he spoofed the IP headers just to make me think he was using Freemail. He sent those emails from your web server. He may very well be our cracker."

"So at first glance anyone examining the header is going to think it's from someplace else," Terry said.

"You know anyone who could do something like this?"

Terry's Adam's apple bobbed up and down on his thin neck. "I know our guys." He shook his head so hard, his glasses skidded down his nose. He shoved them back up. "I know who *could* do it, but I swear that none of them did."

Chris believed him, but he pressed anyway. You never knew what people could remember if pushed. "Anybody on staff come to mind?"

"I know a couple of nurses who seem to know their way around a keyboard."

"Anyone who could do this?"

"Shit, if I knew someone on staff who could do this, I'd hire them myself. They'd be wasted as nurses. I've been trying to talk Laura into coming over to our side, but she says she likes nursing."

"Fine," Chris said, wondering who the hell Laura was. "How accessible are these machines?"

"I supposed a determined visitor could get to one, but, tell me if I'm wrong, doesn't this kind of thing take time? A stranger's going to be noticed..."

"What about a stranger wearing scrubs? Or one of those candy-stripers?"

Terry frowned. "We're not one of the giant medical centers. Most of us have a nodding acquaintance with each other. I still think he'd be noticed."

They continued to pour over the logs. In the same file Chris had discovered the spoofed IP address, he found another reference that intrigued him.

"What's this—another server?"

"Post01? That's our mail server."

"UNIX?"

"Yeah."

"I think he used a sendmail exploit. That's how he gained root access." Root access on a UNIX server was like being God. A root user could do anything. "He used your web server sitting in the DMZ to attack this box inside and from there he could go anywhere." The DMZ was the demilitarized zone where things like web servers were kept out of the vulnerable inner ring. Even if a cracker got to them, it didn't mean they could penetrate the production servers. Unless, like this guy, they were experts at stealth.

Terry swore. "Can we track where he went? Did he leave a footprint?"

"We can check time stamps on the files in question; see if anyone touched them. We'll compare your backups, too, verify their integrity." Chris rubbed a hand through his spiky hair. "Listen, let's take a break. Grab a coffee and work out how we want to approach this."

"Sure. I could use a break."

Only one table was occupied in the cafeteria. Windows lined one wall, looking out onto the main corridor. Overhead several rows of bright fluorescent lights washed the color out of everything. Chris glanced at the other occupants. A slight young man shared the table with a big-bottomed blonde picking at a bowl of wilted greens and an African-American woman emphasizing some point with her coffee spoon.

Terry saw the trio and waved. Only the African-American woman waved back. Both women zeroed in on Chris, and stared at him as he and Terry grabbed coffee and crossed to the other side, to take a table near the far door. Chris resisted the temptation to swing his hips for them. He didn't really mind it when guys looked at him that way. But it always felt weird when the attention came from women.

It wasn't like he'd always looked this way. As a teenager he'd been a skinny nerd, all knees and elbows and acne in a world where the super jock was worshiped. He'd been lousy at sports, sucked at acting and had absolutely no interest in social clubs. He'd been horrified by the feelings that threatened to overwhelm him whenever a good looking guy came near. He hadn't realized what was happening until a senior seduced him in the guy's locker room in his sophomore year.

He knew what that made him.

By the time he graduated, he'd metamorphosed from a scrawny loser into a man who turned heads. There were a lot more encounters like the senior, but by then he'd accepted who he was. In the years he spent at UCLA, then later at CalTech, guys flocked to him, bees to the golden poppy flower, and he reveled in their attention.

Then David came along. There hadn't been anyone since. If he had his way, there wouldn't ever be again.

"That's her," Terry interrupted, and Chris swung around to follow his look. "Laura, the blonde. She's the one I told you about. Knows her way around a computer."

It was the big-bottomed blonde. Chris studied her over the rim of his paper cup.

She looked younger than Chris. Mid-twenties. Make-up did nothing to conceal her tiredness, and her black-rimmed eyes glanced his way without making contact. She hadn't made any headway on the salad, though she still poked at it with her fork.

"What floor does she work on?" Chris asked.

"She works mainly on third. She had some special training in pediatrics and AIDS."

"Come on, let's go meet her," Chris said. "Don't worry, I won't ask any embarrassing questions."

Terry gave him a sour look, but led the way over to the table of three. "Hi, Laura," Terry said. "Kate. Slow night?"

Laura shrugged, her gaze lingering on Chris. "Quiet enough. You're here late."

"Shit happens. Hey, I'd like you to meet Chris. He's gonna be working with me the next few days. Chris, this is Laura Fischer and Kate Johnson." Terry glanced at the janitor. "Sorry, I don't know your name."

"Akeem," he said, offering them a shy smile. "I just started a few weeks ago."

"But he's fitting right in, ain't that right, Akeem?" Kate, the African-American woman, smiled in a proprietary way.

"We better get back," Chris said, knowing this wasn't the time to ask questions. If he wanted to talk to Laura, he'd catch her alone.

"Sure," Terry said. "Talk to you later, Laura. Kate. Akeem." Once they were out of earshot, Terry asked, "What's our next step?"

"More log files. I'd like to take a closer look at your mail server, if that's okay." Chris saw the look on Terry's face. "Hey, we've done pretty good so far."

"You think?"

"I know."

CHAPTER SEVEN

Wednesday 12:35 am, Cove Avenue, Silver Lake, Los Angeles

When Chris let himself into the house it was after midnight. David's car was still in the driveway but Chris knew he couldn't assume David was home. How long had he worked? Chris fumed. Where was he? Had he been out working the whole time Chris had been at the hospital?

In the kitchen he found a plate, a butter knife and a glass in the sink, so clearly David had been home long enough to eat something. But did he go back out again?

Chris rinsed the dirty dishes off and slid them into the dishwasher. Then he wiped the counter down and turned off the downstairs lights as he headed for bed.

Flipping on the bathroom light, he briefly considered a shower, then decided morning was soon enough. A quick brush and floss and he walked out of the bathroom unbuttoning his shirt and stopped dead when he saw David's still form under the covers. Sweeney looked up from Chris's pillow and purred. From the foot of the bed Sergeant barely raised his head off the floor.

So David had come home.

Chris slid out of his jeans and shirt and slipped under the covers, careful not to jostle the sleeping man. Even so, David rolled over, his arm cradling Chris in a loose embrace. His dark eyes blinked open.

"Hey," David said. His smile was warm and sleepy and sexy as hell.

Chris found himself responding to the look in David's eyes.

David eased him over on his back, his arms braced on either side of Chris's head. He lowered his head and trailed a line of fire along Chris's jaw. "'Bout time you came home."

Chris wrapped his hands around David's face, bringing it down until their mouths almost touched. "If I knew you were waiting, I'd have been home hours ago."

"Well, you're here now."

David nibbled at the sensitive skin below Chris's ear. Chris shivered and, shoving David's boxers off, reached between his legs. David groaned.

"Fuck me, David," Chris whispered.

Later, they subside amid snarled bedclothes. Chris played with the damp hairs on David's chest.

"Now we have to take a shower."

David's laughter rumbled through him as his lips played with Chris's salty skin.

"After you."

Wednesday, 6:40 am, Cove Avenue, Silver Lake, Los Angeles

David stood at the end of the bed where Chris lay curled around the depression left by his body. He held one of the new Armani dress shirts Chris bought him for his birthday and stared down at the sleeping form. He knew Chris would be pissed when he realized David had gone back to work yet again. Even Martinez hadn't wanted him back until Friday, though they were desperately short-staffed. He hadn't told Chris he was going in today, either.

He had barely pulled into the lot of the drab, whitewashed Northeast Station when Martinez stepped out of his aging Toyota. David watched him approach. Overhead, the flag hung limply on the flagpole outside the front door. A black and white pulled out of the back parking lot and turned left on San Fernando Road. The sky was brown and still. It was going to be a hot one. Unseasonably hot.

"You sure you're okay, Davey? We could do this another day."

"I'm fine," David snapped. If Martinez started on him, he'd be getting it from two fronts. Chris was bad enough.

"Just asking." Martinez held up his hands in mock surrender. "Just don't want you doing more than you're ready for."

"Sitting around doing nothing is a lot harder than a little work. I rested. That's enough." David glanced behind him. Their meeting with Scott's son wasn't until ten-thirty. "What have you got?"

"An interview with..." Martinez pulled out his notebook and flipped it open. "Father Dalton at Incarnation. Scott's church."

They'd get some background on the victim, if nothing else.

"Priests can be dodgy about talking about parishioners," Martinez warned.

"We're not asking him to divulge her last confession or anything privileged. We just want to know who her friends were. Who she hung out with."

Martinez snorted. "I don't think the Nancy Scotts of this world 'hang out'"

"Her acquaintances then."

"That he might give up. But you, my friend, are at a distinct disadvantage, not being of the faith. It won't score you any brownie points."

"They don't score many with me," David said. He was a little shocked at his own words. It was the first time he had ever disrespected any religion.

"Getting feisty are we, *mijo?* That's not like you."

David refused to answer. His foot was already firmly in his mouth. He didn't need to wedge it in further.

They drove down West Glenoaks Boulevard onto Brand and swung into a near empty parking lot. David braced himself for an interview he wasn't ready for. He really didn't want to talk to a priest who probably knew exactly who and what he was.

Wednesday 8:10 am, Cove Avenue, Silver Lake, Los Angeles

David was a breakfast man. Chris, on the other hand, was happy if he had access to a fresh pot of coffee.

This morning even the coffee left a bitter taste in his mouth. Unbelievable. David had pulled another vanishing stunt.

This time the car was gone.

He'd gone back to work. No doubt with Martinez's encouragement.

Oh, he knew all the excuses. They were short staffed, Martinez would be overwhelmed. Overworked. Chris wouldn't like it if David had to patrol alone. Unmarked or not, cops looked like cops no matter what they drove.

The phone rang. It was David.

"Well, at least you call," Chris said, all too aware of how snippy he sounded.

David sighed. "I have a job to do, Chris, and that's all there is to it. Des called. He wants us to go for dinner tonight."

"I know. Don't change the subject."

David grunted.

"Fine, we'll go to dinner and see his surprise."

"What surprise?"

"Des didn't tell you?" Chris snorted. "He has something to show us. He wouldn't say what."

"Maybe he has a new boyfriend. About time, you said so yourself."

"Sure, but... would he do that and not tell me?"

"Let me see... Des want to one-up drama queen Chris? What do you think?"

"Drama queen? I am not a drama queen. You really think he could have found someone?"

Years ago, Des had been brutally raped and endured the torture of watching his lover murdered by the killer David was pursuing. It had taken months of therapy for Des to recover from the trauma and even longer before he'd have anything to do with a man again. There had been a brief fling with Trevor, a man Chris thought was all wrong for him, but that, thankfully, hadn't lasted. Since then, Chris had set Des up with a few of his friends. He knew Des hated being alone; his nature was to be part of a couple.

"Maybe he's tired of your matchmaking," David said.

Chris bristled. "I don't match-make. I just knew a couple of guys I thought might interest him, that's all. And you're still trying to change the subject."

"Okay." Chris could hear David shift around. "I'm a cop. I'm going to stay a cop. That means the hours are lousy, people I do business with aren't exactly stellar characters and the pay sucks, but you knew all that when you opted in."

"Jesus, you make me sound like an email campaign."

"Sorry, but I don't know how else to say it. I love you, Chris, but I'm not changing my life for you."

Chris knew David had too much integrity for that kind of compromise. It was one of the things he loved about the man, but Jesus, it wasn't easy. David's job scared him spitless.

In the end all he could say was, "I love you too."

Wednesday 9:50 am, Carillon Street, Atwater, Los Angeles

Except for some strategizing about how to handle the coming interview, David and Martinez didn't talk much on the way to Nancy Scott's apartment. What was there to say?

Alice, the deceased woman's friend, came through the front doors of the apartment building five minutes after they pulled into the parking lot. Martinez followed David out of the Crown. At the slam of the car door Alice looked over at them. Her gaze darted around the cypress-lined parking lot before settling on David.

"He's not here yet?" he asked.

"Would you officers like to wait inside? The boy should be along shortly."

"Do you know his name, Mrs. Crandall?"

"Adam," Alice said. "Adam Benjamin, though I'm afraid I don't know his last name—I assume he kept his father's patronymic, though I don't recall if Nancy ever mentioned it."

"Guess we'll have to ask him, won't we?" Martinez said.

They followed her into her tidy apartment. She vanished into the kitchen; David heard the banging of pots and pans, then the clatter of pottery.

David and Martinez stood awkwardly in Alice's living room, eying the beige nightmare surrounding them. Even the paintings on the wall were leeched of color; they were soft, bland pastels.

David gingerly parked himself on a beige sofa, one of two that faced each other across a blond wood and glass coffee table. Martinez took a seat opposite him. His herringbone jacket and puce shirt looked as out of place as the Marlboro man at a society wedding.

Alice returned bearing a wooden tray holding a Russian tea service. It looked old and well used.

He had a feeling Alice didn't entertain much.

"Tea, officers?"

She poured three cups, gently stirred in milk and handed David a cup, then Martinez. The tea was weak; the milk cut whatever bitterness it might have had.

David took a sip then put the tiny flowered cup on the glass coffee table. Alice set the tray down and sat facing them in a gently worn easy chair. Her peach-colored dress pulled up to reveal two skinny, veined legs held primly together. She clasped her hands in her lap and leaned forward.

David instantly knew that she and Nancy Scott had performed this ritual after every Wednesday for as long as Scott had lived here. He also knew something else.

"The boy came here, didn't he, Mrs. Crandall? He picked his mother up here," David asked.

Alice nodded, her orange hair bobbing precariously on her tiny skull. "Every other Wednesday he'd pick his mother up here. We liked to have our tea and Bible reading. Smiling like he always did, but his eyes fair creeped me out."

David knew he wasn't going to make any friends with this upcoming interview. But his gut told him Adam was dirty. He'd come to trust his gut over the years.

When the doorbell rang, David and Martinez stood at the same time. They followed Alice, who opened the door to a slender youth in black jeans and an even blacker T-shirt. The same youth in the photos in Nancy Scott's place, only a couple of years older. Short, dark hair framed a thin face, emphasized by eyes two sizes too large. Put ten pounds of muscles on his skinny frame and he would have been one little hottie, as Chris would say.

"Adam. God bless you, boy," Alice said. "Right on time."

David stepped forward as the boy entered the apartment. "Adam Scott?" he said.

Adam froze, his black eyes looming large in his narrow face. He darted a question at Alice, then stared bug-eyed at David.

"Yeah," he said. "Who are you?"

"Detective David Eric Laine," David said. He flashed his badge, hoping Adam wouldn't ask too many questions right away. "We'd like to ask you few questions, if we could."

Martinez introduced himself.

"Questions? Sure... what's this about?" Adam edged into the room, keeping Alice between him and the detectives. He seemed unable to take his eyes off David. "Where's my mother?"

"Benny—"

The kid winced at Alice's use of the nickname.

"I'm sorry," David said. "I thought you said your name was Adam."

"It's not Benny," Adam said. He threw Alice a dark look.

David could see what the woman meant about his eyes. They were cold.

She opened her mouth to speak and David cut her off before she could say any more. "Thank you, Mrs. Crandall. Is there someplace we could speak to Mr. Scott privately?"

Not hiding her disappointment, Alice led them into her kitchen. "I'll stay in the other room until you tell me you have finished."

David indicated Adam should sit. The boy took the chintz-cushioned chair facing the stove. Martinez pulled a similar chair up beside him and plucked a mint from the glass bowl on the table.

David leaned against the stove.

Adam had to rotate his head ninety degrees to take in both of them. He fixed his gaze on David. "You're that gay cop, aren't you?"

David had heard that question, or similar, less polite ones, enough times to show no outward reaction. He shared a brief glance with Martinez who did not look pleased.

Most gays, when they came out, had the luxury of choosing when and to whom they revealed their secret. David had been outed to the whole world when a violent psychopath tried to destroy Chris. He'd been in the public eye ever since.

"What's this about?" Adam asked.

"We'd just like to ask you a couple of questions about your mother."

"Why don't you go talk to her yourself? She's just down the hall."

"We'll get to that in a minute," David said. "When was the last time you saw her, Mr. Scott?"

Adam's head jerked, he glanced uneasily at Martinez then at David. "My last name's not Scott. It's Baruch."

"Is Baruch your father's name?"

"Yes."

"Where is your father, Mr. Baruch? We may have some questions for him, too—"

"I don't know." Adam's eyes shifted away from David's.

Liar. David didn't challenge him right then. Time enough for that later.

Adam twisted around so that he faced David. "I want to know what's going on. Why are you asking these questions? Has something happened to my mother?"

"When did you last see her, Mr. Baruch?"

"Two weeks ago," Adam whispered. "Wednesday—"

"Your mother diabetic?" Martinez asked.

"Yes—"

"How do you get along with her?" Martinez asked. "Old ladies, they can be a pain. You oughta meet my mother some time."

"We got along fine. Is she sick? Is that why she's not here—?"

"You last saw your mother two weeks ago today?" David asked, making sure he didn't react to Adam's use of the past tense. Just a couple more and he'd have the bastard. "You haven't been back since?"

"I come every two weeks. I'm sure Mrs. Crandall told you that. Will you please tell me what happened to my mother?"

"We're sorry, Mr. Baruch," David said. He stepped away from the stove, aware that between Martinez on Adam's right and his six-four bulk on the young man's left, Adam must be feeling hemmed in. He leaned down and said, "Your mother's dead."

Adam stared at David. His head swung from side to side in denial even while his gaze never left David's face.

"H-how?"

"That's still under investigation."

Adam grew pale. "You think I had something to do with my mother's death?"

Martinez suddenly leaned forward, crowding Adam back into his chair. "I don't know. Did you?"

"No!" Adam's eyes were noticeably wet. "I did not hurt my mother. Please, tell me what happened."

"Your mother was found two days ago in her apartment. She had been dead for several days at that point. We're still looking into the exact cause of death."

"My mother was a very sick woman. Her doctor will tell you that."

"Don't worry, we'll be talking to him," Martinez said. "Right now we're talking to you."

Abruptly Adam stood up. His chair scraped across the linoleum. "No, you're not. I'm going home. You want to talk to me again, call my lawyer."

"Lawyer, huh?" Martinez leisurely pulled a candy cane striped mint out of the bowl and slipped it in his mouth. "What's his name?"

Adam sputtered and flapped his jaw.

"Thought so." Martinez grinned. "I can recommend a couple of good ones."

"My mother is dead!" Adam shouted. "Why aren't you out there trying to find out who killed her?"

David cocked his head sideways, but it was Martinez who responded.

"I don't know as we had established she was murdered," he said. "Interesting."

"Your mother like to eat chocolates?" David asked.

Adam's gaze skidded away from David, then came back, trying to look fierce. "I don't know what you mean."

"It's a simple question. Did your mother eat chocolates?"

"N-no—yes. She wasn't supposed to, but she did sometimes."

"Where were you Saturday and Sunday of last week—?"

"No more questions!" Adam clenched his fists. "When can I get my mother so I can bury her?"

"You'll have to talk to the coroner about that," David said. He fished out a card and wrote a number on the back. "Call here. They'll be able to help you out."

Adam muttered a stiff "thanks" and shoved the card in his jeans pocket, after only the briefest glance. When he stamped out of the kitchen, David and Martinez followed. They met Alice at the front door.

"All done, are you?" she asked. Her pale skin was drawn and her eyes darted between the three invaders. David noted she seemed almost afraid of Adam.

"Thank you, Mrs. Crandall." David held out his hand, which she took gingerly. He glanced at Adam trying to edge past him to the door. "We'll need a way to contact you."

Adam spat out a North Hollywood address and number, then hurried out before they could ask any more questions or demand to see some ID. David stepped into the hallway to watch him exit the building. Adam reached the sidewalk and turned left, away from the parking lot. So he either wasn't driving or he'd parked elsewhere.

"Let's go," he said. "I want to pick up my car at the station."

But by the time they reached the sidewalk, Adam was nowhere in sight. David scanned the street north and south, but there were no pedestrians or moving cars.

"Sonny boy seem all that broken up to you?" In the parking lot Martinez popped open the door to his brown Crown. "Mother's death, gotta be a hard thing for anyone."

"Provided they get along as well as Baruch wants us to think," David said. "You get the feeling he made a point of making sure Crandall saw him come by every two weeks? Like clockwork."

"The loyal, loving son. Alice didn't exactly buy into it."

"Notice he barely shed a tear when we told him she was dead?"

"Nice." Martinez wheeled out of the tree-lined parking lot and headed east toward the station. "Think he's good for it?"

"I'm wondering about this whole religious thing." David beat a tattoo on his thigh. "I always figured mom just switched from, say, being a Presbyterian to Catholicism. Now I'm thinking there's a whole lot more going on."

"Baruch. Adam Baruch. Sounds Jewish. If Nancy Scott married a Jew and they raised their son Jewish, then junior's bound to get ticked off when Mom goes back to the old faith so soon after his father's out of the picture. Gotta seem like a major betrayal."

"Gives him cause to resent her," Martinez said. "Enough to off her?"

"Guess we better find out."

CHAPTER EIGHT

Chris spent the day at the hospital with no more damaging discoveries; he was on his way to grab a bottle of wine for Des's dinner party when he spotted the jewelry store tucked behind the plaza where he parked.

The interior was well lit and smelled of incense that tickled the back of Chris's throat. Almost immediately he spotted the glittering row of pendants spotlighted on their dark, velvet cases.

A thin, delicate Japanese man approached from the other side of the glass case. He eyed Chris with a practiced gaze and must have liked what he saw; the wattage from his smile lit up his face.

"Can I help you, sir?"

Chris pointed out one platinum pendant. "I'd like to look at that one."

Later, after he had selected a couple of bottles of Tantara's Bien Nacido Pinot Noir, he returned to pick up his other purchase, now engraved, and headed home. For once he hoped David hadn't beaten him there.

He was in luck, the house was empty.

After a quick lunch and a long walk down by the reservoir with the dog, he spent the next two hours in the bathroom, waxing and tweezing until his body was as smooth as raw silk. Then he showered and dressed with extra care, new Martin Margiela pants and an aqua sweater that hugged his chest and showed off every line of his carefully honed physique.

In the kitchen he opened a bottle of Bettinelli Chardonnay. He carried the glass into his home office and logged online to check his email.

No more threatening messages from Sandman. Was that good or bad? Had the stunt at the hospital just been a prank gone bad? Had the guy freaked, sent Chris a warning, then skipped?

Sandman was no script kiddie, he—or she, he amended—knew what he was doing. Sandman's actions weren't like the teens who compiled code they found online, which they unleashed as viruses that rarely worked. Most system administrators found them more of an irritation than a real threat; they ate up bandwidth and consumed time cleaning up the mess they left. Weapons of mass annoyance.

Sandman was far beyond that level. The danger he posed was real. He was already responsible for taking one life.

But was he worth pursuing on his own time? David was safe. Why expend energy chasing an ephemeral ghost in the machine? Didn't Chris have enough work?

He heard the front door open and close. David's footsteps echoed across the tiled foyer, first hard, then soft, after he took his shoes off and put his gun and badge in the hall safe.

Chris logged off and stood just as David stuck his head round the corner, his mustache quirking upward as he smiled.

"Hey, it's after five," David said. "Aren't you supposed to be taking this evening off?"

"Hmph, you should talk." Chris kissed him. "Hope you haven't eaten."

"Not unless you count Martinez's donuts." He looked Chris up and down. "You look nice. Got a hot date?"

"Funny," Chris said. "Why don't you grab a shower while I get you a drink."

When David entered the kitchen, hair still damp, Chris had a second glass ready. They shared the last of the Chardonnay, while David read the paper.

Des met them at the door of his Beverly Hills bungalow. His classically beautiful, pale bronze face was wreathed in smiles as he clasped Chris's hands in his and air-kissed him. "Darlings, you came." He repeated the gesture on David, then held the larger man at arm's length while he studied him with knowing eyes. "Have we lost weight? You look marvelous, David. And I must say that suit looks divine on you."

Chris ignored David's rolling eyes and grinned. "He does look good, doesn't he?"

Des guided the two of them into his living room. "You must visit the shop again. I just got the most incredible Brunello Cucinellis in. You'll just die when you see them—"

He broke away to take the wine Chris offered him. He gestured them to sit.

"We'll open this later," he said. "Right now I have something you simply must try."

Under their amused stares the slender African-American man slipped behind his bar, a Fin de Siecle ebony and brown leather piece taking up half the wall. Over it loomed a series of movie posters from the thirties and forties, preserved behind glass on acid-free mats.

Over Des's hairless head, Cary Grant and Joan Fontaine stared down raptly from "Suspicion." On either side of the Hitchcock thriller, Nick and Nora dabbled in mystery and martinis in images from their various Thin Man movies.

Des produced a chrome cocktail set and soon delivered Chris's favorite Cîroc martini. For David he poured a bottle of beer into a tall glass. David watched him, then took the bottle from him. "Tuchers?" he asked. "Where do you find these things?"

"I'm a shopper hon, I can find anything."

David shook his head, but drank the imported beer anyway, since he knew Des refused to stock domestic beer. "Not even for you, sugar," he said, whenever David forgot and asked for a Bud.

"Sit, sit," Des said, herding them toward the pair of Savoy Art Deco club chairs facing the brocade love seat across a walnut-veneered coffee table.

At one time the room had been filled with Louis XIV antiques. Then Kyle, Des's lover, had been murdered and the man who later tried to kill Chris had assaulted Des. The brutality occurred right in this room. Chris wanted Des to sell the place and move someplace, anyplace else, but Des resisted the idea. He had clung to his home through all of Chris's gentle encouragement to move on.

But he sold the furniture.

Chris slipped onto the love seat and pulled David down beside him.

"So what's this big surprise?" Chris asked. "Something really juicy, I hope."

"Oh you'll love it, I know you will." Des had barely parked his delicate rump on the Savoy when he jumped back up, too excited to sit still. "First though, you just have to sample Kozi's sushi. He got it all ready for me, just hold on, I'll go get the first tray—"

Des vanished into the kitchen, a wisp of scented air. He was back almost immediately carrying a massive split bamboo tray on which an array of Japanese delicacies were artfully arranged. There was kappa maki, and nori, crab rolls and soba noodles, along with a bowl after bowl of wasabi, sesame oil and shoyu for dipping.

Chris grabbed a pair of chopsticks and dove in. David gingerly followed suit, though his skills with the sticks were never strong and he favored his fingers when Des refused to allow him to use a fork.

"So are you two all set for next week?" Des asked between bites of nori.

"Next week?" David looked puzzled.

It was Des's turn to roll his eyes. "The party. Have you forgotten already? It's Halloween."

"I don't know, Des—"

"David, you promised." Des looked at Chris. "Didn't he promise?"

"Chris..." David said.

"You did promise," Chris reminded him.

"Oh, you'll have fun, David. Really, inside that gruff bear is a silly old queen just dying to get out and have some fun."

Chris almost burst out laughing at the look on David's face. He patted David's muscular thigh but David wasn't into reassurances.

"Silly old queen?"

Des blushed. "Okay, not so old. It'll be fun, you'll see." He flashed his most beguiling smile. "You did promise."

"Yeah, I guess I did." He glared at Des. "But don't expect me to dress up. I draw the line at that."

Chris and Des traded glances. Without another word Des subsided back into his chair, a smug grin on his dark face.

David didn't look happy at the double-tagged coercion.

Des jumped up again. "Now that that's settled here's my surprise."

Both Chris and David looked where Des was looking with such expectation on his face. A figure appeared in the door to the rear of the bungalow.

Chris's jaw dropped and David gave a grunt of surprise.

Trevor Watson grinned at them both, then slipped up beside Des and took his hand.

"I'm back."

"Since when?" Chris was outraged. He thought Trevor was long gone from Des's life. For the better, he thought. The guy was just so wrong for his best friend. He'd always thought Des had let his grief for the loss of Kyle influence him into a premature relationship with the admittedly good looking man who had almost been Chris's lover before David. "You never told me you were coming back." He realized David was glaring at him. He turned his anger on Des. "You never told me."

"I told you it was a surprise. Not much of a surprise if I tell you ahead of time."

"Good to see you, Trevor," David said flatly. "You in town for a while?"

Trevor put his hand on Des's shoulder and Des looked up at him adoringly. "Maybe permanently."

"Isn't it great?"

Both Chris and David nodded grimly. "Yes, great."

They took their leave soon after. In the car, Chris didn't have to wait long for the outburst he was expecting.

"Did you know about this?"

"No, I'm just as surprised as you are." Chris shifted uneasily in his seat. "Do you think it will work out this time?"

"I hope it does," David growled. When Chris shot him a startled look, he added, "For Des's sake. I didn't like seeing him hurt like last time."

"Maybe I should talk to Trev..." David scowled and Chris reversed himself. "Okay, maybe not a good idea." He drummed his fingers on his leg. "I guess we just wait and see."

David grumpily agreed.

Neither one of them mentioned Des or Trevor the rest of the evening.

♫ ♫ ♫ ♫

Back home, Chris checked his email to see if any emergencies were brewing. Normally he spent one to two hours taking care of business, but tonight he kept one ear cocked for David in the media room down the hall.

Finally he heard the steady tread on the tile stairs. He made a quick perusal of his emails, making sure nothing needed his immediate attention, then logged out and followed David.

He stripped in the bathroom, pulled a towel around his slim hips and entered the bedroom where David was propped up in bed, reading one of his science fiction novels. Reading glasses perched on his nose, David glanced over them at Chris and his smile tightened on his swarthy face.

"Quitting early?"

Chris let his gaze wander over the furred expanse of David's chest. He tried not to linger on the puckered white skin on David's left shoulder where he had been shot saving Chris from the Carpet Killer. The memories were still too painful. He gently covered the scar with his hand. "You could say that."

Before David could react, Chris removed the book from his hands and set it down on the nightstand. Pulling open the top drawer, Chris drew out the black jeweler's case he had stashed there earlier. He flipped it open and withdrew the chain, draping it over David's chest.

David looked down at the St. Michael's medallion. "What's this for?"

Chris trailed the fingers of his left hand over the puckered scar tissue. "It's for this," he said and slid his hand down David's hip, where an assailant had stabbed him with a kitchen knife during an arrest six years ago. "And that."

David shifted under his touch, his breath catching in his throat. "Chris... "

"But mostly it's for this," Chris smoothed the heel of his hand over David's chest, where the cool medal lay over his rapidly beating heart. "Because I love you and I will never do anything to hurt you or bring you harm. I don't ever want you to be jealous of anyone. There's no one in my heart but you."

Before David could answer, Chris planted his lips over the same spot his hand had been. He could feel the furious pumping of David's heart. Chris slid down the length of his body, taking him in his mouth.

David groaned.

David's hands settled on Chris's shoulders, surrendering to his desire. Chris brought him to the brink again and again until

David was nearly mindless with lust. He climaxed with a shout. They embraced until sleep claimed them both.

After several quiet minutes David started snoring.

CHAPTER NINE

Thursday, 7:50 am, Northeast Community Police Station, San Fernando Road, Los Angeles

The next day David shoved open the door to the detectives' room and felt half a dozen pairs of eyes follow him in. The rumor mill had never let up since his precipitous outing years ago. His marriage to Chris had put it into an overdrive that had never abated. Sometimes it was like living in the midst of a pack of hyenas, waiting for their blood lust to overcome caution.

Martinez was already at his desk. His phone pinned under his chin, he sucked back station coffee. He waved David over, hanging up before his partner reached his desk.

"We got our warrant," Martinez said. "You want to head over this morning? Landlord will let us in. He asked us to be there no later than ten."

"Sure."

The other desks filled up as the day shift signed in, phones were answered and keyboards tapped. The smell of bad coffee and too many bodies crammed into a small space filled the narrow detectives' room. Overhead the buzz of a failing fluorescent light did nothing to improve the color of the pale brown walls. Dirty sunlight leached through the blinds and, just outside the window, the cell tower at the rear of the building cast a thin shadow.

David went around to his own desk. He stared down at the mauve box covered with big-eyed kitten graphics on top of his keyboard and sighed. Another prank. He wondered if it was any more imaginative than the pink plastic tampons he had received last month. Or the invitations to join a gay chat line the month before.

David slipped the lid off the box and found it crammed full of fuchsia colored condoms. He rolled his chair back and dumped the box and its contents into the wastebasket. Without a word he turned his monitor on. Unlike Chris, he had never grown comfortable with computers. But his reports wouldn't write themselves, so he might as well spend the waiting time doing paperwork. Behind him he heard Lieutenant McKee talking on the phone in his office. As usual his door was open. McKee didn't believe in shutting himself off from his men. No doubt he would be over soon to check up on him, and make sure his most troublesome detective was really well enough to be back to work.

David opened the blue three-ring binder he'd started on the Scott case. The murder book was distressingly slim. Nearly as empty as the cork-board he shared with Martinez. As the case progressed, it would be covered with the bits and pieces their investigation uncovered.

With any luck their second visit to the woman's apartment would yield something useful.

"Nothing from the ME?"

Martinez shook his head. He tugged at his dimpled golf ball tie. "What do you think about the kid?"

David shrugged. "I'd like to keep him on our radar. He didn't convince me he's grieving."

David's phone rang. He scooped it up. It was Chris.

He kept his voice cool. "What's up?"

Chris's laugh was husky. "I missed you this morning. Why didn't you wake me?"

To distract himself from his body's reaction to Chris's voice, David opened his email program and watched several messages download onto his computer.

Chris sighed. "What time will you be home?"

"I don't know. I'll try to get back early." Out of the corner of his eye David saw McKee leave his office. "Did you call about something in particular?"

"Well, yeah." David could hear the rustle of paper as Chris went through his desk. "I got a call that you wanted to talk to me. Sergeant Sanderson phoned about five minutes ago..."

"Sanderson? I don't know any Sanderson... you sure that was the name?" A new email popped into David's inbox. It was from Chris. "What did he say it was about?"

"He didn't."

"You emailing me, too?" David clicked on the email, which opened into a web link with the words JUST FOR YOU, DAVID. CHECK THIS OUT IT EXPLAINS EVERYTHING. He still couldn't think who Sanderson was. David clicked on it.

"I didn't send you any email—"

David's web browser opened slowly, as usual. The image that filled his screen resolved pixel by pixel, but long before it was done David had seen enough. "Jesus." The blood left his face. "What the hell..."

"David?"

"I'll get back to you," David muttered as he hung up. He refused to focus on the image that filled his monitor even as he moved his mouse to close it. It was clearly a young boy, and he was naked. The web browser ignored his commands to close.

The image changed. The next image was even more explicit. He tried a trick Chris had taught him—Ctrl-Alt-Delete, but where that normally opened the task manager and let him close rogue applications, this time it did nothing, even when he tried the command several times. A new picture, more pornographically explicit than the last, opened up. This one featured a dark-haired naked adult male and a prepubescent male, a boy even younger than the first two. A fourth image began to resolve.

David's heart slammed into his rib cage and he felt light-headed. He hit Backspace, he even tried Start-Shutdown, but his computer refused to respond to any of his commands. Somehow he was trapped in this revolving horror.

His phone rang and he knew it was Chris. He snatched it up. Chris would know how to stop this.

"Chris—"

"You ready to go, Davey?" Martinez came around his desk.

David looked up in alarm as Martinez reached his side. Too late, David fumbled for the off button on his computer. His heartbeat thundered in his ear a dozen times before the machine responded and went down.

Martinez didn't make a sound. David couldn't even hear him breathing. He risked one quick look over his shoulder and the sight of his partner's gray face told him Martinez had seen more than enough.

The two men stared at each other. Harsh throat clearing directly behind the two partners broke their paralysis. David glanced back to find the Lieutenant staring at him from two desks over. The detective manning the desk was also staring. Without looking at anyone in particular, David realized half the desks in the room faced his monitor. How many had seen the images?

"Davey, what the hell's going on?" Martinez whispered.

David shook his head. But before he could open his mouth and tell him it was all a mistake, McKee was beside him.

"I'm going to have to ask you to step away from that computer, Detective Laine." McKee's gaze drilled into his. "You might want to consider contacting your advocate. You can call him from my office."

His advocate. Who the hell was his advocate? David's sluggish brain responded like a drowning swimmer feeling the water close over him one last time. Oh right, Bryan Williams. He had to call Bryan Williams.

When David didn't move, McKee snapped, "Now, Laine."

David reached for his phone. He wasn't going to be browbeaten by McKee before he had a chance to call Bryan. Like it or not, his boss was going to have to wait.

§ § § §

David stood opposite McKee's desk, staring over the Lieutenant's head at the wall full of commendations and citations the lieutenant had received over the years he had headed the Detective table at Northeast.

His desk held several pictures of McKee's wife, a forensic psychologist who often consulted with the department. The pictures included their three children.

"Shut the door, Detective," McKee said. "And take a seat."

David barely closed the door when there was a soft knock on it. McKee got up and took a folder from the uniformed officer who had knocked. He re-shut the door. Again he signaled David to sit. David did so reluctantly.

McKee flipped open the folder, which David realized was his jacket.

"How long have you worked in my department, Detective?" McKee asked.

"Ten years."

"And in those ten years have you ever had any disciplinary action?"

"No."

McKee frowned at him. "Are you forgetting what happened five years ago, then? Or last year when Detective Hernandez was killed?"

"Those matters were investigated and no charges were laid. My jacket is clean."

"Until now."

"My jacket is clean," David insisted, ignoring the dark look McKee gave him.

"Then help me understand," McKee said. "While you're at it, you can explain these, too."

McKee dumped the box of condoms on the desktop.

"No, I can't. And if it's all the same to you, I'd prefer to wait for my advocate before I say anything else."

"You know our forensics people will go through your computer with a fine-toothed comb. What are they going to find, Laine?"

David wondered the same thing. Surely once he shut it down the images would be gone. He hadn't downloaded anything. He wished he could talk to Chris. Chris would know what had happened, including how his name had come up as the sender of that email.

"You're not helping yourself, Laine," McKee said. "Talk to me, and we can clear this whole thing up."

David was saved from answering by a second knock at the door. This time it was Bryan Williams, David's advocate—and the Northeast's Gay and Lesbian Liaison. Bryan was a lanky man, whose red hair and freckled cheeks gave him the look of a small town bumpkin. The look hid a shrewd, calculating mind. He nodded at David, who managed a nod back. Bryan kept him out of trouble during the whole outing fiasco, when David had been in danger of being charged with conduct unbecoming because of his involvement with Chris. Bryan used his not inconsiderable clout in both the gay community and the city to clear David's name and keep his record intact.

Without waiting to be invited, Bryan took the only other chair in the office. He glanced at the condoms, then looked away. "You want to tell me what's going on, Lieutenant? Why has David been dragged in here?"

McKee continued to skim through David's file. He didn't answer Bryan immediately. When his phone rang he snatched it up. "Yes?"

David listened to the one-sided conversation and knew it wasn't good. McKee's face flattened and he stared down at the file folder, taking notes on a yellow legal pad.

"Yes, thank you. Send me the detailed report once you've finished it."

He hung up and steepled his fingers together over the legal pad. His glance slid from David to Bryan.

"Can you explain why forensics found several images of child pornography on your department issued computer, Detective Laine?"

David opened his mouth to explain, but Bryan gripped his arm.

"Don't speak, David. Let me handle this." He turned to McKee. "What are you charging David with?"

"At this point, nothing," McKee said. "But Standards will be investigating our allegations, they'll decide if charges will be laid."

"Allegations of what? What exactly did you find on his computer?"

"Images of underage children engaged in sexual activity."

"Was David in any of these pictures?"

"Irrelevant. Mere possession—"

"Did he download the images to his hard drive?"

McKee looked puzzled and glanced at the notes he had made. "The technician merely mentions finding the images 'cached,' whatever that means. The presence of the images is doubly confounded by these." McKee again held up the box of condoms.

Bryan leaned over and whispered for David's ears only, "What happened? Give me the short version."

David told Bryan how he opened the email purporting to be from Chris and found himself locked in an ever-changing web page and how he couldn't shut it down, no matter what he tried. He also told him about the harassing "jokes" he had faced back to the time he had come out.

"And you never mentioned any of this?" Bryan asked. "It would have helped things now if you had made a formal complaint."

"And be labeled a troublemaker?" David said. "How long do you think I'd survive on the street with that kind of rep?"

"Okay, we'll talk about that later. For now, are you're sure Chris didn't send the email to you?" Bryan was still whispering.

"Of course he didn't. Neither one of us would ever look at that garbage."

"I think I've heard enough of this," Bryan said aloud. "I'm going to look into it. In the meanwhile, don't talk to anyone unless I'm with you." He glared at McKee. "How long until PSB gets involved?"

"They're already involved. They'll set up a meeting over the next few days. Detective Laine will be told when. In the meantime," McKee sighed, "I have no choice but to put you on administrative leave, pending the investigation."

David's heart sank. He had expected this, but had hoped it would be averted at the end. "My cases—"

"Will be reassigned. Go home, Detective. And don't come back until this matter has been adjudicated. Is that clear?"

David stood up, keeping his spine stiff as he led the way toward the door. Bryan followed at his heels.

"Laine."

David turned back.

"I don't want to see you around here. Stay away from the station and stay away from Martinez. We'll be in touch with you about what comes next. Is that clear?"

"Yes, sir."

David stared straight ahead as he and Bryan strode toward the exit. Out of the corner of his eye he saw Martinez rise from his desk, but he didn't slow down. Only when Bryan shut the outer door and dragged him toward the stairwell, did he let his shoulders sag. How could everything go so wrong, so fast?

Bryan kept him moving and within minutes he was behind the wheel of his Chevy. Bryan touched his shoulder through the open window.

"Go home, David. We'll clear this up, I swear. But for now, just go home. Talk to Chris. Maybe he has some ideas we can take to the techies."

"It looks bad, doesn't it?"

"Hey, the homophobes believe we all like little kids anyway. It's not fair and it's never been fair," Bryan sighed. "But I know a couple of PSB guys who are going to love this. Let's hope we don't get one of them adjudicating your case."

David squeezed the steering wheel between clenched fists. "I want to know who the hell did this. And why."

"That's one thing I'll be investigating."

"Are they going to think Chris really sent me that stuff?"

"Some of them will want to think so." Bryan studied David's face. "Don't do anything foolish. You'll only make it worse if you try to get involved, so stay out of it."

"Damn it, man—"

"Let me do my job, David."

"Easy for you to say."

"And a lot easier for me to do if you stay clear of it."

"Fine," David snapped, cranking the key and producing a protesting roar from the Chevy's engine. "I'll leave it in your capable hands—for now."

"I'll call you later. If Chris has any ideas, great. Otherwise *stay out of it.*"

Bryan stepped away from the car and David wheeled out of the lot, roaring away in a cloud of exhaust and hitting thirty before he even reached San Fernando Road.

CHAPTER TEN

"What the hell do you mean they put you on administrative leave?" Chris watched David hunch over the kitchen table, refusing to meet his eyes. "What the fuck is administrative leave?"

"It's PSB's way of telling me to bend over, I'm about to get screwed." David stared into his coffee, wishing for the first time that he had something stronger than the Indonesian stuff Chris favored. A couple of stiff belts of scotch might make this nightmare palatable... He knew that was a path he didn't dare travel—he'd seen too many good cops eat their own weapons once alcohol embraced them. "And right now I don't even understand how it happened, so don't ask."

"Well, tell me what you do know."

So David told him about getting the condoms followed by the email he thought was from Chris, and what happened next.

"There was a link and you said—I mean it said it was important. That it would explain everything, so I clicked on it." David buried his nose in his mug. He felt like an idiot, reliving that moment. He was supposed to notice things. He was a *Detective*, supposedly the crème of the LAPD. How could he be taken in so easily? "I clicked on it and this...garbage started popping up."

"Garbage?"

"Kiddie porn. All pre-adolescent kids." David winced. "With male adults."

"A lot of pictures?"

"Enough." His face flushed as blood rushed to his head. "They kept coming, and I couldn't shut it down. Why the hell is that?"

"You got mouse-trapped."

"What?"

"Mouse-trapped. The web page has code hidden in it that controls how the web page is handled. It's a trick a few unethical programmers developed to trap users on their pages, sometimes just as a gimmick, sometimes to increase revenue—advertisers bill on the number of pages viewed."

"Yeah, well, it trapped me all right. But how did I get it? And who sent it?"

Chris started shaking his head, then suddenly he shot to his feet. "Shit, I can't believe I missed that. How stupid can I get—?"

Before David could ask what he meant, Chris was gone, only to return minutes later with a sheet of scrap of paper. "Sanderson, Sandman—now who's the idiot? I should have seen it—"

"Seen what?" David snapped.

Chris tossed the sheaf of paper down in front of David. "I got these the day you had your overdose at the hospital. Look at the name. Then I get that call today and because he tells me he's a bloody cop I fall for it."

David studied the printouts. Most of it was pure gibberish, but toward the end he spotted what he assumed was the actual message: `MIND YOUR OWN BUSINESS OR ELSE` and `IF YOU MESS WITH ME DAVID MIGHT NOT BE SO LUCKY NEXT TIME`

He raised his head and met Chris's gaze. "And you were going to tell me about this... when?"

Chris fidgeted in his chair. "I tried to trace the poster, but couldn't get anywhere."

"Do you still have the original emails?"

"Sure—"

David got up and paced, too wound up to sit still. "Good. I'll get them to Martinez. They won't mean anything to him, but maybe our tech boys can make something of them."

Chris bristled. "I traced the IP address to Ste. Anne's—it's not the ISP it claims to be. Someone hacked Ste. Anne's and did some IP spoofing to cover their tracks."

David ignored Chris's anger. David didn't care if Chris was right and the LAPD techs couldn't find out anything more. At least Professional Standards Bureau would have to take a good hard look at the facts before them. Would they come to the conclusion that seemed so obvious to David? If they believed that David had been tricked into launching those pages, then even PSB would have to back off.

"I'll need the information about the hospital, too." David pushed his wrought iron chair back. "Let me use your office to call Martinez. Will you be willing to make a statement to our technicians about what you found out? It's all Greek to me. I'd never be able to make any sense out of it."

David left Chris fuming in the kitchen. Once in Chris's office he dialed Martinez's line. After a half a dozen rings it went into voicemail. He hung up without leaving a message. Then he called Martinez's cell.

"Martinez here."

"Don't interrupt, just listen," David said, not wanting Martinez to use his name, in case he wasn't alone. Martinez sounded cool and David had the sinking feeling his partner wished he hadn't called. He'd always known Martinez's tolerance was shallow. He just hadn't expected it to vanish this fast. He repeated what Chris had told him. "The techies will have to talk to Chris for the details, but if they can verify this..."

"You gonna go to Williams with this stuff?"

"I'm not just going to sit here and get railroaded."

"Where do you think that shit came from?" Martinez's voice dropped. "I always heard it was all over the Internet. Guess that's true, but *Dios...*"

"I've never seen anything like that before in my life." David froze, then his own voice grew hoarse. "Is someone saying otherwise? Is someone saying I *like* that stuff?"

"You know gossips, they don't care about the truth..."

"You know me better than that, right?" Except Martinez hadn't even known he was gay for six years of their partnership. Suddenly David wanted off the phone, before one of them blurted out something that would irreparably damage their partnership, if it hadn't been already. "Listen, I have to go. We'll talk later."

He hung up before Martinez fumbled for a response. His next call was to his advocate. He repeated what he had told Martinez and tried to summarize Chris's findings. Someone had to see the same thing he did in the whole convoluted mess.

"Get Chris to document all that, David," Bryan said. "I'll get a tech to come out and secure those emails. Make sure Chris doesn't touch that computer until we get there. We don't want PSB claiming he planted the stuff to help you, though they probably will anyway." Bryan's voice softened. "How are you holding up?"

"Fine." His knuckles were white where they clung to the phone. "Pissed. No, furious."

"Good, hold that thought. As long as you're mad you'll keep on fighting."

Chris entered his office just as David hung up. David gave him the bad news first.

Chris slumped onto the futon he kept in his office for out of town visitors. "And when are they going to come and do this?"

"No idea."

"Great." Chris pulled out his Blackberry. "At least I can check email on this thing." He frowned over the device at David. "What are your plans for the rest of the day? Chase your own tail some more?"

Had Chris overheard his conversation with Martinez? Chris had never been a big fan of David's partner. Would he be happy to see a wedge driven between the two?

The day yawned in front of him. "We still on for supper?"

"Unless you'd rather not." Chris followed David out of his office. "I'm really getting tired of this Sandman." He threw himself onto the living room sofa and stared out the bay window at the distant Mt. Hollywood looming over Griffith Park. Sunlight glittered on the reservoir. "How much priority do you think they'll give to finding him?"

David lowered himself beside Chris, feeling a tightness in his gut from the tensions of the day. He folded his arms over his chest. "Let's see... one disgraced cop and his faggot husband. How much do you think?" David rubbed his face, encountering stubble. He needed to shave again. "What do you think?"

"I think you're blaming yourself for something you had no control over."

"Now why does that sound familiar?"

"Because you're used to delivering the speech, not hearing it." Chris touched David's face. "How does it feel to be on the other side?"

David made a face. "It sucks."

Thursday, 2:35 pm, Cove Avenue, Silver Lake, Los Angeles

Chris was determined that David wasn't going to sit around and stew.

David's advocate, Bryan Williams, hadn't shown up until after lunch. Since David had been outed, Bryan had been a major help during a time of confusion and hostility for both David and Chris. While Chris had been there for David, he hadn't lived his life in the closet and hadn't dealt well with David's reticence. When the conflicts of being a gay cop in a paramilitary organization like the LAPD got to be too much, Bryan was there as only another cop could be.

Chris liked the guy, but his intensity was wearing at times. Bryan was a political animal through and through. Chris wasn't sure he put cream in his coffee without considering the political ramifications of his actions.

But today Chris welcomed him. If anyone would fight tooth and nail for David almost as much as Chris, it would be Bryan. And Bryan knew the ins and outs of the LAPD bureaucracy.

The computer technician had shown up thirty minutes after Bryan. He and Chris spent the next forty minutes dissecting Chris's computer, then going over what Chris found at Ste. Anne's. Bryan told Chris that they would have little trouble getting a warrant for the hospital's computer records. That ought to make him real popular with Terry.

"Then," Bryan said, "we'll get to the bottom of this. I promise you, Chris."

Chris could only hope he was right.

For all that, Chris was glad to see the two men leave. He barely shut the door behind them when he turned his most determined gaze on David, who had come to stand behind him in the foyer.

"Grab your shoes," he said, ignoring David's startled look. "We're going out."

"Out where?"

"Shopping."

"Shopping." David looked pained. Chris ignored him. "Shopping where?"

"Hey, we only got a couple of days till Halloween."

"And I told you I wasn't wearing a costume... What the hell is that smile about?"

Chris took his arm and steered him toward the door, pausing only to grab jackets for both of them, in the event the rain that had been threatening all day came. "Everyone knows how butch you are, hon, but this is one argument you are not going to win, so give it up."

Thursday 7:10 pm, Blujam Cafe, Melrose Avenue, Los Angeles

From the patio of Blujam on Melrose, David watched the usual parade of upscale funk and tourists that flocked to Melrose, the new Beverly Hills according to one gushing review.

David watched it all with a cop's cynical eye. A blue-haired, black-clad guy strolled by, his arm around a pink-haired Latina girl who couldn't have been more than fifteen. They both wore enough metal to make them walking lightning rods. The girl sported tattoos on both cheeks, some kind of Aztec symbol. Or maybe it was Sanskrit. Who knew? Four Japanese tourists, enthralled by the walking art gallery, trailed the duo, snapping pictures.

A trio of older teens came out of Blue Stone with bags of trendy threads. They tottered down Melrose, texting each other in silence. As far as he could see they never said two words to each other, but their thumbs never stopped moving. The tourists out-numbered the locals two to one. Melrose was one of the few popular strolls in L.A. Here cops didn't look at pedestrians with the same jaundiced eye they gave them elsewhere in the city.

Across the table Chris grinned over the rim of his Pinot Noir. He looked slightly ridiculous in the black Stetson he insisted David get to finish off the outfit they had selected from the leather place down Melrose.

"How do I look?" Chris asked, trying to admire himself in the nearest window.

"Like a deranged rodeo queen."

"Very funny." Chris twisted this way and that and tried to see the back of his head. "I don't think black suits me."

David stuffed calamari in his mouth to keep from answering.

"It suits you, though." This time Chris reached into the bag on the chair between them and pulled out the black leather chaps. "As soon as we get home I want you to model this."

"I tried it on in the store. It fit just fine—"

"That was over your jeans. I want it on alone." Chris growled deep in his throat. "Hot daddy... I told you we should have got those boots. You're gonna give this rodeo queen a serious boner."

This conversation was doing the same for David. He shifted uncomfortably in his seat. The part of him that wasn't being aroused by Chris was still fretting over his problems at work. Chris was doing a good job distracting David, but a part of his mind couldn't get over his other problems. What if PSB believed he was guilty? He might not have downloaded those images but they were on his computer. "Can we wait till we get home for this?"

Chris smiled. "Just warming you up to the idea. I find leather really inspiring."

"Well, just be uninspired for now."

"Not a chance, baby." He handed David his glass of ice water. His eyes danced. "Here, cool off with this."

David signaled the server for their bill. He scooped the shopping bag off the chair and held it in front of him as he fished through his wallet for some bills to toss down.

Chris took his arm, and, laughing, led the way down the street to where they parked the car.

And it occurred to David that if Martinez was right, they were going to bury him with gossip. He was glad Chris was driving. He never would have been able to concentrate enough to get them home safely.

What the hell was he supposed to do if he couldn't be a cop anymore?

CHAPTER ELEVEN

Friday, 9:30 am, Cove Avenue, Silver Lake, Los Angeles

Chris loped downstairs, a silk shirt dangling from one hand. He headed straight for the coffee pot and poured a mug. He laced it liberally with cream and sugar, ignoring David's scowl when he bypassed the fruit bowl and grabbed a chocolate chip muffin from the fridge. Shoving the muffin in the microwave, he slid the shirt on, leaving it undone while he set the timer.

"That stuff will make you fat," David said.

"Hasn't yet."

Chris flopped into his chair and fished out the Calendar section of the Times. He peered at David over the paper. "Got plans for today?"

"The garden needs some work," David said. He lowered his own paper. "Why?"

Chris did his best to look innocent, though he knew David could see right through him. He stood up and buttoned his shirt. "I was going to head over to the hospital. Want to tag along? Come on, it'll do you good. Get your mind off your problems."

David smiled mirthlessly. "Like that's going to happen."

"Come on, hon." Chris slid into his lap, looping his arms around his shoulders. "Bryan's good at his job. You always said so. He won't let them screw you." He nuzzled David's throat. "I'm the only one who gets to do that."

∫ ∫ ∫ ∫

David drove.

"That nurse, Laura Fischer, comes on at eleven," Chris said. "I want to see if I can catch her outside of work."

"Think she might be involved?"

"Don't know. Terry seemed kind of protective of her. I know he was lying about her skill level." Chris shrugged. "It probably doesn't mean anything."

David parked near the employee lot. He dropped his visor down and slid on his sunglasses before popping his door open. "I'll be right back." He indicated a tiny saltbox with a broken sign that said *Café Fresco* across the street. Other signs claimed *chilaquiles* and *huevos revueltos* served all day. "Feeling brave?"

"Sure," Chris said. "Cream and—"

"Sugar. I know."

"So much for the mystery."

Chris slid his seatbelt off and pushed his seat back. He scanned the parking lot that was already half-full. A bus braked to a stop several car lengths in front of him and disgorged a dozen passengers. Laura wasn't among them.

David passed the coffee through the open window. "Anything so far?"

"No sign of her— Hold on..."

A banged up black Cavalier pulled up ahead of them. Laura emerged from the passenger's side. Her uniform hugged her hefty frame. Tendrils of dirty blond hair piled atop her head had pulled free and clung to her pale skin.

Chris shrank down in his seat, but Laura never looked their way. She bent down and spoke to the driver, then swung around and headed for the entrance. Chris opened the car door and climbed out, meaning to talk to her privately. But before he stepped onto the curb, Laura was surrounded by a half a dozen women, several of them in outfits like hers. The group entered the hospital together. Chris returned to the car. David grinned at Chris's dismay.

"You need to be quicker there," David said.

Chris stared at the Cavalier. "Think that's her husband?"

David shrugged.

The Cavalier jerked away from the curb with a belch of oily smoke. There was a car that wasn't going to pass its next emission test. Chris glanced at the hospital entrance again, then back at the Cavalier. He wasn't going to get to talk to Laura today, but maybe he could find out something about her anyway.

"Follow him."

"What?" David asked. "Why?"

"You doing anything else right now?"

"That's no reason."

"Just follow him. Please."

David shrugged, but put the Chevy in gear and rolled out after the Cavalier. The two-car caravan turned south on Columbus Avenue then east on Colorado. After nearly ten minutes of trying to keep the vehicle in sight, they followed the Cavalier onto a side street. It turned into the lot of an old post war three story walkup that had fallen on hard times.

David drove past, turning right on the next street, pulling a quick U-turn once they were out of sight. He parked across the street from the apartment building. They watched the driver jump out and trot up the cracked sidewalk.

The figure turned toward them. There was something familiar about that face. Where had he seen it before? Shoulder-length brown hair, prematurely thinning on top, framed a square face that looked sallow in the late October sun. The man wore a faded denim shirt, jeans and black sandals. He looked to be in his twenties.

The door was propped open. Inside were nine mailboxes set in arched openings. It might have been a nice Spanish-style building at one time, but now it was a faded, water-stained memory.

Through the open door they could see the driver pull a handful of flyers out of a bottom mailbox and passed through a second door.

"Okay, Sherlock," David asked. "What now?"

Chris offered an "I don't know, I'm winging it" shrug even as he struggled to remember where he had seen this guy before. The memory remained firmly locked away in his skull. He hopped out of the car and trotted across the empty street. In the front apartment next door, a newer four story building, a tiny furred face peered around a lace curtain and let loose an explosion of high-pitched yaps.

He glanced back; David had climbed out and was standing beside the two-toned Chevy. Behind his shades his gaze was inscrutable, but Chris sensed his amusement. There were worn nametags on each of the mailboxes.

There were three names on the bottom mailbox: C. Than, R. Diego and H. Bolton. The mystery man wasn't Asian or Latino, so he had to be Bolton. He stared at the door Bolton had gone through. Damn, he knew that name and that face. Who was this guy?

Back at the car, he slid in beside David, who lowered his sunglasses and peered at him over the rims. "So," he said. "Was that productive?"

Chris wasn't paying attention. "Can you run those plates?"

The glasses came off completely. David's eyes were flat, the cop gaze Chris hated.

"In case you've forgotten," David said. "I'm taking a little bit of a forced vacation here. Running plates is not exactly on my can-do list."

Not exactly a flat-out no, either. Chris flashed a smile. "What about Bryan?"

David sighed. "I'll call him when we get home."

♪ ♪ ♪ ♪

Bryan arrived half an hour after they got back home. David led them out to the backyard.

The garden David had taken over from Chris's benign neglect was redolent with scented geraniums and California poppies. Deep blue lobelias in pots ringed the stone patio. A low hedge of delicately scented rosemary separated the drought-resistant ground cover from the flagstone patio. A pair of cypress trees that matched the two in the front of the house flanked the rose arbor and provided shade. Two pepper trees finished off the patio décor. In the back of the sloping yard pale, dense night-blooming jasmine crowded against the back fence.

Sergeant sprawled out on the flagstones in the middle of everyone.

Chris handed Bryan a glass of wine and sat beside David on the glider. Bryan sat across from them in one of their newly purchased Adirondack chairs.

"The car is registered to a Herb Bolton," Bryan said. "That name mean anything to you?"

Chris frowned. The name did sound familiar. Just like Bolton's face had. He stared across the rosemary hedge at the bottlebrush tree that still sported fuzzy red spikes. A flick of movement drew his restless gaze; a green and scarlet Ste. Anna's hummingbird flitted from the neighbor's yard and disappeared around the side of the house.

He sat upright so quickly David sloshed wine down the front of his T-shirt. "Bolton! I knew there was something about that name. Wait here—I'll be right back."

He hurried inside, heading straight for his home office where he logged in and got online.

He Googled Herb Bolton and as an afterthought, Hellraiser. If his memory, which had a knack for holding on to the most useless trivia, was right, he definitely knew this guy.

"Aha, I *was* right," he murmured when the screen came back with several hits for both names.

Bolton had been a very bad boy a few years ago. The old headlines gleefully spilled the whole sordid story.

Hollywood man runs wild on other people's money and *Hacker scores big, loses bigger.*

Chris printed off several articles and carried them out to the patio. David and Bryan were deep in conversation and only broke off when Chris sat back down beside David.

"Find what you were looking for?" David asked.

"More. Take a look." Chris handed one article to David and another to Bryan. "Herb Bolton stole a whack of credit cards from some online store. He used the cards to accumulate quite a pile of goodies. Mostly computer equipment, though I understand he treated himself to a trip to Mexico. By the time the Feds rounded him up, he'd spent nearly thirty thousand dollars."

"Outside of the equipment seized, none of it was recovered." David read through the short news article. "Says here he didn't go to Mexico alone, but they had no luck finding any accomplices. Bolton wasn't talking."

Chris and David shared a glance. Then they looked at Bryan.

"There should be records of his traveling companion," David said. "They would have been subpoenaed."

Bryan was nodding. "I'll see what I can dig up. Case is a little stale, though. If they suspect his traveling companion was involved in the credit card theft the case against him—"

"Or her," Chris amended, suspecting he knew exactly who had traveled with Bolton.

"Or her," Bryan continued. "The theft charges would still be open. We could file if we had a suspect. Who are you thinking of?" When Chris didn't answer Bryan persisted. "Well? I need a name if this is going to go anywhere—"

"Can I get back to you on that? I promise I'll tell you, once I know for sure."

Bryan had to leave it at that, though Chris could tell he wasn't impressed. At least David didn't give Laura up.

♫ ♫ ♫ ♫

Bryan left shortly after, promising again to look into the Bolton case. He admonished David to keep his nose clean. "This mess will be cleaned up without your input. You'll only cloud the issue if you get involved."

David assured him he wouldn't.

Once Bryan drove away, Chris retreated to his home office where he worked through his email. After half an hour he emerged and found David in the media room watching college basketball, drinking a Bud.

Chris leaned down to buss his lips. "I gotta go back to Ste. Anne's. I shouldn't be more than a few hours. Late supper? Hamburgers?"

David wasn't much of a cook, but he wielded a mean spatula. He glanced at the Rolex Chris had given him for his fortieth birthday. "Seven good?"

"I'll call if it's not."

It ended up taking nearly six hours but by the time he and Terry wrapped up, they had tracked back on all the areas the hacker had touched and either verified the integrity of the data or were able to replace it with good backups. By the time he returned home the color was long gone from the western sky and the lights up and down the hill ringing the Silver Lake and Ivanhoe reservoirs were on. Light shivered off the placid water.

David fired up the gas barbecue and the patties were in the fridge. Within minutes of Chris's arrival the aroma of searing beef filled the small patio.

Chris grabbed a quick shower, made a salad and by nine-thirty they were seated at the kitchen table, chowing down on mesquite-flavored burgers and drinking beer.

Chris spent all day Saturday at Ste. Anne's. He barely sat down to dinner when his pager went off. Yet another client trying to deal with something their onsite techs couldn't handle. The next ten minutes Chris shoveled food in his mouth while he listened to the technical manager try to explain what was going on.

When he hung up he threw an apologetic look at David. "You mind?"

"Hey, it's your job," David said, even though Chris could tell he did mind.

"I'll be back as soon as I can."

He didn't return until after midnight. On his way home he swung by the hospital, but neither Terry nor Laura were there. He was tempted to drive by Bolton's house but it was already late.

His own house was dark and David was sound asleep, one arm thrown over his head while he snored softly. Chris crawled in beside him and was lulled asleep by the gentle sound of David's breathing, Sweeney's soft purr and Sergeant's snores.

♪ ♪ ♪

Bryan called at six the next morning. The sound dragged Chris out of a deep sleep. It always amazed Chris how David went from dead sleep to wide-awake. He figured it was a cop thing. He still beat him to the phone.

Chris swung around to face David. "Bryan. He's got some information on Herb Bolton. He didn't want to talk on the phone. He'll be here in an hour."

David glanced at the bedside clock and groaned when he saw the time. "Couldn't he have waited for lunch?"

"Come on, lazy bones." Chris snatched the sheet off David's shrinking flesh. "Get dressed. This could be important."

"Not as important as a good night's sleep."

"Let's see what he has to say before we decide that."

David gave up the argument. How could he beat that kind of logic?

While David made coffee, Chris got out an assortment of muffins and arranged them on a tray in the microwave. By the time Bryan rang the front doorbell the coffee was perked and the food warm.

They sat around the kitchen table. Bryan set a thin file folder on the table beside his plate before reaching for a blueberry muffin.

"This is all I could get without raising eyebrows. There's probably more, but this might prove useful in answering some preliminary questions." He shrugged, buttering his muffin. "It's a place to start."

"Before this goes any further I want you to know you don't need to do this, Bryan," David said. "I—we—really appreciate all your help."

Bryan's face grew almost as red as his hair. "Yeah, well, there's not enough of us as it is. I'm not going to let one of the good ones get railroaded by the department's bull-headed beliefs."

"Thanks all the same," David said. "We owe you."

"I'll collect, too." Bryan grinned. "That's one more reason to keep you around. Can't collect if you're off the force."

"Let's see what you've got," David said.

Bryan opened the folder and slid sheets of paper across the table to both Chris and David. "There's a good chance your doer did this sort of thing before. In fact Fraud has a strong suspicion he stole as much as a hundred grand, but all they could nail him on was the thirty. Not a bad haul for a twenty-year-old, either way."

"Any idea who he hung with?" Chris tried reading the police and court reports, but couldn't get past the first few dense lines.

"That's here somewhere... Ah, here we are. The second ticket to Ciudad Juarez, Mexico was in the name of Traci Lords." Bryan grinned. "Think he meant the actress?"

"In his dreams," Chris said. "Mexico? Any idea what he did while he was there?"

"Funny you should ask." Bryan dug out more paper. "Fraud got him good on that. He used a string of stolen cards—maybe he figured the Mexican cops were hicks." He nodded when Chris offered him more coffee. "Now let's see... they booked a room at the Radisson Casa Grande. It's no Beverly Hills Hotel, but it ain't cheap." Bryan glanced down at his paper. "They ordered a lot of room service, but Bolton did take the time out to do some sightseeing. And a little hacking, just to keep his hand in, I guess. Apparently he tried to hack the Casa's database—after a few more credit cards, I guess. He got caught, barely made it out. Feds were waiting for him when he hit LAX."

"And the girl wasn't with him?" Chris asked.

"Her return ticket was never used. The Feds suspect they split up and she found her own way back. He wouldn't give her up, no matter how much they pushed."

"Let's push again. Find out if Laura lives with him now. Talk to some neighbors, see if she was there three years ago."

"Laura?" Bryan asked.

"I think the officers in charge of the investigation would have already done that," David said.

"Maybe, but no one knew about Laura then, did they?" Chris said. "I think I need to go back to Ste. Anne's and talk to these people. If Terry doesn't like it, that's too bad."

"You're going to go snooping around the hospital?"

"Who the hell is Laura?" Bryan demanded. "How does she fit into this case?"

"She might be Bolton's partner. We think they live together."

"And you want to start spying on these people based on the fact they might be lovers?"

"You'd think it was plenty if we could prove she went to Mexico with Bolton," Chris said.

"You can't follow people around until you find what you want. Do the words stalking and harassment mean anything to you?"

"I'm not stalking anyone."

"What do you hope to accomplish that the cops didn't? David has no authority right now!"

"It still makes sense," Chris insisted.

"What do you expect to find?" Bryan snapped.

"See who remembers them around the neighborhood. People might find me easier to talk to than cops—no offense."

So they told Bryan everything they knew up to that point, which wasn't very much. Armed with the new information, Bryan left, promising to keep in touch.

CHAPTER TWELVE

Monday, after a weekend spent avoiding reporters, getting caught in traffic on the way home from a checkup at his doctor's didn't improve David's temper, even if he had been given a clean bill of health. When he finally thumped through the front door and stripped off his jacket, it was nearly four o'clock. Chris was still bent over his laptop.

David grabbed a Bud, which he sucked back while he studied the screen Chris stared at intently. He caught the name Hellraiser.

"Something new?"

Chris frowned. "You mean besides being harassed by reporters?"

David laughed. "Comes with your new notoriety. Anything else?"

"Well, I have been digging around on Bolton. I was right, this guy's done this scam a lot—he's got quite a reputation in the cracker community. His tag is Hellraiser."

"And...?"

"He steals credit card numbers. Sometimes he posts them online so everyone can have a go at them, other times he uses them himself."

"What about the woman?"

"I can't find anything to suggest she's involved in any online scams." Chris got up from his desk, put his hands on the small of his back and stretched. Something creaked. "Jesus, I hate it when that happens."

"You're too much of a bench monkey," David said. "Come on, you need some fresh air. I'll buy you coffee at Mattie's. You can tell me all about this guy on the way."

Until David moved in, Chris had never been much of a walker. He was more of a gym rat. But David liked his strolls and his runs and he had managed to convince Chris to join him on a regular basis—at least walking. Chris refused to take up jogging. With the dog, they got out more often. As long as there was coffee at the end of it, Chris was amenable.

The downhill trip never took more than twenty minutes. They rarely saw any of their neighbors in the gated community. Angelinos weren't known for walking. But their homes were always a visual treat: Craftsman cottages, Spanish *casas* with red-tile roofs, space age boathouses crouched behind stone and wrought iron gates affording glimpses of myrtle trees, eucalyptus, native sycamores, sages and gardens of lush poppies, columbine, and heliotrope. Everywhere ubiquitous palm trees fluttered and rattled in the stiff morning breeze.

Before they knew it they were seated at their usual table on the patio facing Glendale Boulevard, Chris with his cappuccino and David with an extra-large regular. The waiter, a big fan of Sergeant's, slid the dog his usual chew treat. Sergeant spent their half hour there chewing contentedly.

"So what did you find?" David asked. "From what you told me he sounds more than ever like our guy."

Chris dipped into his cappuccino, giving himself a foamy mustache. He licked his lips and frowned. "You'd think so, but I have to wonder..."

"You don't think he's involved?"

"Hellraiser steals credit cards. From everything I've been able to find out about the guy, that's all he's ever done."

"And Laura's just along for the ride."

"She's got no handle that I can see."

"What if the guy decided to branch out, seeing what else he can get away with?"

"Yeah, it sounds plausible, but you don't understand crackers. This guy steals stuff and posts it online. It's his trophy—he likes to use the cards, sure, but his big kick is having all his cracker buddies see what a big success he is."

"I know the mentality. Trophy seekers." David swirled his spoon around in his coffee. "Doesn't he get more accolades if he does something more daring? Doesn't hacking a hospital beat credit card theft?"

"It might," Chris said. "Depending on what he did, but I don't buy it."

"Why?"

"He's not bragging, for one. For another, what did he actually do? Screwed up some patient records? Maybe killed one sick guy. What's to be proud of?"

"Are they really going to care someone died?" David didn't believe for a minute that this guy gave a damn about what he did. Chris was shaking his head.

"No, but it's not spectacular enough, either. If Bolton was responsible he'd have been all over the boards, blowing his horn, making sure everyone knew how ripped he was."

"Maybe he's keeping a low profile because of the trouble he got into last time. He's an adult now, he'd be facing hard time over this charge."

"Point taken." Chris frowned.

"Would he have the skill?"

"Probably. As long as he kept his hand in."

"And he has access, right? Probably goes there all the time to pick up Laura so he's in and out of the hospital. His presence isn't suspicious to anyone."

Chris stared out the window, sliding one manicured finger around the rim of his empty mug. He turned around when their server returned.

"Get you boys anything else?" she asked. "We got a special on coconut cream."

They shook their heads. She nodded and dropped the bill on the scarred linoleum table.

David pulled a five and a two out of his wallet. "Ready?" he asked, picking up Sergeant's leash. He brushed his hand over Chris's spine as they moved toward the sidewalk, briefly pressing against the small of his back. It was as close as he would let himself get to a public display of affection.

After turning off Glendale onto Cove they climbed the hill, passing Mattachine House, the historic site of one of L.A.'s first gay societies. The house Chris inherited from his grandmother was just beyond the crest, overlooking the reservoir. A jogger swung toward them, bronze legs pumping rhythmically down the stairs that separated the Silver Lake side from the Glendale Boulevard side, his white T-shirt molded over perfect abs. Beside him a long-legged Doberman kept pace, toenails clicking on the steps. The jogger glanced at Chris, David, and Sergeant, offering them a knowing smile.

Chris and David both turned to watch the jogger make his way toward Glendale, admiring his muscular backside. Then their eyes met and they burst out laughing.

"Gotcha," Chris said. "If he followed me home, would I be able to keep him?"

"Sure. I wouldn't mind getting another nice big dog. I'm sure Sergeant would love it—"

Chris dug his elbow into David's side. David grunted.

"Dog, my ass. Tell me you were looking at the dog."

David grinned. "Great looking dog. Did you see the legs on that thing?"

"Yeah, I thought so." Chris took David's arm. "If you're up to it, I'd like to go back to the hospital tonight."

David was silent. He'd half expected something like this. He just hadn't thought Chris would go for a direct confrontation. He pulled the house keys out as they entered the courtyard. Unlocking the door, he let Chris slip past him to disable the alarm.

"David—"

"You really think that's a good idea?" David asked, knowing it wasn't, and knowing Chris didn't care.

It was Chris's turn to be silent. Then he sighed. "Yes," he said. "We need to talk to Laura. If she knows you're a cop, she might let something slip. Maybe there's nothing there. She didn't seem like a bad character."

"People can surprise you," David said darkly. He had always tried to keep Chris out of his work. It was a side of his life he didn't think the man he loved needed to experience. Chris cooperated, in his own way. David figured Chris didn't really want to know all the ways people could hurt each other.

$$\int \int \int \int$$

Chris drove. By the time they pulled into the parking lot it was just before eight.

"Let's see if Terry was hedging about Laura." Chris led the way inside. "He said she didn't work that much on the third floor. I think he's lying. I think he knows she had access to the computer."

"We want to catch her as she's going off shift." A phone call had confirmed she was on till eight.

At the hospital they took the elevator to the third floor. Chris wanted to poke around, but David kept him focused on finding Laura.

Chris still managed to peer into several rooms before they reached the nurse's station. The square-faced African-American woman behind the counter looked up when they stopped in front of her. She smiled mechanically, displaying a chipped front tooth. She wore a child's rendering of a flower on her breast, above a nametag that said: Tricia Keeting.

David stepped up to the counter. Her gaze followed him and her eyes narrowed. Chris knew she had made David as a cop.

"We're here to see Laura Fischer," Chris said.

"Is she expecting you?"

David took over. "Doubt it. Where might we find her?"

The smile gone, she looked right, down a darkened corridor. At the far end a shadowy figure of a man stooped over a bucket of water and a mop.

"She's in room three-ten with a patient—you can't go in there—" She sounded panicked when David nodded and moved away from the desk. Chris followed.

"We'll wait outside," David reassured her.

Chris paused by each open door, but outside of the nurse's station there were no other computers visible. Terry said the suspect computer had been on this floor, but had never actually said where. Had it been out in the open for anyone to use? Or tucked away behind locked doors somewhere? Terry, he realized, had been less than forthcoming.

Chris mentioned that to David, who shrugged.

"Pretty typical," he said. "If you were a cop you'd be used to it. Everyone lies."

"I don't expect friends to lie."

"He's protecting his turf. Face it, you're not exactly trying to make him look good."

Laura emerged from a room down the hall. She looked up at their approach, her broad face holding only mild curiosity.

"Ms. Fischer, can we talk to you for just a minute?"

She waited, staring from David to Chris as they drew near. "I know you, don't I?" Her eyebrows lifted. She pinned Chris with a look. "Terry told me you were working for him."

"Do you have a few minutes? We just have a couple of questions."

Now thoroughly puzzled, Laura glanced down the hall towards the nurse's station. Then she checked her watch.

"We know you're off in a few minutes, but this won't take long."

"Sure, I guess. Let me check in with Trish…" She spoke to the African-American nurse briefly then returned. "Can we take this outside? I could use a cigarette."

She eschewed the elevator for a set of stairs that led to an exit tucked around the side of the hospital. It was shielded from the street and the worst of the elements by an overhang and a thicket of dense Japanese boxwood. Cigarette butts littered the exposed earth, despite the presence of a sand-filled container set beside a stone bench. She used the over-sized ashtray to prop the door open.

Without a word Laura lit a cigarette and slid down onto the bench. She pulled her skirt down to cover her knees and peered at Chris through a haze of mentholated smoke.

"Terry know you're here?"

Before he could come up with an answer that might satisfy her obvious suspicions, David cut in, "I'm Detective David Eric Laine. We only have a few questions, Ms. Fischer. Then we'll be out of your hair."

She took a drag on her cigarette. "Detective, huh? What kind of questions?"

"First of all I'd like to understand what you do here," David said. "What is your role?"

"I'm a registered nurse practitioner." She raised one blond eyebrow.

"Been doing that long?" he asked.

"Four years," she said.

"Must be tough sometimes. Being around the sick and dying all day."

Laura's head turned sideways and her glittering eyes studied David. Wondering if he was playing her? Whatever it was she saw satisfied her; she nodded. "It can be. It can also be very rewarding, knowing I make a difference."

David nodded. "How long have you lived with Herb Bolton?"

"Herb? What's he got to do with any of this?"

"We're just following up on some details—"

"Wait a minute," Laura said. "This is about that thing that happened last week, isn't it? That computer break-in." She turned flashing eyes on Chris. "You're not a cop."

"I never said I was—"

"What are you trying to do, blame that shit on Herb? He doesn't have anything to do with that sort of thing anymore. He didn't hack the hospital, and he sure as hell wouldn't hurt anyone."

"Then you won't mind answering our questions, will you, Ms. Fischer," David said.

"I've got nothing to say to you." She threw her half-finished cigarette onto the ground and pulled the ashtray away from the door. She glared at David. "I'll bet you're not even a real cop. Leave me alone. Leave us both alone."

CHAPTER THIRTEEN

Monday 7:40 pm, Ste. Anne's Medical Center, Rowena Avenue, Silver Lake

Back in the car Chris slipped the key into the ignition but didn't turn it.

"Did that suck or did that just plain suck?"

David shrugged. "Interesting reaction."

"Bit of an overreaction."

"She's very protective. Of course, given his history, she's bound to know that sooner or later someone's going to wonder if Herb's involved."

"You think she'll call the station on it?" Chris asked. "If she reports you were here..."

"Too late to worry about that now."

Chris could tell David was worried, and he mentally kicked himself.

"Let's hope nothing comes of it," David said. "I'll call Bryan and give him a heads up. Come on, let's go home. I don't want to miss the game."

Ten minutes later Chris let them back in the house. David grabbed a beer and headed for the media room. Chris puttered around the kitchen for a few minutes but there was nothing to clean up. He didn't feel like watching TV, and the idea of working didn't agree with his frazzled nerves. He knew he'd never be able to concentrate.

He realized what he needed was a physical outlet. He grabbed the car keys and popped his head into the media room. David looked up. The dog was lying at his side, his head on David's slippered feet.

"I'm going down to the gym for a bit. Don't wait up." He paused. "Unless you want to come."

The answer wasn't long in coming; it was the same one he always got. "No, that's okay. You go ahead."

Tuesday 8:10 am, Cove Avenue, Silver Lake, Los Angeles

The next morning David called Bryan. There had been no phone calls from Laura or Herb Bolton that Bryan had heard about. He wasn't happy with David.

"I told you to keep your nose clean."

"Consider it clean," David muttered. "Any word on my case?"

"I think they may be starting to see things our way," Bryan said. "Which means they're not finding what they wanted to. I figure it's only a matter of time before they drop the whole thing and pretend it never happened."

"How about clearing me? Declaring me innocent?"

"You have a rich fantasy life, don't you? Be happy they're not trying harder to pin something on you."

Chris wandered into the kitchen looking half-asleep. He wore nothing but a pair of track pants that rode low, exposing most of his stomach. Bleary-eyed, he poured a mug of coffee, dosed it liberally with cream and sugar, and sank into the chair opposite David. His mug clinked on the Santa Fe table.

David hung up the phone and topped up his coffee. "You overdo it last night?"

"Does it show?" Chris massaged his left shoulder. "Remind me never to get into competition with an eighteen-year-old on the rowing machines."

"Would you listen if I did?"

Chris grunted.

David told him about his call to Bryan.

"So he thinks it will be dropped soon? That is good news. Any idea when?"

"None. The PSB won't rush things, could be a while."

"Assholes," Chris muttered. "Don't they have better things to do?"

Chris finished his coffee and limped back upstairs. The shower came on. Twenty minutes later Chris returned, dressed to go out and looking slightly less miserable.

"I'll be done around four," he said. "Once I get back we can start getting ready."

"Ready?"

Chris impatiently tapped his foot. "You forgot already? Halloween. West Hollywood. Meeting Des. Any of this ringing a bell?"

The Halloween parade. David groaned.

"You promised," Chris said.

He couldn't remember why. Probably because it seemed so far off and it pleased Chris so much. "We don't have to stay late, do we?"

"Why?" Chris asked. "It's not like either of us is working early tomorrow." He brightened. "Come on, it'll be fun. You gotta learn to loosen up, David. It'll do you a world of good."

David had already lost this argument during the very first round weeks ago. With a sigh, he leaned forward and kissed Chris soundly on his open mouth. "What do you want for supper? I could pick up a couple of steaks from the butcher. Some potato salad while I'm at it?"

"Works for me." Chris smiled slyly. "You know, you're going to look so hot tonight, I'll be fighting them off."

David rolled his eyes. "Not in the shape you're in, you won't."

∫∫∫∫

Chris wanted to go all out for the parade. But knowing David's reluctance in going at all, he had toned down his usual off-the-wall indulgence. Leaving David to be the star of their show, he had chosen a sidekick costume.

David looked him up and down before they left the house. "Tonto?" he said. "Isn't that a little... un-pc?"

"Hey, my grandfather was one quarter Cree." Chris smoothed a hand over his skintight buckskin. "Besides, you know what *kemo-sabe* really means?"

"I'm afraid to ask."

Chris smiled. He adjusted his beaded headband and hugged David's bare arm to his chest. "Come on, husband, let's go wow them."

It was barely sunset when they parked David's Chevy at the Pacific Design Center and walked to Santa Monica Boulevard. The usually teeming boulevard had been closed for the annual festivities and now thronged with a different crowd. Rainbow-hued pennants and flags stirred restlessly in the fading light. David saw one California state flag that had been altered to depict a bear in leather, sporting shades and a peaked leather cap. Music pulsed from speakers set up outside clubs and bars; techno, hip-hop and salsa vied for attention above the roar of the thousands who filled the street.

David had heard the expression "not for the faint of heart," but he'd never experienced it literally. The throb of noise was a physical assault, thrumming along his nerve endings and vibrating behind his eyes. He felt light-headed and breathless. His leather vest swung open and he wished he could have worn something under it, but Chris had been adamant. Nothing but leather, though he had conceded that jeans would have to be worn under the chaps for decency.

Each costume was more outrageous than the last. A pair of big-busted drag queens teetered down the street on six-inch spikes, gargantuan boobs thrust out in front of their sequined gowns. One had at least a foot of fire-red hair piled atop her head; the other sported a green Afro the size of a beach ball.

A man who must have weighed three hundred pounds wore nothing but a massive diaper and a pacifier stuffed in his mouth, carrying a three-foot bottle shaped like a penis which he used to squirt white foam over anyone who approached him.

Chris and David expected to meet Des at the Coffee Bean & Tea Leaf. Six leather-clad men watched them approach, their eyes raking David, studying and dismissing him in one cold sweep.

None of them wore an inch more leather than necessary to remain legal. "You'd look hot if you took those jeans off," one hirsute guy said.

"You can ride me anytime, cowboy," said a slender Asian in a skintight angel suit. He stroked David's hip, ignoring Hirsute's scowl. He would have done some more sampling, but Chris pulled David away.

"Tramp," he sniffed, tugging David toward the door. "Come on, there's a Moroccan Mint Latte with my name on it in there."

They entered the coffee house under the watchful gaze of a pair of horse cops. The county Sheriff's office had jurisdiction over West Hollywood, so it was unlikely anyone would be out tonight who would recognize David. He still felt as though they registered him, and he read disapproval in their flat cop eyes.

He shrugged and followed Chris into the café.

The coffee house was standing room only. David bulled his way to the counter, Chris trailing in his wake. Once he caught the eye of a server, he got Chris's latte and a black coffee for himself.

"Omigod, there's Des," Chris said and waved across the packed room.

When Des broke through the crowd David couldn't help it. He stared.

Des was always impeccably dressed; as the owner of an upscale Beverly Hills clothing store it was part of his image.

Not tonight.

Tonight he had donned a pair of skin-tight white pants that rode so low his pubic hair would have shown if he hadn't shaved. His slender, muscular—and equally hairless—chest was barely covered with a tiny, white sleeveless vest. A mask covered the top half of his dark face, but didn't conceal the crimson cat-eyed contacts he wore. David stared hardest at the fine silver chain that connected Des's pierced nipples to his belly button ring.

White and silver feathers dripped off Des's mask and two cat ears perched atop his shaved head. Silver whiskers twitched whenever he moved his mouth. He had draped a white cattail over his left arm. He touched David's arm with diamond-strewn nails that were nearly as long as his fingers.

"You look fabulous, David," Des said. He glanced at Chris. "If we weren't such good friends, I'd give Chrissy a run for his money."

David laughed. "You look pretty good yourself—" He froze when a second figure came up behind Des, possessively putting a fur-covered arm around his bare shoulders.

Trevor had kept to the cat motif. Only he had chosen a tiger outfit that did nothing to conceal a body that clearly saw a lot of gym time. He was covered head to tail with black and orange stripes that should have looked ridiculous instead of sexy and dangerous. David was all too aware that a lot of appreciative eyes followed Trevor as he embraced Chris and kissed him full on the mouth.

David and Des exchanged glances. Des looked amused. David fumed.

"You're still in town," David said when Trevor held out his hand. "Business must be good."

"Couldn't be better," Trevor said. He glanced affectionately at Des. "I think I'll stay a while this time."

A trio of silked and sequined queens who had bathed in uncomplimentary perfumes pressed against them as they tried to get to the counter. David stopped breathing.

"Come on." He tugged Chris's arm. "Let's get out of here before we get stomped to death."

Outside the streets were even more crowded. David was surprised to see a number of families, complete with kids in tow, moving through the sea of costumes. Tiny ghouls and cloaked superheroes clung to their parents, goggle-eyed at the passing parade of color and high camp. Uncostumed tourists captured it all in digital memory; David could imagine the video shows they would play when they went back home.

At least out here the air was breathable. He ignored the sweet smell of marijuana that rode the breeze and the chemical reek of poppers still used by some of the old habitués who hadn't migrated to the more modern roofies or crystal meth. Atop the smell of drugs the air was heavy with testosterone and adrenaline; the crowd grew edgy with just a hint of suppressed violence underlying the raucous laughter. On the fringes of the already volatile crowd a few placard carrying protesters tried to ferment dissension with *God Hates Fags* and *Burn in Hell* that were largely ignored.

The horse cops were still there, and he spotted a couple further down the street, keeping an eye on the protesters. They were smart to use mounted units; a cop on foot wouldn't have a hope in hell if the crowd turned. No doubt a few plainclothes were working the scene, alert for anything out of the ordinary. Tonight they would ignore the pot smokers and the drunks, their job was to watch for signs things were turning ugly.

The four of them moved with the flow of the crowd. Music boomed and shuddered around them. Some enterprising bar owner had mounted several strobes, and they washed the crowded streets with pulsating light. Crimson and green and blinding white, they turned everything into a jittery kaleidoscope of painted shadows and light.

The crowd carried them toward La Cienega. David found it almost as interesting to watch Chris as it was to observe everyone else around them. Chris flirted with everyone he met, running from one costumed character to another like a kid experiencing his first visit to Disneyland. He'd break out into a dance and haul someone off the sidelines to join him. As long as he'd known him, David had envied Chris his ability to grab life with both hands. He never cared what other people thought or said.

David couldn't be that carefree. He still hated it when people looked at him and muttered "faggot" under their breath.

Chris tucked his hand into David's back pocket. After a brief hesitation, David responded by draping his arm over Chris's shoulder. They passed a stage that had been set up by a local radio station where a costume-judging contest drew a raucous throng.

Beyond the stage an alley posted with prominent "No Parking" signs cut between two dark businesses. Over the hip-hop beat from the stage, David heard the deep roar of a large motorcycle engine. The restless crowd pushed them along; they passed the mouth of the alley.

Light flared down the unlit brick corridor. The engine rumble grew in volume and a brilliant red bike scattered the mob on the sidewalk. The motorcycle growled and the driver popped a wheelie. The crowd fell back, screaming.

David stumbled. Chris was wrenched from his arms and he thought he heard Des yelling. The motorcycle driver's full-face visor was as red as his bike and David couldn't see his face, but gut instinct told him the driver was staring straight at Chris and him as it roared past. The bike slewed around, eliciting more screams and panic.

David yelled and grabbed Chris, who nearly went down in the surging mob. David wrenched him to his feet. "Run!" He thrust Chris out of the path of the returning motorcycle.

Something slammed into his side, spinning him around. The motorcycle roar filled his senses. Hot exhaust flooded his lungs and he looked up to see the bike spinning back around.

He lunged to his feet, and threw himself sideways, but the rear tire of the bike flipped around and plowed into his legs, sending him flying backwards. His head smashed against pavement; debris scraped his skin raw. Light flared behind his eyes. Someone's foot slammed into his gut. He was being trampled in the panic.

People were yelling; he recognized Chris's voice. He slid away into dark silence.

CHAPTER FOURTEEN

Tuesday 10:10 pm, Cedars-Sinai Medical Center, Beverly Boulevard, Los Angeles

Chris paced the waiting room. David had been with the emergency doctor for nearly an hour. Des piped up for the third time.

"Honey, he's going to be okay," Des said. "He's not in surgery or anything. He'll be fine."

Chris stopped pacing when a uniformed Sheriff's deputy entered the room. Des and Trevor stood. The deputy looked like he might be eighteen with a face full of baby fuzz. He was distinctly unhappy to be where he was and kept darting nervous glances at the three of them. Des fluttered over to Trevor who gave him a brief hug. The deputy averted his eyes. He looked at Chris.

"Christopher Bellamere?"

Chris nodded. He swept a hand through his hair, encountering the beaded headband he had put on earlier. He dragged it off and stuffed it in his pocket, patting his spiked hair back into place. "I'm Chris. Are you here to see David?"

"I'm Deputy Kenneth Dumont," he said. "I need statements from everyone who was there when the incident occurred." His piercing blue eyes swept over Chris then moved to Des and Trevor, who had joined them. "Were you all there?"

They nodded.

Dumont swept his hand down the hall leading away from the waiting room and its crowd of watchers. "Let's go someplace where we can talk."

They ended up near the stairwell, behind a large Fichus. "Now, tell me what happened," Dumont said, pen poised over a notepad.

"We were just walking down the boulevard," Chris said. "Going with the crowd. This bike came out of nowhere and plowed into us."

"I think he came out of the alley," Des said.

"He?" Dumont asked. "The bike rider was male?"

"I've seen women ride bikes that size before," Des said. "But I think this was a guy. It's just the impression I got. I couldn't see his face or anything."

"What did you see?" Dumont asked. "When you say he came out of nowhere and plowed into you, do you mean deliberately?"

"Oh, yeah," Chris said rubbing his elbow where it had scraped along the pavement. He remembered all too well, the sight and sound of the big machine bearing down on him and David. "I'd say it was deliberate."

Dumont scribbled in his dog-eared notebook. "Any idea why someone would want to do that?"

"Nutcases," Des said darkly. "Wackos who want to kill faggots. You saw those protesters out there. Why aren't you talking to them or does that make your list too long?"

Normally Chris might have agreed with Des, but he had his own ideas about who might have been out to target David and him. He shook his head. "It wasn't the anti-gay crowd. David's LAPD. Homicide detective. David Eric Laine."

"Any reason to think this may be related to something Detective Laine is working on?"

Chris didn't want to say that David wasn't actually working on anything right now. He could just imagine what this guy would think about a cop who was on forced leave because they suspected he was into kiddie porn. Chris could hardly tell him about Bolton and his girlfriend.

"I don't know." He shrugged in answer to Dumont's question. "We don't talk about his work much." Chris knew why David kept him out of that side of his life, and after his brush with it when the Carpet Killer tried to kill him, he didn't mind at all.

"Would you be able to identify the motorcycle?"

They all traded looks. Chris shrugged. "It was big and red. One of those crotch rockets."

"What about the rider?" Dumont asked. "Can you think of anything specific about him? Was he white? African-American? Asian? Thin? Fat?"

"He was covered in leather," Chris said and the other two nodded. "He even had gloves on. He definitely wasn't fat, though. Maybe one fifty? One-sixty?"

"One-sixty," Des said. "Probably around five-eight or nine. I ought to know, I dress men all day."

The deputy looked nonplused until Chris explained. "He owns Samborra's."

"Samborra's?" Dumont asked.

"It's a men's clothing boutique in Beverly Hills."

"Anyone get a license plate?"

"Sorry," Chris said. "It happened so fast."

Dumont didn't cover his disappointment well. He held out a card to Chris. "If you think of anything else, call me."

"Sure, no problem. Can I see David now?"

"The doctor said she'd be right out."

The deputy left. Returning to the waiting room, Chris slipped into the seat Des had vacated. Des sat across from him, squeezed between an overweight woman in a too-large pink and orange muumuu and a fidgety boy who kept kicking his chair.

The doors to the emergency room swung open and a white-coated woman entered the waiting room. "Christopher Bellamere?"

Chris stood up and followed her. He caught up with her at the door. "Is David all right?"

"He sustained no major injuries," the doctor said. "We've made arrangements to have him transferred to Ste. Anne's. I've already been in touch with his doctor, and he'll meet David there."

"But he's okay?"

The doctor glanced at her chart. "All his injuries are superficial. He may sport some bruises for a few days, but there's no internal bleeding or bone fractures and there's no head trauma."

"Why does he have to go back to Ste. Anne's?"

"We received orders." She frowned. "We've been instructed to move him. A Dr. Abrahms requested the transfer."

"If he's okay I can drive him—"

"We're required to send him in an ambulance."

"When will he be going?"

"We should have him there by midnight."

Wednesday, 1:20 am, Ste. Anne's Medical Center, Rowena Avenue, Silver Lake

David blinked his eyes open. He must have dozed off while he waited for Chris. He blinked some more and focused on the figure standing at the end of the bed.

"David?" Chris stepped forward. "You awake, hon?"

"Yeah, I guess," he said. He frowned and looked around the room. "This is getting to be a nasty habit."

"Safer to take up smoking." Chris sat down on the edge of the bed. Anxiety burned tracks along his already frazzled nerves. "Why'd they send you here?"

David shrugged. "They were being overrun at Cedars."

"I was there. They didn't look overrun." Chris told him what the Cedar's doctor told him. "Talk to Abrahms. Something's not right—"

"Now you're being paranoid."

A starched nurse rustled through the door. It was Laura. Chris snapped to his feet.

"You again," she said.

"I won't leave until I know what's happening with David—"

"Chris, it's okay. Go home," David said. "I'll call you in the morning."

"I'm not leaving."

"You can't stay here," Laura said. "Visiting hours are over—"

"He's my husband. You can't kick me out—"

David grabbed his hand. "I need to grab some shut eye. Come back in the morning, you can bring breakfast. How about *huevos revueltas?*"

Laura made a noise in her throat. Chris stepped back from the bed. "I'm going. I don't like it, but I'm going." To David, "I'll bring your clothes."

David looked at the bag that held the ruined leather and jeans he had worn for only a couple of hours. "Guess you better."

Wednesday, 9:45 am, Café Fresco, Rowena Avenue, Silver Lake, Los Angeles

The interior of the *Café Fresco* was redolent with grilled chorizo and beans and the sharp tang of freshly cut cilantro. The girl working the counter was barely out of her teens and looked like she was about nine months pregnant. She moved with surprising grace despite her girth.

He ordered two *huevos revueltas* then flipped his Blackberry out and dialed the hospital switchboard. Within seconds he was talking to David.

"Hey," Chris said. "I'll be there in two. You better not have eaten."

"Hospital food?" David laughed. "You must be joking. I hope you brought clothes."

Chris glanced at his Andiamo carryon stuffed with pants, shirts, boxers and socks. "Of course. Be right there."

Twenty minutes later he stepped outside the little restaurant, a large sack of food swinging against his leg as he waited for traffic to clear before crossing the road. Before he could step off the curb a familiar figure stepped out of the hospital.

Bolton scanned the street and glanced back the way he had come. Seconds later he pulled a Blackberry out and studied the tiny screen.

Even from where he stood outside the restaurant, Chris could see Bolton frown and throw a nervous look behind him. He took the stairs two at a time and trotted down the street. He jumped into the unlocked Cavalier and pealed away.

Chris stared after him for all of two seconds, then swore and darted across the street, narrowly missing being hit by a blue van that pulled to the curb in front of him. Amid squealing tires and a protesting horn, Chris raced up the hospital steps

David! What the hell had Bolton been doing at the hospital? Had Laura told him David was back?

Could they have been responsible for ordering David's return to Ste. Anne's? It had seemed suspicious that David should be transferred from Cedars. Had the two of them tampered with another set of hospital records just to get David back here? Despite David's thought that he was being paranoid, he knew something had been wrong with that. But it didn't make sense. Bolton had never been violent before. Laura was a *nurse*, a healer.

Chris raced through the doorway, pausing briefly to get oriented. He ignored the dark-coated man with a lavish bunch of multi-hued flowers until he was knocked aside by the man, spilling his bag full of food onto the fake terrazzo tile floor. "Hey!" But the hurrying man didn't even pause as he passed through the doors. Chris leaned down to pick his food up. He saw the dark-coated man pull the flowers out of their container, splattering water everywhere, and toss the plastic container into a metal and concrete trash receptacle at the bottom of the steps, then climbed into the waiting blue van that had nearly run Chris over.

Chris's thoughts were still consumed by Bolton. If Bolton meant trouble, then Chris wanted the cops around to deal with it. Hurrying toward the elevators on the other side of the foyer he grabbed his Blackberry, thumbing awkwardly through his address book for Martinez's number. If something was going on David's partner needed to know.

"Shit. Where—" There it was. He hit dial—

A percussive boom slammed him against the elevator door. His head bounced back against the nearest wall, spinning him around. Light and darkness burst in his head. Fire blossomed in the door he had recently passed through and a roar filled his ears. Dust and debris showered down; something slammed into his side. The Blackberry flew out of his grip, skidding across the floor and vanishing into a cloud of debris. His knees buckled and he tumbled down into darkness.

CHAPTER FIFTEEN

Wednesday, 9:50 am, Ste. Anne's Medical Center, Rowena Avenue, Silver Lake, Los Angeles

"What the hell is this I hear about you being in the hospital?" Martinez growled into the phone. "You're off for a couple of days and you forget how to cover your ass? I thought I taught you better."

"Yeah, well they took me by surprise," David said.

"They? Not seeing conspiracies, are you? That's not like you, Davey." David heard Martinez plop into his chair, which he could imagine sagging ponderously under the big Latino's weight.

David changed the subject. "What's happening with PSB's investigation?"

"They tried real hard, but McKee came back today and said it's all a load of crap and they can't prove a thing."

"So I'm in the clear?"

"Clear as rain. Captain's going to make it official tomorrow, and I'm not sure he's too happy about that, but he's gonna do it."

David wasn't surprised to hear that about Captain Fredericks. The man was a notorious homophobe, an attitude tempered by Lieutenant McKee. David was under no illusions that McKee liked him, but he valued a man for the job he performed, not who he slept with. But now, clutching the phone in his fist, David was reluctant to believe what Martinez was saying.

"It's over?"

"Hey man, from the vibes I'm getting, it never even started."

David didn't bother bringing up Martinez's decidedly uncool reaction when he suspected David of downloading kiddie porn. His partner would remember things differently.

"Well, that's got to be good—"

A dull *wump* shook his bed, rattling the metal frame and spilling tepid coffee across his lap. He heard the distant sound of breaking glass.

An alarm wailed. Screams punctuated the rising voices. Footsteps pounded down the corridor and a fire alarm began an ear-splitting howl.

"What the devil?" Martinez asked.

"I don't know." David sat up and barked into the phone, "Alarms. I think you better call this in—"

The phone abruptly went dead. Then he heard the loud blat of a busy signal.

He scrambled to his feet, clutching the receiver. "Martinez!"

He dialed 911. Nothing but the fast busy signal of a line going nowhere.

"Damn—"

Someone ran by the open door, white coat flapping. Abrahms.

"Doctor!" David ignored the pull of wrenched muscles as he scrambled out of bed and hurried into the corridor. "Abrahms, hold it right there."

The doctor slowed and turned. "David, this is not a good time—"

It was hard to feel cop-like with a damp hospital gown barely covering his knees and his ass hanging out the back of the open garment, but David put on his best cop face and stood over Abrahms.

"Do you know what happened?"

Abrahms shook his head. "Something bad." He looked disheveled and shrunken, as though he had taken a savage beating. "I think it was on the main floor."

It was difficult to hear over the screaming alarm. A pair of nurses ran past. Doors slammed and voices rose in confusion.

"I need to get down there and see," David said. "Chris might be there!"

A pair of white-coated women skidded to a stop in front of them. "We need to start evac," the taller of the two said. "The west entrance is clear. We can move the ambulatories down the back flights. I've already got EMTs working to clear out the post ops from ICU. We're short-handed though—"

"David, you can go with these two. They'll move the ambulatory patients outside. You'll be safer there."

In the distance they could hear the approaching shriek of emergency response vehicles and the wail of alarms. Help was coming. But help for what? What had just happened?

David had to find Chris.

Abrahms touched his shoulder. "You should leave, David. We'll take care of things now."

In other words, let the experts do their job. David had been a cop almost all of his adult life. He didn't know how to be anything else. He shook Abrahms' hand off his shoulder.

"I was talking to my partner," he said. "He'll bring more aid. If you're shorthanded I can help."

Abrahms offered him a quick smile of thanks, and glanced down at David's bare legs. "You might want to put something on."

David considered refusing; there was no time. But common sense prevailed. Back in his room, he grabbed the jeans he had been wearing the night before and slipped them on. The knees were torn out, but at least he wasn't flashing his ass anymore. There was no shirt to put on; he had to slip the vest he'd been wearing over his hospital gown.

He put on the heavy black boots he had worn to please Chris and met back up with Abrahms.

"You don't need to do this," Abrahms said.

Every fiber in his being said he had to find Chris, but David couldn't walk away from people who needed him any more than he could stop breathing. Chris understood that.

"Yes," David replied. "I do."

The next hour was a blur of lifting and maneuvering patients from beds to the flexible stretchers that were easier to carry down the stairs. The halls grew crowded with EMTs and hospital staff. Smoke and the stench of burning chemicals seeped from room to room; David was sure he could hear the crackle of approaching flames. He still had no idea what had happened. A gas leak? An electrical transformer blown? Chemical explosion?

Chaos reigned outside. They came out the side door nearest to Rowena. Their position gave them a sweeping view of the front of the hospital. Black smoke billowed from the entrance. Helicopters thumped overhead, waiting their turn to evacuate non-mobile patients. Police, ambulances and fire trucks vied for space on the crowded road. What little green space had existed before was now chewed into gray ruts, while thick hoses snaked across lawns, streets and sidewalks.

Barriers blocked Rowena and Hyperion and the nearest side streets. David could already see reporters pressed up against them, vying for the ideal camera shot or sound bite. David saw the KNBC truck pull in behind KTLA. Whatever it was, was big enough to bring in the network feeds. He also spotted Roz Parnell of the *Times* talking to a uniformed officer who couldn't seem to take his eyes off her chest. David could only hope she wouldn't spot him.

David struggled with his fifth patient-filled stretcher and made it to the waiting ambulance, where an EMT relieved him of his burden. His body, already bruised from the attack the night before, was one massive ache.

Taking deep lung-cleaning breaths, he straightened from where he'd been leaning against the ambulance and braced himself to go back inside. He spotted an EMT at the front of the hospital, walking around the rubble-strewn sidewalk. The technician stopped and knelt, picking something out of the debris. Further on, he saw a roaming uniformed officer gingerly snatch a bunch of flowers from the sidewalk. David stepped toward the side door, prepared to go back inside to assist with the next patient. A hand snaked out, nearly jerking him off his feet.

Martinez glared at him.

"*Dios*, man, you don't give up, do you?"

David sagged back against the van. "How long have you been here?"

"Fifteen-twenty minutes." Martinez eyed the open leather vest David was wearing over his hospital gown, and his torn jeans. He didn't ask. Smart man. "What a mess—"

"Any word on what happened? I heard a blas—"

"Some kind of IED," Martinez said. "The boom boys got their robot and dogs going through the front of the building—I guess they'll tell us what kind it was once they know. There's a lot of rubble blocking the area—"

"Any sign of Chris?" David leaned forward, exhaustion forgotten. "Did you see Chris, Martinez?"

"No, no sign of him. I'm sure he's okay—"

David glanced down the street at the *Café Fresco*, opposite the front entrance, then let his gaze follow the path Chris would have taken with their breakfast. The area was crowded with lookie-loos held back by more barriers, but no Chris. Ice lodged in his chest, numbing his limbs, making breathing difficult.

His gaze snapped back to the *Café Fresco*. A very pregnant woman stood in the doorway of the restaurant. A broad shouldered man stood behind her, towering over the diminutive woman.

David shook off his lethargy and started across the ragged lawn. He darted around a black and white that was parked at a forty-five degree angle to an EMT vehicle loading up patients for transport off-site.

He approached the pregnant woman, all too aware he carried no ID, no badge to prompt answers from anyone.

"Ma'am," he said. "Do you work here?"

"*Si*," she murmured. "For eleven months now." She glanced shyly at the man behind her. "Since we were married."

"What time did you start this morning?"

"*Seis*—six o'clock. Every day we open for breakfast."

David looked at the big, silent man behind her. Did he even speak English? This time David's gaze swept back to where Martinez was helping load evacuees into buses.

"*¿Estubo aqui un hombre esta manana?* Was there a man here this morning?" David asked, adding a description of Chris. "*El hombre tiene cabello rubio, ojos azules, bien parecido y muy bien vestido. I quizas tenia una bolsa.*"

"*¿Bolsa?*"

"Yes," David said. "A bag."

The woman played with the buttons of her blouse where it bulged over her belly. She smiled shyly. She conferred with the man behind her.

"*Si*, he was my last customer." She frowned. "Soon after he left there was a *rugido grande*," she said. "An explosion. *Muy fuerte.*"

"Did you see him after he left? Do you know if he went toward the hospital across the street?"

"*No hici, no.* Sorry."

David met the dark eyes of the man hovering over his wife. "Sir, did you see anything? Did you see this man?"

"*No, no vio nada*," he said and taking his wife's arm he pulled her back into their café.

David spun around and stared at the rubble that had once been the hospital's main entrance. Sour bile filled his throat.

"*Hola*, Davey," Martinez hailed him.

Reluctantly David turned to face his partner.

"McKee says you're back on duty, but you gotta stop down at Northeast to make it formal."

"Chris is in there."

"What?" Martinez came to an abrupt stop in front of him. His face was a mask of confusion. "Chris? Why on earth would he be here?"

"He was bringing me clothes. He stopped to grab breakfast," David waved his bare arm toward the *Café Fresco*. "They confirmed he was there minutes before the blast. Where else would he be?"

Martinez muttered something in Spanish. "I heard they're bringing dogs in. They'll find him, David."

David wasn't going to leave Chris's life in anyone else's hands. "I can't leave until I know he's safe."

A van pulled up behind one of the idling fire trucks and a woman got out. She pulled the rear door of the van open, and seconds later a black lab jumped out. The dog wore a bright yellow coat with big block letters that said "Rescue" over a web harness, which the woman snapped a leash to.

Striding across the street, David made an end-run around the fire truck and approached the woman. Her dog looked up at him.

"Ma'am?"

She took in his bruised face and torn jeans. The lab thumped his tail.

"Sir! You can't come in here." A tall, lanky, uniformed officer David didn't recognize hurried toward him, his hand outstretched. "This is a restricted zone. Please, clear the area."

"I'm—"

"He's with me." Martinez flashed his badge. "Detective Martinez Diego and my partner, David Laine. We have strong reason to believe there's a man in there."

"Who?"

They both swung around to look at the woman with the dog. "Sorry," she said, tightening her hold on the lab's leash. "I'm Sarah Greives, and this is Maverick. Who's missing?"

"My husband, Chris Bellamere." David ran his fingers through his thick hair. Willing them to stop yammering about things that were unimportant. "He called me from here this morning just before this happened." Abruptly David turned and stared hard at Sarah. "This is really a waste of time. He's here."

"Then let's go find him," she said. "If he's here, Detective Laine, Maverick will find him."

David didn't wait for her. He strode across the torn up lawn and up the first set of debris-strewn steps. Behind him he heard the tap-tap of dog toenails against the concrete. Through the ruined front doors he could see the bomb squad clustered around something on the rubble-covered ground that looked like a badly designed go-cart track. Behind him, Martinez directed the uni to start a grid search of the rubble.

"Seek, Maverick," Sarah said. "Find him."

Maverick immediately became all business. Nose to the ground the dog went where Sarah directed, but aside from following her lead, he was clearly working to his own rules.

The blast had brought down most of the front entrance, scattering bricks and mortar everywhere, much of it channeled by the blast where the front door used to be. The worst of the damage was outside. Debris was piled several feet deep; most of the front steps and the doorframe were gone. Dust still hung in the motionless air. It was this area that Sarah had Maverick work.

David grabbed a mask from a hovering EMT and put it on. He moved parallel to Sarah and Maverick, studying the ground, trying to look beyond the destruction. Martinez stayed beside him. Glass and dusty bricks crunched under their feet. David stirred up even more dust; it coated his legs and hair and settled on the exposed skin of his chest and arms. It itched. His eyes stung and he blinked away the grit on his eyelashes. Even through the mask he could smell burnt brick and the odor of cement dust.

The dog kept his nose to the uneven ground, blowing up puffs of dust as he searched. After what seemed like hours, Sarah halted the dog. She produced a handkerchief from her back pocket and the dog obliged her by snorting in to it.

She met David's quizzical gaze. "Fine dust like this, it clogs his nose and he loses the scent."

They worked their way into the front foyer. Soon after that Maverick barked and lay down facing a pile of wood and brick that looked like any other debris. His once black coat was now gray. When he lowered his head and barked dust billowed around his head.

"Over here," Sarah called out. "He's found something."

David scrambled over a shattered wooden beam and dropped to his knees beside the dog. Ignoring the splinters and stone chips that dug into his bare hands, he pulled aside the debris, throwing it behind him. His breath came in shallow grunts. Beside him Maverick grew more excited.

"Chris! Can you hear me?"

Maverick's barks echoed in David's head. Shards of brick sliced into his fingers. He dug deeper, searching frantically, shouting Chris's name as he struggled to reach the bottom.

"I see something!" Sarah called out. Martinez was on his cell, shouting into it.

David spotted the denim-clad leg beyond what had once been drywall and tile. Glass littered the heavy blue material. A wet, red stain darkened the edge of the denim. It looked fresh.

Side by side David and Sarah dug through the rubble, joined by Martinez. Within minutes they had cleared legs and hips and were working on the upper body. Even before he saw his face, David knew it was Chris.

His skin was waxy and pale, and he didn't seem to be breathing. "Chris?"

"Careful," a newly arrived EMT cautioned. "We need to get him out of there with a minimum of movement."

More EMTs arrived, and slowly but inexorably David and the others were pushed aside. He stood helplessly on the sidelines as the professionals removed the last of the debris from the unmoving Chris and eased him onto a stretcher board. They pressed an oxygen mask over his pale face.

"Let's get him out of here," an EMT shouted. "We've got a bus waiting."

While David watched, Chris was rushed down what remained of Ste. Anne's steps and shoved into a waiting ambulance. Sirens rising, the ambulance vanished between a pair of cherry red fire trucks.

CHAPTER SIXTEEN

Wednesday, 1:45 pm, Northeast Community Police Station, San Fernando Road, Los Angeles

David emerged from McKee's office and the first thing he saw was a grinning Martinez.

"You ready to roll, partner?"

David had let Martinez drag him home to change before they raced to USC County General where Chris had just gone into surgery.

At that point Martinez took a phone call. McKee insisted David present himself at the Northeast Station immediately.

After forty minutes with McKee, who made it clear the only reason David still had a job was due to his superior's due diligence and support, David was officially reinstated. David had enough respect for McKee to keep his opinions to himself.

"The only place I'm rolling is back to USC." David threw his partner a sour look. "You can brief me on the way."

Martinez led the way to his car.

"We got the warrant for our victim's place and we got those pictures you were looking for."

"The son? Adam?"

"Yeah. We've got a couple of uniforms visiting all the units in Nancy Scott's apartment with Adam's photo. So far we've got some hits, people saw Adam coming and going, but nobody's too clear about dates or times. People just admit they saw him every week or two."

David slipped back into cop mode with ease. "We'll need to revisit them. Maybe we can jog some memories. What about the tox reports? Any word?"

"I was gonna call them today. They're dragging their feet. They always do when you don't stay on top of 'em."

They agreed that while David was seeing about Chris, Martinez would call CFSI and see if he could drag a preliminary report out of them. Depending on how that went, they would plan the rest of their day. David called the hospital.

Chris was still in surgery.

David waited impatiently for someone to come on the phone. Finally, a woman picked up the extension.

"Detective Laine?" she asked.

"Yes. Can you tell me what happened to Chris?"

"The patient suffered head trauma due to falling debris, some internal bleeding and bruising as well as two cracked ribs."

"What's his condition?"

"He's still in surgery. Once he goes into ICU we'll have to wait for him to regain consciousness so we can assess his mental acuity."

"You suspect brain damage?"

"He was buried in that rubble for an unknown period of time. We have to suspect there was oxygen deprivation. We just don't know for how long, or what damage there might be. We won't know until he wakes up."

"What are the chances of a full recovery?" He knew his agitation was showing "Chris is my husband."

"We're hopeful," she said. "But if you're looking for a firsthand account of what happened, you might be disappointed. Often victims of this sort of trauma suffer permanent short-term memory dysfunction. He might never remember what happened to him today."

David scrubbed his hand through his unruly hair. "Thank you, Doctor. I appreciate your being straight."

"If you need to talk to him, I suggest you come back tomorrow. He might be aware enough to talk then." Her tone grew shrewd.

"But if you want my advice, I'd just let him be for a couple of days. He's likely to be pretty confused when he first wakes up."

"Thank you," David muttered and disconnected after giving her his pager and cell phone number.

The early November sun splashed across the hood of Martinez's mud-brown Crown. "He's still in surgery," he said flatly. David squinted through the window at the street ahead, past a chugging orange, red and white metro bus.

"Let's go talk to some techs then."

"They got a report for us?" David asked. Last he'd talked to anyone at the lab they had nothing for him.

Martinez buffed his knuckles across his chest. "I always deliver."

"I am impressed."

The technician, a tall, robust African-American man, led them into an outer room. He carried two blue folders. His name tag said R. Ronaldson. "You're wanting to see this, then." He flipped open the folder and drew out a thin sheaf of stapled paper, which he handed to David.

He glanced through the document. His attention was immediately riveted by one line.

"Hydrocyanic acid?" David said. "Don't tell me, it was in the chocolates?"

"There was a high degree of lactic acidosis and evidence of pulmonary edema. Your victim ingested roughly three hundred grams of chocolates and at least one hundred and seventy-five milligrams of potassium cyanide."

"Who dosed her?" Martinez muttered.

"Sorry, I don't do whodunit." Ronaldson stuffed the report back into the folder. "I just read the output. I leave the easy stuff to you."

"Anything off the candy wrapper?" David asked. Which was going to be harder, tracing the candy or the poison? Were they still looking at the son? Poisoning was personal. Hard to see it being done by a stranger. Not impossible, but... would Nancy Scott have eaten a box of chocolates handed her by a stranger? "Residue? Fingerprints?"

"High quality cocoa, cocoa butter, hazelnut... If it helps, they were high quality chocolates. Probably European. Sorry, no prints."

"Can you give me a brand?" David asked.

"If you bring me a sample I might be able to match it, but so far I don't think anyone's started a database of chocolates."

"Can you tell us anything else?"

Under David and Martinez's watchful gaze he pulled out another report. "Some hair and fibers were recovered from a carpet." He glanced at the papers he pulled out of the folder. "The bedroom carpet. Not too surprising, most home vacuums suck at getting that kind of stuff." He snorted at his own joke. "One thing you have to keep in mind is that hair's pretty inert. It tends not to break down in a stable environment. So I can't tell you how long they've been there."

"But can you type them?" David asked. He'd worry about proving how the hair got there after he knew who it belonged to.

"Six distinct DNAs. One belongs to your victim. A second, male, is a close relative, so I'm guessing your victim's son. The rest are unknowns."

Meaning they weren't in any database. Neighbors maybe, Alice for sure. No way to test all the possible visitors.

"And then there was the cat hair. Now that was interesting."

"Cat hair?" David glanced at Martinez. "You remember anything about her owning a cat?"

Martinez shook his head. "Where was this hair?"

"That's the interesting part," he said. "It was recovered from the victim's clothing."

"Why is that interesting?" David asked.

"Because that's the only place it was found. If your victim had owned a cat, or even if one had been in her place for a short while, I would expect to find cat hair in the carpet and bedding or chairs."

"So how'd the hair get on her?" David asked. "The killer?"

"Maybe. Could be someone she visited," Martinez said. "But if your killer owns one it's good circumstantial. What color was the thing?"

"Tortoiseshell," Ronaldson said. "So you're looking for a female." At their quizzical look he added, "Sexual dimorphism is a trait linked to the specific sex of an animal. For the most part only female cats can be tortoiseshell."

David nodded. "Still, it only helps us catch a killer if we can find him and his cat."

They left the tech to his equipment and his evidence and made their way outside. A faint, lingering blush of pink stained the western sky.

Before Martinez unlocked the car, they shared a look over the roof.

"We gotta find the son," Martinez said.

"He gave us a contact, didn't he?" David had been out of touch for a while, but he was sure he remembered getting an address and phone number from Adam.

"Yeah. Number was disconnected in September. I sent a couple of uniforms out to the address. Nada."

"He skipped?"

Martinez shrugged and scratched a mole on his neck. "Landlord says he gave his sixty days' notice all regular like. No forwarding, but still, nothing hinky about it as far as the landlord could remember, though he did leave before his sixty days was up. But he was all paid up, so the landlord didn't seem to care. If our guy's running, he sure planned it all out in advance."

"Where'd his mail get diverted to?"

"Didn't. My guess is he already had a mail drop. We'll run DWP and phone searches, see if he transferred anything with him."

David grunted. He looked over his folded hands at the red brick and glass Hertzberg-Davis building. The brand new forensic center was a far cry from the outdated facilities they'd used prior to its opening. His thoughts raced. Maybe Adam *had* planned the poisoning. Except, if he had, why did he come back to his mother's apartment that day? If he was cagey enough to plan this homicide he must have known he'd be the prime suspect. Why not just vanish? He could have been on the other coast before anyone started looking for him.

"If he's still here he must have an agenda," David said, finishing the thought aloud. He thought of Nancy Scott as they had first seen her, lying in her bed, looking like she had just fallen asleep. He swung around to stare hard at Martinez. "I want to go talk to Lopez."

They drove east to Mission Road, struggling through late afternoon traffic, where they found Lopez in her office. She was peering over her glasses at a monitor, working on something and tapping away at her keyboard with two fingers. She looked up when he entered.

"Cyanide," he said, leaning over her desk, palms flat on the scarred metal. "The dosage our victim got, how fast would it hit her?"

"Ingested?"

"Probably in chocolates."

"Ten-fifteen minutes."

"Not instantaneous?"

"No. She'd start to get very ill within those fifteen minutes. She'd feel dizzy, nauseous, maybe even restless."

"Anything else?"

"Rapid onset would cause convulsions and heart failure." Lopez propped her elbows on the desk and laced her fingers together. "The principal toxicity results from the shutting down of cellular respiration. The cells can't get the oxygen they need, so they fail. Tissues with the highest oxygen requirements like the brain and the heart are the most affected by acute cyanide poisoning."

"So she wouldn't just lie down and die?"

"It might be quick, but it's not that gentle," Lopez said. "It's not what I'd call a nice way to die."

"Our victim was arranged all neat and peaceful in her bed, like she'd just dozed off watching TV. From what you've just told me that's about as likely as Martinez suddenly developing a taste for Gucci."

She blinked. "That's not an image for the faint of heart."

"No, I guess it isn't. Thanks, Lopez."

"Anytime."

David rejoined Martinez in the car. Martinez cranked the engine on and rolled down the window.

"Where to?" he asked.

David opened his mouth to say the victim's place when his cell went off. He yanked it off his belt and stared at the text message on the tiny screen. His mouth went dry.

"The hospital," he croaked. "It's the hospital."

Martinez threw the car into gear and they squealed out of the lot in a cloud of burning rubber.

CHAPTER SEVENTEEN

Thick, gummy residue matted Chris's eyelashes and raised tears as he forced them apart. He blinked. All he could see were blurs of dull white and gray. A distant beeping throbbed in his skull.

He turned his head and a crushing pain traced a path of fire from his skull to his hip. He groaned.

A warm hand touched his forehead. "Try not to move, Christopher," a calming female voice said. "You've had a bit of an accident. You're at County General."

"W-what happened?" Chris asked. At least that's what he intended to say. His lips were numb and the words came out as a broken series of grunts.

"Don't," the voice insisted. "Don't speak. Don't move. You're going to be okay."

Chris didn't believe her. As consciousness returned he grew aware of pain that seemed to emanate from every part of his body. "What happened?" This time the words were stronger.

"You had an accident."

"Accident?" Had he been in another car wreck? He couldn't even remember being in the car this time. He struggled through a growing headache to remember anything.

At first when the bizarre images began flashing through his mind he wondered if he was hallucinating. Dark leather. Brilliant lights and loud music. What the hell kind of memory was that?

David!

He bolted upright, pushing aside the hand that tried to hold him down. His vision blurred and his head spun. The room whirled around him. When his stomach turned over he stared up at the thin redhead hovering over him.

"Oh God," he muttered through clenched teeth. "I'm going to—"

She held his head as he emptied his stomach into a bedpan.

"Now," she said briskly as she helped him lie back down. "Didn't I tell you to stop fussing and relax? Nothing is more important right now than getting your rest."

"Where's David?"

"David?" The nurse used a warm damp face cloth to wipe his mouth, throat and eyes. He winced at the sharp pain in his jaw. "Who's David?"

"He's my husband. Is he okay? Was he in the accident too? Where is he?"

"I assure you there was no David—"

"You have to tell me." Chris grabbed the hand holding the cooling cloth. "Is he all right?"

"David is fine. Now you really must rest, Christopher. The doctor will be in to see you shortly, then all this will be straightened out."

The numbness that started in his lips crept down his body. Pain and the memory of pain faded; replaced by a growing lassitude. Something wasn't right. There was something about the "accident" this woman wasn't telling him. A new pain abruptly terminated his worry. It sliced down his left arm; he cried out.

This time when he tried to speak his muscles failed him completely. He watched helplessly as the nurse reached for the call button beside the bed. Her cool fingers gripped his wrist; she smoothed the skin of his brow with the other hand. Then consciousness fled altogether and Chris fell back down into darkness.

Wednesday, 6:40 pm, USC County General, State Street, Los Angeles

David bolted out of the car before Martinez pulled to a stop in front of the main doors. He raced down the corridors toward ICU, ignoring the startled looks, vaguely aware of the hard tension that filled him with suppressed rage.

He should never have left Chris. He should never have let them force him back on active duty while the man he loved lay in a hospital bed, injured, possibly dying.

Chris couldn't die. It was simply unthinkable.

He pushed through the door to the ICU. He knew from experience he wouldn't get past the next set until someone let him in. He thrust his badge into the face of the startled nurse at the desk.

"Detective Laine. I need to speak with Christopher Bellamere's doctor."

The nurse nodded and pulled up something on the computer. She frowned. Her eyes darted back to David. She picked up a phone and spoke low-voiced into it.

"Someone will be right down to see you."

David nodded, but instead of taking one of the stiff, plastic chairs he stood by the desk, though he knew he was unnerving the young nurse.

They were both relieved when a green-garbed surgeon shoved open the inner door. She hastily pulled down her mask.

"David?"

"Detective Laine—" David pulled away from the nurse's station. "How is Chris? I got a message—"

"Chris is strong, he's young and in excellent physical shape. We expect a full recovery."

David felt something leave him then. His rage collapsed like a pile of wet ashes. "Are you sure he's okay? Will there be any permanent damage?"

"I don't expect anything to impede him making a full recovery."

"He's going to be okay?" He wanted to believe her but he'd lived too long in a world of death. He knew how fragile life was. It hit the strong ones as easily as the weak.

"Oh, he won't be doing any strenuous activity for a few days and he'll be bruised and sore for a while longer, but provided he stays clear of falling debris, he'll be just fine."

"When can I see him?"

The doctor brushed a strand of salt and pepper hair off her face. "He's being moved into a private room as we speak. You'll have to wait a few more minutes."

David paced the waiting room waiting for someone to come and tell him what was going on. Martinez joined him. They didn't speak; what was there to say?

"He's been moved. You can see him for ten minutes. I can't allow more than that. He's been heavily sedated."

David followed her behind a curtained alcove. Memories of another bed and another body flooded him. Chris lay under a thin blanket, his pale face slack and motionless. Except for the soft rise and fall of his chest he might have been dead. Like Jairo. The small room was made even smaller by the clutter of machinery. Monitors tracked Chris's vitals. Somewhere down the hall, a woman moaned an unending litany of pain. Whispering voices. The miasma of sickness and disinfectant filled the air.

David shoved the memories of his dead partner aside and held his breath as he approached the bed. "Ten minutes," the doctor said. "No more." Then she pulled the curtain shut and slipped from the room.

David bent over the figure on the bed. He touched Chris's arm, staring at the bruises that mottled his skin from elbow to collarbone. One eye was swollen, the skin already turning an ugly purplish color. Most of his head was encased in thick white bandages.

His eyes were darting around behind closed eyelids; David wondered what he was dreaming about.

"Chris," he said. "Can you hear me?"

At first he assumed Chris hadn't. He slid his fingers over the bandages, feeling the heat from Chris's swollen skin.

"Chris?"

One eye fluttered opened. Light glittered off his dilated pupils.

"Hey, sleepyhead," David whispered. "How do you feel?"

Chris's eyes slid shut again.

David leaned forward. "Chris? Can you hear me?"

The doctor popped her head around the curtain. She frowned when she saw David.

"Sir, I'll have to ask you to leave," she said. "Come back when the patient's a little more responsive."

David knew she was right, but he didn't want to go. He brushed his finger over Chris's swollen mouth.

"I'll be back," he said. "Rest and get stronger. I have some business to take care of, but I will be back. I love you."

He found Martinez lounging in the waiting room, ogling a nurse who didn't seem entirely loath to the attention. David grabbed his partner's arm and hauled him away.

"You want your wife to kill both of us?" David muttered as he dragged Martinez outside. "Come on, I want to find out what's going on with this bombing—"

"We can't," Martinez said. "That was assigned to Bentzen and Krug. The lieutenant specifically said we weren't to go near it."

"That's bull—"

"Orders, Davey. We got paperwork back at Northeast. McKee wants us on it tonight."

"What paperwork?"

"From the old lady's apartment." Martinez shrugged. "Hey, Bentzen's a good man. If anyone can find out what's going on, he can." When David opened his mouth to protest again, Martinez shook his dark head. "Lieutenant's orders, man. I don't think you wanna mess with him on this."

David knew he risked his badge if he did. McKee was a tolerant man, but even he had limits and he had just about reached them with David. The temptation was still there, but in the end he nodded. "Fine," he snapped. "Let's go back and look at this paperwork."

♫ ♫ ♫ ♫

Back at Northeast they dug out the boxes of bills and other documents that had been collected at Nancy Scott's. There were four boxes, all crammed with paper documenting the life of a dead woman.

David pulled out several appointment slips for Scott's doctor. "Anyone ever talk to the doc?" He read the name, "Doctor Vanya Parkov?"

Martinez leaned back in his chair. "The guy was contacted. He wanted to play footsies, until we explained things to him, then he gave us a big fat goose egg. He saw the woman maybe two-three times a year. Says she wasn't one to look after herself, he was always on her to improve her diet, stop the junk food, the usual. He never saw her son."

"She never mentioned her family?" David was skeptical. "Or he didn't know she had any?"

"Apparently he was aware she had a kid, Scott put him down as an emergency contact, but never gave up any other details."

"What about her husband?"

"Nothing," Martinez said. "The old man was out of the picture by the time Parkov started playing doctor with her."

"Out of the picture? Didn't Crandall say she was a widow?"

"Parkov did say that when Scott first came to him she told him her husband was 'gone.'"

"Gone. Dead?"

Martinez shrugged. "It gets better. A few months later she comes in for her bi-yearly visit and she's all in black and it's pretty obvious she's in mourning. Doc doesn't know for who and she was right cagey about it too. Like she didn't want to say. So if he wasn't dead the first time, he died later?"

"The doc asked after her son, I guess thinking maybe he had passed, but Scott assured him her son was just peachy. And she was pretty forthcoming about not having any brothers or sisters or any family for that matter."

"So it had to be the husband." David studied the paper stuffed box in front of him. So many secrets. What was it about people they had to keep so many things hidden? "First they divorce or separate, then he dies? If it was acrimonious it could explain the reticence. When was this anyway?"

Martinez pulled out his own notes and flipped through them. "Couple of years ago as near as the doctor can remember. He did say she seemed to come even less after that, canceled several appointments in fact. I get the impression he'd about written her off."

"Could she have been depressed over the husband's death? Are we looking in the wrong place here? Could she have self-administered the poison?"

"Where would a recluse like her get cyanide? I mean, it's not exactly rare, but it's also not sitting on your local pharmacy shelf." Martinez slipped his notes back into his shirt pocket. "Seems to me she could have got what she needed from her own doctor. A nice prescription for Prozac or Zoloft and she's swinging. Hell, she was diabetic. She just needed to double up on her dosage and it's hello paradise. Besides, isn't she safely in the bosom of the Church? They don't look lightly on suicide."

Martinez was right, of course. Not that it stopped other Catholics from killing themselves, but according to the neighbor, Alice, Scott was unusually devoted. So scratch suicide unless a compelling reason to change his mind came in.

"Let's find the son again," Martinez said. "He can tell us what happened to dear old dad, and how shook up Mom was over it."

They dug back into the boxes. There had to be something on the son in this collection. He was apparently all the family Nancy Scott had possessed.

After nearly an hour of stifling yawns and trying to ignore his muscle aches, David broke down and dry swallowed a couple of Advil, chasing them with station house coffee.

"Lookee here." Martinez held up an opened envelope and a single sheet of paper with a letterhead. "Looks like our boy was accepted to Caltech last year. Think he's still there?"

"Only one way to find out. But it's too late today. Administration offices won't be open this time of night."

Martinez glanced at his watch. "Speaking of time, if I don't hightail it home soon you'll be investigating my homicide. With my luck my wife'd claim justifiable and get some judge I've been up in front of who would agree with her."

David grinned. It was true Martinez tended to alienate the higher ups in the legal profession. He didn't suffer fools gladly, and he especially hated liberal judges.

"Then I guess you better get home before she calls out the dogs," David said. He pulled the second box on his desk closer. "I'll just keep looking for a bit, then I may drop back in to the hospital."

"Then I'll see you tomorrow. And for God's sake, try to get some rest, man."

David nodded at his retreating partner's back. "Right after this whole mess gets settled," he said. "When this whole mess is put to bed and I know Chris is safe, then I'll rest."

CHAPTER EIGHTEEN

Thursday, 6:50 am, Cove Avenue, Silver Lake, Los Angeles

The phone broke through David's restless sleep. Thinking it was Chris, he rolled over and snapped it up.

"Detective Laine? This is Gunderson from the *Times*—"

"No comment."

"What can you tell me about the explosion at Ste. Anne's? Is it true your ah, spouse was injured in the blast—"

"No comment." David snapped and slammed the phone down. Almost immediately it rang again.

"What part of no comment don't you understand?"

"Is this a bad time, Detective? This is Detective Bentzen."

"Bentzen. What can I do for you?"

"Your name came up in my investigation," Bentzen said. He cleared his throat. "I'd like to get together to ask you a few questions."

David had expected this, since he'd been onsite during the crime. He sighed. "Sure. Do you want to meet at Northeast?"

"I have an interview room set up downtown. An hour?"

He grabbed a shower and shave. He arrived at the new LAPD administrative headquarters. The L-shaped, newly finished construction on Spring Street was impressive as hell. Flanked on three sides by City Hall, Caltrans and the venerable Times building, its ten story glass and steel reflecting back the center of downtown L.A. It was surrounded by green space and sculptures that had already triggered controversy. He signed in at the front desk. Bentzen, a muscular silver-blond haired man, came out to meet him and led him to a well-lit interview room on the fourth floor.

David glanced around the room. It was a far cry from what he had grown used to in the old outdated Parker Center. Everything still smelled new.

"We're recording this, that okay with you?"

David shrugged. "Sure."

Bentzen covered the basics quickly: date, time and both their names. Then, "Can you describe what happened yesterday morning at Ste. Anne's Medical Center?"

David thought back. Had it really only been twenty-four hours ago? So little time for so much to change.

"I woke up around seven. Some nurse I'd never seen before came in around seven-thirty, took my blood pressure and temperature." He shrugged. "The usual. She left and they brought my breakfast."

"You eat then?"

"I drank the coffee." He made a face. "Chris was supposed to come by with breakfast for us."

"Chris?"

"Christopher Bellamere," David said, knowing Bentzen knew damn well who Chris was. The whole department knew. "My husband."

"Did he come by?"

"He never made it." David rubbed his face. "He called to tell me he was on his way. My impression was he had just picked up our food—"

"Did he say where he was during this call?"

"No, he just said he'd be there in a couple of minutes. The day before he said he would get breakfast from the *taqueria* across the street."

"So in fact you don't know where he was."

"Except he was there, wasn't he?" David thought of the still figure they had dug out of the rubble. Not moving, not breathing. "He was just coming in when the bomb... when it went off."

Bentzen scratched notes in his pad. "Have you been to see Chris since the accident?"

"Yes. Yesterday."

"He responsive?"

David realized Bentzen must have gone by the hospital hoping to talk to Chris and been turned away. He nodded, knowing what was coming next.

"He tell you anything?" Bentzen asked.

"Sorry, no. He wasn't up to talking."

"What restaurant do you think he went to?"

"Across the street. *Café Fresco.*"

"Ah yes, breakfast. We talked to them," Bentzen said. "They didn't see anything."

"They remembered Chris." David tried a question of his own. "Have you determined the source of the bomb?"

"They used an explosive called NMXFOAM, something relatively new. It looks and feels like shaving cream." Bentzen rubbed his chin. "The foam is perfect for injecting into irregular-shaped cavities. Plug a detonator into it and you're all set. No amount of jostling will set it off."

"What was it delivered in?"

"Flowers." Bentzen tapped his pen on the table. "It seems our bomber was trying to get to the third floor, but when we thought someone had staged an attack on you, we had an officer stationed there. We found remnants of the flowers on the front lawn, we're now assuming he placed the explosive device in a garbage can outside the front door. We found a woman in reception who remembered him coming off the elevator looking upset."

"So she saw him?"

"White male, thirties, early forties. Heavy black beard. She's coming in later today to work with a sketch artist." Bentzen rubbed his chin. "She also noted he spoke with some kind of accent. She thinks it might have been French, but she wasn't sure. She just knew it wasn't Spanish."

David didn't have anyone "French" on his radar. Another lost thread.

"Does anyone remember who he said the flowers were for?"

"Nobody seems to remember." Bentzen narrowed his dark eyes at him. David wasn't sure what he saw there, but Bentzen went on to say softly, "You think it was for you? So you do believe the assault the night before is linked? How?"

"The first attack was on the third floor, too."

"First attack?"

So he hadn't heard of the hospital hack. David told him about the computer attack on the hospital. After a brief pause, he also forced himself to recount what had happened with the phony link and the kiddie porn on his PC. No way to tell if they were related, but David didn't believe in coincidences. Neither, it seemed, did Bentzen.

"And Chris wasn't able to find anything out about this Sandman?"

"Nothing, except that the attack came from inside the hospital." What was the word Chris used? "Spoofed—Sandman spoofed it so it looked like the attack came from somewhere else. Just like he spoofed Chris's email address so I thought that email came from him."

"What about the guy who called Chris, pretending to be a cop?"

"Chris only talked to him once. Apparently the number was blocked so he couldn't trace it." David scrubbed a hand through his hair. "This witness, she's sure she didn't recognize this man? Maybe an ex-patient? A disgruntled employee? The grievance seems to be around the hospital."

"Do you really think so? Perhaps the grievance is with you."

That's ridiculous, David wanted to say. Who the hell would be after him? For what? Instead he asked, "Anyone else see him?"

"We're still interviewing. We've got HR compiling a list of employees, past and present. We'll be interviewing them all, too."

"Any source on the explosives?"

"Still in the lab." Bentzen tapped his Bic against his notebook. The end of the pen was gnawed. "But that stuff's rare. That ought to narrow our search down. If you have no objection, I'd like to talk to Chris as soon as possible."

"The doctors say he may never remember much about what happened that day," he said cautiously, not liking the idea of cops hassling Chris, knowing there was nothing he could do to stop it.

Bentzen nodded. "Yeah, they me told me that, too. But you never know, right?" He shoved the pen into his mouth, then pulled it out again. "After you talked to Chris yesterday morning, what happened?"

"Martinez called." He'd been giving David hell but David didn't feel like sharing that. "We were on the phone when I heard the explosion."

"What happened after that? Were you still on the phone?"

"What? No—the phone went dead."

Bentzen nodded. "All communications were cut," he said. "At first we assumed it was linked to the explosion, but it looks like it was a separate issue."

"A dual pronged attack?"

"Looks that way."

"How were the phones hit?" David asked, though he had his suspicions.

Bentzen looked pleased to deliver the bombshell. "A computer worm was planted in the hospital's network. Apparently it launched an attack timed to coincide with the bomb. Probably why he dumped the thing when he couldn't deliver it where he wanted to. I guess our bomber didn't expect anyone to be talking to a cop. He was counting on a lot of confusion and delay."

"Which means maybe he was there, watching."

"Lot of these guys like to see their handiwork in action."

"Have you canvassed everyone who was in the area at the time?"

"The ones we can find," Bentzen said. "So far a few witnesses have come forward. If our bomber was there, someone must have seen him."

"I guess you get lucky sometimes."

Bentzen shoved the notebook and pen into his shirt pocket. "I don't plan on leaving it to luck. I'll make my own."

He stood up and extended his hand to David across the table. David took it.

"Thank you for coming in on such short notice, Detective."

"I'll let you know if anything else occurs to me."

Bentzen nodded absently. His mind was already on his next step. David saw himself out. He made his way back to his car in the underground parking lot through the corridors of the brand new building that was being touted as state-of-the-art. State-of-the-art or not, it still came down to old-fashioned police work more often than not. He had once aspired to join Robbery Homicide, the elite unit that handled all the complex and notorious crimes in the city. But that had flown out the window when he'd been outed. To the best of his knowledge there were no gay RHD detectives and he was sure that was just the way they wanted it.

Back outside, he slowed as he approached the newly erected monument to fallen LAPD officers. He had been there when it was unveiled. He still remembered the mournful wail of taps as it played in memory of the fallen. At first glance the wall looked solid, only when he got closer did it resolve into over a thousand brass plaques, two hundred and two of them fallen LAPD officers, including the most recent—his partner, Jairo Hernandez, who had died at the hands of a gang thug. He found it easily enough this time, unlike the first time he had looked. He ran his fingers over the engraved metal. Name, rank and day of death. So little to mark a life given in service.

Abruptly he turned away. He didn't need those memories replaying in his head.

Back at USC he found Chris was still unresponsive, though David noted with some relief that most of the machines he'd been hooked into had been removed. Now all he wore was a single heart monitor attached to his chest. His face and arm had blossomed into a kaleidoscope of surly purples and blues and the skin around his eyes looked soft and puffy. A catheter snaked out from under the thin blanket into a half-filled bag.

His eyelids fluttered briefly when David called his name, but they didn't open. David took Chris's hand in his, being careful not to jar the IV line or press on bruised flesh.

"We'll get through this. No matter what."

♫ ♫ ♫ ♫

David was at his desk when Martinez finally strolled in around nine. David looked up from transcribing his latest scratchings into his computer.

"You talk to anybody at Caltech yet?" he asked.

Martinez shook his grizzled head. "You?"

"Got a hold of one of Adam's professors. He said he'd be available to talk to us at ten." David pointedly glanced at his Rolex. "Can we make it?"

"Hey, no prob. We even got time to stop for some decent coffee on the way."

"Let's do it then." David saved his report and logged off. Sliding his jacket off the back of his chair he led the way out of the station. After signing a Crown out they headed east toward California Institute of Technology in Pasadena.

Caltech was the premier technical school in Southern California. Some argued on the whole west coast. David had never visited it. After grabbing coffee at a Starbucks outside of the campus grounds, they went over the directions David's contact had given them.

"He said to meet him in the Powell-Booth Computing Center. He'd be there until eleven. His name is Sanjeeb Narayan." David glanced at his notes again. "He said call him Sanju."

Caltech was a sprawling campus of yellow brick buildings and clean classical lines. It lay in the shadows of the San Gabriel Mountains; golden with the last brush of autumn colors on the slopes. Martinez found parking and they got directions to the Computing Center.

Sanju was a stout bear of a man, his surprisingly lean face wreathed in a silver white beard, his head similarly adorned with an equally white fringe of hair. His hand clasp was fierce; the smile on his face didn't quite reach his eyes.

"How may I help you officers?" he asked.

"I understand you were Adam Baruch's counselor—"

"Yes, yes. That's true, although I knew him as Adam Scott."

David remembered how hostile Adam had been when he had been addressed with his mother's name. What had happened to generate that hostility? He glanced around the public area they were in.

"Is there someplace private we could talk, Mr. Narayan?"

"Yes, yes, of course. But please, call me Sanju." Sanju gestured for them to precede him down the walk. Music wafted through the arcaded walkway, barely heard over the chatter of dozens of student voices. They passed into the shadow of the Jorgensen Laboratory and entered a corridor.

Their footsteps echoed on the tiled floor. Sanju unlocked an unmarked office door and gestured them inside.

"Take a seat, please. I'm sorry, I have no refreshments to offer." He didn't sound remorseful.

"That's okay, sir. We won't take up much of your time." David sank into a Louis Quatorze chair he seriously doubted was real, and glanced quickly at Martinez. "And how long have you been counseling Mr. Scott?" David asked.

"Adam enrolled nearly two years ago. His credentials, including letters of recommendation and test scores, were impeccable," Sanju said. "As you may or may not know, students are admitted only with the Ph.D. as their degree objective and Adam met that criterion without issue. In fact, he took a subject test in his chosen subject and scored exceptionally high, as I recall."

"But...?" David spoke up when it became clear Sanju was stalling. "Did his grades slip?"

Sanju pressed his already thin lips together. They disappeared behind his facial hair. "We all had extremely high hopes for Adam. The boy was brilliant in a way that far surpassed nearly all our students."

David knew that was saying a lot. Caltech was renowned for turning out brilliant, innovative graduates. So what had gone wrong with Adam? And what, if anything, did it have to do with his parents' deaths?

"Sir? Is there any chance we could speak with Adam? If he's in a class, we could wait—"

"I'm sorry, but that will be quite impossible."

"We really won't take long. If you like, we can arrange to meet him after classes—"

"You misunderstand. He's not here."

"Where is he?"

Sanju picked a pewter seal off his desk and stared down at the delicate embossing. "He...left the school at the end of September."

David dropped his indolence and sat up. "He quit?"

Sanju's gaze darted left, his mouth puckered up like he had just bit into a lemon. He nodded.

Liar. Martinez must have seen it too. "He quit? Or was he asked to leave?"

"You have to understand," Sanju said. "We accept a lot of idiosyncrasies in our students. Brilliants minds are often... different than the rest of us. But even the most brilliant mind must have some discipline..."

"What did he do, Mr. Narayan?"

"He broke into the Jet Propulsion Laboratory."

CHAPTER NINETEEN

Thursday, 10:50 am, Caltech, California Boulevard, Pasadena

"What do you mean, he broke into JPL?"

"He hacked one of the JPL servers and vandalized a researcher's web page."

"Was he protesting the site?" David couldn't imagine going to all that trouble unless the guy had some kind of political agenda.

Sanju shook his white head. "I didn't actually see the result, but as I understood it, it was a simple defacement. Some sort of childish cartoon. Nothing that could be construed as controversial or political. At least, not then."

David's hand froze over his notebook. "Not then? He did something controversial later?"

Sanju rubbed the knuckles of his fist over his bearded chin. "I suppose it could be construed as such. At the very least it was in bad taste. I'm sure it played a major factor in his being asked to leave."

"What was it, Professor?"

"When Adam was called before the Student Conduct Committee he showed up wearing a T-shirt that was highly objectionable."

"In what way?" David asked.

When Sanju hesitated Martinez snapped, "Come on, Professor. We can handle it. What did the shirt say?"

"Jew Fascists," Sanju said. His face reddened. "The words were written over the image of a pig being sexually, ah...mounted by a man..."

It was David's turn to frown. "Odd behavior for a Jewish man."

"Jewish? Where did you get the idea Adam was Jewish?"

"From a bad source, I guess," Martinez muttered. "If he wasn't Jewish—"

"His father was Iranian. An expatriate."

"He's Islamic?" David said.

"Statistically it's likely he was Islamic, but there are a number of Christian Iranians."

"Was any of this reported?" David asked.

"Adam seemed sincerely puzzled as to the uproar. He thought it was a lark."

"You didn't agree?"

"I was more concerned with his lack of remorse. He simply didn't comprehend that what he had done was wrong." Sanju seemed to be warming to his topic. "But was he amoral or just another youth railing against intellectual property rights? I don't know. But the decision was made higher up that he be asked to leave."

"What was his demeanor when he was asked to leave?" Sometimes traumas triggered outbursts of rage that could lead to other, more violent attacks.

"He was upset. He didn't understand it. I guess he thought an apology was all he needed."

David nodded. They were going to have to have another talk with Adam Baruch, nee Scott. "Do you have an address on him?"

David wasn't surprised to find it was Nancy Scott's Carillon Street address.

David stood. "Thank you, Professor Narayan. If you should think of anything else..." He handed Sanju his business card. "Please, don't hesitate to call."

Sanju followed them to the door and as soon as they were through it, he locked it behind them. David looked back.

"Guess they don't subscribe to the open door policy here," Martinez said. "I think you got to him there, *mijo*."

"Think so?" David sighed and rubbed his aching ribs. "It doesn't get us any closer to finding him, does it? You think it's worth going after that warrant?"

"Can't hurt. It may produce something."

"The address Adam gave was North Hollywood. Why don't we go and talk with some of the tenants? Maybe somebody saw something we can use."

"Sounds good. Let's grab lunch, then head out. If we get there early enough we may catch folks coming home for the day."

By mutual agreement they decided to leave the vicinity of the campus before they looked for a place to eat. Somehow the prospect of being surrounded by a bunch of boisterous students seemed too exhausting. They grabbed a sandwich at the first greasy spoon they spotted after exiting the Hollywood Freeway in North Hollywood.

The apartment on Vantage was a two story walk-up with pink stucco siding and tattered blue awnings that swayed in the afternoon breeze. A couple of half-dead palms and some languishing geraniums flanked the entrance.

David pulled the unmarked car into a visitor's space. They strode up the path toward the main entrance and buzzed the manager. Huddled in the wilting fronds of the dying palm, a flock of starlings complained.

The apartment manager was a spider-limbed African-American man. He immediately recognized Martinez.

"You back? Thought you were all finished here."

"Got some follow-up questions the boss wants answers to," Martinez said. "You know how it goes when the man upstairs gets involved."

"What kinda questions?"

"Adam Scott, the tenant from 1A," David said. "What can you tell us about him, Mr....?"

"Wayne Briscoe."

Briscoe led them back into his apartment, which smelled of cigarette smoke and the slight sulfurous odor of boiled eggs. All the drapes were pulled shut and the room was encased in shadows. A twenty-one inch TV on a hand-made stand was showing a laugh track filled sitcom. Beside the TV, a two-drawer filing cabinet was half open, stuffed to overflowing with files and folders.

Briscoe jerked open the top drawer and began rifling through the contents. After a couple of minutes he pulled out a thin purple folder.

"This is what Adam filled out." Briscoe reached one long arm across the filing cabinet and snagged a pack of Marlboros. He extracted one and lit it with a gold-plated lighter. "Well, that and his deposit." He grinned, revealing a gap between his yellowed front teeth.

David took the folder and flipped it open. Inside was a single sheet of paper. Adam had filled out the various fields in stiff block letters: name, again Adam Scott; previous address his mother's. David noticed a space for type of car and license plate number. Both were blank.

"Adam didn't have a car?"

Briscoe slipped on a pair of reading glasses and looked where David pointed. "Hmm, didn't notice that. He should have filled it out..." He blew a stream of smoke past David's ear. "Ah, I remember now. He got the car later. He was supposed to register it, guess neither one of us remembered."

"Can you remember what kind of car it was?" David asked.

"It was a green Honda," Briscoe said. "An Accord, a ninety-six. I know that 'cause my ex-wife had one, only she got hers brand new, out of our divorce settlement. Did I get a new car? Hell, no, I'm still driving that piece of shit she stuck me with." He sucked on his cigarette. "Man, I hate Fords worse than anything."

David made a moue of sympathy, like he really cared about the guy's car problems. "Get a license plate?"

Briscoe looked at him as though to say "yeah, right." He lit another cigarette off the first one.

"He a good tenant?" Martinez asked.

"Never late with the rent. Didn't party as far as I could tell. Quiet. Never said boo to anybody." He grinned, showing the gap in his teeth. "Hey, he a serial killer? Isn't that what they always say—quiet, shy, barely knew he was there? Imagine living next door to a serial killer."

Some people watched way too much crime TV. "No sir, we just want to talk to him," David said. He could tell the guy didn't believe him. "He ever mention his family? Mother, father?"

"No." Briscoe tipped his head toward the folder David still held. "Except for what he put in there he never told me nothing."

David studied the form more closely. "Do you have a copy of this?"

"You want it? It's yours. One less thing I gotta find space for."

David glanced at Martinez and nodded. He drew out a business card and passed it over to Briscoe. "If you think of anything else, please call."

"Sure. Anything in particular you looking for?"

"Just tell us anything that comes to you," Martinez said as they rose to leave. "We'll sort it out."

David slipped the folder over to Martinez as he got in the car.

"Anything interesting?"

"Social Security number. Let's see what that gets us."

♪ ♪ ♪ ♪

The SSN got them a single employer and a bank. "Citibank," David said, peering at his computer screen. They'd have to get a financial warrant to see what was in it. He smoothed his fingers over his mustache. "Six weeks at Burger House. Big step down from Caltech."

"Lots of students work slog jobs until they move on to bigger and better," Martinez said. He perched on David's desk, studying the screen over his shoulders.

"Except Adam seems to be moving down, not up."

"We don't have enough to get any of those records subpoenaed. We need more."

"Let's go talk to his ex-boss." David stood up. "Find out why he's not slinging burgers anymore."

"Maybe he insulted a customer this time, instead of a bunch of college liberals. Hold on, let me make a call." Martinez strolled to his desk and scooped his phone up. Minutes later he rejoined David. "We know he had a car. DMV's got to have some kind of record on him. Since we don't know what name he's going under, we'll look for all ninety-six Honda Accords under the name Adam. Maybe we'll get lucky."

David had visions of sorting through that particular list. "And maybe we'll just go blind."

"Hey, bed time reading material. Guaranteed to put an end to insomnia."

"Put you in a coma is more like it," David said.

The Burger House in question was in the general direction of the hospital. He wanted to get in to see Chris before visiting hours were over.

"Let's take our own cars, that way we can split up later."

"Maybe we can grab a burger while we're there." Martinez rubbed his paunch. "*Muero de hambre.*"

David shook his head. Like there was ever a time Martinez wasn't starving. How he put it away without piling on the weight was a mystery David never could solve. Martinez had an easy answer.

"Good genes." He'd always pat his gut. "And a clean conscience."

There was a line at the Burger House counter. The air was heavy with the smell of hot oil, onions and cooking meat. David felt as though a thick coating of grease settled over him, coating his skin.

Martinez studied the overhead menu like he was discovering the true meaning of manna. He ordered two double cheeseburgers and onion rings. David was glad they weren't traveling together. When his turn came, David picked up a Caesar salad. Martinez rolled his eyes. He wove his way through the waiting crowd to find them a seat.

As David handed his cash to the green-haired teen behind the counter, he glanced at her name tag. "Your manager here, Tiffany?"

"Sure, I guess," Tiffany said. "You want fries with that?"

"With a salad?"

She shrugged. "You wanna talk to her?"

"Thanks." When she made no move he added, "Yes, I'd like to talk to her."

Tiffany flipped her lawn-colored hair and went over to talk to a ferret-faced woman who looked like she was sucking stones.

Ferret Face finally broke away from the deep fryer she was watching. "Can I help you?"

David gestured toward Martinez, who was halfway through his first burger. "We'd like to ask you a couple of questions."

"And you are?"

David fished out his badge and watched the stones turn into a pair of boulders. At the same time her eyes narrowed.

"How long have you worked here, Mrs....?"

"Smythe," she said. "Barbara Smythe. I've been the manager here for eight months. Now, what is this about?"

"An ex-employee."

"Ex?"

"Adam Scott," he said. "Or he might have gone by Baruch."

"Adam." She nodded. "Yes, I remember him."

"Remember anything in particular?" Martinez started in on his second burger. David tried not to watch.

"Not really. He wasn't a terribly memorable person."

"Good at his job?" David asked.

"Adequate."

"Adequate?"

"He did his job."

"But only for six weeks," David said.

"That, I'm afraid, was Adam's choice."

"He quit?"

"I suppose that's what you could call it." She frowned and stared at the dirty table next to them that had just been vacated. "The fact is Adam did not show up for his shift one night."

"He call in?"

"He did not. Nor did he quit. He just stopped showing up."

"He come in for his last pay?" Martinez asked.

"He came in when I wasn't here."

"So you have no idea why he left?"

"None."

Didn't want to either. David guessed the fast food industry was pretty transitory. But their records search hadn't shown Adam getting another job. There was a lot of underground work in L.A. Could he have gone that route?

"What was he like to work with?" David asked. "Aside from adequate."

"He came in on time, did his shift. He didn't break any speed records, but no one had any complaints."

Just another minimum wage chump. "Is there anything you do remember about him?"

She considered the question. "When Adam first started, I really did think he might amount to something. He came in with the right attitude and showed what I like to think is management material."

David thought of what Professor Sanju had said about the qualifications Adam had brought with him. Was it a pattern with the guy? "What happened?"

"He grew... I don't know, all I can say is he seemed angry."

"Angry? What did he have to be angry about?"

"He never said. It was just something I sensed."

"Did he ever mention his family?"

"I'm probably not the best person to talk to about this," she said. "My contact with employees is limited to ensuring they do their job and the place runs efficiently. I'm not someone they talk to beyond work."

"Is there someone who might be able to help us?" David asked. "Anyone you might call Adam's friend?"

The manager tapped her short fingernails on the table. Finally she said, "Not friends perhaps, but Tiffany might be able to answer your questions. They were hired around the same time and she went through orientation with Adam."

She turned and swept away. Martinez crammed the last bite of hamburger in his mouth and washed it down with Coke.

Tiffany materialized beside their table. She didn't look thrilled to be there.

"Barbara said you wanted to talk to me."

"You were a friend of Adam's?"

"That geek?" Tiffany sniffed with the sort of disdain only a teenager could muster. "You're joking, right?"

"We're cops," Martinez said. "We don't have a sense of humor. Just how well did you know Adam?"

"We trained together when I first started in this crap hole. He gave me a ride home a couple of times when my old man was too busy to come get me."

She flung her head back in a calculated move that set her breasts bouncing under her green and tan uniform. David had the feeling she knew all too well the power she had over most men. Too bad for her it didn't work on him.

"He ever try anything during those rides?"

"Adam?" She giggled and rolled her eyes. "You're joking, right? He was a geek. A clueless nerd."

Geek. Translate that as computer nut? David wondered if anyone had ever called Chris a geek. He had once claimed he was. David seriously doubted that. "Did he talk about computers with you?" Maybe she was pissed Adam didn't make a pass. Never underestimate a teenage girl's ego. He'd felt the bite a couple of times when he'd ignored their come-ons in high school.

"He barely talked about anything. Like, I tried to talk to him once about this absolutely wild Jynx concert I went to and he like, brushed me off like he'd never even heard of Jynx. I mean, is that gay or what?"

David's eyebrows rose. "Is it?"

"Is it what?"

"Gay?"

"God yes—I mean, Jynx's is so there. They're the best thing outta Seattle since Cobain, ya know?"

David's ignorance left him feeling old. "So Adam never talked to you? Never mentioned his mother or talked about his father, is that right?"

She frowned. "He didn't like her very much."

"Who? His mother?"

"Called her a bitch. Said she'd betrayed him. Pretty harsh words for your mother, right? Hey, I mean my mother can be a hard-core bitch, but she's still, ya know, my mother."

"Did he say how she'd betrayed him?"

"Like you think I asked?"

"Did he ever talk about getting back at her?"

She nodded sagely. "It's about all he did talk about." She did the head flip again. "Me, I'd rather talk about stuff that's important."

"Like Jynx?" David didn't even bother keeping the sarcasm out of his voice.

"Yeah! Junck rock is so cool. And Spence is so hot."

"Well, thank you, Tiffany. You've been very helpful."

"I have?"

"Sure. We'll be in touch if we have any more questions."

"Sure. Like, that's cool."

David gathered up the remains of his supper and brushed past her. Martinez followed. He and Martinez parted company in the parking lot. "We'll pick up where we left off tomorrow," Martinez said. "We're getting closer to him, Davey. I can feel it."

Well, at least one of them could. All David wanted to do was get out to see Chris. His heart wasn't in this investigation. He just hoped Martinez never realized that.

With one last wave, he turned the Chevy towards the hospital.

CHAPTER TWENTY

Thursday, 6:45 pm, USC County General, State Street, Los Angeles

"Well, you're looking a lot better, young man."

Chris tried to glare at the doctor who stood over him, looking too damned perky and upbeat. Regular fucking Pollyanna.

"I'm Dr. Finder," she said. "Do you know where you are, Chris?"

"Sure," he said. "The hospital. USC." He wrinkled his nose. "Hard not to know that."

She reached for his wrist and counted out the beats of his pulse.

"So, doc, am I gonna live?"

"Haven't you heard? No one gets out alive."

"Oh great, my doctor's a philosophy major."

"Minor, actually. Head feel okay? Can you take a deep breath?"

Chris obliged, and winced as shards of pain shot through his chest.

"You got a couple of cracked ribs, so you're going to be sore for a while."

"No shit."

She patted his shoulder. "But you'll live. Maybe even for another six or seven decades."

"Now there's a cheery thought. All old and wrinkled. I always wanted to leave a beautiful corpse."

"Why? You think the worms care?"

"Anyone ever tell you your bedside manner sucks?"

He wished this woman would go away and take her annoying manner with her. There was a tap on the door. Both Chris and the doctor turned.

It was David.

Chris felt the first lifting of his heart since he had woken up. Finder must have been watching his face because the smile she gave him was sly.

"Ah, Detective," she said. "Come to check on your witness?"

"Don't tell her anything," Chris snapped.

Finder glanced at her watch. "What do you know, time for my rounds. I'll see you later, Christopher. Detective."

"What was that all about?" David asked once the door had closed behind her.

"Don't ask." Chris tried to sit up, but pain shot through him and he sank back with a groan.

David was instantly at his side. "What are you trying to do? You can't get up."

Chris blinked away the tears in his eyes. "Hey, don't I get a hug?"

Leaning down, David brushed his lips over Chris's and lightly touched his shoulders.

"I'm not going to break, you know. I may have a few bruises, but I'm not glass." His voice was whispery and Chris knew he wasn't being very convincing. The truth was he felt like shit, but he didn't want to see that mirrored in David's eyes. "Where were you all day?"

"Work."

"You're back? Does that mean they dropped the investigation?"

"It's gone."

"Great."

David studied his face and Chris did his best to look positive. It was good that David had been cleared of those horrible charges, but Chris couldn't get over his dislike of David's job. He couldn't help it; he hated what David did.

He plucked at the blankets folded over his stomach. The thin blue hospital gown felt scratchy against his skin.

"If you want I'll bring your pajamas tomorrow. Is there anything else you'd like?"

"Besides outta here?" Chris muttered. "Really, I could rest so much better in Cozumel." He sighed. "Okay, I guess I could use my razor." He rubbed his blond stubbled cheek. "Shampoo, oh, and don't forget a toothbrush and my floss... That's assuming Hilda the Sadist there lets me do any of that."

"You must be feeling better." David grinned, settling into a chair close to the bed. "You're getting bitchy."

Chris sniffed. "Please, I haven't even warmed up. Speaking of bitchy, I need to call Des. He'll think I fell off the planet or something."

David scooped Chris's hand off the bed and tucked it between his. "Seriously, how do you feel?"

"Sore. Woozy. Honestly, I don't know what they gave me, but I would not recommend it even to my wildest stoner friends. Oh, don't look so deadly serious; I don't have any stoner friends anymore. That was all BD."

"BD?"

"Before David. You reformed me, don't you know? Honestly, if you want to bring me something, bring me something to read. I've got some new journals at home, I can take advantage of this to catch up."

Suddenly he groaned and rubbed his forehead. David leaned forward, his rough face wreathed in concern.

"Where's my Blackberry? My email. My calendar. God, I had the next year mapped out in there."

"I'll look through your effects, but I don't know if it was recovered or not. Don't you keep copies of that stuff?"

Chris frowned. Again his memory showed gaping holes. "I do. I did. But I don't remember if I backed it up before I left the house that day or not."

"I'll look for it. I'll get the hospital staff to check too. But you need to forget work for now. Rest. Maybe Becky can cover for you, do you want me to call her?"

"Would you?"

"Sure."

"Try not to give her too many details. She's such a worry wart."

"And I'm not?"

"But you're cute when you worry. She just turns into my mother." He tried to think of what was critical, then, "Can you ask her to look in on Terry at Ste. Anne's? I wanted to run some more intrusion tests on the outer perimeter. Terry has the documentation. If she can look it over and tweak it if it needs it, I'd appreciate it."

"Consider it done."

Chris could feel sleep nudging at his consciousness. He blinked at David and found his vision blurring. He came back from cracking a huge yawn to find David smiling at him.

"I think you're trying to tell me something. I'll be back as early as I can tomorrow." David leaned down and this time his kiss meant business. Chris's head spun. "Enough talk about work. Rest. I love you."

Chris wanted to reply but his whole head was swathed in cotton, even his tongue wouldn't work. He sank into a soft, welcoming darkness, wondering where the hell his Blackberry was. His dreams were laced with flashes of explosive light and unrecognizable voices that were too distant to hear anything but the menace in them. Finally even they were gone.

David fed an impatient Sergeant and Sweeney and took Sergeant for a twenty minute run. Back home he grabbed a beer from the fridge and they all headed for the media room. Propping his feet up on a footstool he skimmed through the phone's memory for Des's number, temporarily ignoring the blinking message light. He dialed a number and Trevor answered. David kept his voice business-like.

Sweeney jumped into his lap and rubbed his tawny head under David's chin.

"Let me talk to Des."

"David?" Trevor seemed awkward. "Des is right here."

David took a swig of beer. He set the bottle down on one of the agate coasters he had picked up in Palm Springs years ago—BC. Before Chris.

Des picked up the phone.

"David, what's going on? I heard about the bombing. My God, are you okay? You can tell Chris he's such a bitch for not getting back to me. I was so worried about you and no one would say anything—"

"I'm fine, Des," David said. "But Chris is in the hospital—"

When Des settled down enough to listen, David gave him a quick rundown. As Chris had requested, he didn't go into a lot of detail. He assured Des that Chris was going to be just fine.

"He better be," Des huffed. "You tell him if he's not, I'll-I'll take away his Versace frequent shopper card."

Des sobbed into the phone.

David could handle anything but that. "He's going to be fine, Des," he pleaded. "You can go see him tomorrow if you want."

Though how Des would handle the way Chris looked was anyone's guess. It had to be better than thinking he was on death's doorstep.

Trevor came back on.

"How bad is he?"

"He's through the worst of it. If Des does go see him you might want to prepare him. Chris got some pretty nasty-looking cuts and bruises." David plucked at the label of his beer bottle, peeling the edge loose. "He's having some trouble remembering exactly what happened, so don't let Des pester him for details."

"Sure," Trevor said. "He'll be fine. Especially once he knows Chris really will be okay."

"Yeah, well you take care of Des. Tell him not to worry."

Trevor hung up and David immediately called Becky. She answered herself. Unlike Des, she took the news calmly enough. She knew several of Chris's clients and promised to call them the next day. She also promised to drop in to Ste. Anne's and look things over.

"Tell Chris not to worry," she said. "I'll cover for him."

"Thanks, Becky. We owe you."

David replaced the phone and emptied his beer bottle. After the briefest of hesitations he put the empty bottle away and got the dog's leash again. Sergeant bounced toward the front door. They ran for forty minutes this time. Back home David got another beer. He flipped through a dozen TV channels before settling on a country music retrospective of Merle Haggard.

The dog settled in beside him. The cat took up her place on his lap.

$$\int \int \int \int$$

David dropped Chris's clothes and toiletries off before heading in to work. He found Martinez already looking glassy-eyed as he went through the reams of paper DMV kicked back.

"Any luck?" David asked, settling into his chair and flipping on his computer. He glanced around the detectives' cubicles, hoping to see Bentzen, but the blond detective wasn't in the room. Probably settled downtown for good.

"Couple of possibles. I figure we'll put a list together and check 'em all out after." Martinez held up the stack. "You want half?"

David took the proffered papers. Slipping on his reading glasses, he read.

By lunch they had amassed less than a dozen promising names. David decided it would have to do for now. "Let's grab something to eat, then we can start calling."

David took them to Little Thailand, a small hole in the wall place a couple of blocks west of the station. It was nearly always filled with cops; David was hooked on their green curry chicken.

Martinez always tried to surpass himself with hot and mind-numbingly spicy. He challenged the cook at Little Thailand, an ex-cop who had retired on disability, to make something he couldn't handle. So far the guy had failed. But neither one of them would say uncle.

The tall Latina waitress knew David and Martinez by sight. She grinned, revealing a mouthful of braces. "Hey, Bill was just complaining the other day that you guys never came in anymore. I think he was getting bored."

Martinez rubbed his hands together and pretended to study the menu. "What's he got for me today?"

"Got some fresh shrimp in just this morning. He got hold of some of those Naga Jolokia. He's been hoping you'd come in. No one else will try them." She shuddered fiercely. "*Olvídeselo*, I won't even touch those things. *Que picosisimo!*"

Martinez's eyes gleamed. "Bring it on." He grinned at David. "I live for the challenge."

David watched in amazement as Martinez shoveled a plateful of shrimp and rice into his mouth, washed down with milk.

"I can't imagine what that stuff is doing to your stomach."

Martinez burped and waved fumes of chili across the table. "Puts hair on my chest."

David had seen Martinez shirtless in the station's locker room. He was nearly as hairless as Chris.

Bill Maruti, Little Thailand's owner, stopped by their table. The limp that had first put him behind a desk then pushed him into early retirement was noticeable. He must have caught David's look; he grimaced, his dark, scarred face twisting into a scowl.

"Weather's changing. It'll be raining by tomorrow night." He turned gleaming eyes on Martinez, who was visibly sweating. "Want some ice there, Juanita?"

"Ha, you aren't there yet, gimpy."

"You guys busy these days?" Though he had been off the force for ten years, Bill never tired of hearing about their ongoing cases. "Got a hot one?"

It was David's turn to scowl. "Lukewarm and going nowhere," he said.

"Doesn't feel good?" As a cop, he would know that feeling all too well. "Or is it just not coming together like you thought it would?"

"Sometimes I don't think there's anything there to come together," David said. "We couldn't make a case if we threw everything we had in front of a jury and the defense phoned it in."

Bill winced.

"It gets worse," David said. "We had him and we let him walk. Now he's gone ghost."

"It happens. Things fall apart. But if he's going to be the ghost, then maybe it's time for you to be the ghost buster."

"Yeah," Martinez said. "He's found a hole to hide his sorry ass in, and we're gonna find it and drag him out."

Friday, 12:10 pm, USC County General, State Street, Los Angeles

Chris forced himself to finish the bland chicken soup. At least the crackers gave it some body. He glanced at the lime green Jell-O with a jaundiced eye and was grateful when his phone rang. Shoving the tray back, he scooped the receiver up.

It was Becky.

"Hey boss," she said. "You developing a thing for hospitals that you gotta keep going back into them? Too many cute doctors?"

"Hey, no one told me there was a bomb there."

"They usually don't."

"Funny. And I don't even look at the doctors anymore."

"Honey, everybody looks at the doctors."

"Hmph." Chris shoved his spoon into the Jell-O. It jiggled and he made a face. While it tasted bland, it easily slid down his sore throat. "You at work?"

"At Ste. Anne's. Just finishing up those intrusion tests. You'll be happy to know everything is holding up. Terry confirms no more files have been hit and all the restores are golden."

"Thanks, hon. You have no idea how much I appreciate it." He sighed in relief. "Hey, someday I'll figure out a way to pay you back."

"Good. Looking forward to collecting that." Her voice dropped. "I also called Desclan and Third Planet Design just to see if they needed anything, since I knew they were your most active accounts outside of Pharmaden."

A thread of apprehension in her tone put him on instant alert. "What is it, Becky?"

"The CIO at Desclan got a pretty nasty email yesterday, he seems to think it came from you. Dodge over at Third Planet got something too, but he won't say what. Just that it really upset him. He was talking about calling his lawyers until I told him you were in the hospital, and had been for several days. Now he doesn't know what to do."

Goose bumps covered Chris's body. Hesitantly, then with greater strength as anger bubbled through him, he told her about Sandman and the kiddie porn.

"Jesus, do you think that what's happened to Dodge? No wonder he was freaked out."

"That or something worse," Chris said, though he wasn't sure what "worse" could entail. "Whatever it is, this guy is fucking up my life good."

"But why?" Becky asked. "How does he even know about your contacts?"

"I don't—" Chris tried to sit up and grunted at the pain in his ribs. "My Blackberry. It got lost in the rubble."

"I'd say it's not lost now. You better call your provider and freeze that account."

"I will."

"Well you might want to try to do that like yesterday. This guy's on a real tear, from what I've heard."

Chris looked down. Both arms were a mass of dark bruises, starting to turn yellow and green around the edges; his shoulders ached even when he lay still. Just breathing too deeply sent spasms of pain through his chest; moving was a nightmare. How the hell was he supposed to get out of here any time in the near future?

His doctor would never allow it; Chris could just imagine David's reaction if he told him he wanted to go home. But pain or no, he was going to have to get out of here. If he didn't, he wasn't going to have a business left.

He'd worry about explaining it later.

"How did the guy get back in to find my Blackberry, anyway? I don't imagine the cops just let anyone roam around after something like that."

"Unless they thought he belonged," Becky said.

"Listen, Beck, thanks for calling, but I have to go."

"Call me," she said. "I don't care when, day or night. If you need anything at all."

"Thanks, I will."

Chris hung up and immediately called the police station. David wasn't in. So he asked for whoever was in charge of the hospital bombing. Within minutes he was talking to some cop called Bentzen. He vaguely remembered talking to the guy after his surgery. He couldn't for the life of him remember him, beyond that he was almost albino blond.

"Yes, Chris?" Bentzen's voice was deep and soothing. A sexy voice; Chris wondered what he looked like. "How can I help you?"

"Actually, I may be able to help you," Chris said. "I think my Blackberry was picked up by the bomber."

"And what makes you think the bomber got it?"

"He not only took it, but it's definitely the same guy who's been harassing me."

"This is the Sandman, right?" Bentzen asked. "David mentioned him. When did he take your Blackberry?"

"After the bomb," Chris's voice rose. "The guy went back in after the bomb had gone off. Somebody had to have seen him. He probably talked to you guys—if he could get past the cops, then he must have been able to prove he belonged there."

"It was pretty chaotic the first hour. It was more important to get the patients out, they drafted just about everyone who was still ambulatory..." Chris heard the sound of papers rustling. "Thank you, Chris. I promise we'll look into it. Now if I need to speak with you again I can call the hospital, right?"

"What? Oh, sure. Call me here." Not that Chris had any intention of staying put.

CHAPTER TWENTY-ONE

Friday, 10:35 pm, USC County General, State Street, Los Angeles

When Chris awoke again it was dark. His mind was foggy and sluggish. He grabbed his watch off the nightstand. Ten-thirty.

He fell back on the uncomfortable bed with a groan. He missed his own bed; more, he missed David's comforting presence and strong arms. Exhaustion clung to him like a wet blanket. It was all he could do to keep his eyes open.

He knew the exhaustion was his body's way of forcing him to rest. The doctor might be upbeat about his progress; the accident had still taken a serious toll.

Did he really want to risk his health going after the elusive Sandman? What was he going to do if he found him? He couldn't even call David; he had no cell phone, no BlackBerry.

That made his next decision easy. He knew Des would be up; the man never went to sleep before midnight. With a brief hope that he wasn't interrupting something, he dialed his friend's Beverly Hills exchange. He tried not to think of the horrendous charges that were being tacked onto his hospital bill.

Des picked up on the second ring.

"Chris, baby. Oh my God, you're okay!"

"Hey," Chris said, suddenly realizing how long it had been since he had last talked to Des. So much had happened since then. "Yeah, I'm okay. Better all the time."

"You're at home?"

"Ah, no," Chris said reluctantly, knowing exactly how Des was going to take that news. "Not yet—"

"Why are they keeping you there? What's wrong?"

"I'm fine. You gotta believe me—"

"Right. You don't think I haven't talked to David? I know what's going on. I don't believe it. A bomb!" His voice broke. "You could have died."

"Come on, Des. I'm not dead. Not even close."

"You can joke. But it's not funny." Des sniffed. "If you ever do that again, I'll—I'll kill you myself!"

"I'll remember that. Honest, honey, I'm fine." Chris took a deep breath, pushing his exhaustion further back. "I need to ask you a favor."

"Favor? What?"

Chris told him.

"A cell phone? What for?"

Chris had his argument ready. "I can't afford to lose my business. I need to be able to keep in touch—check my email, take messages. They don't do that here. Besides, do you have any idea what they're charging me for these calls?"

"So stay off the phone," Des said, his flamboyance gone, his voice deepening. Chris winced. When Des adopted that tone he wasn't going to be argued with. He wouldn't even listen to Chris's best wheedling. "You need to rest, not be on the phone all day."

"I am resting—"

"Besides," Des's voice grew even more suspicious. "You can't use a cell phone in the hospital. They make you turn them off."

"Des—"

"No, Chrissy. You can take care of your business when you get better. I'm not going to help you kill yourself because you don't know how to let go."

"Damn it, Des—"

"Don't think I don't know you, Christopher Ryan Bellamere. I know you're up to something, so don't try and deny it. I'll come by tomorrow to visit. If you need me to make some phone calls I'll do it then."

Before Chris could marshal another argument Des hung up. Chris swore.

A wave of utter exhaustion drove the last of his will away.

He was asleep before his head hit the stiff pillow that smelled vaguely of his own sweat.

Saturday, 8:45 am, N. Vermont Avenue, East Hollywood

"Adnan Baruq." David read the address from their DMV print out. It was the third Adam-like name with a green Honda they had come to check out.

This one lived in an apartment above a badly lit furniture store stocked with Frank Lloyd Wright and Bauhaus knock offs. The stairs smelled faintly of mildew and urine. They passed a single mailbox with no name on it.

The door at the top of the stairs was propped open with a brick. David nudged it open more with his foot. A second, inner door was shut. The smell of urine was fainter overlaid by pine cleaner. From inside they heard the soft, recorded tones of a woman singing. The words sounded Arabic.

David didn't like the layout of the two doors. They had to stand directly between them when they knocked, and he and Martinez would be exposed to whoever stood behind it. He nodded at Martinez who moved across the hall and rapped sharply on the peeling paint.

Immediately the music cut off. There was movement beyond the door. David held his breath.

"Yes? Who is it?"

David tried to determine if he'd ever heard that voice before. It was muffled by the intervening wood. "The police, Mr. Baruq," he said. "We need to ask you a couple of questions."

"What about?"

"I can't do this through the door," David said. "Let us in and we can talk."

There was silence on the other side. Finally a shuffling of feet. "Okay, give me a minute to get dressed..."

There was the sharp sound of a bolt being thrown then more silence. David and Martinez traded glances.

David struck the door again, more sharply this time. "Adam, open up. We need to talk."

There was a muffled clang. David pushed at the door. It rattled on its hinges but didn't give way.

From further away, an engine roared to life.

Martinez swore. Together they raced down the stairs. David bolted ahead of his partner. His gaze darted left when he emerged onto the street. An alley ran between the furniture store and the Iranian restaurant next door. An older couple, the woman in the traditional black chador, the man in an equally dark suit, paused at the mouth of the alley when David appeared. They looked alarmed and David held up his gold badge. On the street, the air brakes on a diesel truck whooshed and an impatient driver laid on his horn.

The couple stepped back from the alley just as a red Kawasaki roared out, spewing paper, grit and smoke in its wake. The driver popped a wheelie as David reeled back, nearly knocking Martinez over. Martinez grabbed his shoulder, steadying him.

The motorcycle skidded around the truck amid a flurry of horns, screeching tires and the sharp crunch of metal on metal.

"The car," David shouted, knowing it was already too late. "Get back to the car."

They had parked down Fountain, in the same direction the motorcyclist had taken. Not that it mattered. Adam, or Adnan—if that's who the runner was—was long gone by the time they reached the car.

They took off anyway. David darted in front of a slower moving Mazda. He ignored the horn and the finger they got, and slipped in front of a city bus. There was no sign of the motorcycle.

"You get a plate?"

"Partial," Martinez said, already calling it in. "You remember anything about our guy having a motorcycle?"

"No, I don't." The motorcycle had looked familiar. But a red motorcycle? You couldn't throw a dead coyote in L.A without hitting a red motorcycle. As evidence it sucked. They waited for yet another light to change so they could return to Adnan's apartment.

Martinez called in a request for more bodies to come out to assist them. They wanted to secure the building before they headed back to get a warrant that would let them search it.

They were met by two uniformed officers. All four of them walked down the alley. There they found the green Honda, and a fire escape. David dispatched the two officers to canvas the area. When a second backup arrived he instructed them to make sure no one came or went via the fire escape or the front door.

As they drove back to the station where they would initiate the warrant, Martinez called in a Be-On-the-Look-Out for Adam or Adnan Baruq, Baruch, or Scott, including the partial on the motorcycle plate. The BOLO simply said he was a person of interest.

They had to wait until late that afternoon to get their warrant signed by a sitting judge. They hurried back to the apartment, which they found cordoned off with yellow crime scene tape. The four officers had been reduced to two, who reported that no one had approached the building all day. They found the landlord and got the key.

"Let's see what this character left behind," David said.

They left the two unis outside to continue watch on the back exit Adam had used to flee. David and Martinez opened the apartment door. A tortoiseshell kitten appeared, winding around David's feet. He scooped her up. She butted her head against his chest and mewed.

"Guess we know one thing he left."

Adam's apartment was a narrow, L-shaped room. The only furniture was a ladder-back chair and a single bed, carefully made up with a worn blanket. The kitchen consisted of a toaster oven and a single burner hot plate.

The entire apartment was pathologically clean. Whatever Adam had thought of his mother, he had taken her neatness to heart.

David placed the warrant in plain view on top of one of the few flat surfaces in the place, the kitchen counter, and set the kitten down on the floor. The judge they had found to sign the warrant had been very stringent in what they could, and could not, search for. Chocolates or any signs of drugs or chemicals were on the top of David's list.

Martinez started in the kitchen; David pulled on a pair of gloves and began sorting through the bathroom garbage. Aside from a couple of tissues, it was empty. The medicine cabinet contained a bottle of Tylenol, a stick of Right Guard and a half-empty box of Band-Aids. He sorted through the cleaning supplies under the sink. Nothing containing cyanide. Did he really think there would be a bottle with a skull and crossbones on it? The bathtub was as spotless as the rest of the room. Even the toilet looked like it was never used. Only the kitty litter showed any sign of activity.

"You believe this guy? You think if we printed this place we'd find anything?" Martinez muttered when David emerged from the bathroom followed by the cat. "Can't believe he owns a cat."

David pulled the top blanket off the bed and shook it out. He followed with the sheets and flipped the mattress up to peer underneath it. In the shadows a darker square. A small box.

"Hello, what do we have here?" Martinez stooped down to grab the flattened box. He flipped it over in his hand. "Chocolates?"

David eased the mattress back down. He studied the gold-leaf covered box inside and out. There were no chocolates left, but there were half a dozen of the dark wraps matching the ones David had recovered at Nancy Scott's place.

"Looks like Mr. Clean wanted a souvenir," Martinez said.

"Let's get them tested before we jump the gun here. We don't have him yet."

He pulled the nightstand drawer open. The deep drawer was filled with bills and receipts. A quick glance at the bottom ones showed they went back a couple of years. Since he'd been on his own? The guy was a compulsive saver. Good for him.

David sifted through the paper. A receipt for something called the Sweetheart Special from Chocolate Delights caught his eye. It was dated less than two weeks before Nancy Scott's death. If they could trace that box under the mattress to the chocolate Lopez had found in Scott's body, they had Adam nailed.

He showed the receipt to Martinez. "Shows premeditation."

He pulled out a ticket stub. Holding it up into the dim light that poured through the open window, he realized it was a parking ticket. It was dated Halloween.

"He doesn't know West Hollywood, so he parks in the wrong place, gets a ticket. In the meantime he's following Chris and me."

"You really think he tried to run you over?" Martinez asked. "Seems a little in your face for a guy like that."

He had a point. Poisoners were usually a secretive, weasely lot.

"Most of them are women, too," David pointed out. "They don't all follow the pattern. I think this guy's smart—look at his record at Caltech for proof of that—and I think he's adaptable. I guess he considered me more of a threat than I figured."

"So he follows you to West Hollywood and waits for a chance to do some major damage?" Martinez sounded skeptical. David didn't blame him. Even to him it sounded far-fetched. Paranoid. He shrugged and flipped the papers into an evidence box; they'd sort through them later. The kitten sat in his lap and batted at each piece of paper. It wasn't Visa receipts David wanted. He let his gaze roam over the small apartment. There was nothing in it that spoke of Adam's hatred for his mother or of a father betrayed. He got up and moved through the tiny apartment again, letting his cop eyes roam. He folded back a closet door. It held a single dark gray suit, two white shirts and a denim jacket. It smelled of cedar and mothballs. On the top shelf was a large book. He pulled it down and stared at the red and gold engraved cover.

The words *The Qur'an* were highlighted in gold and black.

He showed it to Martinez. "So he is Muslim." He flipped through several pages. "English and something I'm guessing is Arabic."

He put the book back. It wasn't part of the warrant and couldn't be touched.

Neither could the computer he spotted on a rollout cart tucked into the far corner of the closet. Why would anyone hide something like that in a closet? There wasn't even a monitor, though there was a blue network cable plugged into a small blinking box. Chris had something like that. He used it to network his computers.

David's frustration mounted as he realized they couldn't touch it.

"We need to revise our warrant," he muttered.

"On what grounds?" Martinez came to stand beside him. "They're never gonna let that thing in, not based on what we've got."

Martinez was right, except... "What if he used it to research how to poison her? Maybe he even talked it over with someone in one of those chat rooms. His generation, they live on the Internet."

His partner nodded. "That might fly."

"Let's finish up here," David said. "See if there's anything else we want on the amended warrant. Then let's go see if we can find somebody who agrees."

Chapter Twenty-two

Des bounced into the room the next morning, bringing an energy that left Chris exhausted.

Chris knew exactly when Des saw the damage to his face. His friend stiffened and pulled back, briefly averting his eyes. His dark face went gray. Chris had known it would be hard for Des to see him like this. It triggered too many horrific memories of his own assault.

"Don't you ever scare me like that again!"

Chris captured his hand. "I'm okay, Des. They're just bruises."

Des recovered quickly. He waved a perfect French manicured hand at him and deliberately went all camp. "You are absolutely beastly not calling me sooner. What were you thinking?"

Chris brought Des's hand to his face. His dark fingers were cool against Chris's still tender skin. "A little ice, a cucumber masque and I'm good as new. So tell me, how's bad boy Trevor these days?"

"Still bad." Des managed a weak smile. "He wanted to come, but I needed to see you alone."

At one point Chris had wanted to talk to Des about Trevor, about whether this was a good thing. He didn't want to see Des hurt again. But this wasn't the time. Maybe it never would be. Instead he said, "I hope I'm not going to have to fend off a jealous Trevor now. I don't think I'm quite up to that."

Des's laughter this time was more spirited. "Oh, nothing like a little bit of the green-eyed monster to bring out the best in a man. Trevor will be just fine."

With that Des became more businesslike. He opened the bag and handed Chris a bundle of magazines and toiletries. Chris glanced at the latest issues of *The Advocate* and *Out* and grinned. Des was always trying to politicize him. So far he had resisted, but Des was nothing if not stubborn.

He stared at the rest of the stuff and burst out laughing. Along with the miniature bottle of mouthwash, toothpaste, a new toothbrush and a comb, Des had included a small compact, face cleanser, a tube of cover-up, tweezers and a bottle of Aramis. He laughed harder when he held up the avocado masque.

"Great minds."

"I figured David would bring your razor later but you need a toothbrush now," Des said, fussing over the gifts like they were tiny treasures. "And I know how important it is to look your best after this kind of thing."

Chris threw his bandaged arms around Des's slim shoulders. He awkwardly patted his best friend's back, feeling hot tears track down his neck.

"Come on, hon, it's not as bad as that. It looks worse than it is."

"You scared me so much." Then he burst into tears. "I don't want to lose you."

"You're not going to lose me. What a silly idea." Chris squeezed his arm and pressed his mouth against Des's neck, tasting the salt of his tears. "Thank you," he whispered. "You really are a sweetheart."

"Of course I am." Des sat up and hastily wiped his face. "All the queens in Beverly Hills say so."

"Oh, they say it in more places than that." Chris laughed at the pleased expression on Des's fine-boned face. "You're a legend around town."

"Now you're being silly." Des glanced at his watch and sighed. "I wish I could stay but I've got a new shipment of Kenneth Coles coming in. If I'm not there, heaven knows where Clive will put everything. The boy has no common sense. If he wasn't such a cutie I'd dump his pretty little ass tomorrow."

"You just know all your butch customers love him."

Des sniffed. "I'm going to have a talk with David after this is all over. Someone needs to put a leash on you."

"He might like that more than you think." Chris raised his bed. "Listen, you won't get me a phone, fine, I can live with that. But can you lend me twenty? David won't be back till late tomorrow and I can't stomach the crap they try to serve me in here. They tell me I'll be able to get up tomorrow, so I can hit the cafeteria."

"Sure, hon. I can do that."

Chris shoved the bill Des dug out of his wallet and tucked it into his bedside drawer. Des leaned over and kissed him. He smoothed his hand over Chris's beard stubbled face.

"You take care, hon. I love you. Don't ever forget that."

"Like I could."

Five minutes after Des left, Chris was on the phone again. The delivery boy who dropped off the Blackberry two hours later was all smiles at the twenty Chris slipped him. He was only too happy to plug the device in.

Sunday, 2:50 pm, N. Vermont Avenue, East Hollywood

David and Martinez got their amended warrant and returned to Adam's apartment with one of the station techs and a woman from animal control. David helped her secure the kitten, and slipped her his card before she left, "If the cat's not claimed, give me a call." She nodded and left.

This time they did a full search and left with several computer disks and burned CDs as well as the hardware.

David was finishing up when he realized Martinez was no longer in the apartment. He found him on the fire escape crouched over a battered steel box. A mist fell, a gray pall hung low over the city; the winter rains had started early.

Martinez looked up. "You better see this."

He handed David a sheaf of slick photo paper. David remembered seeing a stack of the same paper beside the printer that had also been in the closet. He took the pictures gingerly.

The first image was clearly taken with a telephoto lens at night and it was hard to make out who was in it. The next picture cleared up their identity. It was Chris and him leaving Santo Coyote, a restaurant on Melrose. He tried to remember the last time they had been there. Wasn't it before this mess started? It had been a celebration of Chris's latest contract with Ste. Anne's. It had only been for a week, but Chris thought it would be extended.

David's flesh felt numb as he leafed through the rest of the pictures. As far as he could tell they were all taken that same night, but it was the last one that sent a bolt of fear through him. It showed the two of them outside the door to their Silver Lake home. Chris was looking up at him with that look—the one that always meant the evening was going to end very soon in bed. In fact he seemed to recall they hadn't even made it past the living room that night. It was a very private look and David hated to know that someone was watching that moment.

"He must have parked across the street," he managed to say. "He was right there."

Martinez reached for the pictures before David could drop them, but David wouldn't release them. As he jerked them back, several slips of flimsy paper fell out and fluttered to the wet balcony. He stooped down to grab them.

He stared at them, at first puzzled, then with a knot of fear growing in his gut. The first page was a tax assessor's map of Chris and his home on Cove Avenue. There was a full floor plan and the dimensions of the house Chris had inherited from his grandmother years before.

With stiff fingers he flipped out the next pages. The first was his birth certificate, the one without a father listed. The second one was Chris's.

The final page was the AKC registration the breeder had given them for Sergeant.

Martinez awkwardly patted his partner's shoulder. David brushed his hand off. "He's stalking us." He held the papers up. "This is just to show himself what he can do."

"Fucking power trip," Martinez said. "We're onto the scumbag now. He won't get anywhere near you or Chris."

David slapped the papers and photos against the palm of his hand. "But what was he doing watching us *then*? This is before we caught the Scott squeal. He had no way to know I'd be put on that case—even if you assume he'd already planned to kill her then!"

"So what are you thinking?"

"I don't know." David brushed droplets of rain off his shaggy head and rubbed his face wearily. "But there's something else going on here. I just don't know what yet."

♪ ♪ ♪ ♪

Once they were satisfied there was nothing else in the apartment they could use to bolster their growing case, they returned to the station. David wanted to talk to the technician who had taken in Adam's computer.

He headed to the overcrowded room that had been given over to the techies when computers first started making inroads into police work.

A portly Anglo, who barely looked eighteen, hunched over the equipment from Adam's apartment. His name tag said Brad Dortlander. He glanced up at David's approach.

"This yours?"

"Find anything interesting?"

"Define interesting."

David wished he had Chris there. He might have had more luck communicating with this guy.

"The guy who owned this may have killed his mother," David said. "He also tried to kill... a cop." David almost said "me," but decided to keep it from seeming personal. "You should probably be aware the guy's supposed to be some kind of computer genius. So I don't know what you can expect."

Brad's eyes lit up. "Oh, yeah?" He tried to sound casual, but he'd never make it in Hollywood. "Think it might be booby-trapped?"

David looked askance at the seemingly innocuous machine on Brad's desk. "Booby-trapped? What does that mean?"

"Oh, nothing like you're thinking. It's not going to blow up or anything." Brad snorted and David almost expected milk to shoot out of his nose. "Booby-trapping is an automatically executed shell command that runs whenever a suspicious connection attempt is made to the system. Someone who doesn't know what they're doing will trigger a self-destruct command and wipe the hard drive before they know what hit them."

"Anything you can do to counter it?"

"I'll clone it onto one of our own systems, then generate another SUID. Don't worry, sir. If there's something on there, I'll get it off, without touching or altering the original files."

David got that Dortlander would keep the files safe in case of a trial. Other than that he didn't have a clue what Dortlander was saying, and he wasn't about to ask for a translation.

Instead he nodded sagely. "Good. Ah, carry on, then. You'll let me know as soon as you find something?"

"What? Oh sure." But David could tell Dortlander was already a thousand miles away. Probably buried deep inside the silicon computer chips or copper wires, the same place Chris went at times.

David left him to his incomprehensible activities and rejoined Martinez in a world he was far more comfortable with.

Martinez looked smug as he sat with his phone tucked under his chin. He put the phone down when David came in.

"What did you find?" David asked.

"Our Adam was born in Florida. Jacksonville to be exact. Only the name is Adnan Behnia Baruq," Martinez said. "Mother's name on the birth certificate is Nancy Ellen Baruq, nee Scott. His father is Yousef Baruq."

"And where is Yousef now?"

"Still looking."

David sat down and swiveled his chair around to face Martinez. "So Nancy Scott marries Yousef, presumably converts to Islam and they have a son, Adam. Or Adnan."

"Sounds about right."

"So what happens? How do Nancy and Adnan end up in California with Nancy a devout, church-going Catholic?"

"I'm guessing however it happened, Adnan wasn't happy about the change."

"Did his father share that sentiment?" David wondered. He pulled a pen out of the chipped mug on his desk and began rhythmically tapping it against his knee. "Something's not adding up here."

"Gotta be rough on a guy, losing his wife and kid and then she goes and twists the knife by dumping on his religion, too."

"Why don't you start with the records offices in Florida? I'll start looking around here." David scribbled something on a scrap of paper. "Yousef? How do you spell that?"

Sunday, 7:45 pm, USC County General, State Street, Los Angeles

Chris awoke with a start and swore when he saw the darkness pressing against the barred window of his room. He'd fallen asleep again.

When he tried to move it was as though every muscle in his body chose that precise moment to seize up. He groaned.

"That doesn't sound good."

His doctor's dry voice was the last thing he wanted to hear. But there she was, leaning over him. He saw her wandering gaze flick toward the bedside table where he had stashed the Blackberry and the morphine tablets he had stopped taking.

"Christopher, you really have to understand what your body is going through."

"How's that, doc?" Chris was in no mood for Finder's word games. He just wished she'd go away so he could rest his eyes for a couple of minutes. Then he could get ready for what he had to do.

"More than anything your body needs rest. Complete, uninterrupted rest."

Abruptly she reached over and pulled the drawer open. Seconds later the small brown pills sat in the palm of her hand.

A nurse entered behind her. Finder waved her forward. The nurse inserted a syringe into the IV line.

"What's that?"

"Just something to help you rest. For your own good, Chris."

"I hate it when people tell me something is for my own good."

"Yeah, I agree. Sucks, doesn't it?" She used a penlight to examine his eyes. She rested her fingertips under his rigid jaw. "You're too tense. If you don't want to do something for your sake, how about doing it for David?"

"You're not giving me much choice, are you?" he managed.

Her eyes widened. "Hey, I think you're right."

"And you call yourself a doctor." His eyes began to slide shut as the sedative hit him. "Someone ought to take away your stethoscope."

"Better men than you have tried."

Sunday, 8:45 pm, USC County General, State Street, Los Angeles

David stared at the sleeping figure. Light from the hallway fell across Chris's face, which, despite the yellowing bruises and swollen flesh, looked almost angelic.

David smiled. Angelic and Chris weren't usually two concepts he would have put together, but he looked so peaceful... David reached out tentatively to stroke the hand that lay atop the covers.

"We'll get through this, hon," David murmured. Funny how he never felt comfortable using those kinds of endearments to Chris's face. The words always seemed to stick in his throat. "Not much of a husband, am I? Can't be here for you—"

"Oh, I think Chris knows what he means to you," a voice came through the open door.

David turned. It was Chris's doctor.

"Chris seems like a pretty sharp cookie." Finder entered the room and stood beside him. "He doesn't miss much."

David studied her. "You don't either."

She laid her hand on his shoulder. "He's going to be fine."

"Is that your professional opinion?"

"In my professional opinion Christopher is a pain in the ass."

"Can't argue there—"

"D-David?" Chris said from the bed.

"Yeah, it's me," David kept his voice light. "Who did you expect?"

CHAPTER TWENTY-THREE

David still sat in the molded plastic chair he had taken last night. His head tilted back and his mouth had fallen open in sleep. One hand lay across the bed, still holding Chris's hand.

Chris drank him in. Never had David looked more beautiful to him than at that moment.

A cart rattled in the hall. David sat up with a grunt. His eyes fluttered open and met Chris's.

David stretched and Chris heard something pop. He winced in sympathy. David flashed him a wan smile.

"I'm getting too old for this." David pressed his hands into the small of his back and straightened to more popping sounds. "Think I can find some coffee around here?"

"Bring me a latte if this place is civilized enough to produce them."

David did one better. He'd brought the desired drinks and two blueberry muffins.

Chris attacked his with fervor. He caught David's look. "Hey, how many days of hospital food am I expected to endure?"

"You'll survive."

"You didn't see what they served for supper last night."

David reluctantly took his leave, promising he would return that evening if he could. Chris watched him stride through the door and missed him even before he was out of sight.

Monday, 10:20 am, Northeast Community Police Station, San Fernando Road, Los Angeles

David tracked down Brad, the technician. He was in the same spot, hunched over Adnan's computer and one similar. As far as David could tell the guy hadn't even changed clothes. He was studying a map of the city's center.

"So, was it booby-trapped?" David asked.

"Yes, matter of fact it was." From his smug expression David deduced the traps had been easy to beat. At least by this guy's standards. "I intercepted the shell command before it could run and killed it." He patted the off-white box like it was a puppy. "She gave it all up to me after that. Though from what I can see the guy did regular clean-up, so there's no way to tell how much he already deleted."

"I thought deleted files could be recovered."

"This guy used a high end data scrubber on his deleted files. What is there is pretty recent."

"Guess we surprised him before he had a chance to clean it off completely," David said. "So, what exactly did you find?"

"He had several map searches saved. All like this. Guess he wanted to make sure he could find his way around downtown."

"What else?" David asked, ignoring the guy's feeble attempt at humor. "He must have been protecting more than a couple of maps."

"This guy spent a lot of time at hacker sites. He's no wizard, but he's definitely not a script kiddie, either. It looks like he tried to find what's left of the Legion of Doom and the Masters of Deception, but I doubt that got him anywhere. Those guys are history."

"Talk English, okay?"

Brad shrugged. "Sure, whatever. This guy's got some very interesting tools on this baby," he patted the computer again, "some I've only ever heard of. Plus I found some half-finished code he's been splicing together; I'm still trying to figure that out."

"Code for what?"

"That's what I'm trying to work out. It's not done and the guy didn't do any documentation, so I'm sorting through it line by line, but it looks like a pretty sophisticated worm he's got going there. He's not just launching any simple SYN attacks with this."

"A worm? They can spread, right?"

"That's the whole idea. Worms are self-replicating. Release one of those babies in the wild and it'll jump from system to system until there's nothing left. Pure havoc." Brad sounded impressed. "Of course most worms aren't that well written. They all pretty well fizzle after hitting a few thousand machines. So far Conficker has been about the most successful one. It nailed upward of fifteen million machines."

"Fifteen *million?*" David asked.

"Out of billions of potential targets, that's small stuff. Just imagine how bad it could get if you could infect hundreds of millions of machines. Especially if you start bringing down the major dot com sites."

"What about the stuff this guy is writing?" David waved at the computer on Brad's cluttered desk. "Is it good enough?"

"Haven't finished deconstructing it yet. It's good, but that doesn't mean there aren't major flaws in it. You usually only spot those when you run tests."

"How would you test something like that?"

Brad grinned. "Let it loose and watch what happens."

"Great."

Brad shrugged. "Not many hackers have access to test labs." He swiveled around toward David. "You might be interested to know that your guy here had a second computer, probably a laptop."

"How do you know that?" Visions of the fleeing motorcyclist returned. Had he been carrying a bag? David thought so.

"He's got a workgroup set up. Two machines, this one acted as his server, the other one probably has his newer versions of the code, the one's he's working on right now."

What the hell was Adnan up to? He had hacked the JPL web site, but done nothing except deface it. Was this another attack like that? Get back at the university for kicking him out? Or had he set his sights higher this time?

"I need to know exactly what he was planning to do with that code."

"Like I said," Brad muttered. "I can't tell yet. I need more time."

"Well consider this a priority. I don't want you working on anything else, got it?"

"Sure, yeah, I mean, yes, sir."

∫ ∫ ∫ ∫

David dropped into his chair facing Martinez.

"No luck?"

"Define luck," he muttered, and told Martinez what Brad had found. While he talked he scratched some notes on a legal pad. "He's already hacked one site. Does he intend to do it again? Or is he after more?"

David scrabbled through the evidence boxes on their desks. He dragged out the photos of Chris and himself.

"Adnan was involved in hacking the hospital." He tossed them on the desk in front of Martinez. "That was after Chris was approached to look into the Ste. Anne's situation, so it stands to reason Adnan was responsible for the original hospital attack, the one that brought Chris in. It makes sense Adnan would want to know who they were hiring."

"So he tracked you down to see who the enemy was?"

"It makes perfect sense in light of what happened since then."

"You'll never get the DA to buy that. Not with what we got."

"Then we'll find her more."

Martinez shrugged. "I'm not having a lot of luck tracking this guy's father. It's like he doesn't exist."

"Well we know he does. Let's poke around and keep our ears open."

David began to dig tentatively through the Internet. At first, his searches returned nothing of value, but then something appeared on his screen. A reference to an old article in *The Boulevard Sentinel*, a Los Angeles neighborhood rag. Another hour of further digging found a link to the paper itself.

He opened the link and searched it for the article. It had been written over five years earlier and had to be pulled from the archives. The author, Dick Charles, was a vitriolic, flamboyant writer who clearly wanted his readers to know how strongly he felt on the subject.

The article's title caught David's eye: "The American Disappeared?"

The article itself was no less inflammatory, probably why it had been buried in obscurity.

On September 11, 2001 the world watched in horror as two planes were deliberately flown into the twin towers of the World Trade Center in New York City. Americans were justifiably enraged by this cowardly attack, but what followed at the prison camps in Abu Ghraib and Guantanamo Bay have shown that evil resides on both sides of the ocean...

David was about to take a pass on the article, when a name jumped out at him. Yousef Baruq.

You wouldn't think that a naturalized U.S. citizen would be subject to the whims of a secret military cabal, but the story of Yousef Baruq may very well change your mind.

He quickly skimmed the article, which told the story of Yousef, an Iranian who married an American woman, fathered a son, and became a naturalized citizen before the Al-Qaeda launched their attacks. He was picked up and detained at Guantanamo Bay. The article hinted he had been released, which would explain how Charles had managed to interview him. David doubted too many reporters made it into Guantanamo Bay.

David saved the piece, then launched another search, this time for the writer Dick Charles. He found several more articles Charles wrote for the Sentinel and one that had appeared more recently in another local paper—*L.A. Alternative Press.*

A third search gave him a number for the paper. Flipping his pad to a clean sheet, he dialed. He went from the receptionist to a junior editor to an associate editor in advertising. No one stayed on the line long enough to hear what he wanted before they put him on hold and shuffled him off to yet another faceless voice.

Finally he reached someone who introduced herself as Jane.

"Jane," David said hurriedly before she could put him on hold. "This is the LAPD calling. I need to ask you something."

"LAPD? What do you want?"

She sounded suspicious, but that was better than going into the limbo of hold.

"My name's Detective David Eric Laine. I'm looking for a reporter who did some work for you last year."

"Who would that be?"

David told her.

"Dick Charles? Hold on a minute—"

"Wait—"

But she had dropped him into limbo again. David resigned himself to another wait. He scribbled in his notes. Adnan Baruq. Yousef Baruq. Nancy Scott Baruq. Alice Crandall. Herb Bolton. Laura Fischer. He scratched out the last two names. Then re-added them. Then added one more: Chris.

Was there a link? How was that possible? He traced a line between Herb and Adnan. Two hackers. Three if he added Chris, something he didn't like to do. But honesty required it. How hard would it be for two guys like that to find each other through one of those online places? What about Laura? She was a nurse; Nancy had been a sick woman. Could they have met through Laura's work? That could have been another way for Adnan and Bolton to meet.

Yousef. Where was the father? Somebody at some time seemed to think he might have been a danger to U.S. interests. Had those suspicions ever amounted to anything? That would explain the tension between mother and son, especially if the son remained loyal to his father and his mother turned her back on both of them.

David had the feeling it wouldn't be easy finding out who had been sent to Guantanamo.

But he could find this reporter. See if he had maintained contact with Adnan's father.

Jane finally came back on the line. "Dick is on vacation. He won't be back until the middle of the month."

Even before he hung up he had Dick in the system. It came back with an address in Van Nuys. He swung around to face Martinez. "What are you up to?"

"I've got an appointment with Adnan's landlord. He's gonna take me through the place, see if he can tell me anything I don't already know."

David nodded. "I got a reporter to talk to." He filled Martinez in on what he had found out so far. Martinez nodded when he heard about Guantanamo.

"A nasty piece of business. How 'bout we meet up later and compare notes."

"Dinner at Bill's?" David could run up to visit Chris from there easily enough.

"Suits me."

∫ ∫ ∫ ∫

David took the 134 west, onto the Ventura Freeway and the 405 north to Van Nuys. Rain beat a steady tattoo on the car window as he exited at Sherman Way. It was looking like it was going to be a wet fall.

A middle-aged man in a bathrobe, his wispy fringe of gray hanging down his back in a ponytail, answered David's knock.

"Mr. Charles?"

"Yes?" He looked at David with narrow, rheumy eyes. "Who are you?"

David flashed his badge. Dick looked slightly bemused.

"Okay, what do you want?"

David showed him a printed copy he had made of *The Boulevard Sentinel*'s article with Dick's byline. "You wrote this?"

"Says I did." Charles drew a pair of glasses out of the pocket of his robe. He slipped them on and peered at the paper David handed him. "Yeah, that's one of mine. Where'd you dig that fossil up?"

"You talked to a guy called Yousef Baruq for this article?"

"Yousef? Sure, I remember him. Pathetic old coot." Charles squinted up at the lowering sky. "Listen, you want to come in? Place is a mess, but hey, I'm on vacation."

David followed him into the pale blue Spanish style bungalow that had probably gone up in the early 40's when the Valley's orange groves gave way to urban sprawl. The place was littered with old food containers and bundles of newspapers.

A layer of dust covered most of the surfaces, including a large screen Sony that looked completely out of place amid the Goodwill cast-offs that filled the rest of the room. The TV was off. From another room something operatic played.

Charles cleared some newspapers off the sagging sofa and gestured for David to sit. He did, mindful of his wet clothes.

"What can you tell me about Yousef? When did you speak with him last?"

"Don't recall exactly," Charles said, waving his hand toward him. David caught a whiff of alcohol. "When did I write it?"

"Four years ago," David said. "Do you know which article I'm talking about? Yousef Baruq and Guantanamo Bay."

"Yes, yes, I remember." Charles rubbed thick fingers over his unshaven face. "I got hold of Yousef right after they released him. No one else wanted to hear what we had to say back then, that's why I had to put it in that rag, like anybody ever read it."

"How did you find Mr. Baruq?"

Charles lit up a Camel and let the smoke trickle out of his nose while he stared down at the article in his hand. His fingertips were nicotine stained. "Now that's a funny story," he said. "I was doing a story down in this mission on Western and I met this old character."

"What was he doing down at the Mission?"

"Dying," Charles said and blew out another stream of smoke. "Hey, those were his words. He was pretty blunt when I met him. Said he was dying and the U.S. government killed him and did I want to know his story."

"And you of course said yes."

"Didn't hurt Woodward and Bernstein, now did it? Blasting the government used to get you good coverage. Till we went all Orwellian and shut down the free press."

"So the government killed him? How exactly?"

"That was his story. Me, I figured it was something else. Guy was a last stage junkie with full-blown AIDS."

David felt cold. "How does Guantanamo fit into the story?"

"Ah, that's where it gets interesting."

Charles got up and disappeared into another room, only to return minutes later with a bottle of Jack Daniels. He filled a large tumbler and took a swallow. Thankfully he didn't offer to share.

"Interesting how?" David prodded after several minutes of silence.

"Right, interesting. Yousef was Iranian born, he refugeed to the US after the Shah fell. Found himself a younger US bride and had a son. Right after 9/11 Yousef and his family were living in Florida—the FBI picked him up. Apparently Yousef had just gotten his pilot's license, so of course he fell under suspicion."

"Why of course?"

"Hah, just being Middle-Eastern put you on the radar back then. Being interested in planes, well imagine how that must have looked!"

"Are you saying they had nothing but a vague suspicion?"

"Vague? Try non-existent. But it didn't stop them from holding him for eighteen months. Happened to lots of people. Not all foreign-born, either." Charles topped up his tumbler. His eyes were starting to glaze. His voice dropped and he slurred his words. "They raped him, you know. It took him a while before he admitted to that and he was never comfortable talking about it. Who can blame him, right? Who wants to admit they got buggered by the US military?"

"Is that where he contracted AIDS?"

"He implied it. Once he was released he couldn't get a job—go figure, right? He moved his family back here, but then apparently everything fell apart. He didn't have any more luck finding work here either."

"And the drugs?"

"Who knows?" Charles shrugged and took another healthy swig of whiskey. Some of it dribbled down his chin, unnoticed. "It happens, right? Guy can't handle the pressure...phhtt...he starts mainlining."

If Charles lit another cigarette, David worried he might burst into flames. He glanced uneasily around the room with its paper scattered within easy reach of any flame this drunk triggered.

Would it be poetic justice or a tragic accident?

"How did you interview Mr. Baruq? Did you use a tape recorder?"

"Sure, but do you actually think I kept them? From five years ago?" He laughed and hiccupped. "Get real."

CHAPTER TWENTY-FOUR

Tuesday, 1:55 pm, USC County General, State Street, Los Angeles

Chris pushed his barely touched dinner tray away and eased into a sitting position. The expected pain came and he held himself still until it faded. He took a deep breath and eased his legs over the side of the bed. The floor was a cold shock on his bare feet.

He stared down at his legs and flexed the muscles of his calves. He put more weight on his feet. The coldness crept up his ankles, setting an ache in his bones.

He stood. A brief wave of dizziness swept through him and he closed his eyes until it passed. When he opened them again Finder was standing at the foot of the bed watching him.

"Jesus," he snapped. "Are you stalking me?"

"Everybody needs a hobby," she said. She came around the bed and glanced down. "Nice legs. Are those goose bumps?"

All too aware of his nudity under the thin hospital cover, Chris resisted the urge to sit down and pull the blanket over him. Mustering all the dignity he could manage, he stared her down. "Yes, and if you don't mind I'd like to put something on. David brought my pajamas."

Finder pulled the red silks out of the bag and held them up. She whistled. "I can't wait."

He leaned forward and snatched them out of her hand. "Do you mind?"

"Not at all. If you collapse on me, I'll personally tie you to the bed until you're well enough for David to take home."

"You were a bully in school, weren't you?"

She ignored him. "I know what you want to do, Chris," she said, alarming him until she went on, "and the recovery you want will come, with time. You're young, you're impatient, but you have to give yourself a break. You're not invincible."

"I know."

"Enough said then. I'll leave you alone for now. I'll be in to check on you later."

"I can hardly wait," he said, though the fire had gone out of him and his voice sounded weak, even to his ears.

She closed the blinds to cut out the little bit of light that was coming in and shut the door behind her. The room was dim and quiet, and despite his best efforts to avoid the inevitable, he was asleep in minutes.

Tuesday, 3:10 pm, Western Avenue, Los Angeles

David eased the car to a stop in front of the gray stucco building on Western. The rain had stopped; oily puddles caught the sullen light overhead. A rusted metal screen guarded the door from direct view of the street. There was no sign marking the site, only a hand-written placard that read "God Bless Us."

Stepping around a discarded diaper he pushed the door open and slipped inside.

The interior was dim, which was probably for the best. Someone had tried to conceal the faded and peeling paint on the walls with slabs of whitewashed boards that had been covered with hand-written biblical quotes and crude colored drawings of flowers and crosses.

Past the door a large room opened up. Several sofas and chairs in various states of disintegration lay scattered about; many were occupied. By men, David noted. He didn't see any women. Of the half a dozen men in the room, only one paid any attention to him. The yeasty scent of baking bread did a poor job of masking the odor of unwashed bodies. He felt eyes watching him. Probably already had him made as a cop. Without trying to let on he was looking, David scanned the room.

There, that one. Hot dark eyes looked out of the folds of a hoodie that might once have been pale blue but was now black with grime. There was something vaguely familiar about the face; probably a junkie he had rousted. The area was full of them. He thought of throwing a few questions at him, see if it shook something loose. The guy was obviously spooked—

"*Aquí, lo que le hace quiere?*" A portly Latino man in gray overalls bustled in from a back room. He had the broad, flat face of his Aztecan ancestors. His eyes were wary. "*¿Le puedo ayudar yo?*"

"*¿Habla usted inglés?*" David asked, knowing he'd flounder if he tried to carry on in Spanish. He discreetly handed over his badge while explaining the purpose of his visit. "*Busco a un hombre.*"

The man handed the badge back. "Why?"

"I was told he was here."

The man smiled, showing broad nicotine-stained teeth. "I must ask who then."

"His name is Yousef Baruq." David had kept the article he'd printed off the Internet. He handed it over now. "This reporter came here to interview him."

The man studied the article. "I remember him." He handed the paper back. "I thought having him write about us might help our cause."

"It didn't?"

The man signaled David to follow him. He took David into a tiny cluttered office next door to the kitchen. Here the odors of yeast and cooked cabbage dominated.

"Julian Delgado," the man said, extending his hand. "Will you sit?"

Julian sat behind his "desk," a steel table with a plastic tablecloth thrown over it.

The tiny room was full of potted plants. David brushed aside the fronds of a spider plant and sat in the only other chair in the room, a lawn chair that sagged under his weight.

Julian frowned at something, then jumped up and grabbed a water spritzer off his desk. He sprayed the plants over David's head. A faint mist settled over David. He brushed it off with the back of his hand.

"That man wrote about Yousef like he was a monster. We got threats for weeks afterward. Even bomb threats." He shook his head and squirted a stream of water at a luxuriant potted fern. "All people saw was that he was Iranian and they assumed he masterminded those horrible attacks himself! When they learned he had AIDS some of them rejoiced, as though God had taken time out of punishing sodomites to take care of Yousef personally."

"Do you know where Yousef is now?"

Julian's frown deepened. "I am sorry, Yousef is dead."

David wasn't surprised. Disappointed, but not surprised. "When did he die?"

Julian stared over David's right shoulder. "It would have been over a year ago. In fact I seem to recall it was right after Easter, so that would have been early spring." He tilted his head. "April."

"Do you remember what day?"

"I would need to look at my records..."

David waited. Julian climbed to his feet and crossed to a battered filing cabinet. He rooted through a jumble of folders until he found what he was looking for. He carried a blue folder over and opened it on the desk and slipped on a pair of reading glasses.

After a moment of reading he took the glasses off and met David's gaze. "As I said, April. April twenty-second." He shook his head in sorrow. "That was a hard day. Yousef did not deserve what befell him. I refuse to believe God is so harsh in visiting judgment on those who have done nothing."

"Did you ever meet Mr. Baruq's son, Adnan? He may have gone by Adam."

"Adnan?" Julian cocked his head sideways, like an inquisitive bird. "Was that his name? I recall him now. Quiet boy. He picked his father up here once. I thought he was taking him to a doctor."

"Did he?"

"When Yousef came back that night he was unusually quiet. I thought maybe the news from his doctor wasn't good. I'd been expecting as much—it was obvious the disease was getting the upper hand at that point."

"But something else was going on?"

"If it was, he would never tell me, but yes, I am sure it was something else."

"What about Yousef's wife?"

"He never mentioned her. I got the impression he was alone."

The guy was more astute than he knew. "Did you ever see Adnan after his father was dead?" David couldn't imagine why Adnan would come back to this place, but then nothing about this case made a whole lot of sense.

Julian was nodding. "I've seen him a few times. He did come by about a week after the funeral. He brought me a check for five thousand dollars—said he wanted to thank us for what we had done for his father."

"Something about that bother you?"

"If he had that kind of money, what was his father doing here?"

Tuesday, 2:50 pm, USC County General, State Street, Los Angeles

Chris pulled the jeans up over his bare legs. The denim felt cool against his shrinking skin. The pricey Diesel jeans that had only been a few weeks old were now ripped up one side almost to his knee. Dust from the shattered bricks felt rough against his hands when he tried to brush it off.

His new Blackberry was fully charged; he pulled it out and clipped it to his jeans. His wallet went into his pocket along with the few pain pills he had kept hidden from Finder.

The corridor was empty. He eased the Exit door open, sure the screech of its hinges could be heard all through the hospital. His shoes squeaked on the cement stairs as he descended to ground level.

A slap of cold wet air helped revive him when he stepped outside. He shivered and rubbed the thin material covering his arms, wishing he'd thought to wear his jacket when he'd visited David that day.

He pulled out the Blackberry. After some quick configuring he dialed in to his provider. He ignored the rush of email that populated his inbox. Instead he opened a new email, put in Sandman's address and laboriously typed: *I know who you are.* Then he went out to the front entrance and hailed a cab to take him to Ste. Anne's to pick up his car.

Chris parked the Escape at the bottom of his neighbor's drive. It was unlikely David would be home for hours but he wanted to approach their place carefully.

The house looked empty and there was no Chevy in the driveway.

He let himself into the house, disabling the alarm. Sergeant was pathetically happy to see him. He spent a few minutes he didn't have quieting the dog's excitement. He let the dog out into the backyard.

Then he made his way to his home office. He was pleased to see the police had returned his computer. It only took him a minute to hook everything back up and boot it. While he waited he checked the Blackberry for any replies to his bait. Nothing yet.

It would take more than a single taunt to get Sandman to show his hand.

Chris pulled up Notepad and began typing code, pausing only to consider exactly what he wanted the web bug he was creating to do. He checked his wording carefully, making sure his syntax was correct. He wouldn't have time to test the thing, would have to trust to his skills.

And hope Sandman would let ego and over-confidence affect his judgment and he would take the bait.

He got up at one point to break out the coffee pot and grind up some Indonesian coffee, double strength. Even with the extra jolt of caffeine, exhaustion dragged at him and he had to take frequent breaks to throw cold water on his heated face; once holding his entire head under the icy tap until he shivered with the chill. He let Sergeant back in. The dog seemed to sense something was up and followed him everywhere. He ignored the animal.

Most of the things he wanted the code to do were simple: set a cookie on the computer where it was opened, trap the IP address and computer name, and any user IDs associated with the computer. But he also wanted it to dig deeper and find other cookies that had been downloaded and were still active. This would not only tell him what sites Sandman visited but would reveal whatever name he used to log into them. Maybe he would let slip his real name. Even if he didn't, Chris would have a pattern of usage that would tell him something. Whether it would be useful or not remained to be seen.

Finally it was ready and he constructed the next part of the trap. The email that would get Sandman's attention after the little teaser he had sent earlier.

Chris knew enough from being around David to know that most criminals had huge egos. The Sandman had already proven his weakness with his need to let everyone know what he was doing. Now it was time to play on that weakness.

I know who you are. Soon the cops will know too. You were careless to go back to get my Blackberry. I guess it just proves even the sharpest minds can be stupid at times.

Nobody liked being called stupid, but Chris suspected the Sandman would be outraged by the insult. Outrage, he hoped, would lead to mistakes.

Once the email was sent he constructed the rest of his trap. He set up an online packet sniffer to watch incoming traffic and made sure the results of both the web bug and the sniffer were saved to logs that were emailed directly to an address he could download from anywhere.

Now he could only wait.

But not here. He'd already pushed the limits of his luck by staying here as long as he had.

David rarely visited his office, but Chris still took pains to put it back in the same shape it was when he arrived. He pulled his laptop case out and slid his wallet and Blackberry into the side pockets. He also grabbed a spare jacket out of his office closet, hoping David wouldn't notice. He might see one of his regular jackets missing, but probably didn't know what he had in here. He wished he could have grabbed the Dolce leather, but David would know that was gone for sure.

David was going to find out soon enough he had skipped when he tried to visit the hospital later.

The phone rang and Chris read the call display. It was the hospital.

He gave them enough time to leave their message then he wiped it. If David caught up with him, he'd only insist Chris go back in the hospital without regard to his own personal safety. David figured he could handle any threat Sandman dished out.

Standing up, he nearly fell back in the chair as a wave of pain and dizziness washed over him. He fished around in his pocket for the morphine he had saved and dry swallowed one. He didn't dare take any more, despite the sharp pain that dug into his chest. He had to stay alert.

Beside him Sergeant whined and followed him.

In the laundry room he found a recently washed pair of jeans and a clean T-shirt and changed. The ruined clothes went into the garbage.

CHAPTER TWENTY-FIVE

Tuesday, 6:25 pm, Northeast Community Police Station, San Fernando Road, Los Angeles

Martinez was at his desk when David arrived. He looked up from his keyboard. "You'll never guess who owned the bike."

"Nancy Scott," David said. He peered over Martinez's shoulder. "Not exactly the motorcycle type."

"According to DMV she registered it last year."

"When last year?"

Martinez glanced at his notes. "May. Why, that mean something?"

"Adnan's father died last April. AIDS."

His partner's eyebrow shot up. Before he could comment David went on.

"Yousef told the reporter he got AIDS while he was at Guantanamo. Where, I might add, he was never formally charged with anything."

"Pretty powerful motive for revenge. But what did any of that have to do with his mother?"

"She'd stand to profit more than the son from a wrongful death suit."

Martinez nodded. "Any sign either of them filed?"

"Not that I can find," David said. "But what if it wasn't money he was after?" He parked himself on the edge of Martinez's desk. "What happened to Yousef could incite a lot of anti-American support in the Muslim community. What if somebody got their hooks into Adnan? Promised him revenge on his father and all he'd have to do is use his computer skills to help them out. They'd fund him—it would explain the money for the bike and the shelter. Maybe it made his mother suspicious and she got wind of what he was doing. That's why he killed her."

"If he did poison her. Maybe one of his 'partners' decided to take care of her?"

"I might be able to buy that," Martinez said. "I still got problems with their target. That hospital hardly seems like a likely goal for terrorists like Madrassa or Al-Qaeda."

David shook his head. The Madrassa had grown out of the ashes of the old terrorist groups following 9/11. At first they had been religious schools but their evolution as training facilities for hatred had produced a whole new slate of unrepentant terrorists. "I think the choice was Adnan's. I'll bet you his father died there, right on the same floor I was on. I also think he's only warming up."

"To what?"

"Something a lot more spectacular than blowing the front doors off a hospital." David went around to his desk and sat down. He opened his report. "I think it's time we brought Bentzen in. Our investigation seems to be overlapping his. Maybe he's got something we can use."

Bentzen had left for the day. David left him a voicemail. He wrapped up his report with his visit to the mission and his talk with Julian.

"Unless you got something else I'm calling it a day."

Martinez didn't. David grabbed his jacket and headed for the parking lot.

Traffic on San Fernando Road was heavy. The I5 was at a crawl. It took him over an hour to reach the hospital and another fifteen minutes to find parking. It was just after eight when he reached Chris's room.

The bed was empty. So was the tiny bathroom. Puzzled, David was about to head down to the nurse's station when Dr. Finder entered the room.

"David," she said. "I take it your being here means you haven't heard from Chris."

"I don't understand."

"Chris walked out of here earlier today. Sometime before the dinner cart came around."

What was Chris thinking? "What condition is he in, Doctor?"

"He shouldn't be out there, I can tell you that. He's physically weak. His body needs more time to recover from the surgery and from the trauma he suffered in the bomb attack."

"Any idea why he left?"

"Your guess is as good as mine. Chris wasn't exactly one to share." Finder pulled out the Gap bag David used to bring Chris's toiletries. She withdrew his red silks. "He had these on earlier."

David took the bag and fished through it. All it contained was the silks. "His street clothes are gone."

"Well I guess we know what he was wearing. Would he have gone home?"

David dialed; there was no answer. Chris wouldn't go to all the trouble of getting out of here just to go home. So where was he? He pulled the bedside drawer open. Empty.

David slipped out of the room. The nearest exit was on his left. Ironically, toward the nurse's station. He pulled the door open and peered down the stairs.

Finder followed him. He glanced back at her. "Where does this go?"

"Main floor. There's a side exit that would take him out on the east side of the building."

"He'd have to grab a cab or a bus," David said. Knowing Chris, he'd take a cab.

He barely said goodbye before he hurried back to his own car. It took over an hour to reach Silver Lake and Ste. Anne's.

The front doors of the hospital were draped with a heavy blue tarp, which hung limply in the motionless air. The remnants of crime scene tape were still attached to the metal handrails above the cracked cement steps. He swung around to the parking lot.

Chris's car was gone.

∫ ∫ ∫ ∫

David let himself into the house, knowing before he got past the front door that it was empty. Chris might have been here earlier, but he wasn't in the house now.

The kitchen smelled of coffee. David found a wet filter in the garbage under the sink. Sergeant was agitated and wouldn't leave his side, ignoring him when he told him to go lie down.

But what did Chris do while he was here besides drink coffee? He walked into Chris's office and knew that Chris had been in the room recently. The laptop was missing. He stared down at the desktop computer. Had he come back to get the laptop? What was he doing? Going after the Sandman himself?

He thought of Brad. It took a couple of phone calls but he got the technician's phone number. He answered on the third ring.

"Brad, it's Detective Laine. We spoke yesterday."

"Yeah, I remember. Something wrong?"

"I'd rather you answer that."

There was a telling silence on the other end of the phone. "Uh, I'm not sure—"

"I've got a real puzzle here," David said, knowing he had to hook Brad fast. "I've got a missing man and the computer he used just before he went missing."

"Who?"

"He owns Intelligent Security, does a lot of high-tech work."

"This is his system?"

"Yes."

"What do you want me to do?"

"Find out what he was working on."

David could almost hear Brad shrug. "Bring it in tomorrow," Brad said.

"Not soon enough." David's palms were sweating. "He may be in danger."

"Is this official, sir?"

David stared hard at the blank monitor. He was skirting a gray area now. Chris wasn't his case. He should be turning this over to Bentzen.

Except he wasn't putting Chris's safety in any one else's hands.

"It's official. Will you look at it?"

"You'll bring it here?"

"Sure." David rubbed his damp hand against his pant leg and grabbed a pen from Chris's pen caddy. "Where?"

∫ ∫ ∫ ∫

Brad lived with his parents in Old Pasadena. David drove the Chevy onto the grounds of the gated estate, past a line of torches that led down to the shimmering blue of a classic kidney shaped pool.

The circular drive curved around the front of a white stucco house with an arched doorway opening into a garden courtyard. Low-pitched gable roofs were covered with tiles that looked like dried blood.

David pulled the Chevy up behind a cherry 1954 Jaguar XK120. He came around to the passenger's side and lifted Chris's computer off the seat.

Shoes crunched on the decorative stone walk.

"Bring it around the side," Brad said. "I got my own apartment—I've set up a lab down there."

David followed Brad around the side of the house, through a living willow arch into the house. Brad waved at him to set the computer down on a cluttered workbench.

"Want a beer?"

When David shook his head, Brad got himself a Corona.

"So who is this guy anyway?" Brad swallowed half the beer and wiped his mouth with the sleeve of his T-shirt. "Why's he so important?"

"He's my husband and I think someone's trying to kill him." David gestured at the computer. "How long will this take?"

"Depends what's on it."

"No booby-traps, I guarantee that."

Brad bent over the computer and began hooking up various accessories. Then he powered it on. Eventually it came up to a login screen.

Brad cocked his head at David. "You know the password?"

Fortunately Chris had insisted he learn it. Leaning over Brad's shoulder, David filled in the password field.

Once Brad was in, he started poking around, at random as far as David could tell. But there must have been some rhyme to his meanderings because within minutes he was chuckling.

"This guy's bad."

"What? What do you mean?" David glared at the screen, which was filled with strings of gibberish. "What is it?"

"It's the code behind a web bug. It's a type of spyware, set up to be run on someone else's machine and send back all kinds of information."

"That's illegal, isn't it?"

"Oh, terribly," Brad said gleefully. "Probably breaks a dozen state laws. A few federal ones too."

David was horrified. "What exactly does it do?"

"It collects everything it can from the receiving machine. Names, cookies, email addies, hell, if he'd added a keystroke logger, he'd have an all around data miner."

"Any idea who he sent it to?" Though David already had his suspicions.

Brad confirmed them. "Sandman422@freemail.com is the last address sent to..." He opened the sent mail and verified it. "Yep, that's where he sent the bug. Who's that?"

David's cell rang. He answered it gruffly. It was Martinez.

"They came back with an initial report on the cat hair," Martinez said. "It matches Adnan's cat. If we want an exact DNA match we have to send the samples off to someplace in Texas, I think. I've got an arrest warrant in the works."

"Good," David said. "Let me know when you got it."

He broke the connection and turned back to Brad. "Any way to tell if this web bug was opened at the other end?"

"It's set to email the captured data back to this guy." Brad patted Chris's computer.

"He knew he couldn't stay at home to collect it. What other options does he have?"

"Most accounts now are web enabled. Any Internet café will let you download your messages. A lot of cell phones have the capability, too—"

"Cell phone." But Chris had lost his Blackberry. Except David knew better than to underestimate Chris's resourcefulness.

Tuesday 8:10 pm, The Nosh Pit, Hyperion Avenue, Silver Lake, Los Angeles

Chris found a spot just off Hyperion to park. He moved stiffly, the damp chill in the air playing havoc with his strained joints and muscles. He hobbled down a street bustling with the usual weeknight dinner crowd.

It was too early for the late night drinkers to be out so he wasn't surprised to find The Nosh Pit still quiet, with only a scattering of tables taken and the bar itself half-filled.

Ramsey, the ex-marine owner-bartender, spotted him and grabbed Chris's usual Cîroc off the top shelf. Chris shook his head; a wave of nausea rolled through him.

He eschewed the bar, fearing Ramsey would see too much from there. Instead he picked the table furthest from the light and gingerly eased down into a chair facing away from the bar. He took the Blackberry out and turned it on, waiting for it to find a signal.

Ramsey sent over Chris's favorite server, a sexy little twenty-something Tongan who had blown into town four years before. The slender caramel cutie had proved to be one of Ramsey's more popular servers and recently they had become partners and lovers.

"Drink?"

"Seven-Up." Chris didn't feel up to handling alcohol. God knew what it would do to his poor, drug-riddled body.

The Tongan raised one carefully shaped eyebrow. His botoxed lips twisted into a pout. "No drink?"

"Seven-Up is a drink. Oh, what the hell, I'm feeling brave—toss a lemon slice in there, too."

The Tongan sashayed away. Chris couldn't help it; he watched the gentle swing of the slender hips encased in skintight black pants. He knew his body really was broken up when he didn't feel a thing looking at that tight round butt.

"Since when do you fly solo?"

Chris swung around to find Ramsey standing over him, his thick tattooed arms folded over his chest.

"What the fuck happened to you?" Ramsey asked. "You walk into someone's fist?"

"Nothing like that."

The Tongan came back with his drink. This time it was Ramsey's eyebrows that shot up.

"Solo and dry?"

Chris fished the lemon out and squeezed it into the drink. "David's at work."

"He know you're here?"

Chris threw him a sour grin.

"Really man, what happened to you?" Ramsey looked genuinely concerned. "You sure you should be out here?"

"I'm fine."

"You lie like a rug."

"Don't you have other customers to harass? Cute little wait-boys to take into the back room for a blow job?"

"Stop trying to change the subject. Seriously Chris, what are you doing here? Go home, go to bed."

But Chris wasn't listening. He was watching the tiny screen where a flow of incoming data was beginning to populate his Blackberry. Sandman had taken the bait.

He stored the cookies that were sent. He'd check them out later; see if he could determine where Sandman had been visiting when he'd downloaded them. Right now he was more interested in the guy's browsing history and the stuff stored in his cache.

Chris pulled out his laptop and dug around until he came up with the syncing device. He hooked it up under Ramsey's curious gaze and transferred all the data he'd gathered to the laptop where he could look it over more easily.

He'd already spotted a couple of cracker sites on Sandman's list. That was probably where he had gone to get the code he'd used to hack the hospital the first time. Very few crackers, even the best, wrote all their code from scratch. Why reinvent the wheel?

His BlackBerry beeped, signaling new email. It was from Terry. What could he want?

The message sounded frantic. *I've been trying to reach you. It's urgent. Please call.* He included a cell number Chris didn't recognize.

Chris dialed it. Terry snatched it up on the second ring.

"Yes?"

"Hey, Terry. It's Chris—"

"Christ, man, I've been trying to reach you for hours. You gotta come out here."

Chris was confused. "To the hospital?" That didn't make any sense. The hospital was closed—

"No," Terry whispered. "My place."

Terry lived in Santa Clarita. Chris had been there once for a New Year's party, before he'd ever met David. "Santa Clarita? You gotta be joking."

"It's about David," Terry's voice dropped even lower. Chris strained to hear. "He's in trouble. The kiddie porn was only part of it."

"What do you mean?" How the hell did Terry know about the porn? "Forget it, you're just pulling my chain. Why should I drive out to Santa Clarita?"

Chris disconnected the call. It rang less than a minute later.

"Please man. I gotta talk to you."

Terry sounded damn near hysterical. Chris swallowed past a lump in his throat. Was this really a new threat to David? He wanted to tell Terry to fuck off, but he didn't dare.

"Does this have anything to do with Bolton?"

"Bolton? No, no, it's not Bolton—" Abrupt silence fell. Then: "If you won't come, I'm not sure what they'll do to David. They told me to tell you that."

The cell went dead.

Chris stared at his Blackberry in frustration. He redialed but it went straight to voicemail. He tried again, same result.

Chris looked up to find Ramsey watching him. He started packing away his laptop, keeping the Blackberry out. "I gotta go. If David comes by you didn't see me, okay?"

"You want me to lie to David?"

"Don't lie, just don't tell him I was here."

"You know, David's the best thing that ever happened to you and sometimes I don't think you have the brains to see that," Ramsey said. "Why should I help you fuck it up?"

"You don't think I know he's the best thing?" Chris was stung by the accusation. Of course he loved David. Who the hell could ever doubt that? "I married him, didn't I?"

"I hope you know what you're doing."

"I'm just going to visit an old friend," he lied. "What's the harm in that?"

He hit redial on the way out the door. Voicemail again.

CHAPTER TWENTY-SIX

Tuesday, 8:55 pm East Villa Street, Old Pasadena

David climbed back behind the wheel. He sat there for several minutes, mulling over his next step. Where would Chris go?

At Brad's he had taken advantage of having access to Chris's computer to look up the phone numbers of some of Chris's friends. Outside of Des, none of them had heard from him in days.

David couldn't see Chris getting in the car and driving for any length of time. He'd stick close to home. So where? Mattie's on Glendale where they walked for their coffees? Taix on Sunset? The Nosh Pit? Houston's?

He decided to hit Hyperion first. There were a half a dozen places there that he and Chris frequented, including The Nosh Pit, the bar where circumstances had contrived to bring them together for the first time nearly six years ago.

If he didn't see anything there, he'd circle around to Glendale Boulevard. If that failed, he was at a loss as to where to go next.

He knew he could request a BOLO on Chris's car, but having other cops out looking for his spouse would impress Chris no end. No, David thought, he'd save that drastic option as a last resort.

He threw the car into gear and roared out of the driveway. David was proud of Chris, he knew the guy could out think him a heartbeat, but sometimes he was too smart for his own good. How could he endanger himself just to get back at this guy? Why? Just because he had attacked David? David knew he couldn't take it personally or it would eat at him. Chris had never had any reason to learn that lesson.

Traffic on Hyperion Avenue was picking up with the first of the evening crowds. There was a line-up at Casita del Campo.

David slowed to a crawl, ignoring the impatient honks from those in a hurry behind him.

Each time he spotted a kiwi green Escape he slowed more—or sped up if the car was ahead of him. He cruised by The Nosh Pit and snagged a parking spot that was just being vacated by a Subaru.

Ramsey looked up when he entered and the look that flashed across his face told David he'd hit the jackpot. The flamboyant little queen who served drinks and some heavy duty flirtation seemed disappointed when David said he didn't want anything.

David never took his eyes off Ramsey.

"When was he here?"

He thought Ramsey was going to lie, then he shrugged. "You just missed him. Maybe five minutes ago."

"He say where he was going?"

"He was talking on the phone with someone. Heard him say Santa Clarita. He left here right after that." Ramsey folded his arms over his chest. "He told me not to tell you any of this."

Ramsey was more Chris's friend than his. David was never sure if Ramsey had forgiven him for the heavy-handed way he had conducted his investigation into the Carpet Killer. "So why did you?"

"Chris is doing something even he knows isn't right. If he's in trouble I wouldn't be able to forgive myself."

David held his hand out over the bar. Ramsey took it.

"Thanks," David said.

"Hey, try to keep the guy out of trouble. He's such a magnet for it."

Shaking his head at the truth of that, David hurried back to his car. Heading north towards the I5 he zigzagged through traffic. Taillights flared along the street as traffic ebbed and flowed.

David tailgated a Saturn for a while, until he was able to slip past it and onto the north bound ramp.

The freeway was stop and go traffic. An hour later David spotted a kiwi green Escape and was able to get close enough to read the plate. It was Chris's car. Then the Escape's tail lights flared and the vehicle darted across two lanes of traffic amid a blare of horns, disappearing down the McBean Parkway exit into Santa Clarita. Barely glancing at the traffic behind him David followed.

They passed the California Institute of Arts and David grew even more confused. They didn't know anyone out here. It was classic middleclass suburbia, something Chris detested. Chris's parents lived in Chatsworth and Chris rarely visited them, though as far as David had seen from the two times he had gone with Chris to see them, they were trying hard to accept Chris and his lifestyle. Chris's parents had reached out to them when he and Chris married, something David's parents had not done.

David enjoyed his visits to Chatsworth. He wished he could take Chris to visit his family, but his mother and stepfather would never look on Chris as anything other than an aberration in their son's life. David took Chris home to New Hampshire once. His mother had been cold and disdainful of both Chris and her only son. The trip had been cut short and David never suggested they go again, though he knew Chris wondered why. Chris thought their marriage would change his mother's mind, when David knew nothing would.

David followed Chris past streets with names like Singing Hills Drive and Via Jacara. David nearly lost him at a stoplight, impatiently waiting for it to change while he watched the Escape disappear down Del Monte Drive.

The light changed and David squealed around the corner. His stomach rolled over when he realized the Escape had vanished. He slowed to a crawl, peering anxiously down side streets, looking for the car.

He was about to give up and call LASD at the Magic Mountain substation when he spotted the car in front of a Spanish style adobe brick house. There were several other cars and vans parked up and down the short crescent.

There was no sign of Chris when David pulled the Chevy to the curb two cars down from the empty Escape and turned his lights off. The Spanish-style house was dark, except for a single incandescent bulb hanging above the front door.

David settled in behind the wheel, hunching down in the seat so he would be less obvious. His gaze moved restlessly around the darkened property, searching for movement. He knew he should call the Sheriffs. They wouldn't appreciate him poaching on their turf, but exactly what would he tell them? His husband was sneaking around someone's house and no, he didn't know why?

He caught movement near a five-foot toyon bush on the south side. A figure slipped through the shadows, moving toward the rear of the house. David's view was partially screened by a large fan palm. The nearby chirps of crickets didn't drown out the sonorous hum of traffic on McBean Parkway.

He climbed out of the car. Was Chris looking for a back door? Was he trying to get inside? But why? David wished he could call in the address and find who owned the place, but he had no legitimate reason to make such a call.

His only hope was to catch Chris before he got inside and did something foolish.

No light from the street reached this far. He stepped carefully, doing his best to avoid making noise. Chris had vanished around the corner of the house.

David followed. Along the back wall an inky pit of blackness stained the already dark house. Belatedly David realized it was an open door.

Frowning, he stepped onto the stone patio. The crickets fell silent.

"Chris?" he called softly. "Are you there? Chris—"

The smell washed over him moments before the shadow suddenly detached from the front of the toyon bush. Urine and unwashed flesh. And gasoline. There was a rushing sound. David spun around, instinct kicking in too late. He reached for his

Smith & Wesson. A blow caught him upside the head, throwing him backward. He lurched to his knees; light flared behind his eyes.

He caught a glimpse of the same hot dark eyes he had last seen at the homeless shelter and too late he realized who it was.

"Adnan," he whispered. His fingers closed over the butt of his gun, yanking it out as Adnan again swung whatever he had hit him with the first time. David's head ricocheted off stone and the light in his head exploded into a brilliant kaleidoscope of pain, then nothing.

Tuesday, 9:40 pm, Via Raza, Santa Clarita

When he saw the dark house, Chris wondered if after everything Terry had been pulling his leg.

There was no doorbell. He pounded on the front door and stepped back in alarm when it opened.

He leaned forward and stuck his head inside. "Terry? Hey, it's Chris. You there?"

Silence. Then a rustling sound. Footsteps echoed across hard tile, followed by the clank of something metallic.

"Terry?"

The sound came again. Chris shoved the door open and stepped inside. He fumbled his way down the hall until he found a light switch and flipped it on.

Terry lay propped against the foyer wall. His short hair was drenched in blood. The wall behind him was patterned with gore. Down the hall, half in and half out of another room lay a second body. All he could see were legs, but he knew it was a woman. Terry's wife, Carol? The woman Chris had only met once, years ago. He couldn't see any blood. He knew she was dead without seeing more. His stomach lurched. He had to dig his teeth into his lips to keep from vomiting.

"Terry!" He dropped to his knees, ignoring the blood soaking into his jeans. He fumbled with numb fingers along Terry's throat; there was no pulse.

Chris scrambled to his feet and backed away from the body. The police. He had to call the police. No, he had to call David. He grabbed his Blackberry.

An odd popping sound distracted him while he tried to key in David's number with shaking fingers. He glanced down the hall toward the back of the dark house, trying to ignore the body of Terry's wife. The noise sounded familiar. He went back to his Blackberry, punching in numbers. He'd deal with strange noises later, after he had called David—

The popping, crackling sound grew. All the hairs on his body stood up as he finally recognized it. Fire. Yellow-orange light flickered off the floor tiles and the acrid smell of smoke filled his nostrils, along with another, equally familiar smell. Gasoline.

He stared down at Terry's body. He had to get out of here. But he couldn't leave them to burn. He bent down, hooked his arms under Terry's shoulders and yanked him toward the door. For the first time he understood the expression "dead weight." Chris would have sworn Terry hadn't weighed more than a hundred and eighty, soaking wet, but right now he felt like he was trying to drag around a half a ton. He pulled the body around to face the door, but couldn't get it any further.

Gasping for breath he leaned against the wall and stared down at the body helplessly. His hands were covered in gore. His stomach flipped over again.

Black smoke billowed down the hall, the bitter odor of burning wood, plastic and god knew what else. The gasoline smell grew stronger.

Chris breathed shallowly as he tried one more time to pull Terry toward the front of the house. Pain stabbed through his back and he straightened with a gasp. No way. He wasn't going to be able to get Terry out.

Chris raced for the door and yanked it open. Damp, oxygen-rich air poured into the house. Chris took a deep breath then let it out with a cry. The fire had been as rejuvenated as he was by the blast of fresh air.

The crackling sound became a roar. Fire leaped up the doorframe and curled seductively around a wall light, which exploded into glittering shards of frosted glass.

Chris had never realized fire spread so fast. He barely leaped through the front door when the flames burst out behind him. He smelled burning denim and lurched onto the lawn, where he hastily patted several embers off his jeans. He could feel the pinpricks of heat against his bare skin. His face was covered with greasy sweat and his T-shirt clung to him. Even the cooling night air did not chill his overheated flesh.

He braced his hands on his knees. His chest ached and his breathing was short and labored. He closed his eyes and tried to take deep, cleansing breaths, but each gasp hurt more than the last.

In the distance he heard the rising wail of sirens. One of the neighbors must have called 911. The fire trucks would arrive soon. The cops wouldn't be far behind.

He rolled his head sideways, wondering if he dared try to move.

Pain momentarily forgotten, he stared at the '56 Chevy Two-Tone sport coupe parked at the curb. It couldn't be David's car. David was at work. David was in Los Angeles. He didn't even know Terry, so there was no way he'd know where this place was or that Chris was coming here.

Chris pushed himself upright. On leaden feet he staggered across the lawn and braced himself against the passenger side door, ignoring the smear of blood he left. He immediately spotted David's Ray Bans and the leather steering-wheel cover David had only recently installed.

Chris's knees buckled and he had to grab the door handle to keep from collapsing. What was David doing here? In growing horror Chris turned toward Terry's house just in time to see the front of the roof collapse in a shower of sparks and flame. A wave of heat rolled across the lawn, a fan palm beside the house curled away from the heat and burst into flames.

"No!" Chris lunged away from the car. A fire truck careened around the corner, followed closely by a second.

Chris's feet skidded on the wet grass. The front door was ablaze; he couldn't get in that way. Instead he circled the house looking for another way in. A window, a door. Anything.

Had David gone in after him? Or was he tracking Terry? David kept his business to himself. If he did develop a lead on Terry, he wouldn't tell Chris. But what were the odds of him coming after Terry at the same time Chris was responding to Terry's phone call? Or had the call from Terry come because he knew he was a suspect? Was that why he called Chris? Because he knew David was closing in on him?

It still didn't explain who killed Terry. Or why.

Above the roar of the flames he could hear voices. Footsteps pounded after him and a bulky man in full gear rounded the burning palm and shouted. Chris ignored him.

His foot connected with something on the ground. It skidded away. Puzzled, he looked at what he had kicked. It was some kind of flat dark material, which did not reflect the nearby fire.

He knew what it was even before he snatched it up. He blinked.

It was a gun. He traced the outline of the rectangular barrel and raised writing, knowing even without being able to see it what it said. Smith & Wesson .40. It was David's gun. The one he had bought himself to replace his police issue Beretta. It cost him a small fortune, but he claimed the Smith & Wesson was a better weapon.

Chris raised his head and stared blindly at the burning building. The door was a hole into hell. It was like staring down the maw of a dragon. He stepped toward it.

A voice shouted. Chris spun around and found himself staring into the alarmed face of a fire fighter.

"Sir, you can't be here—"

"Drop the weapon!"

Chris twisted away from the first man only to find himself staring down the barrel of another gun. The deputy holding it didn't look alarmed. She looked grim.

"Drop it, clown."

Chris did as he was told.

"On your stomach," the deputy said. "Hands laced behind your head."

"You don't understand—"

"Now!"

Chris dropped to his knees. The grass felt slimy and cold under the skin of his face. Rough hands grabbed his arms and yanked them behind his back. Hard metal cuffs snicked around his wrists.

"David's in there!"

The deputy dragged him to his feet. She looked even grimmer. "You telling me there's somebody in the house?"

"No—yes, Terry, but that's not who I mean. And his wife. David's in there!" Chris yelled when his arms were wrenched behind him. "David's a cop!"

Something crashed inside the house. A gust of superheated air washed over them. Chris ducked away from it, only to be jerked back. His shoulders ached and his head swam.

"That's his gun. You have to find him—"

Under the watchful gaze of the fire fighter, the deputy hauled Chris to his feet and shoved him toward the street. An ambulance had joined the fire trucks and police cars. A kaleidoscope of multi-colored lights competed with the glow from the fire. With half the population of Santa Clarita watching, the deputy pushed Chris into the back of the black and white idling at the curb.

Hoses snaked out of the fire trucks. Streams of high-pressure water poured into the glowing inferno of Terry's house. Goggled and helmeted fire fighters moved in with axes and hooks.

Chris sat in the back of the black and white staring blankly as chaos unfolded around him.

They left him sitting in the back seat of the deputy's vehicle for over an hour while he watched bedlam reign and begged a deity he had never had much faith in before to keep David safe.

Only when the fire had been reduced to sullen embers did the deputy return. She came back with a tall, hairless Latino man who slid behind the wheel while she took shotgun. Neither of them looked at him, nor spoke, during the ride to the Santa Clarita Valley station on Magic Mountain Parkway.

They led him into a small, well-lit room with four chairs and a steel table. The woman motioned at the chair. "Are you injured? Do you require medical assistance?"

"What? No—" then Chris realized they thought he was bleeding. "It was on Terry—"

The silent Latino took the cuffs off and handed them to his partner. They did a few swabs of his hands, then they both left.

This time he waited for forty minutes. Finally the door reopened. A bull-necked Anglo deputy entered. He was sweating so profusely his pits were soaked through and his thinning hair was plastered to his pale skull. His eyes were pale gray pools.

"Sergeant Clay Ronaldson," he said. "You mind if we tape this?"

"Yes," Chris said. "I do mind. But I expect you'll do it anyway."

The deputy pulled out a chair and sat down. "Can you state your name and address for the record."

Chris did so, then he leaned forward putting his arms on the table. Too late he remembered he was covered in blood. Terry's blood. He snatched his hands away, even though he knew the cop had seen them. "Look," he said quickly. "You have to tell me, did they find anything in the house? Did they find...anybody besides Terry and his wife?"

"Are you IDing the bodies we found in the front hallway as Terry? Terry who? What's his wife's name?" The deputy eyed him and scratched something on his notepad. "You're saying there's a third victim?"

"David's a cop," Chris said. "His car was there—"

"Cop, huh? What's his name then? What unit's he in?"

"David. Detective David Eric Laine. LAPD. Call his partner, Martinez Diego. At the Northeast Station. He'll tell you."

"And the car?"

Chris rubbed his damp hands along his thighs, remembering the blood and grimacing. "It's a '56 Chevy Two-Tone. Yellow and white coupe." He rattled off the license plate.

Ronaldson scribbled in his notepad then got up and opened the door, handing the top sheet to someone on the other side. He came back and sat down.

"You want to tell me where you got the blood on your hands?"

"It was on Terry..." He swallowed past a stone that had settled in his chest. "Please, did you find anyone else there? Carol? Oh, God, David—"

"What were you doing in Santa Clarita, Mr. Bellamere? You here on business or pleasure?"

Chris knew better than to talk to cops. He leaned forward, knotting his fingers together to keep them from shaking. "I'm not talking to you until you call Detective Martinez Diego. He needs to know about David. They're partners. Maybe you'll believe me then."

"Believe what, Mr. Bellamere?"

Chris shook his head.

"Where did the blood come from?"

Chris stared stubbornly at his lap.

Ronaldson sighed. A gust of sour breath wafted across the table. "I'm here right now, Chris. Talk to me. It'll go easier for you if you do."

"You want their number?" Chris asked.

"You're not helping yourself by refusing—"

"Not refusing, just delaying."

"By refusing to answer my questions, you're only hurting yourself." Ronaldson shook his head. "I'm sure Detective Martinez would tell you the same thing."

Proving this guy didn't know Martinez at all.

Ronaldson kept scratching away in his notebook. "Who were you at that house to see? The dead guy or the woman? Was Terry the owner of the house?"

Chris shook his head, feeling a wave of dizziness wash over him. He blinked and forced his eyes to focus. He had to stay alert, when all he wanted to do was close his eyes and sleep for a week. He was seriously beginning to regret leaving the hospital. Even Dr. Finder looked better than this guy.

"Something wrong, Mr. Bellamere?" Ronaldson didn't sound overly alarmed. "You don't look so hot. Something happen to make you feel sick?"

Chris dug his nails into the palm of his hand. His finger nails had crusted blood under them. The pain helped. A little.

"Have you called him yet?"

"Yeah, we called," Ronaldson said. "He said the same thing I've been telling you. Talk to us while we wait for him."

Another thirty minutes passed. Ronaldson went out and returned fifteen minutes later. There was a commotion outside in the hall and Chris looked up when the door flew open. A lean-faced African-American woman wearing lieutenant bars leaned in the room.

"Sergeant," she said curtly, only to be pushed aside by a fuming Martinez whose dark face was suffused with blood.

"What the devil is going on?" Martinez's scowl deepened when he saw Chris. His eyes narrowed into slits. "What the hell are you doing here, Chris? And where in the name of God is David?"

CHAPTER TWENTY-SEVEN

Chris jumped to his feet. "Ask them if they found anyone else in the house. They won't tell me—"

"What house? What's going on?"

Ronaldson pointed a thick finger at Chris. "You, sit." He glared at Martinez. "Detective, if we could talk. *Privately.*"

"You can use my office, Detective," the lieutenant said. "This way, please."

Martinez backed out of the small interrogation room. Ronaldson stood to follow.

"Hey, what about me?" Chris half rose again.

Martinez's face softened. "Just wait here, Chris. I'll sort this out and be back."

Chris sank back down into his chair. While he'd put Martinez up against these sheriff bumpkins any day of the week, he still didn't like it. Not one bit. He was desperate to know where David was, refusing to believe he'd been caught in that fire. David was too smart to let Terry's killer take him by surprise.

But worry gnawed at him. Unable to sit, he paced the narrow confines of the room, skirting the table and chairs in his need to keep moving.

Where was David?

$$\int \int \int \int$$

More time passed. Even his watch slowed to a crawl. Chris kept staring at the door, and the glass wall beside it. Were they watching him even now? What did they expect him to do? Break out into spontaneous confession?

No doubt they thought he had something to do with Terry's death. Under the circumstances he would have suspected himself too.

Would they believe his story that Terry called him? What proof could he offer? The call he had made to Terry's cell might help, if they bothered to trace where Terry's cell was when the call came through. Ramsey could attest to the time he left The Nosh Pit, but unless they could pinpoint Terry's death, he doubted that would prove helpful.

Chris threw his head back and rubbed his forehead with his jacket sleeve. He'd really fucked things up this time.

He spun around when the door cracked open. Martinez slipped into the room.

He shook his grizzled head. Ice formed around Chris's heart.

"David—" he gasped.

Martinez came around to Chris's side of the table and gripped the nearest chair. Hard. His knuckles were white. The chair creaked under his grip. "Where is he, Chris? I've tried calling his cell. He's not responding. You have to tell us everything you know."

"I don't..." Chris wearily sank into the other chair, no longer trying to hide his exhaustion or pain. "Somehow he followed me—I don't know how or why. I swear. He must have got there when I was in the house—"

"What were you doing there?"

Chris glanced at the glass, knowing they were watching on the other side. Ronaldson. Maybe even the lieutenant. Santa Clarita was a small, insular community. It wasn't used to nasty homicides marring that image. They'd want to wrap this up as soon as possible. Even if they dumped it in the lap of an innocent man.

It didn't matter. He had to tell Martinez everything he knew if it meant finding David.

"Terry called me." Chris told him about the work he had done for Terry and the hospital. "He stumbled onto something. I just don't know what." He recounted the conversation he'd had with Terry.

"Could Bolton be the hacker?" Martinez asked. "I thought David had eliminated him."

"He could be," Chris conceded. "But I doubt it. Somebody was in the house with Terry. I heard them."

"They found gas cans by the rear door," Martinez said.

"How did Terry...die?"

"Gunshot to the right front temple. Exited out the back of his skull."

Chris glanced at the mirrored window again. Nausea cramped his gut. Poor Terry. He didn't ask about his wife. He couldn't stand to hear it. Not right now. "What's going to happen to me?"

"They want you to take some tests for combustibles. Your GSR test came back negative, you haven't fired a weapon recently. The blood's problematic." Martinez frowned. "They want a statement, but, the truth?" Martinez sighed. "They're not quite sure what to do with you. They seem willing to believe you weren't involved in Terry's death, but..."

"They want me to be guilty of something," Chris finished for him.

A ghost of a smile crossed Martinez's face. "Something like that."

"Can I leave?"

"They're not arresting you for anything. I can't guarantee that won't change if they find new information. The lieutenant wants to know if you'd take a lie detector test."

"Uh, I don't know..." Chris wished he could talk to a lawyer, but he knew what they'd advise him. No poly. But if it would get him out of here so he could look for David, then he'd do it. "Sure, I guess. Right now?"

"It will have to be set up. Maybe tomorrow."

"So, can I leave now?"

The door opened again and Ronaldson entered. He was sweating even more than the first time, his face looked sheathed in grease. He pushed his limp hair back, where it stuck to his scalp.

"You can go, Mr. Bellamere," he said. "I expect we'll want to talk to you again. Make sure you're available."

"Trust me, I'm not leaving the state."

"Good," Ronaldson said, and held the door open for him. "We'll be in touch."

After they tested his skin and his clothes for gas, which proved negative, and he repeated what he had told Martinez, Chris followed Martinez out of the station to his brown Crown Victoria.

"I got permission from Lieutenant Peters to revisit the scene. I want you to show me where you found David's Smith & Wesson."

They drove back to Terry's. The house was sodden rubble, the lawn trampled to mud. Yellow crime scene tape had been strung around the yard. When they stepped out of the car a sheriff's deputy came around the side of the building. The air stank of fire and gas and death.

"This is a secured crime scene—"

Martinez flashed his badge and after a hasty phone call to the station, they were allowed on the property. Martinez grabbed a torch out of his trunk and followed Chris behind the burnt out house. He kept the powerful light on the ground just in front of them and Chris studied the chewed earth, looking for landmarks.

"It was around here," he finally ventured, kneeling on the wet, trampled ground. Martinez obliged by focusing the light on the ground in front of him.

The small yard was hemmed in by a fence along the back and boxwood hedges on each side. The hedge extended between the two houses almost into the front yard and looked solid as stone in the low light. If David had fallen here, how did the Sandman get him out? Chris hadn't been inside long enough for him to drag David around to the front of the house and into a waiting car. He had to have taken him over the fence or the hedge immediately after the fire.

Chris remembered his efforts to move Terry. Could the Sandman even move a big guy like David?

Chris crawled. The light wavered then began following him.

The ground was torn here; he could imagine heels dragging across the rain-dampened ground. He stared ahead, at a shadowy indent in the boxwood hedge. He waved his arm at Martinez.

"Shine it over there, on the bushes."

Martinez did as he asked. Chris stayed on the ground, knowing he would miss too much if he tried to walk. His left hand skidded on something wet and he sprawled onto his stomach with a soft *umph*. The light vanished and rough hands grabbed him and hauled him to his knees.

"You okay? Chris—"

Chris held up his hand. It was covered in viscous red. "Shit!" He scrambled to his feet and grabbed the torch. The ground at his feet was red with blood. David's blood? The killer's? In the baleful light of the torch, he spotted something metallic. With numb fingers, he lifted the St. Michael's medal he had given to David just last week.

Martinez was instantly on his cell. All Chris heard was "forensics team," and "Code Thirty." He swung the powerful beam of light along the ground toward the hedge while Martinez talked. The dark shadow proved to be one of several ragged holes in the ill-kempt fence. More wet redness stained the outer edges of branches—

"You have to give them the jewelry, Chris," Martinez said. "It's evidence—"

"It's David's."

"You'll get it back."

Chris wanted to refuse, but he knew he couldn't. He clutched the bloody medal against his chest and felt like weeping. Reluctantly he handed it to Martinez, who passed it off to the watching deputy.

"Let's take a look," Martinez said, letting his hand hover over Chris's shoulder. "They dragged him through there." He pointed at the hedge. "Peters is sending a forensics team out. In the meantime don't touch anything."

Chris turned away. He hurried toward the front of the house, rounding the hedge and shining the light down the dark passageway beside the neighboring house.

A car turned onto the street, a van following. Ronaldson hopped out of the lead car. A greyhound-thin Latino man in a tan business suit emerged from the passenger's side. The van discharged three men in baby blue sterile suits lugging spotlights and suitcases. Trailing cables, they set up the lights on the lawn between the burnt house and the hedge.

Within thirty minutes the spots went on, driving away the night. The blood on the trampled ground immediately leaped into focus.

"Over here," Chris called.

When Martinez added his voice, the two deputies left the forensic team to their work and followed Chris and Martinez around the back of the house next door.

"They dragged him through there," Chris pointed.

"They?" Ronaldson looked skeptical.

"David's not a little guy," Martinez said with more patience than Chris could have mustered. "I doubt if anyone short of Andre the Giant could drag him around alone. Not if he was unconscious, and trust me, he wouldn't let anyone drag him around if he wasn't unconscious."

Chris was all too aware of Ronaldson's eyes coming back his way repeatedly. Was he trying to figure out Chris's place in all this? Chris knew he didn't swish, but he also didn't do anything to hide his orientation. Some people picked up on it right away. He suspected Ronaldson was doing just that. With that knowledge, Ronaldson had to wonder at Chris's presence and his obvious distress over David.

Armed with their own powerful torch and a second one Ronaldson had, they had no trouble picking up the trail. Ronaldson lingered at the hole in the hedge; Chris and Martinez were more interested in where the trail went next.

Chris was the first to spot it.

Two distinct round drops of blood on the back doorsteps of the house next door. Chris stared at the door with a crazy kind of hope.

"Jesus, they took him in there."

Ronaldson came over when Martinez called him. He studied the door intently. Then he glanced at Martinez, ignoring Chris. "We canvassed the area. This house came up empty."

"Or they just weren't answering the door," Chris snapped. "Imagine that."

Ronaldson was joined by his partner, who he laconically introduced as *José* Otélo. The two deputies approached the wooden door. Otélo rapped on it sharply. There was no response.

Otélo banged the door a second time, harder. When there was still no response, he glanced at his partner and nodded. Both of them slipped on police issue gloves; Ronaldson tried the door. It opened easily.

Chris suddenly had memories of another door. Would history repeat itself? Would they find another body on the other side?

Would they find David?

He watched the two detectives enter the dark house. Martinez followed, leaving only Chris outside, his legs too weak to carry him.

Suddenly the house was full of lights and there was a flurry of activity and rising voices. Chris bolted up the steps into a tidy, crowded kitchen.

A woman—at least Chris assumed she was a woman, though her face was bloody and her clothes baggy and shapeless—sat in a ladder back chair, her hands bound behind her back with soiled strips of duct tape. More duct tape was in Ronaldson's hand and had obviously just been removed from the captive's face. Otélo was on his cell, calling for an ambulance.

She stared at Chris, wild-eyed, the whites of her eyes standing out against her bloody and bruised face.

A surprisingly gentle Ronaldson knelt by the chair, while Otélo used a pair of scissors to cut the bindings on her hands. "Ma'am? An ambulance is on the way. Can you tell us what happened here?"

Her voice was high-pitched and edged in hysteria. "I was making supper. Gerry's gone to San Diego for a conference so I was just making a bowl of soup."

Chris looked at the stove. There was a blackened pot containing what might have been cream soup. Both pot and soup were ruined, though Chris doubted she would be hungry for anything for a good long time to come.

Otélo got a bottle of cold water from her fridge. She sucked on the bottle greedily. It seemed to help her find her voice.

"They came in the back door. I didn't know what was happening at first. I thought there was three of them, until I saw what they had done to that poor man..."

Chris perked up. *Poor man?* He stepped forward. "What man? What did he look like?"

Ronaldson threw him a dirty look. Chris subsided only when Martinez touched his arm.

"Go ahead, ma'am," Ronaldson said. "What did they look like?"

She shook her head, ringlets of sweat and blood-stiffened hair falling over her pale face. "They wore masks. Those black things, with holes..."

"Balaclavas, ma'am?" Otélo suggested.

She nodded gratefully. "Yes, they wore those. Except the third man. They had him all tied up too."

"Can you describe them? How big were they? Tall, short? Heavy—"

"The one they had tied up was big, the other two were both smaller than him. The one guy wasn't any bigger than me; the other man was burlier, dark haired."

"Anything else?"

She shuddered and wouldn't look at anyone. "He had an accent. Oh, and a beard." Her nose wrinkled. "The smaller man stank."

"Stank, ma'am?"

"Like he hadn't had a shower in weeks."

Otélo wrote that down. "What kind of accent did the other one have?"

Her voice grew small. "I don't know... French, I think. But rough French, not like what you hear on TV." She shook. "I was so sure they were going to kill me."

"You're safe now, ma'am."

She stared up at him as though to ask "Are you sure about that?" but all she did was rub her arms and wipe a tear that leaked from her bruised eye.

"The man who was taped. What can you tell us about him?"

"Like I said, he was big," she said. "They dragged him in here between them and dumped him there—" She indicated another chair at the tiny kitchen table. Chris could see fresh blood on the wooden ladder-back.

"Was he alive?" he whispered.

"Yes, he was. But they had most of his face covered in duct tape. But even with that I could tell they had beaten him pretty bad."

Chris winced but refrained from saying anything more when Martinez's hand tightened painfully on his arm.

"What did they do then?" Ronaldson asked.

"N-nothing." Even she seemed surprised by the admission. "They stood where you are and waited in the dark, made me turn out every light in the place." She twisted the loose fabric of her dressing gown in shaking hands. "We heard the fire trucks and all but they wouldn't let me look, they said no one must know they were here. The doorbell rang after that and the one with the accent took one of my knives out of the drawer and told me if I made a noise he'd kill me."

"What time did they leave, ma'am?" Ronaldson asked.

She glanced at the clock over her stove. It said twelve-thirty. "Maybe two hours ago. I thought to look at the clock after they'd been gone a while. It was just after ten-thirty."

Chris was stunned. That meant the whole time he had been out there with Terry and his wife's body, and later sitting in the sheriff's car, David had been in the house next door. Hurt. Maybe dying.

What did they want with him?

He didn't realize he'd spoken aloud until Martinez answered him.

"Come on, Chris," he said. "Let's take this outside. Let them finish up here." Martinez and Ronaldson shared a glance. "If you're done with him..."

"He can leave," Ronaldson said. "We know where to find him if the need arises."

Reluctantly Chris followed Martinez out of the house, back to his car. They stood beside the unmarked.

"He was in there," Chris murmured. "David was there the whole time—"

"Don't," Martinez said sharply. "That won't help David now."

Chris was about to protest when his Blackberry vibrated. He fumbled for it and studied the tiny screen in confusion, until he remembered the web bug he had sent to the Sandman. He suddenly spun away.

"I have to get home."

"What is it?" When Chris didn't answer, Martinez stepped in front of him. "What's going on, Chris? Talk to me."

At first Chris wasn't going to say anything, then he realized that wasn't fair. Martinez was David's partner. Had been longer than Chris and David had been together. Despite being a loud-mouthed homophobe, Martinez stuck by David when he had been outed so ignominiously. He knew how much that meant to David.

So he told Martinez about his web bug. Martinez frowned.

"What does that mean? You can track him?"

"Not exactly. But I might be able to tell where he's been."

"And that just might let us know where he's going." Martinez jerked his door open. "Well then, what are we waiting for?"

Chris scrambled into his own car and the two vehicles headed back toward the freeway and home.

Chapter Twenty-eight

Wednesday 1:40 am, Cove Avenue, Silver Lake, Los Angeles

Chris put on coffee, knowing he was going to need all the help he could muster in the hours to come. He began to regret going quite so straight once he'd hooked up with David. He really could have used something stronger than caffeine to get through this night. Once the coffee was brewing, he took his laptop and Blackberry into his office. He stopped in the doorway.

Martinez nearly plowed into him. "What?"

"My server's gone." David must have taken it. Why would he do that? Did he suspect what Chris was doing? Then he saw the suspicion darken Martinez's face. He fumbled for a way to cover his admission. The lie came all too easily. "Oh, that's right. They picked it up for service. I'm upgrading it with new SCSI drives. It won't be back until next week."

"Is that going to be a problem?"

Chris frowned. The server had more power than his old laptop, but he was going to have to make do. He mentally crossed his fingers that Martinez wouldn't wonder why a guy who made his living with computers would send his in to a shop to be "upgraded." "Not enough to make a difference. Let's get that coffee first."

Chris filled the biggest mug and topped it up with just enough cream and sugar to make it palatable. Like David, Martinez took his black. It must be a cop thing.

Back in his office he went online, and downloaded everything from his Blackberry. Then he began the tedious task of sorting through the various log files he had created.

The first thing he found was Sandman's IP address. He ran it through Arin, the online database of IP owners, and found it was owned by one of the larger local ISPs. All that meant was that Sandman422 was one of hundreds, if not thousands of customers. Short of cracking their database, no easy trick given their reputation, there was no way to find out any more just from the IP.

Other logs proved more useful. The collection of cookies gathered from every web site Sandman had visited proved very enlightening. Slowly Chris began to get a picture of the elusive man who had haunted his and David's footsteps for so long.

"This actually means something to you?" Martinez peered over his shoulder, his face a mixture of disbelief and the keen distrust of a Luddite.

Chris took a gulp of scalding coffee, trying to blink away the sands of sleep. The trail of heat down his throat did precious little to revive him. He focused his thoughts enough to answer Martinez's question. "A lot, actually. Each one of these," he pointed at a scrap of captured data, "is a session cookie. It tells me not only what web sites he's visited, but when."

"Okay, fine. What does *that* tell you?"

"That this guy's visiting a lot of cracker sites, for one thing," Chris said. "This is one I've heard about. It's got some first rate crackers hanging out there. Black Alice and The Hobbit are two I know of who put their shingles out there."

"We already know this Sandman's a hacker. So he goes to hacker sites. Big deal."

"Depends why he's going there."

"Meaning?"

"Meaning that's where crackers go to get code. And they can get help putting the complex stuff together."

Martinez looked alarmed. "You got any guesses on what he's doing?"

"Ever hear about a book called Black Ice? Guy named Dan Verton wrote it. He concocted a scenario where terrorists launch an attack combining physical and cyber weapons and showed how they could be used to cripple a whole region. Remember the

2003 blackouts back east? Imagine if that had been followed up by a couple of truck bombs hitting a main gas pipeline or two. Or a nuclear plant somewhere. Water, telephones, traffic lights, grocery stores; no food deliveries, no radio stations online to let you know what's happening, no emergency broadcast system—everything shuts down. A guy I knew was out there when it hit. You couldn't even gas up your car to get out of town. If you can trigger a cascade failure you could take out the whole west coast with something like that—"

"And you think that's what this guy's doing?"

"I'm probably reaching," Chris muttered. "But... do you want to take that chance? We know he hacked Ste. Anne's. He has access to explosives. Whatever he's up to, I guarantee it's no good."

"If you can get that out of this," Martinez stabbed a thick finger at the monitor. "What else can you tell?"

Chris kept studying the logs. More cookies. More cracker sites. Then... something else. EBay. An online bank. Chris fired up his Firefox browser and entered the bank's domain name. Back in the log, he extracted the bank cookie. Now he needed to fool the site into accepting the fake cookie as one it had generated. If he could do that...

The bank site opened with an error. Chris swore under his breath.

"That's it, then," Martinez said. "You can't—"

Not so fast, Chris wanted to say. Instead he went into his program files and opened Internet Explorer, which he rarely used. This time the bank site opened into Sandman422's account. Chris stared at the numbers on the screen. He swallowed hard and looked up to find Martinez watching him with flat black eyes.

"Is that what I think it is?"

"Uh, yeah. Listen, maybe you want to go out in the living room or something..." Chris trailed off. "So you don't have to see anything illegal?"

Martinez grunted. "Can you see the name on the account?"

"Should be able to." Chris clicked each tab in turn until he came to one with customer information. He read off the screen. "Adnan Behnia Baruq, Stocker Street..." He looked up to find Martinez had gone very still.

"What was that name?"

"Adnan Ben—"

"That little shit," Martinez said.

"You know him?"

"We've been chasing him all over fucking town." Martinez scrubbed his face furiously.

Chris stared at him. "Why?"

"Bastard killed his mother. Poisoned her." Martinez flicked something off the sleeve of his jacket. "Cyanide."

"From that to building bombs and trying to blow up hospitals?"

"Don't forget the hacking shit. Guy's flexible."

Poison. Chris shivered. There was something so intrinsically evil about someone using poison to kill another human being.

"I'm surprised they expect to get away with it."

"It's not routinely tested for. Unless there's a reason to suspect it or the coroner sees something hinky."

"Hinky?"

"Out of whack. She was diabetic. He was probably thinking we wouldn't see past that."

Chris kept flicking through Sandman—Adnan's—bank site. Nice balance. "Nearly ten grand. This guy's not hurting."

"Especially considering his last job was slinging burgers." Martinez leaned over his shoulder. Chris could smell his sweat; his breath reeked of garlic and onions. "Could he have stolen it?"

Chris shrugged. He opened up the transaction history page and studied the numbers. Not a lot of activity. But a half a dozen five and six thousand dollar deposits and three noticeable withdrawals all in the last month.

"Wonder what he needed..." Chris counted it up in his head, "twelve-thousand dollars for."

"Maybe some of those other...cookies will tell you," Martinez suggested.

"There was that eBay account. Maybe he bought himself some Jesus toast."

Martinez looked at him strangely and Chris shrugged.

"If he was on eBay we may actually be able to see what he bid on—"

The house phone rang. He scooped it up. A male voice asked, "Is David there?"

"W-who is this?"

"Brad Dortlander. I'm the forensics technician for the LAPD."

"Why are you looking for David?"

The guy seemed hesitant. "Ah, he asked me to do some work for him..."

Chris thought of his server. Was that where David had taken it?

"What kind of work?"

"I'm sorry, I can't discuss that—"

"David's not here."

"When do you expect him?"

Chris squeezed his eyes shut. Then they flew open and he glanced at his computer clock. "What are you doing calling him this time of night? What on earth did you find that's so important?"

Chris's mind tracked fast and furious. This guy must have found his web bug and was calling to tell David about it. It hardly mattered now.

"He's not here," Chris repeated.

"Let him know I called—"

"I will." Chris hung up. He glanced at Martinez. "You know a Brad Dortlander?"

"Who?"

"Never mind."

Martinez stabbed his finger at the monitor. "Okay, you said something about finding out what he bought."

"Right." Chris hunched over his laptop and opened eBay. He immediately went to My eBay and selected Sign In. The cookie worked as designed, and populated his login fields with a user ID and password. He hit enter and was in. "Walk in the park," he crowed.

"Well let's walk in and see what our Adnan was up to."

After snooping around the site for several minutes, Chris sat back and rolled his aching head on his neck to relieve the pounding in his skull.

Something called a GeoDuct Conduit, brass caps and sealing tape. Purchased at different times. Chris's skin felt clammy.

"You okay, Chris?" Martinez popped a mint into his mouth. "You're lookin' kinda pale."

"What the hell is this stuff for?" Chris stared at the screen.

Martinez's heavy sigh belied his placid tone. "You got me. Got anything else? He buying fertilizer? Ammonium nitrate? Fuel? Oil?"

"What are those?"

"ANFO. It's what McVeigh used in Oklahoma. Bombing 101 for good old boys."

Chris shivered.

"You know, you really don't look good, Chris. Should they have let you out of the hospital this early?"

Chris shook his head, but he meant it to be more of an "I'm okay, let's get on with it" kind of shake. It was a mistake. His head spun and nausea tightened its grip on him.

"*Dios*, man, you look green."

Chris figured that was apt. He felt green.

Martinez shoved his cuff back and glared at his watch. "Listen, it's late. Why don't we take a short break, come back in say three, four hours. I think we can both use some rest."

Chris rebelled at the idea. But even trying to focus on the big Latino set his already aching head to pounding. He knew Martinez was right. He had to rest.

"Okay if I stretch out there? Save me having to go all the way home and explain to the wife why I can't stay." Martinez pointed to the futon along the far wall. His face scrunched up in distaste at the idea as soon as he mentioned it.

Chris managed a weak grin. "It pulls out. I can get you some sheets—"

"Just show me where they are," Martinez growled. "I'm more domestic than I look."

Chris did just that, then dragged himself up the stairs. He barely paused long enough to strip off his jeans and Tee before he tumbled into bed. He knew he should be weirded out having David's partner bunking in his office, but he couldn't raise any feelings whatsoever. He was out before his head hit the pillow.

Less than five minutes later Martinez was growling at him again, only this time it was to "wake up." Chris thrashed away from him on the bed, but Martinez was persistent. Finally Chris sat up.

"What?"

"It's nearly eight."

Chris grabbed his T-shirt off the floor where he had dropped it and slipped it on.

He looked at the bedside clock. Five hours? He'd been asleep for *five hours*? Sleeping while David—

Panic gibbered behind his façade and it was all he could do not to start screaming. He was hyperventilating.

"Why'd you let me sleep so long?"

Martinez scrubbed his hand through his hair. An indentation on his cheek looked exactly like the watch on his wrist. His eyes were red-rimmed and sunken. They danced away from him and he realized Martinez wasn't doing much better than Chris. "I slept in. Guess that thing was more comfortable than I expected. Either that, or I was more tired."

Chris knew how he felt. Even though he had slept for nearly five hours, he barely felt rested at all. He could have kept on sleeping for hours more.

"Give me ten minutes." A quick shower might help. "If you want, there's a shower downstairs. There are towels in the same closet where the sheets were."

Martinez grunted something and left Chris to his own jumbled thoughts.

Hot water, a fast shave and clean clothes left Chris feeling almost human. He found Martinez sitting at the kitchen table looking uncomfortable.

"What now?"

"Called the station. They got a BOLO out on David and Adnan. If anyone spots either of them they know to approach with caution."

"That's reassuring," Chris muttered.

"No one's going to do anything stupid and put one of their own at risk, if that's what you think."

Chris filled his mug with double-strength coffee and made his way to his office.

He'd left his laptop on and only had to clear the screen saver and log back in. He pulled up the newest logs generated from the connection to Sandman/Adnan's machine. Not a lot of activity, he noted. He told Martinez as much.

"Fits. He *was* otherwise occupied." Martinez sipped his coffee. "Go back to where he bought that equipment. What did he use? A credit card?"

Chris did as directed. "Visa."

Martinez grabbed the office phone and dialed. Before the call could be completed, he hung up. "No, I gotta do this in person." He rubbed a mole on the side of his neck and blinked owlishly at Chris. "I'm going to have to run in to Northeast. I can start the process to get a subpoena for this guy's financials from there better than here. Maybe we can work out where some of that money went. This stuff had to be delivered, right? It might clue us in to where we can find him."

David too, went the unspoken comment. Neither of them wanted to dwell on where David was being held, and under what conditions. Chris figured they both had to keep on believing David was fine. That he only needed finding.

Chris saw Martinez out then locked the front door and visited the kitchen again, where he freshened his coffee, knowing he'd pay for the caffeine overdose later. He returned to his office.

Back on his laptop, reading logs. Line after line of captured code. All he had to do was interpret it.

More session cookies. The machine name and IP address repeated several times. He wished he dared try to remote into Sandman/Adnan's computer, but he knew someone like that would spot Chris in a heartbeat.

Without Martinez peering over his shoulder, Chris opened up the most notorious cracker site Sandman/Adnan had visited. He hadn't told Martinez—or David for that matter—that he kept a handle on several of those sites. Not that he subscribed to cracking, but it never hurt to keep a finger on the pulse. He logged in with his handle, Dark Water Outlaw, and went into the most active forum to see who was online.

Sandman422 wasn't one of them. He did see a couple of names he recognized.

DARK WATER OUTLAW: u c s4ndmn422? Gt something h3 4xd 4

HOBBIT: nt 2d4y

DATA VELOCITY: 54y5 h3 g0t 4 5urpri53 f0r 7h3 m4n

Chris didn't like the sound of that. Carefully he typed, doing his best hakspeak.

DARK WATER OUTLAW: I 5P1IC3D 50M3 MOD5 FOR HIM H3 57I11 N33D 7H3M? He wanted to know if Sandman was still looking for code.

HOBBIT: h3 g07 w47 h3 n33d5 br34k 1ig75 h3 54y5

What the hell did that mean? Sandman already had everything he needed? That really didn't sound good. Chris wondered if these guys had a clue. They'd probably seen bits and pieces of the unfinished code, and weren't sharp enough to put it together.

DATA VELOCITY: (001 gr347 (1 –1 347 (0d3

These guys thought Sandman was writing cool cheat codes for some RPG game. Numbnuts.

DARK WATER OUTLAW: b47713fr0l \l 7 1 –1 41□

HOBBIT: m0r3 1ik3 g74 gr347 (1 –1 337 (0d3 g0il \l g 70 br34k 1igl –1 75 411 0v3r

So it wasn't like Battlefront, the war game, or Halo. These guys thought Sandman was developing new ways to manipulate GTA, the ultra-violent urban video game. But what did they mean by break lights?

Or could it be brake lites? Break lights or brake lights? Chris suspected the former. So how did he plan to break them, and what lights was he talking about?

Chris pushed his chair back, stretching to ease a growing crick in his spine. He sensed these two didn't know anything else. Sandman/Adnan had either deliberately misled them or they had chosen to believe his motives were as simple as theirs. To a lot of them their cyber world was more real than the physical one they were forced to live in. Maybe they couldn't conceive of real evil being done with the simple words they put down in their computers. They were happy to mess up a few thousand corporate computers, or see the name of their latest virus on CNN's nightly news, but for most of them that was as far as their ambition went.

He signed off the cracker site and went back to his captured logs. He had to figure out where this guy was.

If he didn't, Chris had the feeling all hell was going to break loose soon.

Chapter Twenty-nine

David woke slowly. He blinked several times, but couldn't see anything. Something covered his eyes. His hands were bound behind his back. His mouth was taped shut.

He rolled his head sideways, instantly regretting the movement. The bare metal surface beneath him was hot on the exposed skin of his face. The air was overheated and stale. He smelled engine oil, gasoline and his own sweat.

An insectile buzz filled his ear. A fly settled on his open wound and David flinched to drive it away. It came back. He forced himself to ignore it, concentrating on more important things.

He probed through the fog of his memory. Chris in the hospital. No, Chris had disappeared from the hospital. Another memory... taking Chris's computer to Brad.

His cell phone rang.

He twisted his head around, driving the feasting fly away again. He squirmed, pushing down with his bound wrists. He only succeeded in ripping several arm hairs out by the roots. The phone kept ringing. His struggles grew more desperate, until his skin grew slick with sweat and blood and his lungs screamed for oxygen. The tape around his wrists didn't budge. Belatedly he realized his legs were also bound.

Finally, he subsided in exhaustion. The ringing stopped. The first fly returned, joined by a second one. This time they settled on the fresh blood and torn flesh of his wrists.

He groaned. The sound was muffled by the tape over his mouth.

Remember.

He strained his ears, listening, trying to sort out anything that might tell him where he was. Maybe it would trigger a memory that would tell him where he'd been.

Remember.

Brad had found... something on Chris's computer. What was it? He'd called it a web bug. Said it could be used to spy on other machines.

What was Chris doing with a web bug? Had he found the Sandman? But if he had, why was David here... Something must have gone wrong...

His mind hit a wall. No more memories.

He strained to hear anything that would give him a clue to his location. A steady stream of fast moving vehicles overhead suggested a freeway. Which hardly narrowed things down.

His head throbbed. His stomach ached. It had been hours since he'd had anything to eat or drink. Unwanted thoughts of water, cool from the fridge, of steaks, fresh off the backyard grill, and mesclun salad flooded his mind. Thoughts of wine. Which led to the unexpected memory of champagne. A bottle of Mumms. Mumms had become a Christmas Eve tradition with them. The energetic sex that invariably followed the bubbly was another new tradition. Chris had a way of getting past his reserves, even when it came to trying something David never would have considered in his wildest dreams.

Before Chris, sex had been a rare and, by choice, a furtive occurrence. Fearful of exposure, he hid his desires behind a wall of work and lies.

Until Chris forced him to acknowledge everything publicly. Because his desire for the man several years his junior had proved stronger than his secrets.

He heard voices. Loud male voices shouting in rapid Spanish over the steady beep-beep-beep of a truck backing up. A third voice entered the fray, growling something in a heavy Bronx accent almost as incomprehensible as the Spanish.

The voices faded. They were moving off. David snapped into motion. He had to get out of here.

With his arms bound behind his back, it was a struggle to move his upper body. Flexing his shoulders brought with it corresponding pain. His body shifted a couple of inches, rolling him over onto his chest. The stink of old oil and gas, heavier near the floor, stole his breath, making it hard to suck in enough oxygen to keep his head clear.

It would be simple to drift into an uneasy sleep. Rest. Maybe his head would clear up if he got some...

He slammed his head sideways onto the floor, sending a bolt of pain through his skull and down his spine. He couldn't rest. He couldn't expect to lie here and be rescued. No one knew where he was. It was up to him to free himself.

He tugged his arms again. When he encountered nothing, he hunched around, knowing the only way he was going to free himself was by finding a way to cut the bindings. He slammed against the wall again. Behind his gag he grunted.

Spreading his numb fingers, he flexed his leg muscles and began inching his way along the corrugated wall, feeling for an edge, a broken seam. Anything sharp enough to cut his bonds.

He bit at the gag, scraping his face along the floor in an effort to rip off what he assumed was duct tape. It didn't budge. He did it again and again, smashing his face into the floor until blood trickled from his nose and he was forced to stop.

The fly was back. It landed on his cheek, mincing across the bridge of his nose before dipping into his left nostril. Another swipe at the floor drove the insect away.

There were no more voices outside. The hum of traffic grew heavier. Rush hour? It would make sense that it was early in the morning. He had spotted Chris on Hyperion around ten o'clock. He'd followed him to the freeway heading north. Where could Chris have been going? The I5 led past any number of small California communities: Sun Valley, Pacoima, Santa Clarita,

Saugus. None of them stood out in his mind as places where Chris had any interest.

A fresh trickle of blood oozed from his nose. The penetrating smell of blood overwhelmed the stench of oil and gas. The sound of the hungry fly returning was an incessant irritant. He wanted to scream, but couldn't even grunt behind the gag.

The temperature climbed, confirming his feeling that it was coming up to late morning. He doubted the vehicle was in full sun; otherwise it would be even hotter. With the unseasonable heat of Southern California they'd been experiencing lately, he knew it would soon get killing hot.

Wednesday 9:30 am, Cove Avenue, Silver Lake, Los Angeles

Chris stared at the computer screen. Every now and then he broke off long enough to glare at the telephone, which remained stubbornly silent.

Martinez had left over an hour ago, saying he needed a warrant for Adnan's financial records, though what he hoped to find Chris didn't know. As far as he could see, they were just chasing their tails at this point.

Nothing new had come in on Chris's web bug. Adnan was deliberately remaining offline, or he had done all he needed to online. Either way Chris wasn't having any luck figuring out where he was.

Which didn't bode well for finding David.

Chris blinked and tried to focus on the screen. Maybe there was something there he had missed. But when he brought up one of his captured logs he couldn't concentrate on any of it. The words were there, but no matter how many times he read or reread them, they made no sense.

He knew his lack of rest was catching up to him. More than once while studying the words he so desperately needed to understand, his eyes closed of their own volition. He would jerk upright, only to find that several minutes had passed while he wandered in la-la land.

His phone rang. He snatched it up. It was Martinez.

"You gotta come down here right now," he said.

∫∫∫∫

Chris stopped on the way and grabbed two bottles of Red Bull. Still, he waited fifteen minutes while the officious jerk at the front desk found Martinez and they were able to agree that Chris was expected. Finally he got his visitor's badge and, guzzling his first energy booster, followed Martinez.

But instead of taking him through to the detective's room, Martinez led him towards the rear of the building and down a narrow flight of stairs.

The guy who popped out of the unmarked door at the end of the hall looked too young to be a cop. A patchy attempt at facial hair didn't even begin to hide his acne. His name tag said he was Brad Dortlander, IT Forensics.

"Dortlander," Martinez said. "This is Chris. He does that computer stuff too, so I figure he can translate that crap you were telling me earlier."

"Brad." The guy held his hand out. Chris shook it. "I just found a couple of things on Adnan Baruq's machine."

"Tell him what you found," Martinez said.

"I deconstructed a mass of code I found on this PC," Brad gestured back at the room he had come from. "This is some pretty impressive push technology, and I suspect this isn't even the final version."

"And?" Chris urged him on.

"He's got a source route insertion program that will practically rebuild an IP packet so that it avoids almost any IDS. He could get this worm past most firewalls."

Martinez winced. He turned to Chris. "Translation."

"He's figured out a way to make a computer accept a destructive payload without triggering an alarm from an intrusion detection system. He can wipe out a system before anyone knows he's there." Chris turned back to Brad. "But what's he sending in?"

"I did some pattern matching on parts of the code and came up with a Denial of Service attack. I've resolved several IP addresses that appear to be the target. But..."

Brad looked confused. Chris had the feeling he knew why.

"The IP addresses are bogus, aren't they?" He glanced at Martinez. "The attack targets are dummies. He didn't put in the real addresses, just place holders."

Martinez's face fell. "So there's no way to tell who he means to go after?"

"Sorry, no."

"Just what can this kind of attack do?"

"Depends on how well set up it is," Chris said. Brad nodded. "If it's well orchestrated it can bring down a company's infrastructure."

"All their computers, you mean?"

"A lot more than that, these days. Everything's controlled by computers. Power. Phones. Lights..." Chris trailed off and thought of what he had found out at the cracker site. Break lights. "But what's his target?"

He realized he had spoke aloud when both Martinez and Brad leaned forward and said "What?"

Chris outlined his visit to the cracker site and his online "conversation" with Data Velocity and the Hobbit. How they thought the Sandman was working on a game hack, but Chris knew it was something more sinister.

"Well, I may be able to tell you where," Brad said. He spun on his heel and used his passkey to let them in through the unmarked door.

It was the police server room. Several ancient IBM servers hummed away along the far wall. Two newer workstations sat atop a desk to the left of the door.

A third machine, much newer than anything else in the room, sat connected to a keyboard and monitor. Brad nodded at the machine.

"This is Adnan Baruq's server. I've already cloned it onto that hard drive," He indicated one of the IBM workstations. "Along with a few different versions of the code, I found links to several maps."

"Maps?"

"Google Earth, MapQuest," Brad said. "Something called Cartifact. I guess he liked different perspectives."

"Maps of what?" Martinez snapped.

"All the same place, around Temple, 1st, Los Angeles—"

"That's all government buildings," Martinez said. "Federal Courthouse, Detention Center, City Hall, Caltrans... PAB is down there, too."

"PAB?" Chris asked, thinking he'd heard the term before, but not where.

"The new police administration building on Spring."

Now Chris remembered David talking about it. All three men traded glances.

"He's going to knock out the lights?" Brad asked, looking a lot less shocked at the prospect than Martinez. "What? Street lights? Building lights? He's going to shut the power down? But most of these places have generators—"

"Which are also controlled by computers. I think he's planning a lot more than that," Chris said. He gestured at Adnan's server. "Have you combed the slack space for deleted files?"

"I'm running some scans right now, but it's a bit level process, so it's going to be slow."

Brad meant that the software he was using was examining what appeared to be empty space on Adnan's server. Empty space was deceptive; in fact it often contained the remnants of deleted files. Files that, with the right software recovery tools, could be retrieved. Chris explained that to Martinez.

"So we'll be able to read those files?" Martinez asked hopefully.

"Probably. Of course it's a lot to assume they'll actually hold anything important. I'm not really sure we can count on this guy being careless enough to leave incriminating data behind."

"He might have if we surprised him," Martinez said. "I don't think he had time to do anything on his way out the window."

"Can you print those maps?" Chris asked.

Minutes later Brad handed them both hard copies of three maps.

Chris studied his. The Cartifact map was the most informative. It showed the Civic Center between Cesar Chavez Avenue on the north, and Temple to the south, and labeled nearly all the buildings. Chris had spent his entire life in Los Angeles, but didn't go downtown often. A lot of Angelenos didn't. He hadn't realized there were that many government buildings concentrated in such a small area.

He looked over the MSN map. On it a single address had been highlighted: 300 N. Los Angeles Street. A quick look back at the other map confirmed it. The Federal Courthouse.

"That's his target." Chris stabbed a finger at the spot. "That's where he's going to hit."

CHAPTER THIRTY

Wednesday, 10:25 am, Northeast Community Police Station, San Fernando Road, Los Angeles

"The Federal Court?" Martinez glared at the map. "You really think he's going to be able to get anywhere near that place with a bomb?"

"Bomb?" Brad paled. "Who said anything about a bomb? I thought this guy was a hacker."

Chris returned Martinez's glare. "I have no idea how he intends to get the stuff there, I only know he's going to try."

Martinez rubbed the back of his neck. "I better let Bentzen know what we found. He'll want to put out the word."

"Which means we go into a red alert," Chris said.

"Yeah," Martinez said, and Chris could hear the unspoken "duh" in the single word. "That's how we're going to stop him."

"And what does he do to David?" Chris knew the instant the implications of what he had said sank in. "You know this guy's going to kill him."

"Chris—"

"You going to tell me you think he's going to say 'oops, my bad, you're free to go'?" Chris's voice broke. "He's going to *kill* him."

"We'll keep looking for David," Martinez said. "So will the feds. They're not going to want a dead cop on their watch."

"But it won't be a priority, will it? He's collateral damage. The safety of the city outweighs the life of one man."

Martinez had no answer. Chris hadn't expected one. He fell into a chair and dropped his head back against the headrest, staring blindly up at the acoustical tiles on the ceiling.

"He's down there," Chris whispered. "He won't go far from his target. And he's got David somewhere close, too..." He didn't say what he could see on Martinez's face. *Unless he's already dead.*

Abruptly he stood up. "You do what you gotta do, but before you turn it into a circus, I'm going down there."

"I can't let you do that, Chris—"

"You going to arrest me, Detective?"

For a brief moment Chris thought he was going to do just that. Martinez's face was mottled with rage.

"Don't do this, Chris," he said. "Let the experts handle it."

"Experts," Chris almost spat, but bit his tongue and kept silent. Sparing Brad a glance, he headed for the door before Martinez could make a decision they would both regret.

♪ ♪ ♪ ♪

Chris climbed into his Escape and sat unseeing behind the wheel, ignoring the sweat trickling down his face. Finally he put the car in gear and cranked on the AC.

He wasn't sure how much of what he told Martinez was pure bravado, but he couldn't—wouldn't—leave David's rescue in their not-so-delicate hands. Whether or not they meant well—he knew Martinez did, but Martinez wasn't running this show. He'd be lucky if he even got invited along for the ride.

David would be seen as nothing more than collateral damage. No doubt he'd get a hero's funeral, replete with the flag draped coffin and the touching speech from the Chief of Police.

Just like Jairo.

As David's registered partner he'd get the full spousal treatment even if the LAPD had never known what to do with David and certainly wouldn't know what to do with him. Maybe they'd even give him the flag off his coffin.

Well, Chris wasn't ready to write David off quite so fast.

He took the I5 down to the 110 then headed south toward the Civic Center. The skyline towered over him, traffic slowed to a crawl. He got off at Figueroa, past the Health Center, where he turned left on Temple after sitting through two lights. Temple itself was bumper to bumper with lunchtime traffic.

He drove past Los Angeles Street, slowing down to examine 300 North. It was a tall, imposing structure, white against the brilliant cloudless sky. A group of sign carriers protesting some war in some part of the world most of them probably couldn't pick out on a map paraded across the street from the Courthouse. Occasionally one of them would wave a handmade sign in someone's face. Chris found parking on Temple in front of the twenty-two story Roybal Federal building.

He saw why the protesters weren't picketing the federal buildings. A single, empty Homeland Security van was parked two cars behind him. No one who looked like a federal agent was in sight. Were they already on alert?

A woman hurried past him. A scruffy-looking mongrel trotted at her side. The woman jabbered non-stop, her words, as far as Chris could tell, nonsensical. What she lacked in coherence she made up in volume. He could hear her long before she came alongside him. She wore a ratty fur coat over gray sweats. The dog wore an equally scruffy sweater. The dog's eyes met Chris's. It looked resigned.

Ahead of her two men argued, though there wasn't much heat in their words. Their argument must have been an ongoing one. As they drew nearer, Chris heard the name Nixon and "that damned scoundrel, Agnew." Like the woman, they were both overdressed; the one who had taken issue with Agnew wore what once had probably been an expensive suit. It might have been new when Nixon and his reviled running mate first took office. The other one, like the woman, wore a heavy winter coat over several other layers. No doubt all the clothes he owned. As they passed him the miasma of unwashed flesh, urine and shit lingered.

Surely if there was a high alert in place, the streets would have been cleared.

Chris picked up his pace, eager to get clear of this area. He almost wished there was more visible security. Did they think because so many of these homeless people were mentally ill they posed no threat? They couldn't be that naive.

For that matter, what better cover could someone use? No one looked twice at the destitute who littered the streets of Los Angeles. They smelled bad, they talked to themselves and everyone knew they were crazy. Chris had seen people cross the street to avoid them even when they weren't panhandling.

He slowed, no longer trying to flee. Instead he started surreptitiously studying the faces of everyone around him. He tried to keep it casual, knowing some of the more belligerent would take offense if they caught him staring. He remembered the woman in Santa Clarita who had mentioned the way the one man had smelled. Did that mean something?

If Adnan was here, did he have David nearby? But he could hardly conceal an unconscious or bound man, so where could he be?

Couple that with the question of how Adnan planned to deliver the explosives. Judging from the amount of equipment Adnan had purchased, he wasn't going to hand deliver it. That meant a vehicle of some kind.

He wished he could have spent a week combing through Adnan's computer. Just what might he have found? But time was a luxury he no longer had. A luxury David no longer had.

He dragged out his Blackberry and dialed David's cell one more time.

Wednesday, 11:15 am, Civic Center, Los Angeles

The vehicle shook; dragging David out of the fitful half-sleep he had fallen into as the temperature inside the vehicle climbed. The door rattled open and David struggled onto his back. The air that flowed into the cargo area was only marginally cooler than what had been there before. David sucked in as much as he could through his nose.

Even the rich effluence of car exhaust smelled wonderful. It meant he didn't have to smell his own stink.

Somebody climbed into the vehicle bed. The stench hit David almost immediately. Sweat and the rank smell of unwashed flesh and clothes. It brought back a rush of memories. The house in Santa Clarita, following Chris, the man who had attacked him. The brief glimpse he'd had of his assailant. Adnan.

David heard his soft, even breathing. He knew exactly the moment his abductor stood over him. When Adnan knelt, David tried to pull away, though the gesture was futile.

Rough hands jerked him back and wrenched the tape off his mouth. Along with half his mustache.

"Sorry about that." Adnan's familiar voice was gravelly with fatigue and something else—fear? Was what he was doing finally sinking in?

Maybe it wasn't too late to stop this after all.

He strained to hear if Adnan was alone. If his partner was there, Adnan wasn't going to listen to a stranger's plea. Especially a cop's. But all he could hear was Adnan's harsh breathing and his own. Beyond the door he could make out the swish of nearby highway traffic.

"Adnan. Listen to me," David said. "I know what happened to your father. Whatever you're doing, you can stop, it will be all right—"

"Shut up! You don't know anything," Adnan snapped. He pulled David up and shoved something under his nose. "Drink this."

David sputtered as cool water spilled over his closed lips, dribbling down his chin. He hastily opened his mouth and sucked in the liquid. It poured down his parched throat, bringing a coughing fit as some of it went down the wrong way. Too late he remembered the poison Adnan used to kill his mother. Then he realized it didn't matter and he drained the bottle.

"Easy, easy. There's plenty more where that came from."

"Adnan—"

"Shut up, old man. It's hard enough to do this without you trying to fuck with my head."

Do what? David tensed when he heard the snick of a switchblade open. He flinched and tried to pull away, ducking his head down to protect his throat, knowing there were a dozen other places Adnan could stick him that would be just as fatal.

"Hold still!"

David ignored him. He twisted sideways, knocking Adnan's arm aside. Suddenly his hair was being twisted and the knife blade pressed against his throat.

"Hold still or I *will* cut you," Adnan whispered.

David froze, his body going cold as he anticipated the knife sliding in, the pain, then the inevitable shock of death. Instead he was hauled onto his side, the knife blade sawing the bonds that held the tape over his eyes.

Adnan was almost in tears. "It wasn't supposed to go this far," he said. "I just wanted to pay back those bastards for what they did to my father. Not this. Never this—"

Savagely he finished cutting through the tape, tearing it off. David blinked away the tears that flooded his eyes at the shock of light through the open door of what he now realized was a van.

Then his cell phone rang again.

David could see Adnan's tension.

"Answer it, Adnan. Let them know I'm okay. Someone will come. They'll help—"

"Shut up." Adnan dug through David's pocket and extracted the phone.

David held his breath and let it out with a fear-tinged gust of relief when Adnan flipped the thing open and spoke.

"Yes," Adnan snapped.

David could hear Chris's frantic voice on the other end. He shifted on the floor of the vehicle and tried to sit up.

"He is unharmed," Adnan said. "And will be released soon—"

Adnan thrust the phone into David's face.

"Tell him."

"Chris? I'm fine—"

"David! Oh, God, David, where are you—"

Adnan climbed to his feet and stepped toward the back of the truck. David could still hear Chris shouting.

"What are you doing here?" Adnan asked, his voice flat and uneasy. "I thought we agreed—"

David whipped around toward the rear of the van. Through the lingering tears he could make out a dark, broad shouldered silhouette. He didn't need an introduction from Adnan to know it was his partner, the Frenchman.

The Sig Sauer in his hands was pointed at Adnan's gut. In a thick French accent he said, "Our agreement has changed—"

"Hey, what the hell are you doing here?" A thick voice, another accent, lighter. Latino. David shouted out a warning as an orange-vested Caltran's worker appeared behind Adnan's partner, who spun around, weapon coming around in a narrow arc.

The Caltran's worker's eyes bugged out. He backed up, hands coming up in a warding off gesture.

Adnan lunged toward the open door. His partner spun back around, but before he could bring the Sig back on target, Adnan kicked it out of his grip. The knife in his hand flashed and the Frenchman gasped. The gasp became a liquid gurgle. A spray of blood filled the van with the sharp stink of metal.

Adnan stumbled back, the knife falling from his bloody fingers. It clinked against the metal truck bed.

David tasted blood. He rolled onto his knees, his bound hands behind him. He felt, rather than saw, Adnan jump out of the van. Knowing he only had seconds to act, he threw himself forward, feeling the knife handle under his chest.

"Get out of here," Adnan shouted at the Caltran's guy. "I'll shoot."

An agitated Adnan bound back into the van, slamming the door behind him. He scrambled toward the front, but not before David saw that he now held the Sig.

The van engine rumbled to life and the truck shook as it backed slowly out and jolted to an abrupt stop, throwing David back, then forward. The knife skidded out from under him. He tried to roll with it, but the van's sharp movements kept him off balance. The van picked up speed over rough ground, then the wheels whispered with a steady cadence. They were on pavement. Picking up speed.

David began to hear other vehicles alongside them and when they slowed he knew they were traveling through traffic. Surface streets, since their speed was nowhere near enough for highway traveling. The truck slowed, sped up, swerved into another lane. David heard the impatient stutter of horns and brakes squealing on hot pavement, all typical sounds of driving in L.A.

They stopped, the truck idling for a minute or two, then lurching forward again.

Going where?

CHAPTER THIRTY-ONE

Wednesday, 11:30 am, Temple Street, Los Angeles

Chris stared at the silent Blackberry. "David? David!"

He was jostled by someone who reeked of sweat and piss. He fumbled to hang onto the phone.

"David!"

He punched in Martinez's number.

"Diego here."

"Martinez, I talked to him. I talked to David!"

"What? Whoa, slow down, Chris. When did you talk to him? Where is he?"

"I don't know. Can't you trace the call? Our plans are both through Wireless Planet. Call them. There's a GPS on his phone. You can track it."

"They will," Martinez said. "Now, where are you?"

"Downtown." Chris looked around. "Downtown, on... Temple, near Los Angeles."

The crowds pulled Chris along. He left the street people, Homeland Security, and the ragged band of indifferent protesters behind. The suits got newer and Armani and Brut replaced the stink. An errant breeze brought the whiff of Kenneth Cole and he felt an ache at David's familiar fragrance.

South of him the skyline loomed; the seventy-three story First Interstate World Center, the Bank of America and Wells Fargo towers delineating the downtown proper.

He hurried along Temple, driven by demons and the fear that threatened to overwhelm him. He couldn't give in to despair now. He couldn't give up on David. That would be the worst betrayal of all.

He passed the Cathedral of Our Lady of the Angels, the new home of the Los Angeles Archdiocese that had opened to so much media hoopla back in 2002. Ahead the 110 converged with the 101 and the roar of traffic became an overriding hum that grew with each step. He wouldn't find David going that way. He should go back to Los Angeles Street, try and find some pretext to take a closer look at any delivery trucks he saw there.

Chris moved down Temple. A siren screamed ahead of him. A black and white roared up Hope Street and swung west on Temple, a second one followed less than a minute later. An ambulance, its siren ululating into the silent watchfulness that filled the streets, followed.

Chris's heart slammed into his throat. Had David been found? He elbowed his way through the mob. Once he passed Hope, the foot traffic slackened and he picked up his pace, jogging the last block, only slowing when he spotted the kaleidoscope of lights from the emergency vehicles at the mouth of the 101 on-ramp.

A small crowd of onlookers clustered at the south end of the ramp the police had shut down. At first Chris couldn't see anything, then he made out the man-sized shape near the bush-choked verge cut off from the on-ramp by a sagging chain link fence. Swallowing a lump of fear, Chris edged through the crowd to get a better look. A uniformed officer circled the body, snapping pictures. Chris could see enough to know the guy was dead. His black beard was covered with blood, and more blood on the ground had already drawn flies.

"Guy in the back of the van just nailed him and drove off. Never said a word," a gruff voiced Latino in the garb of a Caltran's worker said. "Bastard almost nailed me."

"Jesus, they shoot him?" another orange-vested man whispered.

"Fuck if I know—"

Chris turned to ask the guy who was in the back of what truck when another uniformed cop appeared in their midst.

"Step back, please, people."

Reluctantly the crowd broke up. Chris watched the cops corral them like dogs after sheep and take them off to be interviewed. He knew better than to try to slip away. The cops had made him, and any attempt to disappear would only rouse their suspicion.

He let himself be moved toward the second black and white by a trim, good looking African-American officer. His name tag said Ridley. He looked Chris up and down and Chris knew he was wondering what a guy who looked like him, who clearly wasn't a Caltran's worker, was doing down in this end of town. He wasn't even dressed like the usual downtown crowd with their Prada suits and silk ties, so he couldn't even claim he'd strayed from the office for a little excitement.

Hell, he knew what he looked like to this cop: a Silver Lake twink trolling the wrong part of town.

Chris could hardly tell him the truth; that he was looking for his husband and a truck full of explosives. But he had to say something to the questions he knew were coming once they got the preliminary vital statistics out of him.

"So tell me, Mr. Bellamere," Ridley asked. "What brings you here?"

Chris shrugged. "I heard the sirens and wondered what was going on."

"Just curious, hmm?" Ridley said. "Something must have brought you downtown."

"No, not really." Chris sighed. "Listen. Before we start this dance, you might want to call Detective Martinez Diego at the Northeast. Clear up a couple of things."

"Martinez?"

"Detective—Northeast."

"He someone special to you?"

Chris grinned, knowing what Martinez would make of that assumption. "I'll be sure to tell him you asked."

Ridley wrote something down and stepped back. "We'll be in touch if we have any other questions."

Chris nodded and turned away. That was when he saw the cell phone lying beside a clump of weeds next to the shrouded body. He froze, then edged closer to the yellow crime scene tape.

It couldn't be... It *looked* like David's cell. The blue one Chris had given him last Christmas.

Without thinking he moved toward the barrier of yellow tape. A uniformed shape blocked his way. He ignored Ridley's scowling face and was about to push past him to get to the phone when Ridley blocked him again. He turned away and pressed David's speed dial. Not caring if the cop watched him, he stared at the phone on the ground and waited while his phone connected and began ringing.

On the ground the abandoned phone lit up and Chris barely heard the trill. He spun away and dialed Martinez.

Martinez's impatient voice answered on the fifth ring. As soon as he recognized Chris, the voice changed. "You find something?"

"He was here," Chris shouted. He told Martinez about the cell phone and the dead body. "They got a Caltran's guy who saw it."

"What was the officer's name?"

"Ridley."

"I'll talk to him."

"I'm heading back to Los Angeles Street," Chris said. "Those maps suggest that's his target, right?"

"Chris, stay out of this—"

Chris broke the connection. He looked back the way he had come; no cops were paying him any attention. He hurried down Temple, passing the Ahmanson Theater and the Mark Taper Forum, pausing at Grand for the lights to change. An orange Metro Local bus roared through the intersection. He stopped behind a woman in a severe Donna Karan and a corporate hairdo—the look ruined by a slutty pair of Jimmy Choos. He ignored the temptation to tap her on the shoulder and tell her that Sex and the City was so last decade. Instead he joined the surge of lawyers and clerks as they obeyed the walk sign and hurried to the other side.

At the opposite curb he nearly ran up the woman in the Choos, stumbling to a stop in front of an impatient cab driver who was trying to inch around the corner. Choos had her cell in hand, viciously stabbing the keypad, then holding the misbehaving device to her elegant, diamond-studded ear.

A cab driver found an opening and sped out into traffic, eliciting a barrage of horns as he cut off several vehicles.

Chris sped around Choos, only to have the way blocked a few minutes later by a trio of corporate drones who had stopped to argue about something. He was about to shove his way through them when he caught the gist of their conversation.

"—well that's weird, mine doesn't work either." Drone One tapped his Nokia angrily.

"What the hell—" Drone Two was staring down at his cell with a puzzled frown. "I was talking to Denny and it just cut out. Damn, we were right in the middle of those contract changes we wanted."

"Signal's gone—"

Chris pulled out his own Blackberry and sure enough the search bar was blinking as it tried to pick up an active signal. He looked up, scanning the tops of the nearest buildings. He didn't know where it was, but he knew damned well there was a cell tower nearby. There were probably several. There was no way anyone should be dropping signals here.

Someone slammed into him, nearly pushing him into Drone One. He sidestepped, managing to avoid hitting anyone. Drone One gave him a dirty look, but before Chris could snap back a response a car horn blared, followed almost immediately by a second one. Tires screeched and metal crunched and Chris jerked around to find a heavy black SUV had plowed through the intersection into a Saturn, which folded nearly in half. A second vehicle following the SUV swerved to avoid both vehicles and ended up in the oncoming lane in front of a city bus. The Metro bus slewed out of control and blew through a crowd waiting at the bus stop. Everyone scattered. Chris saw a woman, clipped by the lurching behemoth, go flying into the base of a light pole, where she lay unmoving. If anyone else noticed no one approached her.

More tires squealed as desperate drivers tried to avoid the cars ahead of them, only to add to the growing tangle of metal and fiberglass as they failed to stop in time or were bumped by the driver behind.

People yelled, drivers were pinned in crumpled shells, pedestrians broke up in panicked knots. More horns joined the cacophony.

Only then did Chris notice that in every direction the traffic lights were green. Up and down Temple and Hill and Grand, they had all changed at once. A Caltran's truck jumped the curb and slammed through the courtyard of the Kenneth Hahn Hall of Administration. A plume of black smoke boiled out of the battered engine cowl. The truck sheared off a water hydrant. Water spewed skyward.

Panic fluttered at the back of Chris's mind. He stared blankly at the useless phone in his hand. Adnan! It wasn't the Court House he was after—he had fooled them into thinking that was his target. He was launching a cyber attack instead. Break lights!

"Idiot," Chris muttered. "You goddamned idiot. You should have known..."

He looked around in desperation. He had to warn someone. How many services had Adnan disrupted? He watched in horror as a Tracker climbed onto the sidewalk, trying to maneuver around a crashed SUV, nearly running down a couple with a baby carriage. All around him voices rose in confusion and incipient panic.

Spotting a pay phone near the east side of the Kenneth Hahn building, he shoved through the mob, dodging a bicyclist weaving in and out of stalled cars and bewildered pedestrians. He snatched the phone up and hit 911. His mouth went dry when he heard the rapid pulse of a busy signal. What was it? The Denial of Service attack Brad had spotted? Or had Adnan managed to get an actual worm into the telecommunications system? A DoS could be shut down pretty quickly, but a worm could take hours to clean up, days if it was really efficient. Whatever it was, no one was going to be communicating with the outside in the immediate future. Behind him he heard a car backfire. At least he hoped it was a backfire. If some Neanderthal had brought his gun along to the party, things were going to disintegrate fast.

Further away a man started yelling. Chris heard someone shouting "Terrorists" and "Madrassa" and his heart sank. It wouldn't take too much of that kind of talk to incite a full-blown riot as people tried to flee an imagined terrorist attack.

Chris thought of the cops and paramedics he had left back at the on-ramp. Were they still there? How much time had passed since he left Ridley? Maybe thirty minutes? He knew cops, they wouldn't be done by now.

The streets had grown more crowded as the government and legal offices emptied out. A black-frocked priest shepherded a group of weeping school children back to the Cathedral. Some life lesson: come out for a day and watch a city collapse into chaos. Chris felt an insane urge to giggle. He knew it was hysteria and pressed his mouth shut to contain the impulse. Too many people around him were succumbing, and it wouldn't take much to blow them all over the edge.

He was glad for the hours of gym work he had put in over the years. It gave him the physical strength to push his way through the milling crowd back toward Fremont. When pushing didn't work he cajoled and cursed, but always he moved west.

As he passed Figueroa the crowds grew sparse. Everyone was moving east, drawn by the crowds and the specter of an entertaining sideshow. Most of the traffic that couldn't get down Temple turned north onto Figueroa or tried to get on the 101. Chris started to run.

A black and white careened around the corner of Fremont and slammed on its brakes as it hit a stream of barely moving traffic. Ridley was riding shotgun and he leaped out, hands on his utility belt, as he surveyed the pandemonium in open-mouthed astonishment.

The look changed, his dark face hardened when he caught sight of Chris.

"What the hell are you doing here?"

Chris skidded to a stop a couple of yards from the young cop. Holding a stitch in his side, he took several deep breaths before answering.

"It's a computer attack on the city's infrastructure," Chris gasped. "The phones are down, 911's inaccessible. Can you radio out?"

"What do you mean, an attack?" Ridley looked up in alarm at the nearest tall structures.

"Not that kind of attack," Chris said. "He's using computers."

"He?" Ridley snapped around, his brown eyes drilling into Chris. He stepped closer, his right hand closing over his baton. "You know who's doing this?"

"My husband was investigating it. Like I told you earlier, if you want to know more, talk to Detective Martinez."

An LAPD helicopter roared by overhead, the thunder of its passing drowning out Chris's words. He repeated the last invective.

"Martinez again? Who is this Martinez and what's he to you?"

"He's my husband's partner."

Ridley stared into Chris's eyes, then slowly he dropped his gaze and raked Chris up and down. Finally he raised his head. "Your husband's a cop?"

"Detective from the Northeast." Chris jutted out his chin. "Detective David Eric Laine."

"Laine?"

Chris could tell by the look on Ridley's face that he had heard the name somewhere. As usual, David's infamy preceded him.

Suddenly a wave of dizziness washed over Chris. He lurched forward and Ridley's hard grip on his arm was the only thing that kept him from tipping over.

Chris thought he heard the clunk of a car door and a second set of hands guided him forward. Hands maneuvered him until he was in the back of the black and white. Shit, they were arresting him.

"What's wrong with him?" a strangely musical voice asked.

"Crazy if you ask me," Ridley muttered. His grip on Chris's shoulder tightened. "Said it's some kind of computer attack. And get this: his partner's a cop. Name of Laine."

"Laine?" the musical voice said. "Never heard of her."

"Him," Ridley corrected acidly. "Northeast. Partnered with some dick called Martinez. Don't tell me, you never heard of him either."

Chris heard a click and a musical voice said, "Code thirty, Delta Charlie Three, this is One Adam Sixteen, ten-twenty 101 on-ramp at Temple following up on a one eighty-seven report. There appears to be a serious traffic tie-up around Temple between Hope and Grand. Please advise, Delta Charlie Three. Out."

Chris strained to listen for a response. Another wave of dizziness rolled over him and he lowered his head between his knees to keep from passing out. Through the roaring in his ears he heard the harsh crackle of a broken voice come back over the two-way.

All he caught was "Civic Center traffic grid" and "widespread telecommunications breakdown..." Then he heard Lewis mutter, "Shit."

"What?" Ridley snapped.

"All hell's breaking loose out there. Dispatch is being inundated with 911 calls. A dozen 211s, armed assaults, drive-bys, fires, explosions... Jesus. What the hell is going on?"

"Where?" Ridley asked. "Central?"

"Everywhere. Central, Hollenbeck, Hollywood, Northeast... the boards are lit up everywhere. Traffic lights are out all the way over to Alameda and down to 5th. Total traffic tie-up. Even with the birds up no one can count how many accidents there are." Lewis's voice was tinged with growing unease. "Fire, ambulance, they're all tied up..."

Horror seeped through Chris's numbness. He looked up and met Ridley's gaze. "You're being swatted."

"What?"

"He's swatting you. Triggering an attack on all 911 lines, overloading them. Tying up your emergency services while he does whatever he has planned."

"He was right," Ridley whispered. "The fucking hump was right."

Two fists wrapped around the thin material of Chris's T-shirt and hauled him out of the back of the cruiser, shoving him against the open door. His head spun and shards of light shot through his vision. Ridley's sour breath was hot on his face.

"You better start telling us what's going on before I bust your ass."

Chris didn't try to resist. He told them what he knew about Adnan. After a while they let him sit back down in the rear of the squad car. He sagged in the seat and tipped his head back against the rigid seat rest. His voice grew hoarse with the recitation.

"Let me get this straight," Ridley said. "You think this guy is driving around down here with a van full of explosives and a hostage cop?"

"Yes." What could he say, they either believed him or not. "Except he's probably not driving anymore. He would have parked before he launched his attack."

"I've got a call in to this Detective Martinez. You better hope he corroborates your story."

It was obvious Ridley's heart wasn't in the threat. Chris glanced at him. His face was gray. His partner was on his two-way. When he got off he looked almost as sick as Ridley.

"We're supposed to take up position at the nearest intersection and start working crowd control," Lewis said. "They're sending more units down as they become available. If they become available," he said darkly.

"What about this scrote?" Ridley asked.

"Detective Martinez wants us to bring him along. He'll meet up with us at the secure site. Homeland Security has set up a command post and they want him there."

The only street not clogged with traffic yet was Figueroa. They turned on their lights and sirens and edged down the street and turned left onto 6th Street. The traffic lights were still active there.

"Now you can tell me one thing," Chris said.

"And what would that be?" Ridley asked.

"The van those Caltran's guys saw. Did they see inside it?"

"One guy did." Ridley shrugged. "Why?"

Eagerly Chris leaned forward. "How many people did he see?"

"How many—two, he said he saw two males."

"Oh God." Chris sagged back against the seat and closed his eyes. "David."

"You think that was the missing cop?"

"It was him. It had to be. What did the van look like? Please—"

At first he thought Ridley was going to refuse to tell him any more, then he shrugged again. "Blue, with some kind of flower design on the side panels. We've got a BOLO out on it."

Lewis pulled the black and white to a stop south of 6th on Grand. The twelve story limestone and terra cotta Art Deco office building stood out among the sleeker towers around it.

Ridley and Lewis led him through the ballroom-sized lobby with its 40-foot high pressed tin ceiling and gaudy crystal chandeliers. Their shoes echoed on the marble floor. A suit met them at the front desk where Chris was signed in and handed a temporary pass.

The two beat cops conferred with the suit; Chris figured him for a federal agent. Martinez was noticeable by his absence.

Ridley gestured him over toward the elevators, dark oak paneled and from another era altogether. He approached reluctantly. The fed stood ramrod straight, a grim look of disapproval on his pale, narrow face. Washed out blue eyes slid over Chris and clearly found him wanting.

"We've been instructed to leave you with Special Agent Booker," Ridley said. "Detective Martinez should be along shortly."

Ridley and Lewis hurried out, as though afraid they would be called back if they lingered. Chris watched them go with longing. Ridley was a jerk, but at least he was a jerk Chris could understand.

He breathed an audible sigh of relief when Martinez lumbered into the lobby five minutes later.

Martinez nodded at Chris then turned his attention to the other man. He flashed his ID. "You Booker?"

"Right." Booker showed his blue government ID. "We've got a command post set up on the fifth floor." He looked at Chris again. "This the braniac who's going to fix everything?"

Chris passed over his own ID, which Booker studied closely.

"Let's get upstairs," Martinez said. "I hope your crew has things in place."

CHAPTER THIRTY-TWO

Wednesday, 2:05 pm, Grand Avenue, Los Angeles

They rode the elevator in silence, which suited Chris just fine. All he wanted to do was concentrate on finding David.

On the fifth floor Booker led them to a locked office. He opened the door with a passkey. Half a dozen men who looked like Booker clones glanced up at their entrance.

Chris stared at the bank of computers set up on two steel tables laid end to end. Cables ran everywhere. The screens were full of images. Several were maps of the Civic Center, including what looked like blueprints of the city's pipes and sewer conduits.

Chris sat down at the nearest machine and began running a string of commands on it. He was impressed. On such short notice they'd come up with some pretty decent equipment. Linux, no less. That would help.

"Can you get me into the telecommunications grid?" he asked the nearest agent who looked like he knew his way around a computer.

The fuzzy cheeked kid nodded. "What level?"

"Just get me root access. I'll find what I need." Being logged in as root gave him absolute power over every aspect of the system. Only root could launch commands that could access the system kernel. Adnan would have had to gain the same access to run his programs.

A couple of phone calls and Chris was logged in as a super-user on the grid that controlled the local cell towers.

He ran through another series of commands, scanning files as they came up then grepped through to the next level. He glanced at the young agent. He had a lopsided name tag that said "Troy Schneider."

"Keep your eyes open, Troy. Let me know if you see anything odd."

"Yes, sir," Troy said.

"I'm guessing our cracker replaced a common program with something that would do what he wanted. It'll look like it's supposed to be there, but the time stamp or a bogus signature will give it away. If he tried to tamper with it, I'll find some sign of his activity." Chris stroked the keyboard, calling up yet more lists of files. "Once I figure out which one he's using I can see what it's actually doing."

He almost missed it. The altered program had been a simple key logger, designed to watch who logged in. Now it was doing something entirely different.

The program Adnan had launched was subtle. It isolated the signals generated by cell towers and triggered multi-phasic swings; changing the microwave frequency just enough to shut the cell towers down.

He deconstructed the code as rapidly as he could. Some of it was confusing, he didn't know if it was bad code or if it was his own exhaustion that befuddled him.

"Just stop it," Troy said. "Run the kill command."

Bentzen, the bomb squad detective, entered the room and offered Chris the barest of nods. "We traced the explosives used in the hospital attack back to a known terrorist group," Bentzen said. "Linked to Algerian and Madrassa terrorists. A cell was broken up in Florida a couple of years ago, one prominent member was never found, a French ex-pat called Jean-Gabriel Clavet."

Chris straightened, hands still poised over the keyboard. "The guy who kidnapped David."

"That's what we believe." Bentzen looked uneasy. "His M.O is using an electronic device like a cell phone to trigger his explosives. We think that's what he did at the hospital."

Chris felt the blood drain from his face. He turned to stare at the computer screen, which displayed Adnan's program. "If Adnan is monitoring, he'll know instantly that I've stopped it," he said.

"Hell," Booker said. "He counted on us figuring this out and that our first instinct would be to undo the damage. If he's sticking to his M.O, Jean-Gabriel wants to trigger the attack from a line of sight location. Near enough to let him watch. He apparently has quite a fondness for observing his own handiwork."

Chris was vaguely aware of the others huddled in groups, hashing out all the events of the last few days. Martinez reminded them pointedly that it hadn't originated with the bombing at Ste. Anne's but had started much earlier, with the hospital hacking job and the death of Adnan's mother.

"The guy was stalking David before he ended up in the hospital," Martinez said.

Chris looked up. He blinked the sleep out of his eyes. "What do you mean?"

"We found some photographs..." Martinez suddenly couldn't meet Chris's eyes. "David never told you?"

"No, he missed that little revelation," Chris said icily. "So Adnan was stalking me. Ever since I was hired by Ste. Anne's to find out who hacked their systems. He went after David because of me."

"You can't take responsibility for the actions of a psychopath," Booker said. "And don't doubt for a minute this guy is one. He might be pretending this is about revenge, but the truth is he's just a cold little prick."

Before any of them could respond, Booker's cell rang. He snatched it up.

"Yes? Where? Stationary? Good. If it starts moving call me ASAP."

He flipped the phone shut. "They found a suspicious van. It's located on Los Angeles Street, about a hundred meters from Temple."

"The Federal Court house," Chris said. His mouth was dry and he tried to swallow.

Booker nodded. "Yes."

Chris stared at him. Talk about a cold prick, this guy was an iceberg. But then that wasn't his lover out there at ground zero. Chris turned his back on Booker and his weasel eyes. He bent over the keyboard, his fingers hung in the air over the keys. He tried to focus on the screen, but his eyes kept crossing.

Behind him voices droned on. He heard the words "sharpshooters in place" and "vehicle appears to be empty." Their words hovered just on the edge of his awareness. Belatedly he realized Martinez was calling him.

"We're heading out," he said when Chris finally looked around. "We've got visual confirmation of the van's location."

Chris tried to shake off his fatigue, but it was entrenched. He had finally hit the wall.

"Go home, Chris," Martinez said. "You've done all you can. We've got people moving into place who can handle this."

"While we certainly appreciate your help, Mr. Bellamere," Booker said. "This is a job for experts. No way I'm authorizing a civilian to enter this arena. And that is not open for discussion."

Then they were gone and he heard the elevator door down the hall open.

Chris staggered to his feet. "I'm going home," he muttered.

Spotting the washroom, he pushed through the door and leaned over the sink. He met his own eyes in the mirror and stared at his image.

He looked like he'd aged forty years. His skin was gray and his usually perfectly styled hair was in total disarray. His eyes were bloodshot pools of misery.

He lowered his head into the sink and began scooping handfuls of cold water over his face, not caring if it dribbled down his chest or dampened his shoulders. After a few minutes his head cleared, at least enough to form a solid thought.

Sharpshooters. They were surrounding the van with men with high-powered rifles. They thought the van was empty. But what if David was in the back?

Chris barely glanced at the haggard old man in the mirror before he grabbed some towels and scrubbed his face dry. Then he headed for the elevators.

Chris emerged onto the sidewalk and stared open mouthed at the street in front of him. The cacophony of car horns and the buzz of overhead helicopters were nearly enough to drown out the low roar of voices. Everything north of 6th was a river of deadlocked vehicles crammed between glass and stone canyon walls. Crowds of pedestrians wove through the abandoned cars, guided in some places by horse cops.

South, toward the towering Bank of America, a steady stream of buses had lined up to evacuate everyone on foot. Most of the vehicles still moving did so under the watchful eyes of the cops. There were several abandoned cars and vans on the side of the street.

Edging into the mass, he moved north. He felt like a salmon swimming the wrong way. But that's where David was—

Then something clicked and his mind cleared. He realized what he had seen without registering it: the blue van with a flower design. He jumped out of the way of a horse cop struggling to maintain control. He swung around and stared south.

One Wilshire was one of the world's most interconnected co-location facilities. Hundreds of networks converge at the corner of Wilshire and Grand at this downtown Los Angeles location, bringing together networks from nations around the globe. Over the past decade, it had emerged as the premier communications hub of the Pacific Rim. Chris had done business in the One Wilshire Meet Me room with a couple of his clients.

Sunlight glinted off the blue van parked directly in front of the main doors inset in a half a ton of dark marble. It looked like just another abandoned vehicle.

Had the whole thing been a game? Had Adnan planted the "evidence" suggesting the Federal Courthouse was the target? Jean-Gabriel, who wanted access to a remote trigger, didn't have to depend on Chris or one of the federal techs to "fix" their attack. They never meant to use the disabled cell towers. It was just there to divert them; to keep their attention off the real target.

Chris pushed through the crowd until he was back on the sidewalk. He peered over the heads of the mob to get a better look. If Booker was right, Adnan would want to be within sight of the target to trigger the bomb. Chris needed to let Martinez know. But Martinez's cell was not responding. He was back in the dead zone.

Chris darted around a pair of arguing businesswomen. The front desk was empty and no one challenged him as he entered one of the elevators and punched the fifth floor.

Troy looked up in surprise when he swept back into the room.

"Booker said there's trouble," Chris said. "He needs you downstairs."

Troy frowned. "Why didn't he call?"

"Phones are going out all over." Chris hoped his lies were convincing. "The problem's spreading."

Troy must have believed him. He grabbed his jacket and without a backward glance left the room.

Chris sat down at the same computer he had used before. He logged back in and immediately opened the directory where he had found Adnan's worm. He unpacked the code again and studied it with a different eye. Now he wasn't interested in stopping it, but in using it. Just as he'd expected, Adnan had found a way to target his sites. It was a simple matter to expand the range of attack.

He thought about what he was about to do. Then he thought about David. He took a shuddering breath and launched the recompiled worm.

Nothing dramatic happened. He hadn't expected anything. He hastily shut the computer down, knowing it wouldn't cover his tracks from someone who knew what they were looking for. But Troy was gone, for now. And Chris didn't care what happened after. Not if he found David safe and well.

Back outside he joined the mass of people moving south down Grand. It was immediately obvious Adnan's worm had worked as intended. The lights were out as far as he could see. He could feel the panic moving through the mobs.

He pulled out his Blackberry. The signal band scanned for a signal that wasn't there. His ploy to expand the dead zone had worked. Adnan's cell phone would no longer be able to remotely trigger his bomb.

He jogged down Grand toward One Wilshire, his feet thudding heavily on the harsh concrete, praying he didn't make a misstep. If he fell he had serious doubts he'd be able to get back up again.

He spotted another horse cop. He waved frantically and nearly stumbled into the horse's side. He grabbed the leather straps at the same time a distraught couple clutching a wailing baby slammed into the horse from the other side. The horse sidestepped the trio, and Chris stumbled to his knees. His head ended up between the horse's legs. Only the animal's calmness kept him from being kicked. Two pairs of hands grabbed him none too gently and hauled him upright.

Dimly he could hear the horse cop arguing with someone. All their voices were distant, as though from another room. Even further away he could hear the thump-thump of helicopters and the wail of sirens.

The horse cop stopped arguing with the couple with the baby. His harried look fell on Chris and he frowned.

"All of you need to move toward 7th, they're bringing in buses to get people out—"

Chris jerked away from the solicitous touch of the man who had helped him up. He stared across Grand, and again saw the blue van, still parked in the same spot in front of One Wilshire. Directly behind it was the first of several Metro buses being loaded with scared people. And they wanted to funnel thousands more people down this way?

Chris grabbed the horse's bridle. "Listen to me. They think they've got it figured out. But they're wrong. He tricked them. He tricked all of us—"

"Sir, if you don't move along I'll have you removed from the area."

Chris looked at the radio attached to the cop's uniform. He still clung to the horse. "Are you in communication with anyone in charge? Can you contact Detective Martinez Diego? I know he's in the area, his cell phone's in a dead zone."

"Please step away, sir."

The cop was going to say more but something else caught his eye. He pulled the horse's head around and urged it in the other direction.

Chris surged through the crowd, pushing when he had to, ignoring the irate curses thrown at him when he did.

Ahead of him the crowds grew denser as people thought they were heading toward safety. A white parking ticket fluttered from under the left windshield wiper of the blue van. The traffic cops had probably been in the process of removing the vehicle when the cyber attack had started. Which meant Adnan had put it in place prior to the cascading failures he had set off.

Chris looked towards the facade of One Wilshire. The thirty story structure was not the tallest building in the area. But the two hundred plus telecommunications firms housed inside it helped run the whole state. Destroying it could set back communications throughout southern California and beyond. It could take years to recover.

He cut across the angle of the crowds. A thickset cop with a gray crew cut blocked his path. Now he finds a cop. Just when he didn't want one.

Chris backed away. He couldn't afford to be pulled in by a nervous police officer. "Martinez. Detective Martinez Diego. I need to find him."

The thickset man shrugged. "Move along, buddy, the buses are ahead of you."

Chris kept trudging toward the van. He was shambling now, barely able to maintain a straight line. In case anyone was listening, he repeated, "Detective Martinez Diego. I need to find him."

Hours passed, or maybe it was minutes, he could no longer tell. He kept moving, he no longer knew in what direction. An ambulance roared through the intersection of Grand and 7th, lights blazing. Chris continued toward the van. A dark shadow blocked his path.

"You want to kill yourself, you don't do it on my watch."

Chris focused on the chartreuse shirt two inches from his nose. He blinked and met Martinez's brown eyes, which did not look happy.

"I thought you were told to stay put," Martinez growled.

"What are you doing here?"

"Got this call from a horse cop who said some guy kept babbling my name. I figured it had to be you. I thought I'd better check it out." Martinez made a face. "Besides, it looks like our boy's active again. The area south to 9th is out of power."

Chris shrugged uneasily. "There's a van at the Courthouse?"

"Don't worry, they're still watching it."

"Did anyone check to see if it was empty? I'll bet if they did, they'd find nothing in it."

"Sorry, Chris," Martinez said. "Homeland Security is in charge of that operation. They're calling the shots now."

"Did anyone even check to see if David is inside?"

Martinez put his hand on Chris's arm. "I'm going to take you home, Chris. You can't go on like this—"

"Screw you." Chris shoved Martinez in the chest and made to step around him.

Martinez grabbed him. "I can't believe what a stubborn jerk you are," he snapped. "If I had an ounce of sense I'd cap your ass and keep you in lockup until this whole thing is over."

Chris glared at him. More horse cops and a few on foot moved by, herding the growing throng of people toward the nearby buses. Sitting ducks in the coming conflagration.

"I think they're wrong about the Federal building being the target," Chris said. "I think Adnan decoyed us." Chris pointed out One Wilshire. "I think that's his target. You've got to get people down here to move these people out of here."

"No can do," Martinez said. "Every division this side of Cahuenga is buried under 911 calls. Every patrol car is in play."

"Pull them off."

"Can't. There's no way to tell which ones are legit. We can't take the chance; they all have to be checked out. We're on our own down here."

CHAPTER THIRTY-THREE

David stirred fitfully. He was aware in some dim, still active corner of his mind that the van was no longer moving.

His mouth was beyond dry. The memory of the water Adnan had given him was gone, along with all his fleeting thoughts of food or hope.

He tried to roll over, to ease the growing ache in his shoulders. The jolt of pain roused him enough to become more aware of his surroundings.

He heard the distant whisper of voices outside. They had moved following Adnan's attack on his partner. But they hadn't moved far. Periodically he heard sirens, both police and ambulance, as well as the overhead beat of helicopters. Something was definitely happening outside. He had no idea if it was related to Adnan, though logic said it was.

The voices grew shriller and louder. Sirens came closer. A helicopter swooped low. Had they found him?

But no one came. The van grew hotter as the day progressed. Just his luck the end of the year had proved unseasonably hot. Sweat dripped off his face, stinging his eyes and where the tape had chafed his skin. The stink of blood thickened in the closed space.

He tested his bonds again. His hands were blood-slicked. Maybe some of the fluid had soaked into the tape. He felt it give a bit when he twisted his arms under him, trying to rub them against the floor of the truck. He could feel the knife under his hips.

He braced his legs and twisted his bound arms toward it. The friction created a searing heat. But the bonds slipped. He did it again. More blood poured freely down his arms. Pain tore through him.

The front door of the van opened and Adnan climbed in. He glared at David over the driver's seat. David froze as their eyes met, praying the knife under him wasn't visible.

Adnan showed David a cell phone. "Your boyfriend thinks he's beaten me. Well, I think we'll see about that."

"What do you mean? Chris? What did he do—?"

"It's still going to happen. Especially now."

"Don't, Adnan. You don't have to do this."

"Sure I do." Adnan's face twisted in a forced smile. "I've killed five people already. What's a few more?"

David's insides shrank. So Adnan *had* killed his mother. "Why, Adnan? Your mother—why?"

"I told her. I thought she'd be happy I was avenging my father. But she said it would only help the wrong people. She said I was dishonoring him! She was going to call the police if I didn't stop."

"If people heard what happened to your father, they would understand—"

"Do you take me for a fool, old man? They would only have to hear 'suspected terrorist' and they would kill him all over again."

David winced, knowing there was some truth to his claim. "But not everyone thinks like that now, Adnan. There are people who don't like what's been done at those prison camps. You have to believe they would be outraged at what your father went through—"

Adnan clambered through into the back of the van. He sorted through a metal box by David's head.

"Your boyfriend might have stopped me from triggering it remotely, but if he thinks that's going to stop me, he's as big as fool as you are."

"Adnan—"

Adnan reached over into the front of the van and came back with the Sig Sauer. He pointed it down at David.

"Shut up, old man. Or I will use this."

David shut up. He watched in mounting dismay as Adnan fell to building what even David could recognize as a trigger. He looked around the van, but didn't see anything that looked remotely like an explosive device.

"Where is it?" he whispered. "Where's the bomb?"

Adnan only smiled.

Wednesday, 3:00 pm, One Wilshire, Grand Avenue, Los Angeles

Martinez forced Chris to sit on the nearest curb. He slumped back against the no parking sign and stared at the blue van that Martinez wouldn't let him approach. He almost wished he could just lie back and rest, but he knew if he closed his eyes he would pass out and it would be all over.

So he forced his eyes open and stared dully at the parking ticket that fluttered in the brilliant afternoon sun. He could see the heat wavering off the nearby surfaces and somewhere in his head an alarm went off. Hot. It was so hot.

He shook his head to clear it. Unbidden came memories. Memories of David; David as he had first seen him, all no-nonsense cop, brusque and cold, but even then there had been an underlying feeling of warmth. David cared. He cared about justice, and people and doing the right thing.

Which was a lot more than Chris could say about himself.

But later, when Chris penetrated David's guard, he knew what David really was. A passionate, loving, moral man who would die rather than betray the people he loved. And he loved Chris, something Chris still marveled at.

Lover, friend, husband; Chris never expected he could feel these things for one man. He'd always thought playing the field worked best. No ties. No emotional risks. Cruise the circuit until he found the cutest guy with the biggest dick and spirit him home for a night of hard fucking.

Without even trying, David changed all that. Now Chris couldn't imagine life without him.

Above him, Martinez stared grimly ahead. All Chris could see was the severe set of his mouth and his unblinking eyes.

Suddenly his face changed. His mouth popped open. "Why that little shit."

Chris looked around to see what Martinez was looking at. He saw a slightly built youth open the van door and clamber inside.

Chris climbed to his feet. The kid looked familiar, even in the grungy hoodie he wore over a pair of baggy jeans. "Who is that?"

Martinez ground his teeth together. Together they watched the youth move from the front seat of the van to the rear. The van rocked.

"Martinez."

"That was your hacker."

"That's Adnan? Jesus, you didn't tell me he was a kid—" Chris shut his mouth and stared. The memory came to him. "That's the janitor," he said, his gaze never leaving the van. "From the hospital. That's what Terry figured out. That's why they killed him. Jesus, how old is he?"

"Twenty. But don't let the age fool you. He's a kid who got accepted to CalTech because he's some kind of fucking genius. I wouldn't start underestimating him now."

A horse cop came by, escorting a large group of businessmen. Martinez waved to get his attention. He pulled out his badge as he walked over.

Chris took advantage of Martinez's inattention to stroll toward the rear of the van. The only windows, on the back doors, had been painted over. It was an older model Ford panel van with a simple latch that would pop open the right door, which would then allow the left door to be unlatched and swung open.

Knowing they couldn't see him from inside the van and seeing that Martinez was still engaged with the horse cop, Chris ran his hands over the sides of the van. He hissed and jerked his hand back at the searing heat. Jesus, the thing was an oven. If David was in there he must be cooking. He eased his ear as close as he could to the side panel without touching it.

Hearing muffled voices, the hairs on his neck stood on end. He rubbed his sweating palms along his jeans. He reached up to grab the door handle.

"Get away from the vehicle, Chris," Martinez's voice called out. "Step back immediately."

Chris froze. He shook his head. "Sorry, I can't do that. I have to know if David's in there." Turning, he backed up, until his shoulder blades were pressed against the van door.

Through the sweat that dripped down his face into his eyes he saw Martinez, legs spread in a shooter's stance, arms extended, trained his weapon squarely on him.

"I can't let you open that, Chris. Not until we know what's in there."

Chris stared into Martinez's eyes and saw anger and regret and something else he couldn't quite read. Respect?

"You know I have to do this," Chris said. He fumbled his right hand to the rear door of the van. His heart hammered in his chest and this time the rush of adrenaline didn't wake him up, it left him dizzy. He barely heard the next shouted command.

His fingers closed over the door handle.

"Don't—"

Chris shut his eyes. Wondering if he would hear the shots before the bullets obliterated him. Would Martinez really shoot him? He yanked on the door.

"Hold it right there," Martinez stepped closer. He fractionally lowered his weapon and reached for Chris.

He grabbed Chris's arm. But before Martinez could haul him out of the way, Chris snapped. He jerked away from Martinez and with a yell, swung his fist into Martinez's nose. He yelped when his flesh connected with bone. Taken by surprise, Martinez flew back, his eyes wide in surprise.

Shaking his stinging fist, Chris spun back around. This time he locked both hands around the door handle and yanked. Something thumped on the inside of the van.

The door popped open, releasing a rolling wave of hot air that stank of blood and sweat and the sour reek of adrenaline and unwashed flesh.

Startled, Chris flew back. He tried to hang on, but the handle slipped out of his grip. He stepped away from the van, arms pin-wheeling over his head. One heel hit the curb and he flipped backwards.

He landed flat on his back, the breath exploding out of his lungs.

Before he could suck in a single breath Martinez grabbed him and hauled him upright. He dragged him so close Chris could see dark hair inside Martinez's flaring nose.

"You are more trouble than half the assholes I deal with every day. Now will you—"

His voice trailed off and Chris followed his gaze into the rear of the van.

Adnan, the slight youth they had watched climb into the van earlier, straddled David's head in a gun fighter's stance. The gun he held in one hand visibly shook, as though he was having trouble keeping it steady. The muzzle of the gun was pointed somewhere between David and the open door, as though he was uncertain where he should aim. Chris was afraid to move. Afraid to breath.

Chris's gaze locked on David, then moved back to Adnan. Chris swallowed past renewed terror as he saw that in his other hand Adnan held a brace of wires, the twisted ends separated only by his index finger and thumb. The wires disappeared into the side of the van, which appeared empty except for Adnan himself, and David.

"He's bluffing," Martinez said. He kept his weapon trained on Adnan. His grip was a lot more sure than Adnan's, which did nothing to reassure Chris. "There is no bomb."

"You really want to take that chance, Detective?" Adnan held up the hand gripping the wires. "What if I told you the stuff is like shaving cream. I just filled the panels of the truck with it. It's very stable too." Again he moved his hand, the wires coming perilously close to touching. "Only this can set it off. Instant oblivion."

He looked past them to the thronging streets beyond. "Do you think they'll remember me, Detective?"

"Jesus, man, there are kids out there," Chris said.

"Did they think of that when they took my father away from me? I was only a 'kid' too. But they took him from me and tried to make me believe he was an evil man." Adnan's fist closed on the wires, which writhed like a nest of snakes. "My father never hurt anybody."

"Then tell people that!" Chris couldn't take his eyes off the innocuous-looking wires. "This is only going to make them believe the worst."

"It no longer matters," Adnan said in a flat voice. "Too much has already been done."

Chris met David's gaze again. "No," he whispered. "You can't—"

Two things happened simultaneously. David bolted upright and lunged at Adnan. And a shot was fired.

Chris yelled and scrambling to his feet, dove toward the van. Behind him he heard a grunt and the thump of a body smacking against pavement. He had eyes only for David.

David and Adnan were locked together. The wire Adnan held waved loosely, no longer attached to the side of the van. David had ripped it loose. Adnan dropped the useless wires and now fought for control of the gun.

It was obvious to Chris that David was in trouble. His face was gray with fatigue and he was covered in blood.

Behind him he heard Martinez shout, "Drop it, Adnan. Now—"

Chris didn't wait to see if Adnan would obey. He scrambled into the cargo area and from a half crouch launched himself at the two struggling men.

"Down!" Martinez yelled. "Chris, get down now!"

This time the bullet passed so close Chris could feel the short hairs on the nape of his neck sizzle. In mid-flight he tried to duck and roll at the same time. He slammed into a human body. A sharp woof sent a gust of hot breath past his shoulder. He tried to roll off, but the arms that wrapped around him weren't letting go.

He raised his head and found himself staring into David's green-flecked eyes.

Their hearts thudded together. Chris craned his head up and realized Adnan lay slumped against the driver's seat, a neat bullet hole in the center of his forehead. His eyes were already empty. The gun lay across his lap, still held tightly.

Chris turned back to stare down at David. Their faces were inches apart. Chris could see every pore on his face, every hair of his mustache, half of which was gone. His face, always rough from childhood acne, looked abraded. His eyes looked weary, but amused. "Hey," he whispered.

"We really gotta stop doing this," Chris said. His breath ruffled David's hair.

"What, and miss all this excitement?" David muttered as he closed his eyes. But his grip on Chris never loosened.

Chris rolled his wheelchair into David's room, startling an orderly who had been delivering clean towels and a carafe of water. Chris grinned at the young hunk and fluttered his fingers in a gesture of dismissal.

"Run along, sweetie," he said. "I'll take care of him now."

The orderly left, though not without a few backward glances that Chris took firmly to heart. Once more he was attracting the right kind of attention. The bags under his eyes were history and he'd wrangled a haircut out of Des, who had talked his favorite stylist into visiting the hospital. He'd taken care of David too, and now it was just up to Chris to shave him every day, though David was making serious noises about doing it himself. Chris was reluctant to give the job up. Shaving David was his way of reassuring himself they were both safe.

David was propped up in the bed, his pajamas open to the waist. Chris admired the expanse of furry chest.

"Hey," David said.

"Hey yourself. How you feeling?"

"Good." When Chris left the chair, he sat on the edge of the bed David reached out and took hold of his hand. "You?"

"They're letting me out tomorrow. Finder's giving me a clean bill of health. All I need to do is rest, and I can do that at home just as easily as here."

"Well, good." Only David didn't look all that happy.

"Hey, I've already talked to your doctor. They want to keep you in at least another few days, but then you can come home too." Chris stroked his cheek, now mostly back to normal, the marks from his ordeal fading. "I'll be here every day to visit. Has Martinez been in to see you?"

"Yeah, he came by," David said. "They dismantled the truck. Adnan wasn't lying when he said he'd filled it with that foam. Every panel. God knows how much damage it would have done. Homeland isn't talking. Guess they don't want anyone to know how effective it is."

Chris tightened his grip on David's hand.

"It was Jean-Gabriel who delivered the bombs in the flowers," David said. He pulled Chris's hand open, stroking the palm. "Terry put it together and realized what Adnan was doing. But they were one step ahead of him and they grabbed him and his wife and forced him to make that call to you. I really think Adnan was a reluctant terrorist at best. He wanted someone to pay for what they did to his father, but he was having trouble with the idea of killing so many innocent people. But once he'd killed his mother and Jean-Gabriel he no longer thought he had a choice." David shook his head. "I don't think he killed Terry or his wife. That one's on his partner. That only added to his guilt."

"How much trouble did Martinez get into?" Chris asked. "I mean, doing that... I'm just so sorry I hit him."

David grinned. "He still can't believe you did either. He got chewed a new one by the Lieutenant and if he hadn't taken a bullet it might have gone harder on him. McKee still had to make an example of him. I think Booker, the Homeland Security guy, forced his hand on that. But his suspension's a light one. Only a week, with pay. He's taking his kids to Disneyland. So they love you, even if their father isn't your favorite fan right now." David tried to look stern. "Just be thankful he's not pressing charges. Hitting an officer is a serious offense."

"Hmph, he should know better than to come between you and me."

David just shook his head.

Chris helped David climb out of bed and enter the bathroom. At the sink, David washed his hands and studied his reflection in the mirror. He stroked his mustache and tilted his head from side to side. He spoke with resignation.

"Lot's more gray there." He ran his finger along what was left of his moustache and the new hairs that were growing in. "Look at that. Pure white."

Chris drew David's head down and nibbled his mouth, slipping his tongue between David's lips. David returned the kiss with an ardor that left Chris breathless. "Don't you dare pluck that out—ten more will come to its funeral."

David framed Chris's face with his big hands. "Would you mind?"

"What do you think?" Chris whispered. "Go ahead, ask me to prove it. I don't mind. I'll spend the rest of my life proving I love you, gray hair or no hair. I don't care."

"Still, maybe it's time to get rid of it." David grinned tiredly. "Everyone keeps saying I look like a seventies porn star."

"Before my time. But if you want to take it off, I could get used to seeing your upper lip. Come on, you need to rest."

Once back in bed, Chris tucked him in. David yawned.

"Okay, sleepyhead. Before you go off to happy land I got something for you."

David watched Chris as he reached into the deep pocket of his silk robe. His eyes widened when he saw what Chris held in his hand.

"You gotta be more careful next time. Leaving this thing lying around, someone might think you didn't care."

David touched the St. Michael's medal as Chris slipped it over his head.

"I got it to keep you safe." Chris leaned in and kissed him, making sure it was a kiss he wouldn't forget. "But you gotta wear it for it to work."

"You make sure you talk to Abrahms," David whispered. "If I don't get out of here soon there's going to be trouble."

"Oh, we'll be talking. Believe it."

David pulled him down for another mind-numbing kiss.

PAT BROWN was born in Canada, which she is sure explains her intense dislike of all things cold and her constant striving to escape to someplace warm. Her first move took her to Los Angeles, and her fate was sealed. To this day she has a love/hate relationship with L.A, a city that was endlessly fascinating. L.A. Heat and the even darker L.A. Boneyard grew out of those dark, compelling days.

She wrote her first book at 17 – an angst ridden tome about a teenage girl hooked up with a drug user and went off the deep end. All this from a kid who hadn't done anything stronger than weed. She read her first positive gay book then too, The Lord Won't Mind, by Gordon Merrick and had her eyes open to a whole other world (which didn't exist in ultra conservative vanilla plain London, Ontario). Visit Pat on the internet at: http://www.pabrown.ca/

THE TREVOR PROJECT

The Trevor Project operates the only nationwide, around-the-clock crisis and suicide prevention helpline for lesbian, gay, bisexual, transgender and questioning youth. Every day, The Trevor Project saves lives though its free and confidential helpline, its website and its educational services. If you or a friend are feeling lost or alone call The Trevor Helpline. If you or a friend are feeling lost, alone, confused or in crisis, please call The Trevor Helpline. You'll be able to speak confidentially with a trained counselor 24/7.

The Trevor Helpline: 866-488-7386

On the Web: http://www.thetrevorproject.org/

THE GAY MEN'S DOMESTIC VIOLENCE PROJECT

Founded in 1994, The Gay Men's Domestic Violence Project is a grassroots, non-profit organization founded by a gay male survivor of domestic violence and developed through the strength, contributions and participation of the community. The Gay Men's Domestic Violence Project supports victims and survivors through education, advocacy and direct services. Understanding that the serious public health issue of domestic violence is not gender specific, we serve men in relationships with men, regardless of how they identify, and stand ready to assist them in navigating through abusive relationships.

GMDVP Helpline: 800.832.1901

On the Web: http://gmdvp.org/

THE GAY & LESBIAN ALLIANCE AGAINST DEFAMATION / GLAAD EN ESPAÑOL

The Gay & Lesbian Alliance Against Defamation (GLAAD) is dedicated to promoting and ensuring fair, accurate and inclusive representation of people and events in the media as a means of eliminating homophobia and discrimination based on gender identity and sexual orientation.

On the Web: http://www.glaad.org/

GLAAD en español: http://www.glaad.org/espanol/bienvenido.php

Stimulate yourself.
READ.
www.manloveromance.com
THE HOTTEST M/M EROTIC AUTHORS & WEBSITES ON THE NET